The Green Mummy

Fergus Hume

The Green Mummy

ISBN: 979-8-88942-486-4

CONTENTS

CONTENTS

CHAPTER I

THE LOVERS

"I am very angry," pouted the maid.

"In heaven's name, why?" questioned the bachelor.

"You have, so to speak, bought me."

"Impossible: your price is prohibitive."

"Indeed, when a thousand pounds—"

"You are worth fifty and a hundred times as much. Pooh!"

"That interjection doesn't answer my question."

"I don't think it is one which needs answering," said the young man lightly; "there are more important things to talk about than pounds, shillings, and sordid pence."

"Oh, indeed! Such as—"

"Love, on a day such as this is. Look at the sky, blue as your eyes; at the sunshine, golden as your hair."

"Warm as your affection, you should say."

"Affection! So cold a word, when I love you."

"To the extent of one thousand pounds."

"Lucy, you are a—woman. That money did not buy your love, but the consent of your step-father to our marriage. Had I not humored his whim, he would have insisted upon your marrying Random."

Lucy pouted again and in scorn.

"As if I ever would," said she.

"Well, I don't know. Random is a soldier and a baronet; handsome and agreeable, with a certain amount of talent. What objection can you find to such a match?"

"One insuperable objection; he isn't you, Archie—darling."

"H'm, the adjective appears to be an afterthought," grumbled the bachelor; then, when she merely laughed teasingly after the manner of women, he added moodily:

"No, by Jove, Random isn't me, by any manner of means. I am but a poor artist without fame or position, struggling on three hundred a year for a grudging recognition."

"Quite enough for one, you greedy creature."

"And for two?" he inquired softly.

"More than enough."

"Oh, nonsense, nonsense, nonsense!"

"What! when I am engaged to you? Actions speak much louder

1

than remarks, Mr. Archibald Hope. I love you more than I do money."

"Angel! angel!"

"You said that I was a woman just now. What do, you mean?"

"This," and he kissed her willing lips in the lane, which was empty save for blackbirds and beetles. "Is any explanation a clear one?"

"Not to an angel, who requires adoration, but to a woman who—Let us walk on, Archie, or we shall be late for dinner."

The young man smiled and frowned and sighed and laughed in the space of thirty seconds—something of a feat in the way of emotional gymnastics. The freakish feminine nature perplexed him as it had perplexed Adam, and he could not understand this rapid change from poetry to prose. How could it be otherwise, when he was but five-and-twenty, and engaged for the first time? Threescore years and ten is all too short a time to learn what woman really is, and every student leaves this world with the conviction that of the thousand sides which the female of man presents to the male of woman, not one reveals the being he desires to know. There is always a deep below a deep; a veil behind a veil, a sphere within a sphere.

"It's most remarkable," said the puzzled man in this instance.

"What is?" asked the enigma promptly.

To avoid an argument which he could not sustain, Archie switched his on to the weather.

"This day in September; one could well believe that it is still the month of roses."

"What! With those wilted hedges and falling leaves and reaped fields and golden haystacks, and—and—"

She glanced around for further illustrations in the way of contradiction.

"I can see all those things, dear, and the misplaced day also!"

"Misplaced?"

"July day slipped into September. It comes into the landscape of this autumn month, as does love into the hearts of an elderly couple who feel too late the supreme passion."

Lucy's eyes swept the prospect, and the spring-like sunshine, revealing all too clearly the wrinkles of aging Nature, assisted her comprehension.

"I understand. Yet youth has its wisdom."

"And old age its experience. The law of compensation, my dearest. But I don't see," he added reflectively, "what your remark and my answer have to do with the view," whereat Lucy declared that his wits wandered.

2

Within the last five minutes they had emerged from a sunken lane where the hedges were white with dust and dry with heat to a vast open space, apparently at the World's-End. Here the saltings spread raggedly towards the stately stream of the Thames, intersected by dykes and ditches, by earthen ramparts, crooked fences, sod walls, and irregular lines of stunted trees following the water-courses. The marshes were shaggy with reeds and rushes, and brown with coarse, fading herbage, although here and there gleamed emerald-hued patches of water-soaked soil, fit for fairy-rings. Beyond a moderately high embankment of turf and timber, the lovers could see the broad river, sweeping eastward to the Nore, with homeward-bound and outward-faring ships afloat on its golden tide. Across the gleaming waters, from where they lipped their banks to the foot of low domestic Kentish hills, stretched alluvial lands, sparsely timbered, and in the clear sunshine clusters of houses, great and small, factories with tall, smoky chimneys, clumps of trees and rigid railway lines could be discerned. The landscape was not beautiful, in spite of the sun's profuse gildings, but to the lovers it appeared a Paradise. Cupid, lord of gods and men, had bestowed on them the usual rose-colored spectacles which form an important part of his stock-in-trade, and they looked abroad on a fairy world. Was not SHE there: was not HE there: could Romeo or Juliet desire more?

From their feet ran the slim, straight causeway, which was the King's highway of the district—a trim, prim line of white above the picturesque disorder of the marshes. It skirted the low-lying fields at the foot of the uplands and slipped through an iron gate to end in the far distance at the gigantic portal of The Fort. This was a squat, ungainly pile of rugged gray stone, symmetrically built, but aggressively ugly in its very regularity, since it insulted the graceful curves of Nature everywhere discernible. It stood nakedly amidst the bare, bleak meadows glittering with pools of still water, with not even the leaf of a creeper to soften its menacing walls, although above them appeared the full-foliaged tops of trees planted in the barrack-yard. It looked as though the grim walls belted a secret orchard. What with the frowning battlements, the very few windows diminutive and closely barred, the sullen entrance and the absence of any gracious greenery, Gartley Fort resembled the Castle of Giant Despair. On the hither side, but invisible to the lovers, great cannons scowled on the river they protected, and, when they spoke, received answer from smaller guns across the stream. There less extensive forts were concealed amidst trees and masked by turf embankments, to watch and guard the golden argosies of London commerce.

3

Lucy, always impressionable, shivered with her hand in that of Archie's, as she stared at the landscape, melancholy even in the brilliant sunshine.

"I should hate to live in Gartley Fort," said she abruptly. "One might as well be in jail."

"If you marry Random you will have to live there, or on a baggage wagon. He is R.G.A. captain, remember, and has to go where glory calls him, like a good soldier."

"Glory can call until glory is hoarse for me," retorted the girl candidly. "I prefer an artist's studio to a camp."

"Why?" asked Hope, laughing at her vehemence.

"The reason is obvious. I love the artist."

"And if you loved the soldier?"

"I should mount the baggage wagon and make him Bovril when he was wounded. But for you, dear, I shall cook and sew and bake and—"

"Stop! stop! I want a wife, not a housekeeper."

"Every sensible man wants the two in one."

"But you should be a queen, darling."

"Not with my own consent, Archie: the work is much too hard. Existence on six pounds a week with you will be more amusing. We can take a cottage, you know, and live, the simple life in Gartley village, until you become the P.R.A., and I can be Lady Hope, to walk in silk attire."

"You shall be Queen of the Earth, darling, and walk alone."

"How dull! I would much rather walk with you. And that reminds me that dinner is waiting. Let us take the short cut home through the village. On the way you can tell me exactly how you bought me from my step-father for one thousand pounds."

Archie Hope frowned at the incurable obstinacy of the sex. "I didn't buy you, dearest: how many times do you wish me to deny a sale which never took place? I merely obtained your step-father's consent to our marriage in the near future."

"As if he had anything to do with my marriage, being only my step-father, and having, in my eyes, no authority. In what way did you get his consent—his unnecessary consent," she repeated with emphasis.

Of course it was waste of breath to argue with a woman who had made up her mind. The two began to walk towards the village along the causeway, and Hope cleared his throat to explain—patiently as to a child.

"You know that your step-father—Professor Braddock—is crazy on the subject of mummies?"

Lucy nodded in her pretty wilful way. "He is an Egyptologist."

4

"Quite so, but less famous and rich than he should be, considering his knowledge of dry-as-dust antiquities. Well, then, to make a long story short, he told me that he greatly desired to examine into the difference between the Egyptians and the Peruvians, with regard to the embalming of the dead."

"I always thought that he was too fond of Egypt to bother about any other country," said Lucy sapiently.

"My dear, it isn't the country he cares about, but the civilization of the past. The Incas embalmed their dead, as did the Egyptians, and in some way the Professor heard of a Royal Mummy, swathed in green bandages—so he described it to me."

"It should be called an Irish mummy," said Lucy flippantly. "Well?"

"This mummy is in possession of a man at Malta, and Professor Braddock, hearing that it was for sale for one thousand pounds—"

"Oh!" interrupted the girl vivaciously, "so this was why father sent Sidney Bolton away six weeks ago?"

"Yes. As you know, Bolton is your step-father's assistant, and is as crazy as the Professor on the subject of Egypt. I asked the Professor if he would allow me to marry you—"

"Quite unnecessary," interpolated Lucy briskly.

Archie passed over the remark to evade an argument.

"When I asked him, he said that he wished you to marry Random, who is rich. I pointed out that you loved me and not Random, and that Random was on a yachting cruise, while I was on the spot. He then said that he could not wait for the return of Random, and would give me a chance."

"What did he mean by that?"

"Well, it seems that he was in a hurry to get this Green Mummy from Malta, as he feared lest some other person should snap it up. This was two months ago, remember, and Professor Braddock wanted the cash at once. Had Random been here he could have supplied it, but as Random was away he told me that if I handed over one thousand pounds to purchase the mummy, that he would permit our engagement now, and our marriage in six months. I saw my chance and took it, for your step-father has always been an obstacle in our path, Lucy, dear. In a week Professor Braddock had the money, as I sold out some of my investments to get it. He then sent Bolton to Malta in a tramp steamer for the sake of cheapness, and now expects him back with the Green Mummy."

"Has Sidney bought it?"

"Yes. He got it for nine hundred pounds, the Professor told me, and is bringing it back in The Diver—that's the same tramp steamer in which he went to Malta. So that's the whole story, and you can

5

see there is no question of you being bought. The thousand pounds went to get your father's consent."

"He is not my father," snapped Lucy, finding nothing else to say.

"You call him so."

"That is only from habit. I can't call him Mr. Braddock, or Professor Braddock, when I live with him, so `father' is the sole mode of address left to me. And after all," she added, taking her lover's arm, "I like the Professor; he is very kind and good, although extremely absent-minded. And I am glad he has consented, for he worried me a lot to marry Sir Frank Random. I am glad you bought me."

"But I didn't," cried the exasperated lover.

"I think you did, and you shouldn't have diminished your income by buying what you could have had for nothing."

Archie shrugged his shoulders. It was vain to combat her fixed idea.

"I have still three hundred a year left. And you were worth buying."

"You have no right to talk of me as though I had been bought."

The young man gasped. "But you said—"

"Oh, what does it matter what I said. I am going to marry you on three hundred a year, so there it is. I suppose when Bolton returns, my father will be glad to see the back of me, and then will go to Egypt with Sidney to explore this secret tomb he is always talking about."

"That expedition will require more than a thousand pounds," said Archie dryly. "The Professor explained the obstacles to me. However, his doings have nothing to do with us, darling. Let Professor Braddock fumble amongst the dead if he likes. We live!"

"Apart," sighed Lucy.

"Only for the next six months; then we can get our cottage and live on love, my dearest."

"Plus three hundred a year," said the girl sensibly then she added, "Oh, poor Frank Random!"

"Lucy," cried her lover indignantly.

"Well, I was only pitying him. He's a nice man, and you can't expect him to be pleased at our marriage."

"Perhaps," said Hope in an icy tone, "you would like him to be the bridegroom. If so, there is still time."

"Silly boy!" She took his arm. "As I have been bought, you know that I can't run away from my purchaser."

"You denied being bought just now. It seems to me, Lucy, that I am to marry a weather-cock."

6

"That is only an impolite name for a woman, dear. You have no sense of humor, Frank, or you would call me an April lady."

"Because you change every five minutes. H'm! It's puzzling."

"Is it? Perhaps you would like me to resemble Widow Anne, who is always funereal. Here she is, looking like Niobe."

They were strolling through Gartley village by this time, and the cottagers came to their doors and front gates to look at the handsome young couple. Everyone knew of the engagement, and approved of the same, although some hinted that Lucy Kendal would have been wiser to marry the soldier-baronet. Amongst these was Widow Anne, who really was Mrs. Bolton, the mother of Sidney, a dismal female invariably arrayed in rusty, stuffy, aggressive mourning, although her husband had been dead for over twenty years. Because of this same mourning, and because she was always talking of the dead, she was called "Widow Anne," and looked on the appellation as a compliment to her fidelity. At the present moment she stood at the gate of her tiny garden, mopping her red eyes with a dingy handkerchief.

"Ah, young love, young love, my lady," she groaned, when the couple passed, for she always gave Lucy a title as though she really and truly had become the wife of Sir Frank, "but who knows how long it may last?"

"As long as we do," retorted Lucy, annoyed by this prophetic speech.

Widow Anne groaned with relish. "So me and Aaron, as is dead and gone, thought, my lady. But in six months he was knocking the head off me."

"The man who would lay his hand on a woman save in the way of—"

"Oh, Archie, what nonsense, you talk!" cried Miss Kendal pettishly.

"Ah!" sighed the woman of experience, "I called it nonsense too, my lady, afore Aaron, who now lies with the worms, laid me out with a flat-iron. Men's fit for jails only, as I allays says."

"A nice opinion you have of our sex," remarked Archie dryly.

"I have, sir. I could tell you things as would make your head waggle with horror on there shoulders of yours."

"What about your son Sidney? Is he also wicked?"

"He would be if he had the strength, which he hasn't," exclaimed the widow with uncomplimentary fervor. "He's Aaron's son, and Aaron hadn't much to learn from them as is where he's gone too," and she looked downward significantly.

"Sidney is a decent young fellow," said Lucy sharply. "How dare you miscall your own flesh and blood, Widow Anne? My father

7

thinks a great deal of Sidney, else he would not have sent him to Malta. Do try and be cheerful, there's a good soul. Sidney will tell you plenty to make you laugh, when he comes home."

"If he ever does come home," sighed the old woman.

"What do you mean by that?"

"Oh, it's all very well asking questions as can't be answered nohow, my lady, but I be all of a mubble-fubble, that I be."

"What is a mubble-fubble?" asked Hope, staring.

"It's a queer-like feeling of death and sorrow and tears of blood and not lifting your head for groans," said Widow Anne incoherently, "and there's meanings in mubble-fumbles, as we're told in Scripture. Not but what the Perfesser's been a kind gentleman to Sid in taking him from going round with the laundry cart, and eddicating him to watch camphorated corpses: not as what I'd like to keep an eye on them things myself. But there's no more watching for my boy Sid, as I dreamed."

"What did you dream?" asked Lucy curiously.

Widow Anne threw up two gnarled hands, wrinkled with age and laundry work, screwing up her face meanwhile.

"I dreamed of battle and murder and sudden death, my lady, with Sid in his cold grave playing on a harp, angel-like. Yes!" she folded her rusty shawl tightly round her spare form and nodded, "there was Sid, looking beautiful in his coffin, and cut into a hash, as you might say, with—"

"Ugh! ugh!" shuddered Lucy, and Archie strove to draw her away.

"With murder written all over his poor face," pursued the widow. "And I woke up screeching with cramp in my legs and pains in my lungs, and beatings in my heart, and stiffness in my—"

"Oh, hang it, shut up!" shouted Archie, seeing that Lucy was growing pale at this ghoulish recital, "don't be fool, woman. Professor Braddock says that Bolton'll be back in three days with the mummy he has been sent to fetch from Malta. You have been having nightmare! Don't you see how you are frightening Miss Kendal?"

"'The Witch' of Endor, sir—"

"Deuce take the Witch of Endor and you also. There's a shilling. Go and drink yourself into a more cheery frame of mind."

Widow Anne bit the shilling with one of her two remaining teeth, and dropped a curtsey.

"You're a good, kind gentleman," she smirked, cheered at the idea of unlimited gin. "And when my boy Sid do come home a corpse, I hope you'll come to the funeral, sir."

"What a raven!" said Lucy, as Widow Anne toddled away in the direction of the one public-house in Gartley village.

8

"I don't wonder that the late Mr. Bolton laid her out with a flat-iron. To slay such a woman would be meritorious."

"I wonder how she came to be the mother of Sidney," said Miss Kendal reflectively, as they resumed their walk, "he's such a clever, smart, and handsome young man."

"I think Bolton owes everything to the Professor's teaching and example, Lucy," replied her lover. "He was an uncouth lad, I understand, when your step-father took him into the house six years ago. Now he is quite presentable. I shouldn't wonder if he married Mrs. Jasher."

"H'm! I rather think Mrs. Jasher admires the Professor."

"Oh, he'll never marry her. If she were a mummy there might be a chance, of course, but as a human being the Professor will never look at her."

"I don't know so much about that, Archie. Mrs. Jasher is attractive."

Hope laughed. "In a mutton-dressed-as-lamb way, no doubt."

"And she has money. My father is poor and so—"

"You make up a match at once, as every woman will do. Well, let us get back to the Pyramids, and see how the flirtation is progressing."

Lucy walked on for a few steps in silence. "Do you believe in Mrs. Bolton's dream, Archie?"

"No! I believe she eats heavy suppers. Bolton will return quite safe; he is a clever fellow, not easily taken advantage of. Don't bother any more about Widow Anne and her dismal prophecies."

"I'll try not to," replied Lucy dutifully. "All the same, I wish she had not told me her dream," and she shivered.

9

CHAPTER II

PROFESSOR BRADDOCK

There was only one really palatial mansion in Gartley, and that was the ancient Georgian house known as the Pyramids. Lucy's step-father had given the place this eccentric name on taking up his abode there some ten years previously. Before that time the dwelling had been occupied by the Lord of the Manor and his family. But now the old squire was dead, and his impecunious children were scattered to the four quarters of the globe in search of money with which to rebuild their ruined fortunes. As the village was somewhat isolated and rather unhealthily situated in a marshy country, the huge, roomy old Grange had not been easy to let, and had proved quite impossible to sell. Under these disastrous circumstances, Professor Braddock—who described himself humorously as a scientific pauper—had obtained the tenancy at a ridiculously low rental, much to his satisfaction.

Many people would have paid money to avoid exile in these damp waste lands, which, as it were, fringed civilization, but their loneliness and desolation suited the Professor exactly. He required ample room for his Egyptian collection, with plenty of time to decipher hieroglyphics and study perished dynasties of the Nile Valley. The world of the present day did not interest Braddock in the least. He lived almost continuously on that portion of the mental plane which had to do with the far-distant past, and only concerned himself with physical existence, when it consisted of mummies and mystic beetles, sepulchral ornaments, pictured documents, hawk-headed deities and suchlike things of almost inconceivable antiquity. He rarely walked abroad and was invariably late for meals, save when he missed any particular one altogether, which happened frequently. Absent-minded in conversation, untidy in dress, unpractical in business, dreamy in manner, Professor Braddock lived solely for archaeology. That such a man should have taken to himself a wife was mystery.

Yet he had been married fifteen years before to a widow, who possessed a limited income and one small child. It was the opportunity of securing the use of a steady income which had decoyed Braddock into the matrimonial snare of Mrs. Kendal. To put it plainly, he had married the agreeable widow for her money, although he could scarcely be called a fortune-hunter. Like Eugene

Aram, he desired cash to assist learning, and as that scholar had committed murder to secure what he wanted, so did the Professor marry to obtain his ends. These were to have someone to manage the house, and to be set free from the necessity of earning his bread, so that he might indulge in pursuits more pleasurable than money-making. Mrs. Kendal was a placid, phlegmatic lady, who liked rather than loved the Professor, and who desired him more as a companion than as a husband. With Braddock she did not arrange a romantic marriage so much as enter into a congenial partnership. She wanted a man in the house, and he desired freedom from pecuniary embarrassment. On these lines the prosaic bargain was struck, and Mrs. Kendal became the Professor's wife with entirely successful results. She gave her husband a home, and her child a father, who became fond of Lucy, and who—considering he was merely an amateur parent—acted admirably.

But this sensible partnership lasted only for five years. Mrs. Braddock died of a chill on the liver and left her five hundred a year to the Professor for life, with remainder to Lucy, then a small girl of ten. It was at this critical moment that Braddock became a practical man for the first and last time in his dreamy life. He buried his wife with unfeigned regret—for he had been sincerely attached to her in his absent-minded way—and sent Lucy to a Hampstead boarding school. After an interview with his late wife's lawyer to see that the income was safe, he sought for a house in the country, and quickly discovered Gartley Grange, which no one would take because of its isolation. Within three months from the burial of Mrs. Braddock, the widower had removed himself and his collection to Gartley, and had renamed his new abode the Pyramids. Here he dwelt quietly and enjoyably—from his dry-as-dust point of view—for ten years, and here Lucy Kendal had come when her education was completed. The arrival of a marriageable young lady made no difference in the Professor's habits, and he hailed her thankfully as the successor to her mother in managing the small establishment. It is to be feared that Braddock was somewhat selfish in his views, but the fixed idea of archaeological research made him egotistical.

The mansion was three-story, flat-roofed, extremely ugly and unexpectedly comfortable. Built of mellow red brick with dingy white stone facings, it stood a few yards back from the roadway which ran from Gartley Fort through the village, and, at the precise point where the Pyramids was situated, curved abruptly through woodlands to terminate a mile away, at Jessum, the local station of the Thames Railway Line. An iron railing, embedded in moldering stone work, divided the narrow front garden from the road, and on either side of the door—which could be reached by five shallow steps—grew two small yew trees, smartly clipped and trimmed into cones of dull green. These yews possessed some magical significance, which Professor Braddock would occasionally explain to chance visitors interested in occult matters; for, amongst other things Egyptian, the archaeologist searched into the magic of the Sons of Khem, and insisted that there was more truth than superstition in their enchantments.

Braddock used all the vast rooms of the ground floor to house his collection of antiquities, which he had acquired through many laborious years. He dwelt entirely in this museum, as his bedroom adjoined his study, and he frequently devoured his hurried meals amongst the brilliantly tinted mummy cases. The embalmed dead populated his world, and only now and then, when Lucy insisted, did he ascend to the first floor, which was her particular abode. Here was the drawing-room, the dining-room and Lucy's boudoir; here also were sundry bedrooms, furnished and unfurnished, in one of which Miss Kendal slept, while the others remained vacant for chance visitors, principally from the scientific world. The third story was devoted to the cook, her husband—who acted as gardener—and to the house parlor maid, a composite domestic, who worked from morning until night in keeping the great house clean. During the day these servants attended to their business in a comfortable basement, where the cook ruled supreme. At the back of the mansion stretched a fairly large kitchen garden, to which the cook's husband devoted his attention. This was the entire domain belonging to the tenant, as, of course, the Professor did not rent the arable acres and comfortable farms which had belonged to the dispossessed family.

Everything in the house went smoothly, as Lucy was a methodical young person, who went by the clock and the almanac. Braddock little knew how much of his undeniable comfort he owed to her fostering care; for, prior to her return from school, he had been robbed right and left by unscrupulous domestics. When his step-daughter arrived he simply handed over the keys and the housekeeping money—a fixed sum—and gave her strict instructions not to bother him. Miss Kendal faithfully observed this injunction, as she enjoyed being undisputed mistress, and knew that, so long as her step-father had his meals, his bed, his bath and his clothes, he required nothing save the constant society of his beloved mummies, of which no one wished to deprive him. These he dusted and cleansed and rearranged himself. Not even Lucy dared to invade the museum, and the mere mention of spring cleaning drove the Professor into displaying frantic rage, in which he used bad language.

On returning from her walk with Archie, the girl had lured her step-father into assuming a rusty dress suit, which had done service for many years, and had coaxed him into a promise to be present at dinner. Mrs. Jasher, the lively widow of the district, was coming, and Braddock approved of a woman who looked up to him as the one wise man in the world. Even science is susceptible to judicious flattery, and Mrs. Jasher was never backward in putting her admiration into words. Female gossip declared that the widow wished to become the second Mrs. Braddock, but if this was really the case, she had but small chance of gaining her end. The Professor had once sacrificed his liberty to secure a competence, and, having acquired five hundred a year, was not inclined for a second matrimonial venture. Had the widow been a dollar heiress with a million at her back he would not have troubled to place a ring on her finger. And certainly Mrs. Jasher had little to gain from such a dreary marriage, beyond a collection of rubbish—as she said—and a dull country house situated in a district inhabited solely by peasants belonging to Saxon times.

Archie Hope left Lucy at the door of the Pyramids and repaired to his village lodgings, for the purpose of assuming evening dress. Lucy, being her own housekeeper, assisted the overworked parlor maid to lay and decorate the table before receiving the guests. Thus Mrs. Jasher found no one in the drawing-room to welcome her, and, taking the privilege of old friendship, descended to beard Braddock in his den. The Professor raised his eyes from a newly bought scarabeus to behold a stout little lady smiling on him from the doorway. He did not appear to be grateful for the interruption, but Mrs. Jasher was not at all dismayed, being a man-hunter by profession. Besides, she saw that Braddock was in the clouds as usual, and would have received the King himself in the same absent-minded manner.

"Pouf! what an abominal smell!" exclaimed the widow, holding a flimsy lace handkerchief to her nose. "Kind of camphor-sandal-wood charnel-house smell. I wonder you are not asphyxiated. Pouf! Ugh! Bur-r-r

The Professor stared at her with cold, fishy eyes. "Did you speak?"

"Oh, dear me, yes, and you don't even ask me to take a chair. If I were a nasty stuffy mummy, now, you would be embracing me by, this time. Don't you know that I have come to dinner, you silly man?" and she tapped him playfully with her closed fan.

"I have had dinner," said Braddock, egotistic as usual.

"No, you have not." Mrs. Jasher spoke positively, and pointed to a small tray of untouched food on the side table. "You have not

13

even had luncheon. You must live on air, like a chameleon—or on love, perhaps," she ended in a significantly tender tone.

But she might as well have spoken to the granite image of Horus in the corner. Braddock merely rubbed his chin and stared harder than ever at the glittering visitor.

"Dear me!" he said innocently. "I must have forgotten to eat. Lamplight!" he looked round vaguely. "Of course, I remember lighting the lamps. Time has gone by very rapidly. I am really hungry." He paused to make sure, then repeated his remark in a more positive manner. "Yes, I am very hungry, Mrs. Jasher." He looked at her as though she had just entered. "Of course, Mrs. Jasher. Do you wish to see me about anything particular?"

The widow frowned at his inattention, and then laughed. It was impossible to be angry with this dreamer.

"I have come to dinner, Professor. Do try and wake up; you are half asleep and half starved, too, I expect."

"I certainly feel unaccountably hungry," admitted Braddock cautiously.

"Unaccountably, when you have eaten nothing since breakfast. You weird man, I believe you are a mummy yourself."

But the Professor had again returned to examine the scarabeus, this time with a powerful magnifying glass.

"It certainly belongs to the twentieth dynasty," he murmured, wrinkling his brows.

Mrs. Jasher stamped and flirted her fan pettishly. The creature's soul, she decided, was certainly not in his body, and until it came back he would continue to ignore her. With the annoyance of a woman who is not getting her own way, she leaned back in Braddock's one comfortable chair—which she had unerringly selected—and examined him intently. Perhaps the gossips were correct, and she was trying to imagine what kind of a husband he would make. But whatever might be her thoughts, she eyed Braddock as earnestly as Braddock eyed the scarabeus.

Outwardly the Professor did not appear like the savant he was reported to be. He was small of stature, plump of body, rosy as a little Cupid, and extraordinarily youthful, considering his fifty-odd years of scientific wear and tear. With a smooth, clean-shaven face, plentiful white hair like spun silk, and neat feet and hands, he did not look his age. The dreamy look in his small blue eyes was rather belied by the hardness of his thin-lipped mouth, and by the pugnacious push of his jaw. The eyes and the dome-like forehead hinted that brain without much originality; but the lower part of this contradictory countenance might have belonged to a prize-fighter. Nevertheless, Braddock's plumpness did away to a

14

considerable extent with his aggressive look. It was certainly latent, but only came to the surface when he fought with a brother savant over some tomb-dweller from Thebes. In the soft lamplight he looked like a fighting cherub, and it was a pity—in the interests of art—that the hairless pink and white face did not surmount a pair of wings rather than a rusty and ill-fitting dress suit.

"He's nane sa dafty as he looks," thought Mrs. Jasher, who was Scotch, although she claimed to be cosmopolitan. "With his mummies he is all right, but outside those he might be difficult to manage. And these things," she glanced round the shadowy room, crowded with the dead and their earthly belongings. "I don't think I would care to marry the British Museum. Too much like hard work, and I am not so young as I was."

The near mirror—a polished silver one, which had belonged, ages ago, to some coquette of Memphis—denied this uncomplimentary thought, for Mrs. Jasher did not look a day over thirty, although her birth certificate set her down as forty-five. In the lamplight she might have passed for even younger, so carefully had she preserved what remained to her of youth. She assuredly was somewhat stout, and never had been so tall as she desired to be. But the lines of her plump figure were still discernible in the cunningly cut gown, and she carried her little self with such mighty dignity that people overlooked the mortifying height of a trifle over five feet. Her features were small and neat, but her large blue eyes were so noticeable and melting that those on whom she turned them ignored the lack of boldness in chin and nose. Her hair was brown and arranged in the latest fashion, while her complexion was so fresh and pink that, if she did paint—as jealous women averred—she must have been quite an artist with the hare's foot and the rouge pot and the necessary powder puff.

Mrs. Jasher's clothes repaid the thought she expended upon them, and she was artistic in this as in other things. Dressed in a crocus-yellow gown, with short sleeves to reveal her beautiful arms, and cut low to display her splendid bust, she looked perfectly dressed. A woman would have declared the wide-netted black lace with which the dress was draped to be cheap, and would have hinted that the widow wore too many jewels in her hair, on her corsage, round her arms, and ridiculously gaudy rings on her fingers. This might have been true, for Mrs. Jasher sparkled like the Milky Way at every movement; but the gleam of gold and the flash of gems seemed to suit her opulent beauty. Her slightest movement wafted around her a strange Chinese perfume, which she obtained—so she said—from a friend of her late husband's who was in the British Embassy at Pekin. No one possessed this especial perfume

15

but Mrs. Jasher, and anyone who had previously met her, meeting her in the darkness, could have guessed at her identity. With a smile to show her white teeth, with her golden-hued dress and glittering jewels, the pretty widow glowed in that glimmering room like a tropical bird.

The Professor raised his dreamy eyes and laid the beetle on one side, when his brain fully grasped that this charming vision was waiting to be entertained. She was better to look upon even than the beloved scarabeus, and he advanced to shake hands as though she had just entered the room. Mrs. Jasher—knowing his ways—rose to extend her hand, and the two small, stout figures looked absurdly like a pair of chubby Dresden ornaments which had stepped from the mantelshelf.

"Dear lady, I am glad to see you. You have—you have"—the Professor reflected, and then came back with a rush to the present century—"you have come to dinner, if I mistake not."

"Lucy asked me a week ago," she replied tartly, for no woman likes to be neglected for a mere beetle, however ancient.

"Then you will certainly get a good dinner," said Braddock, waving his plump white hands. "Lucy is an excellent housekeeper. I have no fault to find with her—no fault at all. But she is obstinate—oh, very obstinate, as her mother was. Do you know, dear lady, that in a papyrus scroll which I lately acquired I found the recipe for a genuine Egyptian dish, which Amenemha—the last Pharaoh of the eleventh dynasty, you know—might have eaten, and probably did eat. I desired Lucy to serve it to-night, but she refused, much to my annoyance. The ingredients, which had to do with roasted gazelle, were oil and coriander seed and—if my memory serves me—asafoetida."

"Ugh!" Mrs. Jasher's handkerchief went again to her mouth. "Say no more, Professor; your dish sounds horrid. I don't wish to eat it, and be turned into a mummy before my time."

"You would make a really beautiful mummy," said Braddock, paying what he conceived was a compliment; "and, should you die, I shall certainly attend to your embalming, if you prefer that to cremation."

"You dreadful man!" cried the widow, turning pale and shrinking. "Why, I really believe that you would like to see me packed away in one of those disgusting coffins."

"Disgusting!" cried the outraged Professor, striking one of the brilliantly tinted cases. "Can you call so beautiful a specimen of sepulchral art disgusting? Look at the colors, at the regularity of the hieroglyphics—why, the history of the dead is set out in this magnificent series of pictures." He adjusted his pince-nez and began

16

to read, "The Osirian, Scemiophis that is a female name, Mrs. Jasher—who—"

"I don't want to have my history written on my coffin," interrupted the widow hysterically, for this funereal talk frightened her. "It would take much more space than a mummy case upon which to write it. My life has been volcanic, I can tell you. By the way," she added hurriedly, seeing that Braddock was on the eve of resuming the reading, "tell me about your Inca mummy. Has it arrived?"

The Professor immediately followed the false trail. "Not yet," he said briskly, rubbing his smooth hands, "but in three days I expect The Diver will be at Pierside, and Sidney will bring the mummy on here. I shall unpack it at once and learn exactly how the ancient Peruvians embalmed their dead. Doubtless they learned the art from—"

"The Egyptians," ventured Mrs. Jasher rashly.

Braddock glared. "Nothing of the sort, dear lady," he snorted angrily. "Absurd, ridiculous! I am inclined to believe that Egypt was merely a colony of that vast island of Atlantis mentioned by Plato. There—if my theory is correct—civilization begun, and the kings of Atlantis—doubtless the gods of historical tribes—governed the whole world, including that portion which we now term South America."

"Do you mean to say that there were Yankees in those days?" inquired Mrs. Jasher frivolously.

The Professor tucked his hands under his shabby coattails and strode up and down the room warming his rage, which was provoked by such ignorance.

"Good heavens, madam, where have you lived?" he exclaimed explosively—"are you a fool, or merely an ignorant woman? I am talking of prehistoric times, thousands of years ago, when you were probably a stray atom embedded in the slime."

"Oh, you horrid creature!" cried Mrs. Jasher indignantly, and was about to give Braddock her opinion, if only to show him that she could hold her own, when the door opened.

"How are you, Mrs. Jasher?" said Lucy, advancing.

"Here am I and here is Archie. Dinner is ready. And you—"

"I am very hungry," said Mrs. Jasher. "I have been called an atom of the slime," then she laughed and took possession of young Hope.

Lucy wrinkled her brow; she did not approve of the widow's man-annexing instinct.

CHAPTER III

A MYSTERIOUS TOMB

One member of the Braddock household was not included in the general staff, being a mere appendage of the Professor himself. This was a dwarfish, misshapen Kanaka, a pigmy in height, but a giant in breadth, with short, thick legs, and long, powerful arms. He had a large head, and a somewhat handsome face, with melancholy black eyes and a fine set of white teeth. Like most Polynesians, his skin was of a pale bronze and elaborately tattooed, even the cheeks and chin being scored with curves and straight lines of mystical import. But the most noticeable thing about him was his huge mop of frizzled hair, which, by some process, known only to himself, he usually dyed a vivid yellow. The flaring locks streaming from his head made him resemble a Peruvian image of the sun, and it was this peculiar coiffure which had procured for him the odd name of Cockatoo. The fact that this grotesque creature invariably wore a white drill suit, emphasized still more the suggestion of his likeness to an Australian parrot.

Cockatoo had come from the Solomon Islands in his teens to the colony of Queensland, to work on the plantations, and there the Professor had picked him up as his body servant. When Braddock returned to marry Mrs. Kendal, the boy had refused to leave him, although it was represented to the young savage that he was somewhat too barbaric for sober England. Finally, the Professor had consented to bring him over seas, and had never regretted doing so, for Cockatoo, finding his scientific master a true friend, worshipped him as a visible god. Having been captured when young by Pacific black-birders, he talked excellent English, and from contact with the necessary restraints of civilization was, on the whole, extremely well behaved. Occasionally, when teased by the villagers and his fellow-servants, he would break into childish rages, which bordered on the dangerous. But a word from Braddock always quieted him, and when penitent he would crawl like a whipped dog to the feet of his divinity. For the most part he lived entirely in the museum, looking after the collection and guarding it from harm. Lucy—who had a horror of the creature's uncanny looks—objected to Cockatoo waiting at the table, and it was only on rare occasions that he was permitted to assist the harassed parlormaid. On this night the Kanaka acted excellently as a butler, and crept softly round the

18

table, attending to the needs of the diners. He was an admirable servant, deft and handy, but his blue-lined face and squat figure together with the obtrusively golden halo, rather worried Mrs. Jasher. And, indeed, in spite of custom, Lucy also felt uncomfortable when this gnome hovered at her elbow. It looked as though one of the fantastical idols from the museum below had come to haunt the living.

"I do not like that Golliwog," breathed Mrs. Jasher to her host, when Cockatoo was at the sideboard. "He gives me the creeps."

"Imagination, my dear lady, pure imagination. Why should we not have a picturesque animal to wait upon us?"

"He would wait picturesquely enough at a cannibal feast," suggested Archie, with a laugh.

"Don't!" murmured Lucy, with a shiver. "I shall not be able to eat my dinner if you talk so."

"Odd that Hope should say what he has said," observed Braddock confidently to the widow. "Cockatoo comes from a cannibal island, and doubtless has seen the consumption of human flesh. No, no, my dear lady, do not look so alarmed. I don't think he has eaten any, as he was taken to Queensland long before he could participate in such banquets. He is a very decent animal."

"A very dangerous one, I fancy," retorted Mrs. Jasher, who looked pale.

"Only when he loses his temper, and I'm always able to suppress that when it is at its worst. You are not eating your meat, my dear lady."

"Can you wonder at it, and you talk of cannibals?"

"Let us change the conversation to cereals," suggested Hope, whose appetite was of the best—"wheat, for instance. In this queer little village I notice the houses are divided by a field of wheat. It seems wrong somehow for corn to be bunched up with houses."

"That's old Farmer Jenkins," said Lucy vivaciously; "he owns three or four acres near the public-house and will not allow them to be built over, although he has been offered a lot of money. I noticed myself, Archie, the oddity of finding a cornfield surrounded by cottages. It's like Alice in Wonderland."

"But fancy any one offering money for land here," observed Hope, toying with his claret glass, which had just been refilled, by the attentive Cockatoo, "at the Back-of-Beyond, as it were. I shouldn't care to live here—the neighborhood is so desolate."

"All the same you do live here!" interposed Mrs. Jasher smartly, and with a roguish glance at Lucy.

Archie caught the glance and saw the blush on Miss Kendal's face.

"You have answered your question yourself, Mrs. Jasher," he—said, smiling. "I have the inducement you hint at to remain here, and certainly, as a landscape painter, I admire the marshes and sunsets. As an artist and an engaged man I stop in Gartley, otherwise I should clear out. But I fail to see why a lady of your attractions should—"

"I may have a sentimental reason also," interrupted the widow, with a sly glance at the absent-minded Professor, who was drawing hieroglyphics on the table-cloth with a fork; "also, my cottage is cheap and very comfortable. The late Mr. Jasher did not leave me sufficient money to live in London. He was a consul in China, you know, and consuls are never very well paid. I will come in for a large income, however."

"Indeed," said Lucy politely, and wondering why Mrs. Jasher was so communicative. "Soon I hope."

"It may be very soon. My brother, you know—a merchant in Pekin. He has come home to die, and is unmarried. When he does die, I shall go to London. But," added the widow, meditatively and glancing again at the Professor, "I shall be sorry to leave dear Gartley. Still, the memory of happy hours spent in this house will always remain with me. Ah me! ah me!" and she put her handkerchief to her eyes.

Lucy telegraphed to Archie that the widow was a humbug, and Archie telegraphed back that he quite agreed with her. But the Professor, whom the momentary silence had brought back to the present century, looked up and asked Lucy if the dinner was finished.

"I have to do some work this evening," said the Professor.

"Oh, father, when you said that you would take a holiday," said Lucy reproachfully.

"I am doing so now. Look at the precious minutes I am wasting in eating, my dear. Life is short and much remains to be done in the way of Egyptian exploration. There is the sepulchre of Queen Tahoser. If I could only enter that," and he sighed, while helping himself to cream.

"Why don't you?" asked Mrs. Jasher, who was beginning to give up her pursuit of Braddock, for it was no use wooing a man whose interests centered entirely in Egyptian tombs.

"I have yet to discover it," said the Professor simply; then, warming to the congenial theme, he glanced around and delivered a short historical lecture. "Tahoser was the chief wife and queen of a famous Pharaoh—the Pharaoh of the Exodus, in fact."

"The one who was drowned in the Red Sea?" asked Archie idly.

"Why, yes—but that happened later. Before pursuing the

20

Hebrews,—if the Mosaic account is to be believed,—this Pharaoh marched far into the interior of Africa,—the Libya of the ancients,—and conquered the natives of Upper Ethiopia. Being deeply in love with his queen, he took her with him on this expedition, and she died before the Pharaoh returned to Memphis. From records which I discovered in the museum of Cairo, I have reason to believe that the Pharaoh buried her with much pomp in Ethiopia, sacrificing, I believe, many prisoners at her gorgeous funeral rites. From the wealth of that Pharaoh—for wealthy he must have been on account of his numerous victories—and from the love he bore this princess, I am confident—confident," added Braddock, striking the table vehemently, "that when discovered, her tomb will be filled with riches, and may also contain documents of incalculable value."

"And you wish to get the money?" asked Mrs. Jasher, who was rather bored.

The Professor rose fiercely. "Money! I care nothing for money. I desire to obtain the funeral jewelry and golden masks, the precious images of the gods, so as to place them in the British Museum. And the scrolls of papyrus buried with the mummy of Tahoser may contain an account of Ethiopian civilization, about which we know nothing. Oh, that tomb,—that tomb!" Braddock began to walk the room, quite forgetting that he had not finished his dinner. "I know the mountains whose entrails were pierced to form the sepulchre. Were I able to go to Africa, I am certain that I should discover the tomb. Ah, with what glory would my name be covered, were I so fortunate!"

"Why don't you go to Africa, sir, and try?" asked Hope.

"Fool!" cried the Professor politely. "To fit out an expedition would take some five thousand pounds, if not more. I would have to penetrate through a hostile country to reach the chain of mountains I speak of, where I know this precious tomb is to be found. I need supplies, an escort, guns, camels, and all the rest of it. A leader must be obtained to manage the fighting men necessary to pass through this dangerous zone. It is no easy task to find the tomb of Tahoser. And yet if I could—if I could only get the money," and he walked up and down with his head bent on his breast.

Mrs. Jasher was used to Braddock's vagaries by this time, and merely continued to fan herself placidly.

"I wish I could help you with the expedition," she said quietly. "I should like to have some of that lovely Egyptian jewelry myself. But I am quite a pauper, until my brother dies, poor man. Then—" She hesitated.

"What then?" asked Braddock, wheeling.

"I shall aid you with pleasure."

21

"It's a bargain!" Braddock stretched out his hand.

"A bargain," said Mrs. Jasher, accepting the grasp somewhat nervously, for she had not expected to be taken so readily at her word. A glance at Lucy revealed her nervousness.

"Do sit down, father, and finish your dinner," said that young lady. "I am sure you will have more than enough to do when the mummy arrives."

"Mummy—what mummy?" murmured Braddock, again beginning to eat.

"The Inca mummy."

"Of course. The mummy of Inca Caxas, which Sidney is bringing from Malta. When I strip that corpse of its green bandages I shall find—"

"Find what?" asked Archie, seeing that the Professor hesitated.

Braddock cast a swift look at his questioner.

"I shall find the peculiar mode of Peruvian embalming," he replied abruptly, and somehow the way in which he spoke gave Hope the impression that the answer was an excuse. But before he could formulate the thought that Braddock was concealing something, Mrs. Jasher spoke frivolously.

"I hope your mummy has jewels," she said.

"It has not," replied Braddock sharply. "So far as I know, the Inca race never buried their dead with jewels."

"But I have read in Prescott's History that they did," said Hope.

"Prescott! Prescott!" cried the Professor contemptuously, "a most unreliable authority. However, I'll promise you one thing, Hope, that if there are any jewels, or jewelry, you shall have the lot."

"Give me some, Mr. Hope," cried the widow.

"I cannot," laughed Archie; "the green mummy belongs to the Professor."

"I cannot accept such a gift, Hope. Owing to circumstances I have been obliged to borrow the money from you; otherwise the mummy would have been acquired by some one else. But when I find the tomb of Queen Tahoser, I shall repay the loan."

"You have repaid it already," said Hope, looking at Lucy.

Braddock's eyes followed his gaze and his brows contracted. "Humph!" he muttered, "I don't know if I am right in consenting to Lucy's marriage with a pauper."

"Oh, father!" cried the girl, "Archie is not a pauper."

"I have enough for Lucy and me to live on," said Hope, although his face had flushed, "and, had I been a pauper I could not have given you that thousand pounds."

"You will be repaid—you will be repaid," said Braddock, waving his hand to dismiss the subject. "And now," he rose with a yawn, "if this tedious feast is at an end, I shall again seek my work."

Without a word of apology to the disgusted Mrs. Jasher, he trotted to the door, and there paused.

"By the way, Lucy," he said, turning, "I had a letter to-day from Random. He returns in his yacht to Pierside in two or three days. In fact, his arrival will coincide with that of The Diver."

"I don't see what his arrival has to do with me," said Lucy tartly.

"Oh, nothing at all—nothing at all," said Braddock airily, "only I thought—that is, but never mind, never mind. Cockatoo, come down with me. Good night! Good night!" and he disappeared.

"Well," said Mrs. Jasher, drawing along breath, "for rudeness and selfishness, commend me to a scientist. We might be all mud, for what notice he takes of us."

"Never mind," said Miss Kendal, rising, "come to the drawing-room and have some music. Archie, will you stop here?"

"No. I don't care to sit over my wine alone," said that young gentleman, rising. "I shall accompany you and Mrs. Jasher. And Lucy," he stopped her at the door, through which the widow had already passed, "what did your father mean by his hints concerning Random?"

"I think he regrets giving his consent to my marriage with you," she whispered back. "Did you not hear him talk about that tomb? He desires to get money for the expedition."

"From Random? What rubbish! Sooner than that—if our marriage is stopped by the beastly business—I'll sell out and—"

"You'll do nothing of the sort," interrupted the girl imperiously; "we must live if we marry. You have given my father enough."

"But if Random lends money for this expedition?"

"He does so at his own risk. I am not going to marry Sir Frank because of my step-father's requirements. He has no rights over me, and, whether he consents or not, I marry you."

"My darling!" and Archie kissed her before they followed Mrs. Jasher into the drawing-room. All the same, he foresaw trouble.

CHAPTER IV

THE UNEXPECTED

For the next two or three days, Archie felt decidedly, worried over his projected marriage with Lucy. Certainly he had—to put it bluntly—purchased Braddock's consent, and that gentleman could scarcely draw back from his plighted word, which had cost the lover so much. Nevertheless, Hope did not entirely, trust the Professor, as, from the few words which he had let drop at the dinner party, it was plain that he hankered after money with which to fit out the expedition in search of the mysterious tomb to which he had alluded. Archie knew, as did the Professor, that he could not supply the necessary five thousand pounds without practically ruining himself, and already he had crippled his resources in paying over the price of the green mummy. He had fondly believed that Braddock would have been satisfied with the relic of Peruvian humanity; but it seemed that the Professor, having got what he wanted, now clamored for what was at present beyond his reach. The mummy was his property, but he desired the contents of Queen Tahoser's tomb also. This particular moon, which he cried for, was a very expensive article, and Hope did not see how he could gain it.

Unless—and here came in the cause of Archie's worry—unless the five thousand pounds was borrowed from Sir Frank Random, the Professor would have to content himself with the Maltese mummy. But from what the young man had seen of Braddock's longing for the especial sepulchre, which he desired to loot, he believed that the scientist would not readily surrender his whim. Random could easily lend or give the money, since he was extremely rich, and extremely generous, but it was improbable that he would aid Braddock without a quid pro quo. As the sole desire of the baronet's heart was to make Lucy his wife, it could easily be guessed that he would only assist the Professor to realize his ambition on condition that the savant used his influence with his step-daughter. That meant the breaking of the engagement with Hope and the marriage of the girl to the soldier. Of course such a state of things would make Lucy unhappy; but Braddock cared very little for that. To gratify his craze for Egyptian research, he would be willing to sacrifice a dozen girls like Lucy.

Undoubtedly Lucy would refuse to be passed along from one man to another like a bale of goods, and Archie knew that, so far as in her lay, she would keep to her engagement, especially as she denied Braddock's right to dispose of her hand. All the same, the Professor, in spite of his cherubical looks, could make himself extremely disagreeable, and undoubtedly would do so if thwarted. The sole course that remained, should Braddock begin operations to break the present engagement, would be to marry Lucy at once. Archie would willingly have done so, but pecuniary difficulties stood in the way. He had never told any one of these, not even the girl he loved, but they existed all the same. For many years he had been assisting needy relatives, and thus had hampered himself, in spite of his income. By sheer force of will, so as to force Braddock into giving him Lucy, he had contrived to secure the necessary thousand pounds, without confusing the arrangements he had made to pay off certain debts connected with his domestic philanthropy; but this brought him to the end of his resources. In six months he hoped to be free to have his income entirely to himself, and then—small as it was—he could support a wife. But until the half year elapsed he could see no chance of marrying Lucy with any degree of comfort, and meanwhile she would be exposed to the persecutions of the Professor. Perhaps persecutions is too harsh a word, as Braddock was kind enough to the girl. Nevertheless, he was pertinacious in gaining his aims where his pet hobby was concerned, and undoubtedly, could he see any chance of obtaining the money from Random by selling his step-daughter, he would do so. Assuredly it was dishonorable to act in this way, but the Professor was a scientific Jesuit, and deemed that the end justified the means, when any glory to himself and gain to the British Museum was in question.

"But I may be doing him an injustice," said Archie, when he was explaining his fears to Miss Kendal on the third day after the dinner party. "After all, the Professor is a gentleman, and will probably hold to the bargain which he has made."

"I don't care whether he does or not," cried Lucy, who had a fine color and a certain amount of fire in her eyes. "I am not going to be bought and sold to forward these nasty scientific schemes. My father can say what he likes and do what he likes, but I marry you—to-morrow if you like."

"That's just it," said Archie, flushing, "we can't marry."

"Why?" she asked, much astonished.

Hope looked at the ground and drew patterns with his cane-point in the sand. They were seated in the hot sunshine—for the Indian summer still continued—under a moldering brick wall, which ran around the most delightful of kitchen gardens. This was situated at the back of the Pyramids, and contained a multiplicity of pot herbs and fruit trees and vegetables. It resembled the Fairy Garden in Madame D'Alnoy's story of The White Cat, and in the autumn yielded a plentiful crop of fine-flavored fruit. But now the trees were bare and the garden looked somewhat forlorn for lack of greenery. But in spite of the lateness of the season, Lucy often brought a book to read under the glowing wall, and there ripened like a peach in the warm sunshine. On this occasion she brought Archie into the old-world garden, as he had hinted at confidences. And the time had come to speak plainly, as Hope began to think that he had not treated Lucy quite fairly in hiding from her his momentarily embarrassed position.

"Why can't we marry at once?" asked Lucy, seeing that her lover held his peace and looked confused.

Hope did not reply directly. "I had better release you from your engagement," he said haltingly.

"Oh!" Lucy's nostrils dilated and she threw back her head scornfully. "And the other woman's name?"

"There is no other woman. I love you and you only. But—money."

"What about money? You have your income!"

"Oh yes—that is sure, small as it is. But I have incurred debts on behalf of an uncle and his family. These have embarrassed me for the moment, and so I cannot see my way to marrying you for at least six months, Lucy." He caught her hand. "I feel ashamed of myself that I did not tell you of this before. But I feared to lose you. Yet, on reflection, I see that it is dishonorable to keep you in the dark, and if you think that I have behaved badly—"

"Well, I do in a way," she interrupted quickly, "as your silence was quite unnecessary. Don't treat me as a doll, my dear. I wish to share your troubles as well as your joys. Come, tell me all about it."

"You are not angry?"

"Yes, I am—at your thinking I loved you so little as to be biased against our marriage because of money troubles. Pooh!" she flicked away a speck of dust from his coat, "I don't care that for such things."

"You are an angel," he cried ardently.

"I am a very practical girl just now," she retorted. "Go on, confess!"

Archie, thus encouraged, did so, and it was a very mild confession that she heard, involving a great deal of unnecessary sacrifice in helping a pauper uncle. Hope strove to belittle his good deeds as much as possible, but Lucy saw plainly the good heart that had dictated the giving up of his small income for some years. When in possession of all the facts, she threw her arms around his neck and kissed him.

"You are a silly old boy," she whispered. "As if what you tell me could make any difference to me!"

"But we can't be married for six months, dearest."

"Of course not. Do you believe that I as a woman can gather together my trousseau under six months? No, my dear. We must not marry in haste to repent at leisure. In another half year you will enjoy your own income, and then we can marry."

"But meanwhile," said Archie, after kissing her, "the Professor will bother you to marry Random."

"Oh no. He has sold me to you for one thousand pounds. There! There, do not say a single word. I am only teasing you. Let us say that my father has consented to my marriage with you, and cannot withdraw his word. Not that I care if he does. I am my own mistress."

"Lucy!"—he took her hands again and looked into her eyes— "Braddock is a scientific lunatic, and would do anything to forward his aims with regard to this very expensive tomb, which he has set his heart on discovering. As I can't lend or give the money, he is sure to apply to Random, and Random—"

"Will want to marry me," cried Lucy, rising. "No, my dear, not at all. Sir Frank is a gentleman, and when he learns that I am engaged to you, he will simply become a dear friend. There, don't worry any more about the matter. You ought to have told me of your troubles before, but as I have forgiven you, there is no more to be said. In six months I shall become Mrs. Hope, and meanwhile I can hold my own against any inconvenience that my father may cause me."

"But—" He rose and began to remonstrate, anxious to abase himself still further before this angel of a maiden.

She placed her hand over his mouth. "Not another word, or I shall box your ears, sir—that is, I shall exercise the privilege of a wife before I become one. And now," she slipped her arm within his, "let us go in and see the arrival of the precious mummy."

"Oh, it has arrived then."

"Not here exactly. My father expects it at three o'clock."

"It is now a quarter to," said Archie, consulting his watch. "As I have been to London all yesterday I did not know that The Diver had arrived at Pierside, How is Bolton?"

Lucy wrinkled her brows. "I am rather worried over Sidney," she said in an anxious voice, "and so is my father. He had not appeared."

"What do you mean by that?"

"Well," she looked at the ground in a pondering manner, "my father got a letter from Sidney yesterday afternoon, saying that the ship with the mummy and himself on board had arrived about four o'clock. The letter was sent on by special messenger and came at six."

"Then it arrived in the evening and not in the afternoon?"

"How particular you are!" said Miss Kendal, with a shrug. "Well, then, Sidney said that he could not bring the mummy to this place last night as it was so late. He intended—so he told my father in the letter—to remove the case containing the mummy ashore to an inn near the wharf at Pierside, and there would remain the night so as to take care of it."

"That's all right," said Hope, puzzled. "Where's your difficulty?"

"A note came from the landlord of the inn this morning, saying that by direction of Mr. Bolton—that is Sidney, you know—he was sending the mummy in its case to Gartley on a lorry, and that it would arrive at three o'clock this afternoon."

"Well?" asked Hope, still puzzled.

"Well?" she rejoined impatiently. "Can't you see show strange it is that Sidney should let the mummy out of his sight, after guarding it so carefully not only from Malta to England, but all the night in Pierside at that hotel? Why doesn't he bring the mummy here himself, and come on with the lorry?"

"There is no explanation—no letter from Sidney Bolton?"

"None. He wrote yesterday, as I stated, saying that he would keep the case in the hotel, and send it on this morning."

"Did he use the word `send,' or the word `bring'?"

"He said 'send.'"

"Then that shows he did not intend to bring it himself."

"But why should he not do so?"

"I daresay he will explain when he appears."

"I am very sorry for him when he does appear," said Lucy seriously, "for my father is furious. Why, this precious mummy, for which so much has been paid, might have been lost."

"Pooh! Who would steal a thing like that?"

"A thing like that is worth nearly one thousand pounds," said Lucy in a dry tone, "and if anyone got wind of it, stealing would be easy, since Sidney, as appears likely, has sent on the case unguarded."

"Well, let us go in and see if Sidney arrives with the case."

They passed out of the garden and sauntered round to the front of the house. There, standing in the roadway, they beheld a ponderous lorry with a rough-looking driver standing at the horses' heads. The front door of the house was open, so the mummy case had apparently arrived before its time, and had been taken to Braddock's museum while they were chatting in the kitchen garden.

"Did Mr. Bolton come with the case?" asked Lucy, leaning over the railings and addressing the driver.

"No one came, miss, except myself and my two mates, who have taken the case indoor." The driver jerked a coarse thumb over his shoulder.

"Was Mr. Bolton at the hotel, where the case remained for the night?"

"No, miss—that is, I dunno who Mr. Bolton is. The landlord of the Sailor's Rest told me and my mates to take the case to this here house, and we done it. That's all I know, miss."

"Strange," murmured Lucy, walking to the front door. "What do you think, Archie? Isn't it strange?"

Hope nodded. "But I daresay Bolton will explain his absence," said he, following her. "He will arrive in time to open the mummy case along with the Professor."

"I hope so," said Miss Kendal, who looked much perplexed. "I can't understand Sidney abandoning the case, when it might so easily have been stolen. Come in and see my father, Archie," and she passed into the house, followed by the young man, whose curiosity was now aroused. As they entered the door, the two men who had taken in the case blundered out and shortly drove away on the lorry towards Jessum railway station.

In the museum they found Braddock purple with rage and swearing vigorously. He was staring at a large packing case, which had been set up on end against the wall, while beside him crouched Cockatoo, holding chisels and hammers and wedges necessary to open the treasure trove.

"So the precious mummy has arrived, father," said Lucy, who saw that the Professor was furious. "Are you not pleased?"

"Pleased! pleased!" shouted the angry man of science. "How can I be pleased when I see how badly the case has been treated? See how it has been bruised and battered and shaken! I'll have an action against Captain Hervey of The Diver if my mummy has been injured. Sidney should have taken better care of so precious an object."

"What does he say?" asked Archie, glancing round the museum to see if the delinquent had arrived.

"Say!" shouted Braddock again, and snatching a chisel from Cockatoo. "Oh, what can he say when he is not here?"

"Not here?" said Lucy, more and more surprised at the unaccountable absence of Braddock's assistant. "Where is he, then?"

"I don't know. I wish I did; I'd have him arrested for neglecting to watch over this case. As it is, when he comes back I'll dismiss him from my employment. He can go back to his infernal laundry work along with his old witch of a mother."

"But why hasn't Bolton come back, sir?" asked Hope sharply.

Braddock struck a furious blow at the head of the chisel which he had inserted into the case.

"I want to know that. He brought the case to the Sailor's Rest, and should have come on with it this morning. Instead of doing so, he tells the landlord—a most unreliable man—to send it on. And my precious mummy—the mummy that has cost nine hundred pounds," cried Braddock, working furiously, and battering the chisel as though it were Bolton's head, "is left to be stolen by any scientific thief that comes along." While the Professor, assisted by Cockatoo, loosened the lid of the packing case, a mild voice was heard at the door. Lucy turned, as did Archie, to see Widow Anne curtseying on the threshold of the door.

Braddock himself took no notice of her entrance, being occupied with his task, and even while doing it swore scientifically under his breath. He was furious against Bolton for neglect of duty, and Hope rather sympathized with him. It was a serious matter to have left a valuable object like the green mummy to the rough care of laborers.

"I beg your pardon, my lady," whimpered Widow Anne, who looked more lean and rusty and dismal than ever; "but has my Sid come? I saw the cart and the coffin. Where's my boy?"

"Coffin! coffin!" bellowed Braddock angrily between thunder blows. "What do you mean by calling this case a coffin?"

"Well, it do hold one of them camphorated corps, sir," said Mrs. Bolton with another curtsey. "My boy Sid told me as much, afore he went to them furren parts."

"Have you seen him since he returned?" questioned Lucy, while Braddock and Cockatoo strained at the lid, now nearly off.

"Why, I ain't set eyes on him," moaned the widow dismally, "and summat tells me as I never will."

"Don't talk rubbish, woman," said Archie tartly, for he did not wish Lucy to be upset again by this ancient ghoul.

"Woman indeed, sir. I'd have you know,—oh!" the widow jumped and quavered as the lid of the packing case fell on the floor with a bang. "Oh lor, sir, the start you did give me!"

But Braddock had no eyes for her, and no ears for anyone. He pulled lustily at the straw packing, and soon the floor was littered with rubbish. But no green case appeared, and no mummy. Suddenly Widow Anne shrieked again.

"There's my Sid—dead—oh, my son, dead! dead!"

She spoke truly. The body of Sidney Bolton was before them.

CHAPTER V

MYSTERY

After that one cry of agony from Widow Anne, there was silence for quite one minute. The terrible contents of the packing case startled and terrified all present. Faint and white, Lucy clung to the arm of her lover to keep herself from sinking to the ground, as Mrs. Bolton had done. Archie stared at the grotesque rigidity of the body, as though he had been changed into stone, while Professor Braddock stared likewise, scarcely able to credit the evidence of his eyes. Only the Kanaka was unmoved and squatted on his hams, indifferently surveying the living and the dead. As a savage he could not be expected to have the nerves of civilized man.

Braddock, who had dropped chisel and hammer in the first movement of surprise, was the quickest to recover his powers of speech. The sole question he asked, revealed the marvelous egotism of a scientist, nominated by one idea. "Where is the mummy of Inca Caxas?" he murmured with a bewildered air.

Widow Anne, groveling on the floor, pulled her gray locks into wild confusion, and uttered a cry of mingled rage and grief. "He asks that? he asks that?" she cried, stammering and choking, "when he has murdered my poor boy Sid."

"What's that?" demanded Braddock sharply, and recovering from a veritable stupor, which the disappearance of the mummy and the sight of his dead assistant had thrown him into. "Kill your son: how could I kill your son? What advantage would it have been to me had I killed your son?"

"God knows! God knows!" sobbed the old woman, "but you—"

"Mrs. Bolton, you are raving," said Hope hastily, and strove to raise her from the floor. "Let Miss Kendal take you away. And you go, Lucy: this sight is too terrible for your eyes."

Lucy, inarticulate with nervous fear, nodded and tottered towards the door of the museum; but Widow Anne refused to be lifted to her feet.

"My boy is dead," she wailed; "my boy Sid is a corp as I saw him in my dream. In the coffin, too, cut to pieces—"

"Rubbish! rubbish!" interrupted Braddock, peering into the depths of the packing case. "I can see no wound."

Mrs. Bolton leaped to her feet with an agility surprising in so

31

aged a woman. "Let me find the wound," she screamed, throwing herself forward.

Hope caught her back and forced her towards the door. "No! The body must not be disturbed until the police see it," he said firmly.

"The police—ah, yes, the police," remarked Braddock quickly, "we must send for the police to Pierside and tell them my mummy has been stolen."

"That my boy has been murdered," screeched Widow Anne, waving her skinny arms, and striving to break from Archie. "You wicked old devil to kill my darling Sid. If he hadn't gone to them furren parts he wouldn't be a corp now. But I'll have the lawr: you'll be hanged, you—you—"

Braddock lost his patience under this torrent of unjust accusations and rushed towards Mrs. Bolton, dragging Cockatoo by the arm. In less time than it takes to tell, he had swept both Archie and the widow out into the hall, where Lucy was trembling, and Cockatoo, by his master's order, was locking the door.

"Not a thing shall be touched until the police come. Hope, you are, a witness that I have not meddled with the dead: you were present when I opened the packing case: you have seen that a useless body has been substituted for a valuable mummy. And yet this old witch dares—dares—" Braddock stamped and grew incoherent from sheer rage.

Archie soothed him, leaving go of Widow Anne's arm to do so. "Hush! hush!" said the young man quietly, "the poor woman does not know what she is saying. I'll go for the police and—"

"No," interrupted the Professor sharply; "Cockatoo can go for the inspector of Pierside. I shall call in the village constable. Meanwhile you keep the key of the museum," he dropped it into Hope's breast-pocket, "so that you and the police may be sure the body has not been touched. Widow Anne, go home," he turned angrily on the old creature, who was now trembling after her burst of rage, "and don't dare to come here again until you ask pardon for what you have said."

"I want to be near my poor boy's corp," wailed Widow Anne, "and I'm very sorry, Perfesser. I didn't mean to—"

"But you have, you witch. Go away!" and he stamped.

But by this time Lucy had recovered her self-possession, which had been sorely shaken by the sight of the dead. "Leave her to me," she observed, taking Mrs. Bolton's arm, and leading her towards the stairs. "I shall take her to my room and give her some brandy. Father, you must make some allowance for her natural grief, and—"

Braddock stamped again. "Take her away! take her away!" he

cried testily, "and keep her out of my sight. Is it not enough to have lost an invaluable assistant, and a costly mummy of infinite historical and archaeological value, without my being accused of— of—oh!" The Professor choked with rage and shook his hand in the air.

Seeing that he was unable to speak, Lucy seized the opportunity of the lull in the storm, and hurried the old woman, sobbing and moaning, up the stairs. By this time the shrieks of Mrs. Bolton, and the wordy wrath of Braddock, had drawn the cook and her husband, along with the housemaid, from the basement to the ground floor. The sight of their surprised faces only added to their master's anger, and he advanced furiously.

"Go downstairs again: go down, I tell you!"

"But if there's anything wrong, sir," ventured the gardener timidly.

"Everything is wrong. My mummy has been lost: Mr. Bolton has been murdered. The police are coming, and—and—" He choked again.

But the servants waited to hear no more. The mere mention of the words "murder" and "police" sent them, pale-faced and startled, down to the basement, where they huddled like a flock of sheep. Braddock looked around for Hope, but found that he had opened the front door, and had vanished. But he was too distracted to think why Archie had gone, and there was much to do in putting things straight. Beckoning to Cockatoo, he stalked into a side room, and scribbled a pencil note to the inspector of police at Pierside, telling him of what had happened, and asking him to come at once to the Pyramids with his underlings. This communication he dispatched by Cockatoo, who flew to get his bicycle. In a short time he was riding at top speed to Brefort, which was on this side of the river; facing Pierside. There he could ferry across to the town and deliver his terrible message.

Having done all that he could until the police came, Braddock walked out of the front door and into the roadway to see if Archie was in sight. He could not see the young man, but, as luck would have it, and by one of those coincidences which are much more common than is suspected, he saw the Gartley doctor walking briskly past.

"Hi!" shouted the Professor, who was purple in the face and perspiring profusely. "Hi, there, Dr. Robinson! I want you. Come! come! hurry, man, hurry!" he ended in a testy rage, and the doctor, knowing Braddock's eccentricities, advanced with a smile. He was a slim, dark, young medical practitioner with an amiable countenance, which argued of no mighty intelligence.

33

"Well, Professor," he remarked quietly, "do you want me to attend you for apoplexy? Take your time, my dear sir—take your time." He patted the scientist on the shoulder to soothe his clamorous rage. "You are already purple in the face. Don't let your blood rush to your head."

"Robinson, you're a—a—a fool!" shouted Braddock, glaring at the suave looks of the doctor. "I am in perfect health, damn you, sir."

"Then Miss Kendal—?"

"She is quite well also. But Bolton—?"

"Oh!" Robinson looked interested. "Has he returned with your mummy?"

"Mummy," bellowed Braddock, stamping like an insane Cupid—"the mummy hasn't arrived."

"Really, Professor, you surprise me," said the doctor mildly.

"I'll surprise you more," growled Braddock, dragging Robinson into the garden and up the steps.

"Gently! gently! my dear sir," said the doctor, who really began to think that much learning had made the Professor mad. "Didn't Bolton—?"

"Bolton is dead, you fool."

"Dead!" The doctor nearly tumbled backward down the steps.

"Murdered. At least I think he is murdered. At all events he arrived here to-day in the packing case, which should have contained my green mummy. Come in and examine the body at once. No," Braddock pushed back the doctor just as fiercely as he had dragged him forward, "wait until the constable comes. I want him to see the body first, and to observe that nothing has been touched. I have sent for the Pierside inspector to come. There will be all sorts of trouble," cried Braddock despairingly, "and my work—most important work—will be delayed, just because this silly young ass Sidney Bolton chose to be murdered," and the Professor stormed up and down the hall, shaking impotent arms in the air.

"Good heavens!" stammered Robinson, who was young in years and somewhat new to his profession, "you—you must be mistaken."

"Mistaken! mistaken!" shouted Braddock with another glare. "Come and see that poor fellow's body then. He is dead, murdered."

"By whom?"

"Hang you, sir, how should I know?"

"In what way has he been murdered? Stabbed, shot, or—"

"I don't know—I don't know! Such a nuisance to lose a man like Bolton—an invaluable assistant. What I shall do without him I really don't know. And his mother has been here, making no end of a fuss."

34

"Can you blame her?" said the doctor, recovering his breath. "She is his mother, after all, and poor Bolton was her only son."

"I am not denying the relationship, confound you!" snapped the Professor, ruffling his hair until it stood up like the crest of a parrot. "But she needn't—ah!" He glanced through the open door, and then rushed to the threshold. "Here is Hope and Painter. Come in—come in. I have the doctor here. Hope, you have the key. You observe, constable, that Mr. Hope has the key. Open the door: open the door, and let us see the meaning of this dreadful crime."

"Crime, sir?" queried the constable, who had heard all that was known from Hope, but now wished to hear what Braddock had to say.

"Yes, crime: crime, you idiot! I have lost my mummy."

"But I thought, sir, that a murder—"

"Oh, of course—of course," gabbled the Professor, as if the death was quite a minor consideration. "Bolton's dead—murdered, I suppose, as he could scarcely have nailed himself down in a packing case. But it's my precious mummy I am thinking of, Painter. A mummy—if you know what a mummy is—that cost me nine hundred pounds. Go in, man. Go in and don't stand there gaping. Don't you see that Mr. Hope has opened the door. I have sent Cockatoo to Pierside to notify the police. They will soon be here. Meanwhile, doctor, you can examine the body, and Painter here can give his opinion as to who stole my mummy."

"The assassin stole the mummy," said Archie, as the four men entered the museum, "and substituted the body of the murdered man."

"That is all A B C," snapped Braddock, issuing into the vast room, "but we want to know the name of the assassin, if we are to revenge Bolton and get back my mummy. Oh, what a loss!—what a loss! I have lost nine hundred pounds, or say one thousand, considering the cost of bringing Inca Caxas to England."

Archie forebore to remind the Professor as to who had really lost the money, as the scientist was not in a fit state to be talked to reasonably, and seemed much more concerned because his Peruvian relic of humanity had been lost than for the terrible death of Sidney Bolton. But by this time Painter—a fair-haired young constable of small intelligence—was examining the packing case and surveying the dead. Dr. Robinson also looked with a professional eye, and Braddock, wiping his purple face and gasping with exhaustion, sat down on a stone sarcophagus. Archie, folding his arms, leaned against the wall and waited quietly to hear what the experts in crime and medicine would say.

The packing case was deep and wide and long, made of tough

35

teak and banded at intervals with iron bands. Within this was a case of tin, which, when it held the mummy, had been soldered up; impervious to air and water. But the unknown person who had extracted the mummy, to replace it by a murdered man's body, had cut open the tin casing with some sharp instrument. There was straw round the tin casing and straw within, amongst which the body of the unfortunate young man was placed. Rigor mortis had set in, and the corpse, with straight legs and hands placed stiffly by its side, lay against the back of the tin casing surrounded more or less by the straw packing, or at least by so much as the Professor had not torn away. The face looked dark, and the eyes were wide open and staring. Robinson stepped forward and ran his hand round the neck. Uttering an ejaculation, he removed the woollen scarf which the dead man had probably worn to keep himself from catching cold, and those who looked on saw that a red-colored window cord was tightly bound about the throat of the dead.

"The poor devil has been strangled," said the doctor quietly. "See: the assassin has left the bow-string on, and had the courage to place over it this scarf, which belonged to Bolton."

"How do you know that, sir?" asked Painter heavily.

"Because Widow Anne knitted that scarf for Bolton before he went to Malta. He showed it to me, laughingly, remarking that his mother evidently thought that he was going to Lapland."

"When did he show it to you, sir?"

"Before he went to Malta, of course," said Robinson in mild surprise. "You don't suppose he showed it to me when he returned. When did he return to England?" he asked the Professor, with an afterthought.

"Yesterday afternoon, about four o'clock," replied Braddock.

"Then, from the condition of the body"—the doctor felt the dead flesh—"he must have been murdered last night. H'm! With your permission, Painter, I'll examine the corpse."

The constable shook his head. "Better wait, sir, until the inspector comes," he said in his unintelligent way. "Poor Sid! Why, I knew him. He was at school with me, and now he's dead. Who killed him?"

None of his listeners could answer this question.

CHAPTER VI

THE INQUEST

Like a geographical Lord Byron, the isolated village of Gartley awoke one morning to find itself famous. Previously unknown, save to the inhabitants of Brefort, Jessum, and the surrounding country, and to the soldiers stationed in the Fort, it became a nine days' centre of interest. Inspector Date of Pierside arrived with his constables to inquire into the reported crime, and the local journalists, scenting sensation, came flying to Gartley on bicycles and in traps. Next morning London was duly advised that a valuable mummy was missing, and that the assistant of Professor Braddock, who had been sent to fetch it from Malta, was murdered by strangulation. In a couple of days the three kingdoms were ringing with the news of the mystery.

And a mystery it proved, to be, for, in spite of Inspector Date's efforts and the enterprise of Scotland Yard detectives summoned by the Professor, no clue could be found to the identity of the assassin. Briefly, the story told by the newspapers ran as follows:

The tramp steamer Diver—Captain George Hervey in command—had berthed alongside the Pierside jetty at four o'clock on a Wednesday afternoon in mid-September, and some two hours later Sidney Bolton removed the case, containing the green mummy, ashore.

As it was impossible to carry the case to the Pyramids on that night, Bolton had placed it in his bedroom at the Sailor's Rest, a mean little public-house of no very savory reputation near the water's edge. He was last seen alive by the landlord and the barmaid, when, after a drink of harmless ginger-beer, he retired to bed at eight, leaving instructions to the landlord—overheard by the barmaid—that the case was to be sent on next day to Professor Braddock of Gartley. Bolton hinted that he might leave the hotel early and would probably precede the case to its destination, so as to advise Professor Braddock—necessarily anxious—of its safe arrival. Before retiring he paid his bill, and deposited in the landlord's hand a small sum of money, so that the case might be sent across stream to Brefort, thence to be taken in a lorry to the Pyramids. There was no sign, said the barmaid and the landlord, that Bolton contemplated suicide, or that he feared sudden death.

37

His whole demeanor was cheerful, and he expressed himself exceedingly glad to be in England once more.

At eleven on the ensuing morning, a persistent knocking and a subsequent opening of the door of Bolton's bedroom proved that he was not in the room, although the tumbled condition of the bed-clothes proved that he had taken some rest. No one in the hotel thought anything of Bolton's absence, since he had hinted at an early departure, although the chamber-maid considered it strange that no one had seen him leave the hotel. The landlord obeyed Bolton's instructions and sent the case, in charge of a trustworthy man, to Brefort across the river. There a lorry was procured, and the case was taken to Gartley, where it arrived at three in the afternoon. It was then that Professor Braddock, in opening the case, discovered the body of his ill-fated assistant, rigid in death, and with a red window cord tightly bound round the throat of the corpse. At once, said the newspapers, the Professor sent for the police, and later insisted that the smartest Scotland Yard detectives should come down to elucidate the mystery. At present both police and detectives were engaged in searching for a needle in a haystack, and so far had met with no success.

Such was the tale set forth in the local and London and provincial journals. Widely as it was discussed, and many as were the theories offered, no one could fathom the mystery. But all agreed that the failure of the police to find a clue was inexplicable. It was difficult enough to understand how the assassin could have murdered Bolton and opened the packing case, and removed the mummy to replace it by the body of his victim in a house filled with at least half a dozen people; but it was yet more difficult to guess how the criminal had escaped with so noticeable an object as the mummy, bandaged with emerald-hued woollen stuff woven from the hair of Peruvian llamas. If the culprit was one who thieved and murdered for gain, he could scarcely sell the mummy without being arrested, since all England was ringing with the news of its disappearance; if a scientist, impelled to robbery by an archaeological mania, he could not possibly keep possession of the mummy without someone learning that he possessed it. Meanwhile the thief and his plunder had vanished as completely as if the earth had swallowed both. Great was the wonder at the cleverness of the criminal, and many were the solutions offered to account for the disappearance. One enterprising weekly paper, improving on the Limerick craze, offered a furnished house and three pounds a week for life to the fortunate person who could solve the mystery. As yet no one had won the prize, but it was early days yet, and at least five thousand amateur detectives tried to work out the problem.

Naturally Hope was sorry for the untimely death of Bolton, whom he had known as an amiable and clever young man. But he was also annoyed that his loan of the money to Braddock should have been, so to speak, nullified by the loss of the mummy. The Professor was perfectly furious at his double loss of assistant and embalmed corpse, and was only prevented from offering a reward for the discovery of the thief and assassin by the painful fact that he had no money. He hinted to Archie that a reward should be offered, but that young man, backed by Lucy, declined to throw away good money after bad. Braddock took this refusal so ill, that Hope felt perfectly convinced he would try and wriggle out of his promise to permit the marriage and persuade Lucy to engage herself to Sir Frank Random, should the baronet be willing to offer a reward. And Hope was also certain that Braddock, a singularly obstinate man, would never rest until he once more had the mummy in his possession. That the murderer of Sidney Bolton should be hanged was quite a minor consideration with the Professor.

Meanwhile Widow Anne had insisted on the dead body being taken to her cottage, and Braddock, with the consent of Inspector Date, willingly agreed, as he did not wish a newly dead corpse to remain under his roof. Therefore, the remains of the unfortunate young man were taken to his humble home, and here the body was inspected by the jury when the inquest took place in the coffee-room of the Warrior Inn, immediately opposite Mrs. Bolton's abode. There was a large crowd round the inn, as people had come from far and wide to hear the verdict of the jury, and Gartley, for the first and only time in its existence, presented the aspect of an August Bank Holiday.

The Coroner—an elderly doctor with a short temper; caused by the unrealized ambition of a country practitioner—opened the proceedings by a snappy speech, in which he set forth the details of the crime in the same bold fashion in which they had been published by the newspapers. A plan of the Sailor's Rest was then placed before the jury, and the Coroner drew the attention of the twelve good and lawful men to the fact that the bedroom occupied by deceased was on the ground floor, with a window looking out on to the river, merely a stone-throw away.

"So you will see, gentlemen," said the Coroner, "that the difficulty of the assassin in leaving the hotel with his plunder was not so great as has been imagined. He had merely to open the window in the quiet hours of the night, when no one was about, and pass the mummy through to his accomplice, who probably waited without. It is also probable that a boat was waiting by the bank of the river, and the mummy having been placed in this, the assassin

39

and his friend could row away into the unknown without the slightest chance of discovery."

Inspector Date—a tall, thin, upright man with an iron jaw and a severe expression—drew the Coroner's attention to the fact that there was no evidence to show that the assassin had an accomplice.

"What you have stated, sir, may have occurred," rasped Date in a military voice, "but we cannot prove the truth of your assumption, since the evidence at our disposal is merely circumstantial."

"I never suggested that it was anything else," snapped the Coroner. "You waste time in traversing my statements. Say what you have to say, Mr. Inspector, and produce your witnesses—if you have any."

"There are no witnesses who can swear to the identity of the murderer," said Inspector Date coldly, and determined not to be ruffled by the apparent antagonism of the Coroner. "The criminal has vanished, and no one can guess his name or occupation, or even the reason which led him to slay the deceased."

Coroner: "The reason is plain. He wanted the mummy."

Inspector: "Why should he want the mummy?"

Coroner: "That is what we wish to find out."

Inspector: "Exactly, sir. We wish to learn the reason why the murderer strangled the deceased."

Coroner: "We know that reason. What we wish to know is why the murderer stole the mummy. And I would point out to you, Mr. Inspector, that, as yet, we do not even know the sex of the assassin. It might be a woman who murdered the deceased."

Professor Braddock, who was seated near the door of the coffee-room, being even more irascible than usual, rose to contradict.

"There isn't a scrap of evidence to show that the murderer was a woman."

Coroner: "You are out of order, sir. And I would point out that, as yet, Inspector Date has produced no witnesses."

Date glared. He and the Coroner were old enemies, and always sparred when they met. It seemed likely, that the peppery little Professor would join in the quarrel and that there would be a duel of three; but Date, not wishing for an adverse report in the newspapers as to his conduct of the case, contented himself with the glare aforesaid, and, after a short speech, called Braddock. The Professor, looking more like a cross cherub than ever, gave his evidence tartly. It seemed ridiculous to his prejudiced mind that all this fuss should be made over Bolton's body, when the mummy; was still missing. However, as the discovery of the criminal would assuredly lead to the regaining of that precious Peruvian relic, he curbed his wrath and answered the Coroner's questions in a fairly amiable fashion.

And, after all, Braddock had very little to tell. He had, so he stated, seen an advertisement in a newspaper that a mummy, swathed in green bandages, was to be sold in Malta; and had sent his assistant to buy it and bring it home. This was done, and what happened after the mummy left the tramp steamer was known to everyone, through the medium of the press.

"With which," grumbled the Professor, "I do not agree."

"What do you mean by that?" asked the Coroner sharply.

"I mean, sir," snapped Braddock, equally sharply, "that the publicity given by the newspapers to these details will probably place the assassin on his guard."

"Why not on her guard?" persisted the Coroner wilfully.

"Rubbish! rubbish! rubbish! My mummy wasn't stolen by a woman. What the devil would a woman want with my mummy?"

"Be more respectful, Professor."

"Then talk sense, doctor," and the two glared at one another.

After a moment or two the situation was adjusted in silence, and the Coroner asked a few questions, pertinent to the matter in hand.

"Had the deceased any enemies?"

"No, sir, he hadn't, not being famous enough, or rich enough, or clever enough to excite the hatred of mankind. He was simply an intelligent young man, who worked excellently when supervised by me. His mother is a washerwoman in this village, and the lad brought washing to my house. Noting that he was intelligent and was anxious to rise above his station, I engaged him as my assistant and trained him to do my work."

"Archaeological work?"

"Yes. I don't wash, whatever Bolton's mother may, do. Don't ask silly questions."

"Be more respectful," said the Coroner again, and grew red. "Have you any idea as to the name of anyone who desired to obtain possession of this mummy?"

"I daresay dozens of scientists in my line of business would have liked to get the corpse of Inca Caxas. Such as—" and he reeled out a list of celebrated men.

"Nonsense," growled the Coroner. "Famous men like those you mention would not murder even for the sake of obtaining this mummy."

"I never said that they would," retorted Braddock, "but you wanted to hear who would like to have the mummy; and I have told you."

The Coroner waived the question.

"Was there any jewelry on the mummy likely to attract a thief?" he asked.

"How the devil should I know?" fumed the Professor. "I never unpacked the mummy; I never even saw it. Any jewelry buried with Inca Caxas would be bound up in the bandages. So far as I know those bandages were never unwound."

"You can throw no light on the subject?"

"No, I can't. Bolton went to get the mummy and brought it home. I understood that he would personally bring his precious charge to my house; but he didn't. Why, I don't know."

When the Professor stepped down, still fuming at what he considered were the unnecessary questions of the Coroner, the young doctor who had examined the corpse was called. Robinson deposed that deceased had been strangled by means of a red window cord, and that, from the condition of the body, he would judge death had taken place some twelve hours more or less before the opening of the packing case by Braddock. That was at three o'clock on Thursday afternoon, so in witness's opinion the crime was committed between two and three on the previous morning.

"But I can't be absolutely certain as to the precise hour," added witness; "at any rate poor Bolton was strangled after midnight and before three o'clock."

"That is a wide margin," grumbled the Coroner, jealous of his brother-practitioner. "Were there any, other wounds on the body?"

"No. You can see for yourself, if you have inspected the corpse."

The Coroner, thus reproved, glared, and Widow Anne appeared after Robinson retired. She stated, with many sobs, that her son had no enemies and was a good, kind young man. She also related her dream, but this was flouted by the Coroner, who did not believe in the occult. However, the narration of her premonition was listened to with deep interest by those in the court. Widow Anne concluded her evidence by asking how she was to live now that her boy Sid was dead. The Coroner professed himself unable to answer this question, and dismissed her.

Samuel Quass, the landlord of the Sailor's Rest, was next called. He proved to be a big, burly, red-haired, red-whiskered man, who looked like a sailor. And indeed a few questions elicited the information that he was a retired sea-captain. He gave his evidence gruffly but honestly, and although he kept so shady a public-house, seemed straightforward enough. He told much the same tale as had appeared in the newspapers. In the hotel on that night there was only himself, his wife and two children, and the staff of servants. Bolton retired to bed saying that he might start early for Gartley, and paid one pound to get the case taken across to river and placed on a lorry. As Bolton had vanished next morning, Quass obeyed instructions, with the result which everyone knew. He also stated that he did not know the case contained a mummy.

"What did you think it contained?" asked the Coroner quickly.

"Clothes and curios from foreign parts," said the witness coolly.

"Did Mr. Bolton tell you so?"

"He told me nothing about the case," growled the witness, "but he chatted a lot about Malta, which I know well, having put into that port frequent when a sailor."

"Did he hint at any rows taking place at Malta?"

"No, he didn't."

"Did he say that he had enemies?"

"No, he didn't."

"Did he strike you as a man who was in fear of death?"

"No, he didn't," said the witness for the third time. "He seemed happy enough. I never thought for one moment that he was dead until I heard how his body had been found in the packing case."

The Coroner asked all manner of questions, and so did Inspector Date; but all attempts to incriminate Quass were vain. He was bluff and straightforward, and told—so far as could be judged—everything he knew. There was nothing for it but to dismiss him, and Eliza Flight was called as the last witness.

She also proved to be the most important, as she knew several things which she had not told to her master, or to the reporters, or even to the police. On being asked why she had kept silence, she said that her desire was to obtain any reward that might be offered; but as she had heard that there would be no reward, she was willing to tell what she knew. It was an important piece of evidence.

The girl stated that Bolton had retired to bed at eight on the ground floor, and the bedroom had a window—as marked in the plan—which looked on to the river a stone-throw distant. At nine or a trifle later witness went out to have a few words with her lover. In the darkness she saw that the window was open and that Bolton was talking to an old woman muffled in a shawl. She could not see the woman's face, nor judge of her stature, as she was stooping down to listen to Bolton. Witness did not take much notice, as she was in a hurry to see her lover. When she returned past the window at ten o'clock it was closed and the light was extinguished, so she thought that Mr. Bolton was asleep.

"But, to tell the truth," said Eliza Flight, "I never thought anything of the matter at all. It was only after the murder that I saw how important it was I should remember everything."

"And you have?"

"Yes, sir," said the girl, honestly enough. "I have told you everything that happened on that night. Next morning—" She hesitated.

"Well, what about next morning?"

"Mr. Bolton had locked his door. I know that, because a few minutes after eight on the night before, not knowing he had retired. I tried to enter the room and make ready the bed for the night. He sang out through the door—which was locked, for I tried it—that he was in bed. That was a lie also, as after nine I saw him talking to the woman at the window."

"You previously said an old woman," said the Coroner, referring to his notes. "How do you know she was old?"

"I can't say if she was old or young," said the witness candidly; "it's only a manner of speaking. She had a dark shawl over her head and a dark dress. I couldn't say if she was old or young, fair or dark, stout or lean, tall or short. The night was dark."

The Coroner referred to the plan.

"There is a gas-lamp near the window of the bedroom. Did you not see her in that light?"

"Oh, yes, sir; but just for a moment. I took very little notice. Had I known that the gentleman was to be murdered, I should have taken a great deal of notice."

"Well, about this locked door?"

"It was locked over-night, sir, but when I went next morning, it was not locked. I knocked and knocked, but could get no answer. As it was eleven, I thought the gentleman was sleeping very long, so I tried to open the door. It was not locked, as I say—but," added witness with emphasis, "the window was snibbed and the blind was down."

"That is natural enough," said the Coroner. "Mr. Bolton, after his interview with the woman, would of course snib the window, and pull down the blind. When he went away next morning he would unlock the door."

"Begging your pardon, sir, but, as we know, he didn't go away next morning, being in the packing case, nailed down."

The Coroner could have kicked himself for the very natural mistake he had made, for he saw a derisive grin on the faces around him, and particularly on that of Inspector Date.

"Then the assassin must have gone out by the door," he said weakly.

"Then I don't know how he got out," cried Eliza Flight, "for I was up at six and the front and back doors of the hotel were locked. And after six I was about in passages and rooms doing my work,

44

and master and missus and others were all over the place. How could the murderer walk out, sir, without some of us seeing him?"

"Perhaps you did, and took no notice?"

"Oh, sir, if a stranger was around we should all have taken notice."

This concluded the evidence, which was meagre enough. Widow Anne was indeed recalled to see if Miss Flight could identify her as the woman who, had been talking to Bolton, but witness failed to recognize her, and the widow herself proved, by means of three friends, that she had been imbibing gin at home on the night and at the hour in question. Also, there was no evidence to connect this unknown woman with the murder, and no sound—according to the unanimous testimony of the inmates of the Sailor's Rest—had been heard in the bedroom of Bolton. Yet, as the Coroner observed, there must have been some knocking and hammering and ripping going on. But of this nothing could be proved, and although several witnesses were examined again, not one could throw light on the mystery. Under these circumstances the jury could only bring in a verdict of wilful murder against some person or persons unknown, which was done. And it may be mentioned that the cord with which Bolton had been strangled was identified by the landlord and the chamber-maid as belonging to the blind of the bedroom window.

"Well," said Hope, when the inquest was over, "so nothing can be proved against anyone. What is to be done next?"

"I'll tell you after I have seen Random," said the Professor curtly.

45

CHAPTER VII

THE CAPTAIN OF THE DIVER

The day after the inquest, Sidney Bolton's body was buried in Gartley churchyard. Owing to the nature of the death, and the publicity given to the murder by the press, a great concourse of people assembled to witness the interment, and there was an impressive silence when the corpse was committed to the grave. Afterwards, as was natural, much discussion followed on the verdict at the inquest. It was the common opinion that the jury could have brought in no other verdict, considering the nature of the evidence supplied; but many people declared that Captain Hervey of The Diver should have been called. If the deceased had enemies, said these wiseacres, it was probable that he would have talked about them to the skipper. But they forgot that the witnesses called at the inquest, including the mother of the dead man, had insisted that Bolton had no enemies, so it is difficult to see what they expected Captain Hervey to say.

After the funeral, the journals made but few remarks about the mystery. Every now and then it was hinted that a clue had been found, and that the police would sooner or later track down the criminal. But all this loose chatter came to nothing, and as the days went by, the public—in London, at all events—lost interest in the case. The enterprising weekly paper that had offered the furnished house and the life income to the person who found the assassin received an intimation from the Government that such a lottery could not be allowed. The paper, therefore, returned to Limericks, and the amateur detectives, like so many Othellos, found their occupation gone. Then a political crisis took place in the far East, and the fickle public relegated the murder of Bolton to the list of undiscovered crimes. Even the Scotland Yard detectives, failing to find a clue, lost interest in the matter, and it seemed as though the mystery of Bolton's death would not be solved until the Day of Judgment.

In the village, however, people still continued to be keenly interested, since Bolton was one of themselves, and, moreover, Widow Anne kept up a perpetual outcry about her murdered boy. She had lost the small weekly sum which Sidney had allowed her out of his wages, so the neighbors, the gentry of the surrounding country, and the officers at the Fort sent her ample washing to do.

46

Widow Anne in a few weeks had quite a large business, considering the size of the village, and philosophically observed to a neighbor that "It was an ill wind which blew no one any good," adding also that Sidney was more good to her dead than alive. But even in Gartley the villagers grew weary of discussing a mystery which could never be solved, and so the case became rarely talked about. In these days of bustle and worry and competition, it is wonderful how people forget even important events. If a blue sun arose to lighten the world instead of a yellow one, after nine days of wonder, man would settle down quite comfortably to a cerulean existence. Such is the wonderful adaptability of humanity.

Professor Braddock was less forgetful, as he always bore in mind the loss of his mummy, and constantly thought of schemes whereby he could trap the assassin of his late secretary. Not that he cared for the dead in any way, save from a strictly business point of view, but the capture of the criminal meant the restitution of the mummy, and—as Braddock told everyone with whom he came in contact—he was determined to regain possession of his treasure. He went himself to the Sailor's Rest, and drove the landlord and his servants wild by asking tart questions and storming when a satisfactory answer could not be supplied. Quass was glad when he saw the plump back of the cross little man, who so pertinaciously followed what everyone else had abandoned.

"Life was too short," grumbled Quass, "to be bothered in that way."

The wooing of Archie and Lucy went on smoothly, and the Professor showed no sign of wishing to break the engagement. But Hope, as he confided to Lucy, was somewhat worried, as his pauper uncle, on an insufficient borrowed capital, had begun to speculate in South African mines, and it was probable that he would lose all his money. In that case Hope fancied he would be once more called upon to make good the avuncular loss, and so the marriage would have to be postponed. But it so happened that the pauper uncle made some lucky speculative shots and acquired money, which he promptly reinvested in new mines of the wildcat description. Still, for the moment all was well, and the lovers had a few halcyon days of peace and happiness.

Then came a bolt from the blue in the person of Captain Hervey, who called a fortnight after the funeral to see the Professor. The skipper was a tall, slim man, lean as a fasting friar, and hard as nails, with closely clipped red hair, mustache of the same aggressive hue, and an American goatee. He spoke with a Yankee accent, and in a truculent manner, sufficiently annoying to the fiery Professor. When he met Braddock in the museum, the two became enemies at the first glance, and because both were bad-tempered and obstinate, took an instant dislike to one another. Like did not draw to like in this instance.

"What do you want to see me about?" asked Braddock crossly. He had been summoned by Cockatoo from the perusal of a new papyrus to see his visitor, and consequently was not in the best of tempers.

"I've jes' blew in fur a trifle of chin-music," replied Hervey with an emphatic U.S.A. accent.

"I'm busy: get out," was the uncomplimentary reply.

Hervey took a chair and, stretching his lengthy legs, produced a black cheroot, as long and lean as himself.

"If you were in the States, Professor, I'd draw a bead on you for that style of lingo. I'm not taking any. See!" and he lighted up.

"You're the captain of 'The Diver'?"

"That's so; I was, that is. Now, I've shifted to a dandy wind-jammer of sorts that can run rings round the old barky. I surmise I'm off for the South Seas, pearl-fishing, in three months. I'll take that Kanaka along with me, if y'like, Professor," and he cast a side glance at Cockatoo, who was squatting on his hams as usual, polishing a blue enameled jar from a Theban tomb.

"I require the services of the man," said Braddock stiffly. "As to you, sir: you've been paid for your business in connection with Bolton's passage and the shipment of my mummy, so there is no more to be said."

"Heaps more! heaps, you bet," remarked the man of the sea placidly, and controlling a temper which in less civilized parts would have led him to wipe the floor with the plump scientist. "My owners were paid fur that racket: not me. No, sir. So I've paddled into this port to see if I can rake in a few dollars on my own."

"I've no dollars to give you—in charity, that is."

"Huh! An' who asked charity, you bald-headed jelly-bag?"

Braddock grew scarlet with fury. "If you speak to me like that, you ruffian, I'll throw you out."

"What?—you?"

"Yes, me," and the Professor stood on tip-toe, like the bantam he was.

"You make me smile, and likewise tired," murmured Hervey, admiring the little man's pluck. "See here, Professor, touching that mummy?"

"My mummy: my green mummy. What about it?" Braddock rose to the fly thrown by this skilful angler.

"That's so. What will you shell out if I pass along that corpse?"

"Ah!" The Professor again stood on tip-toe, gasping and purple in the face. He almost squeaked in the extremity of his anger. "I knew it."

"Knew what?" demanded the skipper, genuinely surprised.

"I knew that you had stolen my mummy. Yes, you needn't deny it. Bolton, like the silly fool he was, told you how valuable the mummy was, and you strangled the poor devil to get my property."

"Go slow," said the captain, in no wise perturbed by this accusation. "I would have you remember that at the inquest it was stated that the window was locked and the door was open. How then could I waltz into that blamed hotel and arrange for a funeral? 'Sides, I guess shooting is mor'n my line than garrotting. I leave that to the East Coast Yellow-Stomachs."

Braddock sat down and wiped his face. He saw plainly enough that he had not a leg to stand on, as Hervey was plainly innocent.

"'Sides," went on the skipper, chewing his cheroot, "I guess if I'd wanted that old corpse of yours, I'd have yanked Bolton overside, and set down the accident to bad weather. Better fur me to loot the case aboard than to make a fool of myself ashore. No, sir, H.H. don't run 'is own perticler private circus in that blamed way."

"H.H. Who the devil is H.H.?"

"Me, you bet. Hiram Hervey, citizen of the U.S.A. Nantucket neighborhood for home life. And see, don't you get m'hair riz, or I'll scalp."

"You can't scalp me," chuckled Braddock, passing his hand over a very bald head. "See here, what do you want?"

"Name a price and I'll float round to get back your verdant corpse."

"I thought you were going to the South Seas?"

"In three months, pearl-fishing. Lots of time, I reckon, to run this old circus I want you to finance."

"Have you any suspicions?"

"No, 'sept I don't believe in that window business."

"What do you mean?" Braddock sat upright.

"Well," drawled the Yankee, "y'see, I interviewed the gal as told that perticler lie in court."

"Eliza Flight. Was it a lie she told?"

"Well, not exactly. The window was snibbed, but that was done after the chap who sent your pal to Kingdom Come had got out."

"Do you mean to say that the window was locked from the outside?" asked Braddock, and then, when Hervey nodded, he exclaimed "Impossible!"

"Narry an impossibility, you bet. The chap who engineered the circus was all-fired smart. The snib was an old one, and he yanked a piece of string round it, and passed the string through the crack between the upper and lower sash of the window. When outside he pulled, and the snib slid into place. But he left the string on the ground outside. I picked it up nex' day and guessed the racket he'd been on. I tried the same business and brought off the deal."

"It sounds wonderful and yet impossible," cried Braddock, rubbing his bald head and walking excitedly to and fro. "See here, I'll come along with you and see how it's done."

"You bet you won't, unless you shell out. See here"—Hervey leaned forward—"from that window business it's plain that no one inside the shanty corpsed your pal. The chap as did it entered and left by the window, and made tracks with that old corp you want. Now you pass along five hundred pounds—that's English currency, I reckon—and I'll smell round for the robber."

"And where do you think I can obtain five hundred pounds?" asked the Professor very dryly.

"Well, I guess if that blamed corpse is worth it, you'll be willing to trade. Y'don't live in this shanty for nothing."

"My good friend, I have enough to live on, and obtain this house at a small rent on account of its isolation. But I can no more find the sum of five hundred pounds than fly."

Hervey rose and straightened his legs.

"Then I guess I'd best be getting back to Pierside."

"One moment, sir. Did anything happen on the voyage?—did Bolton say anything likely to lead you to suppose that he was in danger of being robbed and murdered?"

"No," said the skipper musingly, and pulling his goatee. "He told me that he had secured the old corpse, and was bringing it home to you. I didn't talk much to Bolton; he wasn't my style."

"Have you any idea who killed him?"

"No, I ain't."

"Then how do you propose to find the criminal who has the mummy?"

"You give me five hundred pounds and see," said Hervey coolly.

"I haven't got the money."

"Then I reckon you don't get the corpse. So long," and the skipper strolled towards the door. Braddock followed him.

"You have a clue?"

"No, I've got nothing; not even that five hundred pounds you make such a fuss over. It's a wasted day with H.H., I surmise. Wait!" He scribbled on a card and flung it across the room. "That's my Pierside address if you should change your blamed mind."

The Professor picked up the card. "The Sailor's Rest! What, are you stopping there?" Then, when Hervey nodded, he cried violently,

"Why, I believe you have a clue, and stop at the hotel to follow it up."

"Maybe I do and maybe I don't," retorted the captain, opening the door with a jerk; "anyhow, I don't hunt for that corpse without the dollars."

When Hiram Hervey departed, the Professor raged up and down the room so violently that Cockatoo was cowed by his anger. Apparently this American skipper knew of something which might lead to the discovery of the assassin and incidentally to the restoration of the green mummy to its rightful owner. But he would not make a move unless he was paid five hundred pounds, and Braddock did not know where to procure that amount. Having long since made himself acquainted with Hope's financial condition, he knew well that there was no chance of getting a second check in that quarter. Of course there was Random, whom he had heard casually had returned from his yachting cruise, and was now back again at the Fort. But Random was in love with Lucy, and would probably only give or lend the money on condition that the Professor helped him with his wooing. In that case, since Lucy was engaged to Hope, there would be some difficulty in altering present conditions. But having arrived at this point of his somewhat angry meditations, Braddock sent Cockatoo with a message to his step-daughter, saying that he wished to see her.

"I'll see if she really loves Hope," thought the Professor, rubbing his plump hands. "If she doesn't, there may be a chance of her throwing him over to become Lady Random. Then I can get the money. And indeed," soliloquized the Professor virtuously, "I must point out to her that it is wrong of her to make a poor marriage, when she can gain a wealthy husband. I will only be doing my duty by my dear dead wife, by preventing her wedding poverty. But girls are so obstinate, and Lucy is a thorough girl."

His amiable anxiety on behalf of Miss Kendal was only cut short by the entrance of the young lady herself. Professor Braddock then showed his hand too plainly by evincing a strong wish to conciliate her in every way. He procured her a seat: he asked after her health: he told her that she was growing prettier every day, and in all ways behaved so unlike his usual self, that Lucy became alarmed and thought that he had been drinking.

"Why have you sent for me?" she asked, anxious to come to the point.

"Aha!" Braddock put his venerable head on one side like a roguish bird and smiled in an infantine manner. "I have good news for you."

"About the mummy?" she demanded innocently.

51

"No, about flesh and blood, which you prefer. Sir Frank Random has arrived back at the Fort. There!"

"I know that," was Miss Kendal's unexpected reply. "His yacht came to Pierside on the same afternoon as The Diver arrived."

"Oh, indeed!" said the Professor, struck by the coincidence, and with a stare. "How do you know?"

"Archie met Sir Frank the other day, and learned as much."

"What?" Braddock struck a tragic attitude. "Do you mean to say that those two young men speak to one another?"

"Yes. Why not? They are friends."

"Oh!" Braddock became roguish again. "I fancied they were lovers of a certain young lady who is in this room."

By this time Lucy was beginning to guess what her step-father was aiming at, and grew correspondingly angry.

"Archie is my sole lover now," she remarked stiffly. "Sir Frank knows that we are engaged and is quite ready to be the friend of us both."

"And he calls that love. Idiot!" cried the Professor, much disgusted. "But I would point out to you, Lucy—and I do so because of my deep affection for you, dear child—that Sir Frank is wealthy."

"So is Archie—in my love."

"Nonsense! nonsense! That is mere foolish romance, He has no money."

"You should not say that. Archie had money to the extent of one thousand pounds, which he gave you."

"One thousand pounds: a mere nothing. Consider, Lucy, that if you marry Random you will have a title."

Miss Kendal, whose patience was getting exhausted, stamped a very neat boot.

"I don't know why you talk in this way, father."

"I wish to see you happy."

"Then your wish is granted: you do see me happy. But I won't be happy long if you keep bothering me to marry a man I don't care two straws about. I am going to be Mrs. Hope, so there."

"My dear child," said the Professor, who always became paternal when most obstinate, "I have reason to believe that the green mummy can be discovered and poor Sidney's death avenged if a reward of five hundred pounds is offered. If Hope can give me that money—"

"He will not: I shall not allow him to. He has lost too much already."

"In that case I must apply to Sir Frank Random."

"Well, apply," she snapped, being decidedly angry; "it's none of my business. I don't want to hear anything about it."

52

"It is your business, miss," cried Braddock, growing angry in his turn and becoming very pink; "you know that only by getting you to marry Random can I procure the money."

"Oh!" said Lucy coldly. "So this is why you sent for me. Now, father, I have had enough of this. You gave your consent to Archie being engaged to me in exchange for one thousand pounds. As I love him I shall abide by the word you gave. If I had not loved him I should have refused to marry him. You understand?"

"I understand that I have a very obstinate girl to deal with. You shall marry as I choose."

"I shall do nothing of the sort. You have no right to dictate my choice of a husband."

"No right, when I am your father?"

"You are not my father: merely my step-father—merely a relation by marriage. I am of age. I can do as I like, and intend to."

"But, Lucy," implored Braddock, changing his tune, "think."

"I have thought. I marry Archie."

"But he is poor and Random is rich."

"I don't care. I love Archie and I don't love Frank."

"Would you have me lose the mummy for ever?"

"Yes, I would, if my misery is to be the price of its restoration. Why should I sell myself to a man I care nothing about, just because you want a musty, fusty old corpse? Now I am going." Lucy walked to the door. "I shan't listen to another word. And if you bother me again, I shall marry Archie at once and leave the house."

"I can make you leave it in any case, you ungrateful girl," bellowed Braddock, who was purple with rage, never having a very good temper at the best of times. "Look what I have done for you!"

Miss Kendal could have pointed out that her step-father had done nothing save attend to himself. But she disdained such an argument, and without another word opened the door and walked out. Almost immediately afterwards Cockatoo entered, much to the relief of the Professor, who relieved his feelings by kicking the unfortunate Kanaka. Then he sat down again to consider ways and means of obtaining the necessary mummy and still more necessary money.

CHAPTER VIII

THE BARONET

Sir Frank Random was an amiable young gentleman with—as the saying goes—all his goods in the shop window. Fair-haired and tall, with a well-knit, athletic figure, a polished manner, and a man-of-the-world air, he strictly resembled the romantic officer of Bow Bells, Family Herald, Young Ladies' Journal fiction. But the romance was all in his well-groomed looks, as he was as commonplace a Saxon as could be met with in a day's march. Fond of sport, attentive to his duties as artillery captain, and devoted to what is romantically known as the fair sex, he sauntered easily through life, very well contented with himself and with his agreeable surroundings. He read fiction when he did read, and those weekly papers devoted to sport; troubled his head very little about politics, save when they had to do with a possible German invasion, and was always ready to do any one a good turn. His brother-officers declared that he was not half a bad sort, which was high praise from the usually reticent service man. His capacity may be accurately gauged by the fact that he did not possess a single enemy, and that every one spoke well of him. A mortal who possesses no quality likely to be envied by those around him is certain to belong to the rank and file of humanity. But these unconsidered units of mankind can always console themselves with the undoubted fact that mediocrity is invariably happy.

Such a man as Random would never set the Thames on fire, and certainly he had no ambition to perform that astounding feat. He was fond of his profession and intended to remain in the army as long as he could. He desired to marry and beget a family, and retire, when set free from soldiering, to his country seat, and there perform blamelessly the congenial role of a village squire, until called upon to join the respectable corpses in the Random vault. Not that he was a saint or ever could be one. Neither black nor white, he was simply gray, being an ordinary mixture of good and bad. As theology has provided no hereafter for gray people, it is hard to imagine where the bulk of humanity will go. But doubts on this point never troubled Random. He went to church, kept his mouth shut and his pores open and vaguely believed that it would be all right somehow. A very comfortable if superficial philosophy indeed.

It can easily be guessed that Random's somewhat colorless

personality would never attract Lucy Kendal, since the hues of her own character were deeper. For this reason she was drawn to Hope, who possessed that aggressive artistic temperament, where good and bad, are in violent contrast. Random took opinions from books, or from other people, and his mind, like a looking-glass, reflected whatever came along; but Hope possessed opinions of his own, both right and wrong, and held to these in the face of all verbal opposition. He could argue and did argue, when Random simply agreed. Lucy had similar idiosyncrasies, inherited from a clever father, so it was just as well that she preferred Archie to Frank. Had the latter young gentleman married her, he would have dwindled to Lady Random's husband, and would have found too late that he had domesticated a kind of imitation George Eliot. When he congratulated Archie on his engagement somewhat ruefully, he little thought what an escape he had had.

But Professor Braddock, who did not belong to the gray tribe, knew nothing of this, as his Egyptological studies did not permit him time to argue on such commonplace matters. He therefore failed in advance when he set out to persuade Random into renewing his suit. As the fiery little man afterwards expressed himself, "I might as well have talked to a mollusc," for Random politely declined to be used as an instrument to forward the Professor's ambition at the cost of Miss Kendal's unhappiness. The interview took place in Sir Frank's quarters at the Fort on the day after Hervey had called to propose a search for the corpse. And it was during this interview that Braddock learned something which both startled and annoyed him.

Random, at three o'clock, had just changed into mufti, when the Professor was announced by his servant. Braddock, determined to give his host no chance of denying himself, followed close on the man's heels, and was in the room almost before Sir Frank had read the card. It was a bare room, sparsely furnished, according to the War Office's idea of comfort, and although the baronet had added a few more civilized necessities, it still looked somewhat dismal. Braddock, who liked comfort, shook hands carelessly with his host and cast a disapproving eye on his surroundings.

"Dog kennel! dog kennel!" grumbled the polite Professor. "Bare desolation like a damned dungeon. You might as well live in the Sahara."

"It would certainly be warmer," replied Random, who knew the scientist's snappy ways very well. "Take a chair, sir!"

"Hard as bricks, confound it! Hand me over a cushion. There, that's better! No, I never drink between meals, thank you. Smoke? Hang it, Random, you should know by this time that I dislike making a chimney of my throat! There! there! don't fuss. Take a seat and listen to what I have to say. It's important. Poke the fire, please: it's cold."

Random placidly did as he was told, and then lighted a cigar, as he sat down quietly.

"I am sorry to hear of your trouble, sir.'"

"Trouble! trouble! What particular trouble?"

"The death of your assistant."

"Oh yes. Silly young ass to get killed. Lost my mummy, too: there's trouble if you like."

"The green mummy." Random looked into the fire, "Yes. I have heard of the green mummy."

"I should think you have," snapped Braddock, warming his plump hands. "Every penny-a-liner has been talking about it. When did you return?"

"On the same day that that steamer with the mummy on board arrived," was Random's odd reply.

The Professor stared suspiciously. "I don't see why you should date your movements by my mummy," he retorted.

"Well, I had a reason in doing so."

"What reason?"

"The mummy—"

"What about it?—do you know where it is?" Braddock started to his feet, and looked eagerly at the calm face of his host.

"No, I wish I did. How much did you pay for it, Professor?"

"What's that to you?" snapped the other, resuming his seat.

"Nothing at all. But it is a great deal to Don Pedro de Gayangos."

"And who the deuce is he? Some Spanish Egyptologist?"

"I don't think he is an Egyptologist, sir."

"He must be, if he wants my mummy."

"You forget, Professor, that the green mummy comes from Peru."

"Who denied that it did, sir? You are illogical—infernally so." The little man rose and straddled on the hearth-rug, with his back to the fire and his hands under his coat-tails. "Now, sir," he said, glaring at the young man like a school-master—"what the deuce are you talking about? Out with it: no evasion."

"Oh, hang it, Professor, don't jump down my throat, spurs and all," said Random, rather annoyed by this dictatorial tone.

"I never wear spurs: go on, sir, and don't argue."

Sir Frank could not help laughing, although he knew that it was useless to induce Braddock to be civil. Not that the Professor, meant to be rude, especially as he desired to conciliate Random. But long

56

years of fighting with other scientists and of having his own scientific way had turned him into a kind of school-master, and every one knows that they are the most domineering of the human race.

"It's a long story," said the baronet, with a shrug and a smile.

"Story! story! What story?"

"'That which I am about to tell you." And then

Random began hurriedly, so as to prevent further arguments of an unprofitable kind. "I was at Genoa with my yacht, and there stopped on shore at the Casa Bianca."

"What place is that?"

"An hotel. I there met with a certain Don Pedro de Gayangos and his daughter, Donna Inez, He was a gentleman from Lima, and had come to Europe in search of the green mummy."

Braddock stared.

"And what did this confounded Spaniard want with my green mummy?" he demanded indignantly. "How did he know of its existence?—what reason had he to try and obtain it? Answer, sir."

"I shall let Don Pedro answer himself," said Random dryly. "He arrives in a couple of days, and intends to take rooms at the Warrior Inn along with his daughter. Then you can question him, Professor."

"I question you," snapped Braddock angrily.

"And I am answering to the best of my ability. Don Pedro told me nothing beyond the fact that he wanted the mummy, and had come to Europe to get it. In some way he learned that it was in Malta and was for sale."

"Quite so: quite so," rasped the Professor. "He saw the advertisement in the newspapers, as I did, and wanted to buy it over my head."

"Oh, he wanted to buy it right enough, and wired to Malta," said Random, "but in reply he received a letter stating that it had been sold to you and was being taken to England on The Diver. I followed The Diver in my yacht and arrived at Pierside an hour after she did."

"Ah!" Braddock glared. "I begin to see light. This infernal Spaniard was on board, and wanted my mummy. He knew that Bolton had taken it to the Sailor's Rest and went there to kill the poor lad and get my—"

"Nothing of the sort," interrupted Sir Frank impatiently. "Don Pedro remained behind in Genoa, intending to write and ask if you would sell him the mummy. I wrote and told him of the murder of your assistant and related all that had happened. He wired to me that he was coming to England at once, as—as I told you. He will be in Gartley in a couple of days. That is the whole story."

"It is a sufficiently strange one," grumbled Braddock, frowning. "What does he want with my mummy?"

"I cannot tell you. But if you will sell—"

"Sell! sell! sell!" vociferated Braddock furiously.

"Don Pedro will give you a good price," finished Random calmly.

"I haven't got the mummy," said the Professor, sitting down and wiping his pink head, "and if I had, I certainly would not sell. However, I'll hear what this gentleman has to say when he arrives. Perhaps he can throw some light on the mystery of this crime."

"I am perfectly certain that he cannot, sir. Don Pedro—as I said—was left behind in Genoa."

"Humph!" said the Professor, unconvinced. "He could easily employ a third party."

Random rose, looking and feeling annoyed.

"I assure you that Don Pedro is a gentleman and a man of honor. He would not stoop to—"

"There! there!" Braddock waved his hands. "Sit down: sit down."

"You shouldn't say such things, Professor."

"I say what I desire to say," retorted the old gentleman tartly; "but we can dismiss the subject for the time being."

"I am only too glad to do so," said Random, who was ruffled out of his usual calm by the veiled accusation which Braddock had brought against his foreign friend, "and to get to a more agreeable subject, tell me how Miss Kendal is keeping."

"She is ill, very ill," said the Professor solemnly.

"Ill? Why, Hope, whom I met the other day, said that she was feeling very well and very happy."

"So Hope thinks, because he has forced her into an engagement."

Random started to his feet.

"Forced her? Nonsense!"

"It isn't nonsense, and don't dare to speak like that to me, sir. I repeat that Lucy—poor child—is breaking her heart for you."

The young man stared and then broke into a hearty laugh.

"Pardon me, sir, but that is impossible."

"It isn't, confound you!" said Braddock, who did not like being laughed at. "I know women."

"You don't know your daughter."

"Step-daughter, you mean."

"Ah, perhaps the more distant relationship accounts for your ignorance of her character," said Random dryly. "You are quite wrong. I was in love with Miss Kendal, and asked her to be my wife

58

before I went on leave. She refused me, saying that she loved Hope, and because of her refusal I took my broken heart to Monte Carlo, where I lost much more money than I had any right to lose."

"Your broken heart seems to have mended quickly," said Braddock, who was trying to suppress his wrath at this instance of Lucy's duplicity, for so he considered it.

"Oh, pooh, it's only my way of speaking," laughed the young man. "If my heart had been really broken I should not have mentioned the fact."

"Then you did not love Lucy, and you dared to play fast and loose with her affections," raged Braddock, stamping.

"You are quite wrong," said Sir Frank sharply; "I did love Miss Kendal, or I should certainly not have asked her to be my wife. But when she told me that she loved another man, I stood aside as any fellow would."

"You should have insisted on—"

"On nothing, sir. I am not the man to force a woman to give me a heart which belongs to another person. I am very glad that Miss Kendal is engaged to Hope, as he is a capital fellow, and will make her a better husband than I ever could have made her. Besides," Random shrugged his shoulders, "one nail drives another out."

"Humph! That means you love another."

"I am not bound to tell you my private affairs, Professor."

"Quite so: quite so; but Inez is a pretty and romantic name."

"I don't know what you are talking about, sir," said Random stiffly.

Braddock chuckled, having read the truth in the flush which had crept over Random's tanned face.

"I ask your pardon," he said elaborately. "I am an old man, and I was your father's friend. You must not mind if I have been a trifle inquisitive."

"Say no more, sir: that is all right."

"I don't agree with you, Random. Things are not all right and never will be until my mummy is discovered. Now you can help me."

"In what way?" asked the other uneasily.

"With money. Understand, my boy," added the Professor in a genial way which he knew well how to assume, "I should have preferred Lucy becoming your wife. However, since she prefers Hope, there's no more to be said on that score. I therefore will not make the offer I came here to make."

"An offer, sir?"

"Yes! I fancied that you loved Lucy and were broken-hearted by the news of her engagement to Hope. I therefore intended to ask

59

you to give me, or rather lend me, five hundred pounds on condition that I helped you to—"

"Stop, Professor," said Random, coloring, "I should never have bought Miss Kendal as my wife on those terms."

"Of course! of course! and—as I say—there is no more to be said. I shall therefore agree to Lucy's engagement to Hope"— Braddock carefully omitted to say that he had already agreed and had been paid one thousand pounds to agree—"and will congratulate you when you lead Donna Inez to the altar."

"I never said anything about Donna Inez, Professor Braddock."

"Of course not: modern reticence. However, I can see through a brick wall as well as most people. I understand, so let us drop the subject, my boy. And this five hundred pounds—"

"I cannot lend it to you, Professor. The fact is, I lost heaps of coin at Monte Carlo, and am not in a position to—"

"Very good, let us shelve that also," said Braddock with apparent heartiness, although he was really very angry at his failure. "I am sorry, though, as I wish to get back the mummy and to revenge poor Sidney Bolton's death."

"How can the five hundred do that?" asked Random with interest.

"Well," drawled the Professor with his eyes on the young man's attentive face, "Captain Hervey of The Diver came to me yesterday and proposed to search for the assassin and his plunder on condition that I paid him five hundred pounds. I am, as you know, very poor for a scientist, and so I wished to borrow the five hundred from you on condition that Lucy—"

"We won't talk of that again," said Random hurriedly; "but do you mean to say that this Captain Hervey knows of anything likely to solve this mystery?"

"He says that he does not, and merely proposes to search. From what I have seen of the man I should think that he had all the capacities of a good bloodhound and would certainly succeed. But he will not move a step without money."

"Five hundred pounds," murmured Random thoughtfully, while the Professor watched him closely. "I can tell you how to obtain it."

"How? In what way?"

"Don Pedro seems to be rich, and he wants the mummy," said the baronet. "So when he comes here ask him to—"

"Certainly not: certainly not," raged Braddock, clapping on his hat in a fury. "How dare you make such a proposition to me, Random! If this Don Pedro offers the reward and Hervey finds the mummy, he will simply hand it over to your friend."

"He can scarcely do that, since you have bought the mummy. But Don Pedro is willing to purchase it from you."

"Humph!" Braddock moved to the door, thinking. "I shall reserve my decision until this man arrives. Good day," and he departed.

Random did not attempt to detain him, as he was somewhat weary of the Professor's vagaries. He knew very well that Braddock would call on Don Pedro when he came to the Warrior Inn, and join forces with him in searching for the lost goods. And the train of thought initiated by the Professor's visit led Random to a certain drawer, whence he took the photograph of a splendid-looking beauty. To this he pressed his lips. "I wonder if your father will give you to me in exchange for that mummy," he thought, and kissed the pictured face again.

CHAPTER IX

MRS. JASHER'S LUCK'

Some weeks had now elapsed since the death and burial of Sidney Bolton, and the excitement had simmered down to a gentle speculation as to who had killed him. This question was discussed in a half-hearted manner round the winter fires of Gartley, but gradually people were ceasing to interest themselves in a crime, the mystery of which would apparently never be solved. Life went on in the village and at the Pyramids much in the same way, save that the Professor attended along with Cockatoo to his museum and did not engage another assistant.

Archie and Lucy were perfectly happy, as they looked forward to being married in the spring, and Braddock showed no desire to interfere with their engagement. They knew, of course, that he had called upon Sir Frank, but were ignorant of what had taken place. Random himself called at the Pyramids to congratulate Miss Kendal on her engagement, and seemed so very pleased that she was going to marry the man of her choice, that, woman-like, she grew rather annoyed. As the baronet had been her lover, she thought that he should wear the willow for her sake. But Random showed no disposition to do so, therefore Lucy shrewdly guessed that his broken heart had been mended by another woman. The Professor could have confirmed the truth of this from the hints which Random had given him, but he said nothing about his interview with the young man, nor did he mention that a Spanish gentleman from Peru was seeking for the famous green mummy.

Considerably vexed that Random should be so cheerful, Lucy cast round to learn the truth. She could scarcely ask the baronet himself, and Archie professed himself unable to explain. Miss Kendal did not dream of cross-examining Braddock, as it never entered her mind that the dry-as-dust scientist would know anything. It then occurred to this inquisitive young lady that Mrs. Jasher might be aware of Random's secret, which made him so cheerful. Sir Frank was a great friend of the plump widow, and frequently went to take afternoon tea at her small house, which was situated no great distance from the Fort. In fact, Mrs. Jasher entertained the officers largely, as she was hospitable by nature, and liked to have presentable men about her for flirting purposes. With good-looking youth she assumed the maternal air, and in the role of a clever woman of the world professed to be the adviser of one and all. In this way she became quite a favorite, and her little parlor—she liked the old English word—was usually, well filled at the hour of afternoon tea.

Twice already Lucy had called on Mrs. Jasher after the commotion caused by the crime, as she wished to speak to her about the same; but on each occasion the widow proved to be absent in London. However, the third visit proved to be more lucky, for Mrs. Jasher was at home, and expressed herself happy to see the girl.

"So good of you to come and see me in my little wooden hut," said the widow, kissing her guest.

And Mrs. Jasher's cottage really was a little wooden hut, being what was left of an old-fashioned farmhouse, built before the stone age. It lay on the verge of the marshes in an isolated position and was placed in the middle of a square garden, protected from the winter floods by a low stone wall solidly built, but of no great height. The road to the Fort ran past the front part of the garden, but behind the marshes spread towards the embankment, which cut off the view of the Thames. The situation was not an ideal one, nor was the cottage, but money was scarce with Mrs. Jasher, and she had obtained the whole place at a surprisingly small rental. The house and grounds were dry enough in summer, but decidedly damp in winter. Therefore, the widow went to a flat in London, as a rule, for the season of fogs. But this winter she had made up her mind—so she told Lucy—to remain in her own little castle and brave the watery humors of the marshes.

"I can always keep fires burning in every room," said Mrs. Jasher, when she had removed her guest's hat and had settled her for a confidential talk on the sofa. "And after all, my dear, there is no place like home."

The room was small, and Mrs. Jasher was small, so she suited her surroundings excellently. Also, the widow had the good taste to furnish it sparsely, instead of crowding it with furniture; but what furniture there was could not be improved upon. There were Chippendale chairs, a Louis Quinze table, a Sheridan cabinet, and a satin-wood desk, hand-painted, which was said to have been the property of the unhappy Marie Antoinette. Oil-paintings adorned the rose-tinted walls, chiefly landscapes, although one or two were portraits. Also, there were water-colored pictures, framed and signed caricatures, many plates of old china, and rice-paper adornments from Canton. The room was essentially feminine, being filled with Indian stuffs, with silver oddments, with flowers, and with other trifles. The walls, the carpet, the hangings, and the upholstery of the arm-chairs were all of a rosy hue, so that Mrs.

63

Jasher looked as young as Dame Holda in the Venusberg. A very pretty room and a very charming hostess, was the verdict of the young gentlemen from the Fort, who came here to flirt when they were not serving their country.

Mrs. Jasher in a tea-rose tea-gown for afternoon tea—she always liked to be in keeping—rang for that beverage dear to the feminine heart, and lighted a rose-shaded lamp. When a glow as of dawn spread through the dainty room, she settled Lucy on the sofa near the fire, and drew up an arm-chair on the other side of the hearth-rug. Outside it was cold and foggy, but the rose-hued curtains shut out all that was disagreeable in the weather, and in the absence of male society, the two women talked more or less confidentially. Lucy did not dislike Mrs. Jasher, even though she fancied that the lively widow was planning to become the mistress of the Pyramids.

"Well, my dear girl," said Mrs. Jasher, shading her face from the fire with a large fan, "and how is your dear father after his late terrible experiences?"

"He is perfectly well, and rather cross," replied Lucy, smiling.

"Cross?"

"Of course. He has lost that wretched mummy."

"And poor Sidney Bolton."

"Oh, I don't think he cares for poor Sidney's death beyond the fact that he misses his services. But the mummy cost nine hundred pounds, and father is much annoyed, especially as Peruvian mummies are somewhat hard to obtain. You see, Mrs. Jasher, father wishes to see the difference between the Peruvian and Egyptian modes of embalming."

"Ugh! How gruesome!" Mrs. Jasher shuddered. "But has anything been discovered likely to show who killed this poor lad?"

"No, the whole thing is a mystery."

Mrs. Jasher looked into the fire over the top of the fan.

"I have read the papers," she said slowly, "and have gathered what I could from what the reporters explained. But I intend to call on the Professor and hear all that evidence which did not get into the papers."

"I think that everything has been made public. The police have no clue to the murderer. Why do you want to know?"

Mrs. Jasher made a movement of surprise.

"Why, I am the Professor's friend, of course, my dear, and naturally I want to help him to solve this mystery."

"There is no chance, so far as I can see, of it ever being solved," said Lucy. "It's very sweet of you, of course, but were I you I should not talk about it to my father."

"Why?" asked Mrs. Jasher quickly.

"Because he thinks of nothing else, and both Archie and I are trying to get him off the subject. The mummy is lost and poor Sidney is buried. There is no more to be said."

"Still, if a reward was offered—"

"My father is too poor to offer a reward, and the Government will not do so. And as people will not work without money, why—" Lucy completed her sentence with a shrug.

"I might offer a reward if the dear Professor will let me," said the widow unexpectedly.

"You! But I thought that you were poor, as we are."

"I was, and I am not very rich now. All the same, I have come in for some thousands of pounds."

"I congratulate you. A legacy?"

"Yes. You remember how I told you about my brother who was a Pekin merchant. He is dead."

"Oh, I am so sorry."

"My dear, what is the use of being sorry. I never cry over spilt milk, or assume a virtue which I have not. My brother and I were almost strangers, as we lived apart for so many years. However, he came home to die at Brighton, and a few weeks ago—just after this murder took place, in fact—I was summoned to his death-bed. He lingered on until last week and died in my arms. He left me nearly all his money, so I will be able to help the Professor."

"I don't see why you should," said Lucy, wondering why Mrs. Jasher did not wear mourning for the dead.

"Oh yes, you do see," remarked the widow, raising her eyes and rubbing her plump hands together. "I want to marry your father."

Lucy did not express astonishment, as she had understood this for a long time.

"I guessed as much."

"And what do you say?"

Miss Kendal shrugged her shoulders.

"If my step-father," she emphasized the word—"if my step-father consents, why should I mind? I am going to marry Archie, and no doubt the Professor will be lonely."

"Then you do not disapprove of me as a mother."

"My dear Mrs. Jasher," said Lucy, coldly, "there is no relationship between me and my step-father beyond the fact that he married my mother. Therefore you can never be my mother. Were I stopping on at the Pyramids, that question might arise, but as I become Mrs. Hope in six months, we can be friends—nothing more."

"I am quite content with that," said Mrs. Jasher in a

businesslike way. "After all, I am no sentimentalist. But I am glad that you do not mind my marrying the Professor, as I don't want you to prevent the match, my dear."

Lucy laughed.

"I assure you that I have no influence with my father, Mrs. Jasher. He will marry you if he thinks fit and without consulting me. But," added the girl with emphasis, "I do not see what you gain in becoming Mrs. Braddock."

"I may become Lady Braddock," said the widow, dryly. Then, in answer to the open astonishment on Lucy's face, she hastened to remark: "Do you mean to say that you don't know your father is heir to a baronetcy?"

"Oh, I know that," rejoined Miss Kendal. "The Professor's brother, Sir Donald Braddock, is an old man and unmarried. If he dies without heirs, as it seems likely, the Professor will certainly take the title."

"Well, then, there you are!" cried Mrs. Jasher, in her liveliest tone. "I want to give my legacy for the title and preside over a scientific salon in London."

"I understand. But you will never get my father to live in London."

"Wait until I marry him," said the little woman shrewdly. "I'll make a man of him. I know, of course, that mummies and sepulchral ornaments and those sort of horrid things are dull, but the Professor will become Sir Julian Braddock, and that is enough for me. I don't love him, of course, as love between two elderly people is absurd, but I shall make him a good wife, and with my money he can take his proper position in the scientific world, which he doesn't occupy at present. I would rather he had been artistic, as science is so dull. However, I am getting on in years and wish to have some amusement before I die, so I must take what I can get. What do you say?"

"I am quite agreeable, as, when I leave, someone must look after my father, else he will be shamefully robbed by everyone in household matters. We are good friends, so why not you as well as another."

"You are a dear girl," said Mrs. Jasher with a sigh of relief, and kissed Lucy fondly. "I am sure we shall get on excellently."

"At a distance. The artistic world doesn't touch on the scientific, you know. And you forget, Mrs. Jasher, that my father wishes to go to Egypt to explore this mysterious tomb."

Mrs. Jasher nodded.

"Yes, I promised, when I came in for my brother's money, to help the Professor to fit out his expedition. But it seems to me that the money will be better spent in offering a reward so that the mummy can be found."

"Well," said Lucy, laughing, "you can give the Professor his choice."

"Before marriage, not after. He needs to be managed, like all men."

"You will not find him easy to manage," said Lucy dryly. "He is a very obstinate man, and quite feminine in his persistency."

"H'm! I recognize that he is a difficult character, and between you and me dear, I should not marry him but for the title. It sounds rather like an adventuress talking in this way, but, after all, if he makes me Lady Braddock I can give him enough money to let him realize his desire of getting the mummy back. It's six of one and half a dozen of the other. And I'll be good to him: you need not fear."

"I am quite sure that, good or bad, the Professor will have his own way. It is not his happiness I am thinking of so much as yours."

"Really. Here is the tea. Put the table near the fire, Jane, between Miss Kendal and myself. Thank you. The muffins on the fender. Thank you. No, there is nothing more. Close the door when you go out."

The tea equippage having been arranged, Mrs. Jasher poured out a cup of Souchong, and handed it to her guest, resuming the subject of her proposed marriage meanwhile.

"I don't see why you should be anxious about me, dear. I am quite able to look after myself. And the Professor seems to be kind-hearted enough."

"Oh, he is kind-hearted when he gets his own way. Give him his hobby and he will never bother you. But he won't live in London, and he will not consent to this salon you wish to institute."

"Why not? It means fame to him. I shall gather round me all the scientists of London and make my house a centre of interest. The Professor can stop in his laboratory if he likes. As his wife, I can do all that is necessary. Well, my dear"—Mrs. Jasher took a cup of tea—"we need not talk the subject threadbare. You do not disapprove of my marriage with your step-father, so you can leave the rest to me. If you can give me a hint of how to proceed to bring about this marriage, of course I am not above taking it."

Lucy glanced at the tea-gown.

"As you will have to tell the Professor that your brother is dead to account for possessing the money," she said pointedly, "I should advise you to go into mourning. Professor Braddock will be shocked otherwise."

"Dear me, what a tender heart he must have!" said Mrs. Jasher flippantly. "My brother was very little to me, poor man, so he cannot be anything to the Professor. However, I shall adopt your advice, and, after all, black suits me very well. There"—she swept her hands across the tea-table—"that is settled. Now about yourself?"

"Archie and I marry in the springtime."

"And your other admirer, who has come back?"

"Sir Frank Random?" said Lucy, coloring.

"Of course. He called to see me a day or so ago, and seems less broken-hearted than he should be."

Lucy nodded and colored still deeper.

"I suppose some other woman has consoled him."

"Of course. Catch a modern man wearing the willow for any girl, however dear. Are you angry?"

"Oh no, no."

"Oh yes, yes, I think," said the widow, laughing, "else you are no woman, my dear. I know I should be angry to see a man get over his rejection so rapidly."

"Who is she?" asked Lucy abruptly.

"Donna Inez de Gayangos."

"A Spaniard?"

"I believe so—a colonial Spaniard, at least—from Lima. Her father, Don Pedro de Gayangos, met Sir Frank in Genoa by chance."

"Well?" demanded Lucy impatiently.

Mrs. Jasher shrugged her plump shoulders.

"Well, my dear, can't you put two and two together. Of course Sir Frank fell in love with this dark-hued angel."

"Dark-hued! and I am light-haired. What a compliment!"

"Perhaps Sir Frank wanted a change. He played on white and lost, and therefore stakes his money on black to win. That's the result of having been at Monte Carlo. Besides, this young lady is rich, I understand, and Sir Frank—so he told me—lost much more money at Monte Carlo than he could afford. Well, you don't look pleased."

Lucy roused herself from a fit of abstraction.

"Oh yes, I am pleased, of course. I suppose, as any woman would, I felt rather hurt for the moment in being forgotten so soon. But, after all, I can't blame Sir Frank for consoling himself. If I am married first, he shall dance at my wedding: if he is married first, I shall dance at his."

"And you shall both dance at mine," said Mrs. Jasher. "Why, there is quite an epidemic of matrimony. Well, Donna Inez arrives here with her father in a day, or so. They stop at the Warrior Inn, I believe."

"That horrid place?"

"Oh, it is clean and respectable. Besides, Sir Frank can hardly

68

ask them to stop in the Fort, and I have no room in this bandbox of mine. However, the two of them—Donna Inez and Frank, I mean—can come here and flirt; so can you and Archie if you like."

"I fear four people in this room would not do," laughed Lucy, rising to take her leave. "Well, I hope Sir Frank will marry this lady and that you will become Mrs. Braddock. Only one thing I should like to know."

"And that is?"

"Why was the mummy stolen. It was not valuable save to a scientist."

"By that argument a scientist must be the murderer and thief," said Mrs. Jasher. "However, we shall see. Meanwhile, live every moment of love's golden hours: they never return."

"That is good advice; I shall take it and my leave," said Lucy, and departed in a very happy frame of mind.

CHAPTER X

THE DON AND HIS DAUGHTER

Professor Braddock was usually the most methodical of men, and timed his life by the clock and the almanac. He rose at seven, summer and winter, to partake of a hearty breakfast, which served him until dinner came at five thirty. Braddock dined at this unusual hour—save when there was company—as he did not eat any luncheon and scorned the very idea of afternoon tea. Two meals a day, he maintained, was enough for any man who led a sedentary life, as too much food was apt to clog the wheels of the intellect. He usually worked in his museum—if the indulgence of his hobby could be called work—from nine until four, after which hour he took a short walk in the garden or through the village. On finishing his dinner he would glance over some scientific publication, or perhaps, by way of recreation, play a game or two of patience; but at seven invariably retired into his own rooms to renew work. Retirement to bed took place at midnight, so it can be guessed that the Professor got through an enormous quantity of work during the year. A more methodical man, or a more industrious man did not exist.

But on occasions even this enthusiast wearied of his hobby, and of the year's routine. A longing to see brother scientists of his own way of thinking would seize him, and he would abruptly depart for London, to occupy quiet lodgings, and indulge in intercourse with his fellow-men. Braddock rarely gave early intimation of his urban nostalgia. At breakfast he would suddenly announce that the fit took him to go to London, and he would drive to Jessum along with Cockatoo to catch the ten o'clock train to London. Sometimes he sent the Kanaka back; at other times he would take him to town; but whether Cockatoo remained or departed, the museum was always locked up lest it should be profaned by the servants of the house. As a matter of fact, Braddock need not have been afraid, for Lucy—knowing her step-father's whims and violent temper—took care that the sanctity of the place should remain inviolate.

Sometimes the Professor came back in a couple of days; at times his absence would extend to a week; and on two or three occasions he remained absent for a fortnight. But whenever he returned, he said very little about his doings to Lucy, perhaps deeming that dry scientific details would not appeal to a lively young lady. As soon as he was established in his museum again, life at the Pyramids would resume its usual routine, until Braddock again felt the want of a change. The wonder was, considering the nature of his work, and the closeness of his application, that he did not more often indulge in these Bohemian wanderings.

Lucy, therefore, was not astonished when, on the morning after her visit to Mrs. Jasher, the Professor announced in his usual abrupt way that he intended to go to London, but would leave Cockatoo in charge of his precious collection. She was somewhat disturbed, however, as, wishing to forward the widow's matrimonial aims, she had invited her to dinner for the ensuing night. This she told her step-father, and, rather to her surprise, he expressed himself sorry that he could not remain.

"Mrs. Jasher," said Braddock hastily, drinking his coffee, "is a very sensible woman, who knows when to be silent."

"She is also a good housekeeper, I believe," hinted Miss Kendal demurely.

"Eh, what? Well? Why do you say that?" snapped Braddock sharply.

Lucy fenced.

"Mrs. Jasher admires you, father."

Braddock grunted, but did not seem displeased, since even a scientist possessing the usual vanity of the male is not inaccessible to flattery.

"Did Mrs. Jasher tell you this?" he inquired, smiling complacently.

"Not in so many words. Still, I am a woman, and can guess how much another woman leaves unsaid." Lucy paused, then added significantly: "I do not think that she is so very old, and you must admit that she is wonderfully well preserved."

"Like a mummy," remarked the Professor absently; then pushed back his chair to add briskly: "What does all this mean, you minx? I know that the woman is all right so far as a woman can be: but her confounded age and her looks and her unexpressed admiration. What are these to an old man like myself?"

"Father," said Lucy earnestly, "when I marry Archie I shall, in all probability, leave Gartley for London."

"I know—I know. Bless me, child, do you think that I have not thought of that? If you were only wise, which you are not, you would marry Random and remain at the Fort."

"Sir Frank has other fish to fry, father. And even if I did remain at the Fort as his wife, I still could not look after you."

"Humph! I am beginning to see what you are driving at. But I can't forget your mother, my dear. She was a good wife to me."

"Still," said Lucy coaxingly, and becoming more and more the

71

champion of Mrs. Jasher, "you cannot manage this large house by yourself. I do not like to leave you in the hands of servants when I marry. Mrs. Jasher is very domesticated and—"

"And would make a good housekeeper. No, no, I don't want to give you another mother, child."

"There is no danger of that, even if I did not marry," rejoined Lucy stiffly. "A girl can have only one mother."

"And a man apparently can have two wives," said Braddock with dry humor. "Humph!"—he pinched his plump chin—"it's not a bad idea. But of course I can't fall in love at my age."

"I don't think that Mrs. Jasher asks for impossibilities."

The Professor rose briskly.

"I'll think over it," said he. "Meanwhile, I am going to London."

"When will you be back, father?"

"I can't say. Don't ask silly questions. I dislike being bound to time. I may be a week, and I may be only a few days. Things can go on here as usual, but if Hope comes to see you, ask Mrs. Jasher in, to play chaperon."

Lucy consented to this suggestion, and Braddock went away to prepare for his departure. To get him off the premises was like launching a ship, as the entire household was at his swift heels, packing boxes, strapping rugs, cutting sandwiches, helping him on with his overcoat and assisting him into the trap, which had been hastily sent for to the Warrior Inn. All the time Braddock talked and scolded and gave directions and left instructions, until every one was quite bewildered. Lucy and the servants all sighed with relief when they saw the trap disappear round the end of the road in the direction of Jessum. In addition to being a famous archaeologist, the Professor was assuredly a great nuisance to those who had to do with his whims and fancies.

For the next two or three days Lucy enjoyed herself in a quiet way with Archie. In spite of the lateness of the season, the weather was still fine, and the artist took the opportunity of the pale sunshine to sketch a great deal of the marsh scenery. Lucy attended him as a rule when he went abroad, and sometimes Mrs. Jasher, voluble and merry, would come along with them to play the part of chaperon. But the girl noticed that Mrs. Jasher's merriment was forced at times, and in the searching morning light she appeared to be quite old. Wrinkles showed themselves on her plump face and weary lines appeared round her mouth. Also, she was absent-minded while the lovers chattered, and, when spoken to, would return to the present moment with a start. As the widow was now well off as regards money, and as her scheme to marry Braddock was well on the way to success—for Lucy had duly reported the

Professor's attitude—it was difficult to understand why Mrs. Jasher should look so worried. One day Lucy spoke to her on the subject. Random had strolled across the marshes to look at Hope sketch, and the two men chatted together, while Miss Kendal led the little widow to one side.

"There is nothing the matter, I hope," said Lucy gently.

"No. Why do you say that?" asked Mrs. Jasher, flushing.

"You have been looking worried for the last few days."

"I have a few troubles," sighed the widow—"troubles connected with the estate of my late brother. The lawyers are very disagreeable and make all sorts of difficulties to swell their costs. Then, strangely enough, I am beginning to feel my brother's death more than I thought I should have done. You see that I am in mourning, dear. After what you said the other day I felt that it was wrong for me not to wear mourning. Of course my poor brother and I were almost strangers. All the same, as he has left me money and was my only relative, I think it right to show some grief. I am a lonely woman, my dear."

"When my father comes back you will no longer be lonely," said Lucy.

"I hope not. I feel that I want a man to look after me. I told you that I desired to marry the Professor for his possible title and in order to form a salon and have some amusement and power. But also I want a companion for my old age. There is no denying," added Mrs. Jasher with another sigh, "that I am growing old in spite of all the care I take. I am grateful for your friendship, dear. At one time I thought that you did not like me."

"Oh, I think we get on very well together," said Lucy somewhat evasively, for she did not want to say that she would make the widow an intimate friend, "and, as you know, I am quite pleased that you should marry my step-father."

"So pleasant to think that you look at my ambition in that light," said Mrs. Jasher, patting the girl's arm. "When does the Professor return?"

"I cannot say. He refused to fix a date. But he usually remains away for a fortnight. I expect him back in that time, but he may come much earlier. He will come back when the fancy takes him."

"I shall alter all that, when we are married," muttered Mrs. Jasher with a frown. "He must be taught to be less selfish."

"I fear you will never improve him in that respect," said Lucy dryly, and rejoined the gentlemen in time to hear Random mention the name of Don Pedro de Gayangos.

"What is that, Sir Frank?" she asked.

Random turned toward her with his pleasant smile.

73

"My Spanish friend, whom I met at Genoa, is coming here to-morrow."

"With his daughter?" questioned Mrs. Jasher roguishly.

"Of course," replied the young soldier, coloring. "Donna Inez is quite devoted to her father and never leaves him."

"She will one day, I expect," said Hope innocently, for his eyes were on his sketch and not on Random's face, "when the husband of her choice comes along."

"Perhaps he has come along already," tittered Mrs. Jasher significantly.

Lucy took pity on Random's confusion.

"Where will they stay?"

"At the Warrior Inn. I have engaged the best rooms in the place. I fancy they will be comfortable there, as Mrs. Humber, the landlady, is a good housekeeper and an excellent cook. And I don't think Don Pedro is hard to please."

"A Spaniard, you say," remarked Archie idly. "Does he speak English?"

"Admirably—so does the daughter."

"But why does a Spaniard come to so out-of-the-way a place?" asked Mrs. Jasher, after a pause.

"I thought I told you the other day, when we spoke of the matter," answered Sir Frank with surprise. "Don Pedro has come here to interview Professor Braddock about that missing mummy."

Hope looked up sharply.

"What does he know about the mummy?"

"Nothing so far as I know, save that he came to Europe with the intention of purchasing it, and found himself forestalled by Professor Braddock. Don Pedro told me no more than that."

"Humph!" murmured Hope to himself. "Don Pedro will be disappointed when he learns that the mummy is missing."

Random did not catch the words and was about to ask him what he had said, when two tall figures, conducted by a shorter one, were seen moving on the white road which led to the Fort.

"Strangers!" said Mrs. Jasher, putting up her lorgnette, which she used for effect, although she had remarkably keen sight.

"How do you know?" asked Lucy carelessly.

"My dear, look how oddly the man is dressed."

"I can't tell at this distance," said Lucy, "and if you can, Mrs. Jasher I really do not see why you require glasses."

Mrs. Jasher laughed at the compliment to her sight, and colored through her rouge at the reproof to her vanity. Meanwhile, the smaller figure, which was that of a village lad leading a tall gentleman and a slender lady, pointed toward the group round

74

Hope's easel. Shortly, the boy ran back up to the village road, and the gentleman came along the pathway with the lady. Random, who had been looking at them intently, suddenly started, having at length recognized them.

"Don Pedro and his daughter," he said in an astonished voice, and sprang forward to welcome the unexpected visitors.

"Now, my dear," whispered the widow in Lucy's ear, "we shall see the kind of woman Sir Frank prefers to you."

"Well, as Sir Frank has seen the kind of man I prefer to him," retorted Lucy, "that makes us quite equal."

"I am glad these new-comers talk English," said Hope, who had risen to his feet. "I know nothing of Spanish."

"They are not Spanish, but Peruvian," said Mrs. Jasher.

"The language is the same, more or less. Confound it! here is Random bringing them here. I wish he would take them to the Fort. There's no more work for the next hour, I suppose," and Hope, rather annoyed, began to pack his artistic traps.

On a nearer view, Don Pedro proved to be a tall, lean, dry man, not unlike Dore's conception of Don Quixote. He must have had Indian blood in his veins, judging from his very dark eyes, his stiff, lank hair, worn somewhat long, and his high cheek-bones. Also, although he was arrayed in puritanic black, his barbaric love of color betrayed itself in a red tie and in a scarlet handkerchief which was twisted loosely round a soft slouch hat, It was the hat and the brilliant red of tie and handkerchief which had caught Mrs. Jasher's eye at so great a distance, and which had led her to pronounce the man a stranger, for Mrs. Jasher well knew that no Englishman would affect such vivid tints. All the same, in spite of this eccentricity, Don Pedro looked a thorough Castilian gentleman, and bowed gravely when presented to the ladies by Random.

"Mrs. Jasher, Miss Kendal, permit me to present Don Pedro de Gayangos."

"I am charmed," said the Peruvian, bowing, hat in hand, "and in turn, allow me, ladies, to introduce my daughter, Donna Inez de Gayangos."

Archie was also presented to the Don and to the young lady, after which Lucy and Mrs. Jasher, while not appearing to look, made a thorough examination of the lady with whom Random was in love. No doubt Donna Inez was making an examination on her own account, and with the cleverness of the sex the three women, while chatting affably, learned all that there was to be learned from the outward appearance of each other in three minutes. Miss Kendal could not deny but what Donna Inez was very beautiful, and frankly admitted—inwardly, of course—her own inferiority. She was merely

75

pretty, whereas the Peruvian lady was truly handsome and quite majestic in appearance.

Yet about Donna Inez there was the same indefinite barbaric look as characterized her father. Her face was lovely, dark and proud in expression, but there was an aloofness about it which puzzled the English girl. Donna Inez might have belonged to a race populating another planet of the solar system. She had large black, melting eyes, a straight Greek nose and perfect mouth, a well-rounded chin and magnificent hair, dark and glossy as the wing of the raven, which was arranged in the latest Parisian style of coiffure. Also, her gown—as the two women guessed in an instant—was from Paris. She was perfectly gloved and booted, and even if she betrayed somehow a barbaric taste for color in the dull ruddy hue of her dress, which was subdued with black braid, yet she looked quite a well-bred woman. All the same, her whole appearance gave an observant onlooker the idea that she would be more at home in a scanty robe and glittering with rudely wrought ornaments of gold. Perhaps Peru, where she came from, suggested the comparison, but Lucy's thoughts flew back to an account of the Virgins of the Sun, which the Professor had once described. It occurred to her, perhaps wrongly, that in Donna Inez she beheld one who in former days would have been the bride of some gorgeous Inca.

"I fear you will find England dull after the sunshine of Lima," said Lucy, having ended a swift examination.

Donna Inez shivered a trifle and glanced around at the gray misty air through which the pale sunshine struggled with difficulty.

"I certainly prefer the tropics to this," she said in musical English, "but my father has come down here on business, and until it is concluded we shall remain in this place."

"Then we must make things as bright as possible for you," said Mrs. Jasher cheerfully, and desperately anxious to learn more of the new-comers. "You must come to see me, Donna Inez—yonder is my cottage."

"Thank you, madame: you are very good."

Meanwhile Don Pedro was talking to the two young men.

"Yes, I did arrive here earlier than I expected," he was remarking, "but I have to return to Lima shortly, and I wish to get my business with Professor Braddock finished as speedily as possible."

"I am sorry," said Lucy politely, "but my father is absent."

"And when will he return, Miss Kendal?"

"I can scarcely say—in a week or a fortnight."

Don Pedro made a gesture of annoyance.

"It is a pity, as I am so very pressed for time. Still, I must

76

remain until the Professor returns. I am so anxious to hear if the mummy has been found."

"It is not found yet," said Hope quickly, "and never will be."

Don Pedro looked at him quietly.

"It must be found," said he. "I have come all the way from Lima to obtain it. When you hear my story you will not be surprised at my desire to regain the mummy."

"Regain it?" echoed Hope and Random in one breath.

Don Pedro nodded.

"The mummy was stolen from my father," he said.

CHAPTER XI

THE MANUSCRIPT

It was certainly strange how constantly the subject of the missing mummy came uppermost. Since it had disappeared and since the man who had brought it to England was dead, it might have been thought that nothing more would be said about the matter. But Professor Braddock harped incessantly on his loss—which was perhaps natural—and Widow Anne also talked a great deal as to the possibility of the mummy, being found, as she hoped to learn by that means the name of the assassin who had strangled her poor boy. Now Don Pedro de Gayangos appeared with the strange information that the weird relic of Peruvian civilization had been stolen from his father. Apparently fate was not inclined to let the matter of the lost mummy drop, and was working round to a denouement, which would possibly include the solution of the mystery of Sidney Bolton's death. Yet, on the face of it, there appeared to be no chance of the truth becoming known.

Of course, when Don Pedro announced that the Mummy had formerly belonged to his father, every one was anxious to hear how it had been stolen. The Gayangos family were established in Lima, and the embalmed body of Inca Caxas had been purchased from a gentleman residing in Malta. How, then, had it crossed the water, and how had Don Pedro learned its whereabouts, only to arrive too late to secure his missing property? Mrs. Jasher was especially anxious to learn these things, and explained her reasons to Lucy.

"You see, my dear," she said to the girl on the day after Don Pedro's arrival in Gartley, "if we learn the past of that horrid mummy, we may gain a clue to the person who desired possession of the nasty thing, and so may hunt down this terrible criminal. Once he is found, the mummy may be secured again, and should I be able to return it to your father, out of gratitude he would certainly marry me."

"You seem to think that the assassin is a man," said Lucy dryly; "yet you forget that the person who talked to Sidney through the window of the Sailor's Rest was a woman."

"An old woman," emphasized Mrs. Jasher briskly: "quite so."

Lucy contradicted.

"Eliza Flight did not say if the woman was old or young, but merely stated that she wore a dark dress and a dark shawl over her head. Still, this mysterious woman was connected in some way with the murder, else she would not have been speaking to Sidney."

"I don't follow you, my dear. You talk as though poor Mr. Bolton expected to be murdered. For my part, I hold by the verdict of wilful murder against some person or persons unknown. The truth is to be found, if anywhere, in the past of the mummy."

"We can discover nothing about that."

"You forget what Don Pedro said, my dear," remarked Mrs. Jasher hastily, "that the mummy had been stolen from his father. Let us hear what he has to say and we may find a clue. I am anxious that the Professor should regain the green mummy for reasons which you know of. And now, my hear, can you come to dinner to-night?"

"Well, I don't know." Miss Kendal hesitated. "Archie said that he would look in this evening."

"I shall ask Mr. Hope also, my love. Don Pedro is coming and his daughter likewise. Needless to say Sir Frank will follow the young lady. We shall be a party of six, and after dinner we must induce Don Pedro to relate the story of how the mummy was stolen."

"He may not be inclined."

"Oh, I think so," replied; Mrs. Jasher quickly. "He wants to get the mummy back again, and if we discuss the subject we may see some chance of securing it."

"But Don Pedro will not wish it to be restored to my father."

Mrs. Jasher shrugged her plump shoulders.

"Your father and Don Pedro can arrange that themselves. All I desire is, that the mummy should be found. Undoubtedly it belongs by purchase to the Professor, but as it has been stolen, this Peruvian gentleman may claim it. Well?"

"I shall come and Archie also," assented Lucy, who was beginning to be interested in the matter. "The affair is somewhat romantic."

"Criminal, my dear, criminal," said Mrs. Jasher, rising to take her leave. "It is not a matter I care to mix myself up with. Still"—she laughed—"you know, why I am doing so."

"If I had to take all this trouble to gain a husband," observed Lucy somewhat acidly, "I should remain single all my life."

"If you were as lonely as I am," retorted the plump widow, "you would do your best to secure a man toy look after you. I should prefer a young and handsomer husband—such as Sir Frank Random, for instance but, as beggars cannot be choosers, I must content myself with old age, a famous scientist, and the chance of a possible title. Now mind, dear, to-night at seven—not a minute later," and she bustled away to prepare for the reception of her guests.

It seemed to Lucy that Mrs. Jasher was taking a great deal of trouble to become Mrs. Braddock, especially as the Professor's brother might live for many a long day yet, in which case the widow would not gain the title she coveted for years. However, the girl rather sympathized with Mrs. Jasher, who was a companionable soul, and fond of society. Circumstances condemned her to a somewhat lonely life in an isolated cottage in a rather dull neighborhood, so it was little to be wondered at that she should strive to move heaven and earth—as she was doing—in the hope of escaping from her solitude. Besides, although Miss Kendal did not wish to make a close companion of the widow, yet she did not dislike her, and, moreover, thought that she would make Professor Braddock a very presentable wife. Thinking thus, Lucy was quite willing to forward Mrs. Jasher's plans by inducing Don Pedro to tell all he knew about this missing mummy.

Thus it came about that six people assembled in the tiny pink parlor of Mrs. Jasher at the hour of seven o'clock. It required dexterous management to seat the whole company in the dining room, which was only a trifle larger than the parlor. However, Mrs. Jasher contrived to place them round her hospitable board in, a fairly comfortable fashion, and, once seated, the dinner was so good that no one felt the drawbacks of scanty elbow room. The widow, as hostess, was placed at the head of the table; Don Pedro, as the eldest of the men, at the foot; and Sir Frank, with Donna Inez, faced Archie and Lucy Kendal. Jane, who was well instructed in waiting by her mistress, attended to her duties admirably, acting both as footman and butler. Lucy, indeed, had offered Mrs. Jasher the services of Cockatoo to hand round the wine, but the widow with a pretty shudder had declined.

"That dreadful creature with his yellow mop of hair gives me the shivers," she declared.

Considering the isolation of the district, and the narrow limits of Mrs. Jasher's income, the meal was truly, admirable, being well cooked and well served, while the table was arrayed like an altar for the reception of the various dishes. Whatever Mrs. Jasher might be as an adventuress, she certainly proved herself to be a capital housekeeper, and Lucy foresaw that, if she did become Mrs. Braddock, the Professor would fare sumptuously, for the rest of his scientific life. When the meal was ended the widow produced a box of superfine cigars and another of cigarettes, after which she left the gentlemen to sip their wine, and took her two young friends to chatter chiffons in the tiny parlor. And it said much for Mrs.

80

Jasher's methodical ways that, considering the limited space, everything went—as the saying goes—like clockwork. Likewise, the widow had proved herself a wonderful hostess, as she kept the ball of conversation rolling briskly and induced a spirit of fraternity, uncommon in an ordinary dinner party.

During the meal Mrs. Jasher had kept off the subject of the mummy, which was the excuse for the entertainment; but when the gentlemen strolled into the parlor, feeling well fed and happy, she hinted at Don Pedro's quest. As the night was cold and the Peruvian gentleman came from the tropics, he was established in a well padded arm-chair close to the sea-coal fire, and with her own fair hands Mrs. Jasher gave him a cup of fragrant coffee, which was rendered still more agreeable to the palate by the introduction of a vanilla bean. With this and with a good cigar—for the ladies gave the gentlemen permission to smoke—Don Pedro felt very happy and easy, and complimented Mrs. Jasher warmly on her capability of making her fellow-creatures comfortable.

"It is altogether comfortable, madame," said Don Pedro, rising to make a courtly bow. In fact, so agreeable was the foreigner that Mrs. Jasher dreamed for one swift moment of throwing over the dry-as-dust scientist to become a Spanish lady of Lima.

"You flatter me, Don Pedro," she said, waving a wholly unnecessary fan out of compliment to her guest's Spanish extraction. "Indeed, I am very glad that you are pleased with my poor little house."

"Pardon, madame, but no house can be poor when it is a casket to contain such a jewel."

"There!" said Lucy somewhat satirically to the young men, while Mrs. Jasher blushed and bridled, "what Englishman could turn such a compliment? It reminds one of Georgian times."

"We are more sober now than my fathers were then," said Hope, smiling, "and I am sure if Random thought for a few minutes he could produce something pretty. Go on, Random."

"My brain is not equal to the strain after dinner," said Sir Frank.

As for Donna Inez, she did not speak, but sat smiling quietly in her corner of the room, looking remarkably handsome. As a young girl Lucy was pretty, and Mrs. Jasher was a comely widow, but neither one had the majestic looks of the Spanish lady. She smiled, a veritable queen amidst the gim-crack ornaments of Mrs. Jasher's parlor, and Sir Frank, who was fathoms deep in love, could not keep his eyes off her face.

For a few minutes the conversation was frivolous, quite the Shakespeare and musical glasses kind of speech. Then Mrs. Jasher, who had no idea that her good dinner should be wasted in charming nothings, introduced the subject of the mummy by a reference to Professor Braddock. It was characteristic of her cleverness that she did not address Don Pedro, but pointed her speech at Lucy Kendal.

"I do hope your father will return with that mummy," she observed, after a dexterous allusion to the late tragedy.

"I don't think he has gone to look for it," replied Miss Kendal indifferently.

"But surely he desired to get it back, after paying nearly one thousand pounds for it," said Mrs. Jasher, with well-feigned astonishment.

"Oh, of course; but he would scarcely look for it in London."

"Has Professor Braddock gone to search for the mummy?" asked Don Pedro.

"No," answered Lucy. "He is visiting the British Museum to make some researches in the Egyptian department."

"When do you expect him back, please?"

Lucy shrugged her shoulders.

"I can't say, Don Pedro. My father comes and goes as the whim takes him."

The Spanish gentleman looked thoughtfully into the fire.

"I shall be glad to see the Professor when he returns," he said in his excellent, slow-sounding English. "My concern about this mummy is deep."

"Dear me," remarked Mrs. Jasher, shielding her fair cheek with the unnecessary fan, and venturing on a joke, "is the mummy a relative?"

"Yes, madame," replied Don Pedro, gravely and unexpectedly.

At this every one, very naturally, looked astonished—that is, all save Donna Inez, who still preserved her fixed smile. Mrs. Jasher took a mental note of the same, and decided that the young lady was not very intelligent. Meanwhile Don Pedro continued his speech after a glance round the circle.

"I have the blood of the royal Inca race in my veins," he said with pride.

"Ha!" murmured the widow to herself, "then that accounts for your love of color, which is so un-English;" then she raised her voice. "Tell us all about it, Don Pedro," she entreated; "we are usually so dull here that a romantic story excites us dreadfully."

"I do not know that it is very romantic," said Don Pedro with a polite smile, "and if you will not find it dull—"

"Oh, no!" said Archie, who was as anxious as Mrs. Jasher to hear what was to be said about the mummy. "Come, sir, we are all attention."

Don Pedro bowed again, and again swept the circle with his deep-set eyes.

"The Inca Caxas," he remarked, "was one of the decadent rulers of ancient Peru. At the Conquest by the Spaniards, Inca Atahuallpa was murdered by Pizarro, as you probably know. Inca Toparca succeeded him as a puppet king. He died also, and it was suspected that he was slain by a native chief called Challcuchima. Then Manco succeeded, and is looked upon by historians as the last Inca of Peru. But he was not."

"This is news, indeed," said Random lazily. "And who was the last Inca?"

"The man who is now the green mummy."

"Inca Caxas," ventured Lucy timidly.

Don Pedro looked at her sharply. "How do you come to know the name?"

"You mentioned it just now, but, before that, I heard my father mention it," said Lucy, who was surprised at the sharpness of his tone.

"And where did the Professor learn the name?" asked Don Pedro anxiously.

Lucy shook her head.

"I cannot say. But go on with the story," she continued, with the naive curiosity of a child.

"Yes, do," pleaded Mrs. Jasher, who was listening with all her ears.

The Peruvian meditated for a few minutes, then slipped his hand into the pocket of his coat and brought out a discolored parchment, scrawled and scribbled with odd-looking letters in purple ink somewhat faded.

"Did you ever see this before?" he asked Lucy, "or any manuscript like it?"

"No," she answered, bending forward to examine the parchment carefully.

Don Pedro again swept an inquiring eye round the circle, but everyone denied having seen the manuscript.

"What is it?" asked Sir Frank curiously.

Don Pedro restored the manuscript to his pocket.

"It is an account of the embalming of Inca Caxas, written by his son, who was my ancestor."

"Then you are descended from this Inca?" said Mrs. Jasher eagerly.

"I am. Had I my rights I should rule Peru. As it is, I am a poor gentleman with very little money. That," added Don Pedro with emphasis, "is why I wish to recover the mummy of my great ancestor."

"Is it then so valuable?" asked Archie suddenly. He was thinking of some reason why the mummy should have been stolen.

"Well, in itself it is of no great value, save to an archaeologist," was Don Pedro's reply; "but I had better tell you the story of how it was stolen from my father."

"Go on, go on," cried Mrs. Jasher. "This is most interesting."

Don Pedro plunged into his story without further preamble.

"Inca Caxas held his state amidst the solitudes of the Andes, away from the cruel men who had conquered his country. He died and was buried. This manuscript,"—he touched his pocket—"was written by his son, and details the ceremonies, the place of sepulchre, and also gives a list of the jewels with which the mummy was buried."

"Jewels," murmured Hope under his breath. "I thought as much."

"The son of Inca Caxas married a Spanish lady and made peace with the Spaniards. He came to live at Cuzco, and brought with him, for some purpose which the manuscript does not disclose, the mummy of his father. But the manuscript was lost for years, and although my family—the De Gayangoses—became poor, no member of it knew that, concealed in the corpse of Inca Caxas, were two large emeralds of immense value. The mummy of our royal ancestor was treated as a sacred thing and venerated accordingly. Afterwards my family came to live at Lima, and I still dwell in the old house."

"But how was the mummy stolen from you?" asked Random curiously.

"I am coming to that," said Don Pedro, frowning at the interruption. "I was not in Lima at the time; but I had met the man who stole the precious mummy."

"Was he a Spaniard?"

"No," answered Don Pedro slowly, "he was an English sailor called Vasa."

"Vasa is a Swedish name," observed Hope critically.

"This man said that he was English, and certainly spoke like an Englishman, so far as I, a foreigner, can tell. At that time, when I was a young man, civil war raged in Peru. My father's house was sacked, and this Vasa, who had been received hospitably by my father when he was shipwrecked at Callao, stole the mummy, of Inca Caxas. My father died of grief and charged me to get the mummy back. When peace was restored to my unhappy country I tried to recover the venerated body of my ancestor. But all search proved vain, as Vasa had disappeared, and it was supposed that, for some reason, he had taken the embalmed body out of the country. It was when the mummy was lost that I unexpectedly came across the manuscript, which detailed the funeral ceremonies of Inca Caxas, and on learning about the two emeralds I was naturally more anxious than ever to discover the mummy and retrieve my fallen fortunes by means of the jewels. But, as I said, all search proved vain, and I afterward married, thinking to settle down on what fortune remained to me. I did live quietly in Lima for years until my wife died. Then with my daughter I came to Europe on a visit."

"To search for the mummy?" questioned Archie eagerly.

"No, sir. I had given up all hope of finding that. But chance placed a clue in my hands. At Genoa I came across a newspaper, which stated that a mummy in a green case—and a Peruvian mummy at that—was for sale at Malta. I immediately made inquiries, thinking that this was the long-lost body of Inca Caxas. But it so happened that I was too late, as already the mummy had been sold to Professor Braddock, and had been taken to England on board The Diver by Mr. Bolton. Chance, which had pointed out the whereabouts of the mummy, also brought me at Genoa into relations with Sir Frank Random"—Don Pedro bowed his head to the baronet—"and, as it appeared that he knew Professor Braddock, I thankfully accepted his offer to introduce me. Hence I am here, but only to hear that the mummy is again lost. That is all," and the Peruvian gentleman dramatically waved his arm.

"A strange story," said Archie, who was the first to speak, "and it certainly solves at least one part of the mystery."

"What is that?" demanded Mrs. Jasher quickly.

"It shows that the mummy was stolen on account of the emeralds."

"Pardon me, but that is impossible, sir," said Don Pedro, drawing up his lean figure. "No one but myself knew that the mummy held two emeralds in its dead hands, and I learned that only a few years ago from the manuscript which I had the honor of showing you."

"There is that objection assuredly," replied Hope with composure. "Yet I can hardly believe that any man would risk his neck to steal so remarkable a mummy, which he would have a difficulty in disposing of. But did this assassin know of the emeralds, he would venture much to gain them, since jewels can be disposed of with comparative ease, and cannot easily be traced."

"All the same," said Random, looking up, "I do not see how the assassin could have learned that the jewels were wrapped in the bandages."

"Humph!" said Hope, glancing at De Gayangos, "perhaps there is more than one copy of this manuscript you speak of."

"Not to my knowledge."

"The sailor Vasa might have copied it."

"No." Don Pedro shook his head. "It is written in Latin, since a Spanish priest taught the son of Inca Caxas, who wrote it, that language. I do not think that Vasa knew Latin. Also, if Vasa had copied the manuscript, he would have stripped the mummy to procure the jewels. Now, in the newspaper advertisement it stated that the bandages of the mummy were intact, as also was the verdant case. No," said Don Pedro decisively, "I am quite of opinion that Vasa, and indeed everyone else, was ignorant of this manuscript."

"It seems to me," suggested Mrs. Jasher, "that it would be best to find this sailor."

"That," remarked De Gayangos, "is impossible. It is twenty years since he disappeared with the mummy. Let us drop the subject until Professor Braddock returns to discuss it with me." And this was accordingly done.

CHAPTER XII

A DISCOVERY

Three days went by, and Professor Braddock still remained absent in London, although an occasional letter to Lucy requested such and such an article from the museum to be forwarded, sometimes by post and on other occasions by Cockatoo, who traveled up to town especially. The Kanaka always returned with the news that his master was looking well, but brought no word of the Professor's return. Lucy was not surprised, as she was accustomed to Braddock's vagaries.

Meanwhile Don Pedro, comfortably established at the Warrior Inn, wandered about Gartley in his dignified way, taking very little interest in the village, but a great deal in the Pyramids. As the Professor was absent, Lucy could not ask him to dinner, but she did invite him and Donna Inez to afternoon tea. Don Pedro was anxious to peep into the museum, but Cockatoo absolutely refused to let him enter, saying that his master had forbidden anyone to view the collection during his absence. And in this refusal Cockatoo was supported by Miss Kendal, who had a wholesome dread of her step-father's rage, should he return and find that a stranger had been making free of his sacred apartments. The Peruvian gentleman expressed himself extremely disappointed, so much so, indeed, that Lucy fancied he believed Braddock had the green mummy hidden in the museum, in spite of the reported loss from the Sailor's Rest.

Failing to get permission to range through the rooms of the Pyramids, Don Pedro paid occasional visits to Pierside and questioned the police regarding the Bolton murder. From Inspector Date he learned nothing of any importance, and indeed that officer expressed his belief that not until the Day of judgment would the truth become known. It then occurred to De Gayangos to explore the neighborhood of the Sailor's Rest, and to examine that public-house himself. He saw the famous window through which the mysterious woman had talked to the deceased, and noted that it looked across a stony, narrow path to the water's edge, wherefrom a rugged jetty ran out into the stream for some little distance. Nothing would have been easier, reflected Don Pedro, than for the assassin to enter by the window, and, having accomplished his deed, to leave in the same way, bearing the case containing the mummy. A few steps would carry the man and his burden to a waiting boat, and once the craft slipped into the mists on the river, all trace would be lost, as had truly happened. In this way the Peruvian gentleman believed the murder and the theft had been accomplished, but even supposing things had happened as he surmised, still, he was as far as ever from unraveling the mystery.

While Don Pedro searched for his royal ancestor's corpse, and incidentally for the thief and murderer, his daughter was being wooed by Sir Frank Random. Heaven only knows what he saw in her—as Lucy observed to young Hope—for the girl had not a word to say for herself. She was undeniably handsome, and dressed with great taste, save for stray hints of barbaric delight in color, doubtless inherited from her Inca ancestors. All the same, she appeared to be devoid of small talk or great talk, or any talk whatsoever. She sat and smiled and looked like a handsome picture, but after her appearance had satisfied the eye, she left much to be desired. Yet Sir Frank approved of her stately quietness, and seemed anxious to make her his wife. Lucy, in spite of the fact that he had so speedily got over her refusal to marry him, was anxious that he should be happy with Donna Inez, whom he appeared to love, and afforded him every opportunity of meeting the lady, so that he might prosecute his wooing. All the same, she wondered that he should desire to marry an iceberg, and Donna Inez, with her silent tongue and cold smiles, was little else. However, as Frank Random was the chief party concerned in the love-making—for Donna Inez was merely passive—there was no more to be said.

Sometimes Hope came to dine at the Pyramids, and on these occasions Mrs. Jasher was present in her character of chaperon. As Miss Kendal was helping the widow to marry Professor Braddock, she in her turn did her best to speed Archie's wooing. Certainly the young couple were engaged and there was no understanding to be brought about. Nevertheless, Mrs. Jasher was a useful article of furniture to be in the room when they were together, for Gartley, like all English villages, was filled with scandalmongers, who would have talked, had Hope and Lucy not employed Mrs. Jasher as gooseberry. Sometimes Donna Inez came with the widow, while her father was hunting for the mummy in Pierside, and then Sir Frank Random would be sure to put in an appearance to woo his Dulcinea in admiring silence. Mrs. Jasher declared that the two must have made love by telepathy, for they rarely exchanged a word. But this was all the better, as Archie and Lucy chattered a great deal, and two pair of magpies—Mrs. Jasher declared—would have been too much for her nerves. She made a very good chaperon, as she allowed the young people to act as they pleased, only sanctioning the meetings by her elderly presence.

One evening Mrs. Jasher was due to dinner, and Hope had already arrived. No one else was expected, as Don Pedro had taken his daughter to the theatre at Pierside and Sir Frank had gone to London in connection with his military duties. It was a bitterly cold night, and already a fall of snow had hinted that there was to be a real English Christmas of the genuine kind. Lucy had prepared an excellent dinner for three, and Archie had brought a set of new patience cards for Mrs. Jasher, who was fond of the game. While the widow played, the lovers hoped to make love undisturbed, and looked forward to a happy evening. But there was one drawback, for although the dinner hour was supposed to be eight o'clock, and it was now thirty minutes past, Mrs. Jasher had not arrived. Lucy was dismayed.

"What can be keeping her?" she asked Archie, to which that young gentleman replied that he did not know, and, what was more, he did not care. Miss Kendal very properly rebuked this sentiment. "You ought to care, Archie, for you know that if Mrs. Jasher does not come to dinner, you will have to go away."

"Why should I?" he inquired sulkily.

"People will talk."

"Let them. I don't care."

"Neither do I, you stupid boy. But my father will care, and if people talk he will be very angry."

"My dear Lucy," and Archie put his arm round her waist to say this, "I don't see why you should be afraid of the Professor. He is only your step-father, and you aren't so very fond of him as to mind what he says. Besides, we can marry soon, and then he can go hang."

"But I don't want him to go hang," she replied, laughing. "After all, the Professor has always been kind to me, and as a step-father has behaved very well, when he could easily have made himself disagreeable. Another thing is that he can be very bad tempered when he likes, and if I let people talk about us—which they will do if they get a chance—he will behave so coldly to me, that I shall have a disagreeable time. As we can't marry for ever so long, I don't want to be uncomfortable."

"We can marry whenever you like," said Hope unexpectedly.

"What, with your income so unsettled?"

"It is not unsettled."

"Yes, it is. You will help that horrid spendthrift uncle of yours, and until he and his family are solvent I don't see how we can be sure of our money."

"We are sure of it now, dearest. Uncle Simon has turned up trumps after all, and so have his investments."

"What do you mean exactly?"

"I mean that yesterday I received a letter from him saying that he was now rich, and would pay back all I had lent him. I went up to London to-day, and had an interview. The result of that is that I am some thousands to the good, that Uncle Simon is well off for the rest of his life and will require no more assistance, and that my three hundred a year is quite clear for ever and ever and ever."

"Then we can marry," cried Miss Kendal with a gasp of delight.

"Whenever you choose—next week if you like."

"In January then—just after Christmas. We'll go on a trip to Italy and return to take a flat in London. Oh, Archie, I am sorry I thought so badly of your uncle. He has behaved very well. And what a mercy it is that he will require no more assistance! You are sure he will not."

"If he does, he won't get it," said Hope candidly. "While I was a bachelor I could assist him; but when I am married I must look after myself and my wife." He gave Lucy a hug. "It's all right now, dear, and Uncle Simon has behaved excellently—far better than I expected. We shall go to Italy for the honeymoon and need not hurry back until we—well, say until we quarrel."

"In that case we shall live in Italy for the rest of our lives," said Lucy with twinkling eyes; "but we must come back in a year and take a studio in Chelsea."

"Why not in Gartley? Remember, the Professor will be lonely."

"No, he won't. Mrs. Jasher, as I told you, intends to marry him."

"He might not wish to marry her"

"That doesn't matter," rejoined Lucy, with the cleverness of a woman. "She can manage to bring the marriage about. Besides, I want to break with the old life here, and begin quite a new one with you. When I am your wife and Mrs. Jasher is my step-father's, everything will be capitally arranged."

"Well, I hope so," said Archie heartily, "for I want you all to myself and have no desire to share you with anyone else. But I say," he glanced at his watch; "it is getting towards nine o'clock, and I am desperately hungry. Can't we go to dinner?"

"Not until Mrs. Jasher arrives," said Lucy primly.

"Oh, bother—!"

Hope, being quite exasperated with hunger, would have launched out into a speech condemning the widow's unpunctuality, when in the hall below the drawing-room was heard the sound of the door opening and closing. Without doubt this was Mrs. Jasher arriving at last, and Lucy ran out of the room and down the stairs to welcome her in her eagerness to get Archie seated at the dinner table. The young man lingered by the open door of the drawing-room, ready to welcome the widow, when he heard Lucy utter an exclamation of surprise and became aware that she was ascending the stairs along with Professor Braddock. At once he reflected there would be trouble, since he was in the house with Lucy, and lacked the necessary chaperon which Braddock's primitive Anglo-Saxon instincts insisted upon.

"I did not know you were returning to-night," Lucy was saying when she re-entered the drawing-room with her step-father.

"I arrived by the six o'clock train," explained the Professor, unwinding a large red scarf from his neck, and struggling out of his overcoat with the assistance of his daughter. "Ha, Hope, good evening."

"Where have you been since?" asked Lucy, throwing the Professor's coat and wraps on to a chair.

"With Mrs. Jasher," said Braddock, warming his plump hands at the fire. "So you must blame me that she is not here to preside at dinner as the chaperon of you young people."

Lucy and her lover glanced at one another in surprise. This light and airy tone was a new one for the Professor to take. Instead of being angry, he seemed to be unusually gay, and looked at them in quite a jocular manner for a dry-as-dust scientist.

"We waited dinner for her, father," ventured Lucy timidly.

"Then I am ready to eat it," announced Braddock. "I am extremely hungry, my dear. I can't live on love, you know."

"Live on love?" Lucy stared, and Archie laughed quietly.

"Oh yes, you may smile and look astonished;" went on the Professor good-humoredly, "but science does not destroy the primeval instincts entirely. Lucy, my dear," he took her hand and patted it, "while in London and in lodgings, it was borne in upon me forcibly how lonely I was and how lonely I would be when you married our young friend yonder. I had intended to come down to-morrow, but to-night, such was my feeling of loneliness that I considered favorably your idea that I should find a second helpmate in Mrs. Jasher. I have always had a profound admiration for that lady, and so—on the spur of the moment, as I may say—I decided to come down this evening and propose."

"Oh," Lucy clapped her hands, very well satisfied with the unexpected news, "and have you?"

"Mrs. Jasher," said the Professor gravely, "did me the honor to promise to become my wife this evening."

"She will become your wife this evening?" said Archie, smiling.

Braddock, with one of those odd twists of humor which were characteristic of him, became irascible.

"Confound it, sir, don't I speak English," he snapped, with his eyes glaring rebuke. "She promised this evening to become Mrs. Braddock. We shall marry—so we have arranged—in the springtime, which is the natural pairing season for human beings as well as for birds. And I am glad to say that Mrs. Jasher takes a deep interest in archaeology."

"And, what is more, she is a splendid housekeeper," said Lucy.

The temporary anger of the Professor vanished. He drew his step-daughter towards him and kissed her on the cheek.

"I believe that I have to thank you for putting the idea into my head," said he, "and also—if Mrs. Jasher is to be believed—for aiding her to see the mutual advantage it would be to both of us to marry. Ha," he released Lucy and rubbed his hands, "let us go to dinner."

"I am very glad," said Miss Kendal heartily.

"So am I, so am I," replied Braddock, nodding. "As you very truly observed, my child, the house would have gone to rack and ruin without a woman to look after my interests. Well," he took the arms of the two young people, "I really think that we must have a bottle of champagne on the strength of it."

Shortly the trio were seated at the table, and Braddock explained that Mrs. Jasher, being overcome by his proposal, had not been able to face the ordeal of congratulations.

"But she will come to-morrow," said he, as Cockatoo filled three glasses.

"Indeed, I shall congratulate her to-night," said Lucy obstinately. "As soon as dinner is over, I shall go with Archie to her house, and tell her how pleased I am."

"It is very cold for you to be out, Lucy dear," urged Archie anxiously.

"Oh, I can wrap up warmly," she answered.

Strange to say, the Professor made no objection to the excursion, although Hope quite expected such a stickler for etiquette to refuse permission to his step-daughter. But Braddock seemed rather pleased than otherwise. His proposal of marriage seemed to have put him into excellent humor, and he raised his glass with a chuckle.

"I drink to your happiness, my dear Lucy, and to that of Mrs. Jasher's."

"And I drink to Archie's and to yours, father," she replied. "I am glad that you will not be lonely when we are married. Archie and I wish to become one in January."

"Yes," said Hope, finishing his champagne, "my income is now all right, as my uncle has paid up."

"Very good, very good. I make no objection," said Braddock

placidly. "I will give you a handsome wedding present, Lucy, for you may have heard that my future wife has money left to her by her brother, who was lately a merchant in Pekin. She is heart and hand with me in our proposed expedition to Egypt."

"Will you go there for the honeymoon, sir?" asked Hope.

"Not exactly for the honeymoon, since we are to be married in spring, and my expedition to the tomb of Queen Tahoser cannot start until the late autumn. But Mrs. Braddock will come with me. That is only just, since it will be her money which will furnish the sinews of war."

"Well, everything is arranged very well," said Lucy. "I marry Archie; you, father, make Mrs. Jasher your wife; and I suspect Sir Frank will marry Donna Inez."

"Ha!" said Braddock with a start, "the daughter of De Gayangos, who has come here for the missing mummy. Mrs. Jasher told me somewhat of that, my dear. But I shall see Don Pedro myself to-morrow. Meanwhile, let us eat and drink. I must go down to the museum, and you—"

"We shall go to congratulate Mrs. Jasher," said Lucy.

So it was arranged, and shortly Professor Braddock retired into his sanctum along with the devoted Cockatoo, who displayed lively joy on beholding his master once more. Lucy, after being carefully wrapped up by Archie, set out with that young man to congratulate the bride-elect. It was just half-past nine when they started out.

The night was frosty and the stars twinkled like jewels in a cloudless sky of dark blue. The moon shone with hard brilliance on the ground, which was powdered with a light fall of snow. As the young people walked briskly through the village, their footsteps rang on the frosty earth and they scrunched the snow in their quick tread. The Warrior Inn was still open, as it was not late, and lights shone from the windows of the various cottages. When the two, following the road through the marshes, emerged from the village, they saw the great mass of the Fort bulking blackly against the clear sky, the glittering stream of the Thames, and the marshes outlined in delicate white. The fairy world of snow and moonlight appealed to Archie's artistic sense, and Lucy approving of the same, they did not hurry to arrive at their destination.

But shortly they saw the squarely fenced acre of ground near the embankment, wherein Mrs. Jasher's humble abode was placed. Light shone through the pink curtains of the drawing-room, showing that the widow had not yet retired. In a few minutes the lovers were at the gate and promptly entered. It was then that one of those odd things happened which would argue that some people are possessed of a sixth sense.

93

Archie closed the gate after him, and, glancing right and left, walked up the snowy path with Lucy. To the right was a leafless arbor, also powdered with snow, and against the white bulked a dark form something like a coffin. Hope out of curiosity went up to it.

"What the deuce is this?" he asked himself; then raised his voice in loud surprise. "Lucy! Lucy! come here!"

"What is it?" she asked, running up.

"Look"—he pointed to the oddly shaped case—"the green mummy!"

CHAPTER XIII

MORE MYSTERY

Neither Lucy nor Archie Hope had ever seen the mummy, but they knew the appearance which it would present, as Professor Braddock, with the enthusiasm of an archaeologist, had often described the same to them. It appeared, according to Braddock, that on purchasing the precious corpse in Malta, his dead assistant had written home a full description of the treasure trove. Consequently, being advised beforehand, Hope had no difficulty in recognizing the oddly shaped case, which was made somewhat in the Egyptian form. On the impulse of the moment he had proclaimed this to be the long-lost mummy, and when a closer examination by the light of a lucifer match revealed the green hue of the coffin wood, he knew that he was right.

But what was the mummy in its ancient case doing in Mrs. Jasher's arbor? That was the mute question which the two young people asked themselves and each other, as they stood in the chilly moonlight, staring at the grotesque thing. The mummy had disappeared from the Sailor's Rest at Pierside some weeks ago, and now unexpectedly appeared in a lonely garden, surrounded by marshes. How it had been brought there, or why it should have been brought there, or who had brought it to such an unlikely place, were questions hard to answer. However, the most obvious thing to do was to question Mrs. Jasher, since the uncanny object was lying within a stone-throw of her home. Lucy, after a rapid word or two, went to ring the bell, and summon the lady, while Archie stood by the arbor, wondering how the mummy came to be there. In the same way George III had wondered how the apples got into the dumplings.

Far and wide spread the marshes, flatly towards the shore of the river on one side, but on the other sloping up to Gartley village, which twinkled with many lights on the rising ground. Some distance away the Fort rose black and menacing in the moonlight, and the mighty stream of the Thames glittered like polished steel as it flowed seaward. As there were only a few leafless trees dotted about the marshy ground, and as that same ground, lightly sprinkled with powdery snow, revealed every moving object for quite a mile or so, Hope could not conceive how the mummy case, which seemed heavy, could have been brought into the silent garden

95

without its bearers being seen. It was not late, and soldiers were still returning through Gartley to the Fort. Then, again, some noise must have been caused by so bulky an object being thrust through the narrow wicket, and Mrs. Jasher, inhabiting a wooden house, which was a very sea-shell for sound, might have heard footsteps and voices. If those who had brought the mummy here—and there was more than one from the size of the case—could be discovered, then the mystery of Sidney Bolton's death would be solved very speedily. It was at this moment of his reflections that Lucy returned to the arbor, leading Mrs. Jasher, who was attired in a tea-gown and who looked bewildered.

"What are you talking about, my dear?" she said, as Lucy led her towards the arbor. "I declare I was ever so much astonished, when Jane told me that you wished to speak to me. I was just writing a letter to the lawyer who has my poor brother's property in hand, announcing my engagement to the Professor. Mr. Hope? You here also. Well, I'm sure."

Lucy grew impatient at all this babble.

"Did you not hear what I said, Mrs. Jasher?" she cried irritably. "Can't you use your eyes? Look! The green mummy is in your arbor."

"The—green—mummy—in—my—arbor," repeated Mrs. Jasher, like a child learning words of one syllable, and staring at the black object before which the three were standing.

"As you see," said Archie abruptly. "How did it come here?"

He spoke harshly. Of course, it was absurd to accuse Mrs. Jasher of knowing anything about the matter, since she had been writing letters. Still, the fact remained that a mummy, which had been thieved from a murdered man, was in her arbor, and naturally she was called upon to explain.

Some suspicion in his tone struck the little woman, and she turned on him with indignation.

"How did it come here?" she repeated. "Now, how can I tell, you silly boy. I have been writing to my lawyer about my engagement to Mr. Braddock. I daresay he has told you."

"Yes," chimed in Miss Kendal, "and we came here to congratulate you, only to find the mummy."

"Is that the horrid thing?" Mrs. Jasher stared with all her eyes, and timidly touched the hard green-stained wood.

"It's the case—the mummy is inside."

"But I thought that the Professor opened the case to find the body of poor Sidney Bolton," argued Mrs. Jasher.

"That was a packing case in which this"—Archie struck the old-world coffin—"was stored. But this is the corpse of Inca Caxas,

96

about which Don Pedro told us the other night. How does it come to be hidden in your garden?"

"Hidden." Mrs. Jasher repeated the word with a laugh. "There is not much hiding about it. Why, every one can see it from the path."

"And from the door of your house," remarked Hope significantly. "Did you not see it when you took leave of Braddock?"

"No," snapped the widow. "If I had I should certainly have come to look. Also Professor Braddock, who is so anxious to recover it, would not have allowed it to remain here."

"Then the case was not here when the Professor left you to-night?"

"No! He left me at eight o'clock to go home to dinner."

"When did he arrive here?" questioned Hope quickly.

"At seven. I am sure of the time, for I was just sitting down to my supper. He was here an hour. But he said nothing, when he entered, of any mummy being in the arbor; nor when he left me at the door and I came to say good-bye to him—did either of us see this object. To be sure," added Mrs. Jasher meditatively, "we did not look particularly in the direction of this arbor."

"I scarcely see how any one entering or leaving the garden could fail to see it, especially as the snow reflects the moonlight so brightly."

Mrs. Jasher shivered, and taking the skirt of her tea-gown, flung it over her carefully attired head,

"It is very cold," she remarked irritably. "Don't you think we had better return to the house, and talk there?"

"What!" said Archie grimly, "and leave the mummy to be carried away as mysteriously as it has been brought. No, Mrs. Jasher. That mummy represents one thousand pounds of my money."

"I understood that the Professor bought it himself."

"So he did, but I supplied the purchase money. Therefore I do not intend that this should be lost sight of again. Lucy, my dear, you run home again and tell your father what we have found. He had better bring men, to take it to his museum. When it is there, Mrs. Jasher can then explain how it came to be in her garden."

Without a word Lucy set off, walking quickly, anxious to fulfill her mission and gladden the heart of her step-father with the amazing news.

Archie and Mrs. Jasher were left alone, and the former lighted a cigarette, while he tapped the mummy case, and examined it as closely as the pale gleam of the moonlight permitted. Mrs. Jasher made no move to enter the house, much as she had complained of the cold. But perhaps she found the flimsy skirt of the tea-gown sufficient protection.

"It seems to me, Mr. Hope," said she very tartly, "that you suspect my having a hand in this," and she tapped the mummy coffin also.

"Pardon me," observed Hope very politely, "but I suspect nothing, because I have no grounds upon which to base my suspicions. But certainly it is odd that this missing mummy should be found in your garden. You will admit that much."

"I admit nothing of the sort," she rejoined coolly. "Only myself and Jane live in the cottage, and you don't expect that two delicate women could move this huge thing." She tapped the case again. "Moreover, had I found the mummy I should have taken it to the Pyramids at once, so as to give Professor Braddock some pleasure."

"It will certainly be an acceptable wedding present," said Archie sarcastically.

"Pardon me," said Mrs. Jasher in her turn, "but I have nothing to do with it as a present or otherwise. How the thing came into my arbor I really cannot say. As I told you, Professor Braddock made no remark about it when he came; and when he left, although I was at the door, I did not notice anything in this arbor. Indeed I cannot say if I ever looked in this direction."

Archie mused and glanced at his watch.

"The Professor told Lucy that he came by the six train: you say that he was here at seven."

"Yes, and he left at eight. What is the time now?"

"Ten o'clock, or a few minutes after. Therefore, since neither you nor Braddock saw the mummy, I take it that the case was brought here by some unknown people between eight o'clock and a quarter to ten, about which time I arrived here with Lucy."

Mrs. Jasher nodded.

"You put the matter very clearly," she observed dryly. "You have mistaken your vocation, Mr. Hope, and should have been a criminal lawyer. I should turn detective were I you."

"Why?" asked Archie with a start.

"You might ascertain my movements on the night when the crime was committed," snapped the little widow. "A woman muffled in a shawl, in much the same way as my head is now muffled in my skirt, talked to Bolton through the bedroom window of the Sailor's Rest, you know."

Hope expostulated.

"My dear lady, how you run on! I assure you that I would as soon suspect Lucy as you."

"Thank you," said the widow very dryly and very tartly.

"I merely wish to point out," went on Archie in a conciliatory tone, "that, as the mummy in its case—as appears probable—was brought into your garden between the hours of eight and ten, less fifteen minutes, that you may have heard the voices or footsteps of those who carried it here."

"I heard nothing," said Mrs. Jasher, turning towards the path. "I had my supper, and played a game or two of patience, and then wrote letters, as I told you before. And I am not going to stand in the cold, answering silly questions, Mr. Hope. If you wish to talk you must come inside."

Hope shook his head and lighted a fresh cigarette.

"I stand guard over this mummy until its rightful owner comes," said he determinedly.

"Ho!" rejoined Mrs. Jasher scornfully: she was now at the door. "I understood that you bought the mummy and therefore were its owner. Well, I only hope you'll find those emeralds Don Pedro talked about," and with a light laugh she entered the cottage.

Archie looked after her in a puzzled way. There was no reason to suspect Mrs. Jasher, so far as he saw, even though a woman had been seen talking to Bolton on the night of the crime. And yet, why should the widow refer to the emeralds, which were of such immense value, according to Don Pedro? Hope glanced at the case and shook the primitive coffin, anxious for the moment to open it and ascertain if the jewels were still clutched grimly in the mummy's dead hands. But the coffin was fastened tightly down with wooden pegs, and could only be opened with extreme care and difficulty. Also, as Hope reflected, even did he manage to open this receptacle of the dead, he still could not ascertain if the emeralds were safe, since they would be hidden under innumerable swathings of green-dyed llama wool. He therefore let the matter rest there, and, staring at the river, wondered how the mummy had been brought to the garden in the marshes.

Hope recollected that experts had decided the mode in which the mummy had been removed from the Pierside public-house. It had been passed through the window, according to Inspector Date and others, and, when taken across the narrow path which bordered the river, had been placed in a waiting boat. After that it had vanished until it had re-appeared in this arbor. But if taken by water once, it could have been taken by water again. There was a rude jetty behind the embankment, which Hope could easily see from where he stood. In all probability the mummy had been landed there and carried to the garden, while Mrs. Jasher was busy with her supper and her game of cards and her letters. Also, the path from the shore to the house was very lonely, and if any care had been exercised, which was probable, no one from the Fort road or from the village street could have seen the stealthy conspirators bringing their weird burden. So far Hope felt that he could argue excellently. But who had brought the mummy to the garden and why had it been brought there? These questions he could not answer so easily, and indeed not at all.

While thus meditating, he heard, far away in the frosty air, a puffing and blowing and panting like an impatient motor-car. Before he could guess what this was, Braddock appeared, simply racing along the marshy causeway, followed closely by Cockatoo, and at some distance away by Lucy. The little scientist rushed through the gate, which he flung open with a noise fit to wake the dead, and lunged forward, to fall with outstretched arms upon the green case. There he remained, still puffing and blowing, and looked as though he were hugging a huge green beetle. Cockatoo, who, being lean and hard, kept his breath more easily, stood respectfully by, waiting for his master to give orders, and Lucy came in quietly by the gate, smiling at her father's enthusiasm. At the same moment Mrs. Jasher, well wrapped up in a coat of sables, emerged from the cottage.

"I heard you coming, Professor," she called out, hurrying down the path.

"I should think the whole Fort heard the Professor coming," said Hope, glancing at the dark mass. "The soldiers must think it is an invasion."

But Braddock paid no heed to this jocularity, or even to Mrs. Jasher, to whom he had been so lately engaged. All his soul was in the mummy case, and as soon as he recovered his breath, he loudly proclaimed his joy at this miraculous recovery of the precious article.

"Mine! mine!" he roared, and his words ran violently through the frosty air.

"Be calm, sir," advised Hope—"be calm."

"Calm! calm!" bellowed Braddock, struggling to a standing position. "Oh, confound you, sir, how can I be calm when I find what I have lost? You have a mean, groveling soul, Hope, not the soaring spirit of a collector."

"There is no need to be rude to Archie, father," corrected Lucy sharply.

"Rude! Rude! I am never rude. But this mummy." Braddock peered closely at it and rapped the wood to assure himself it was no phantom. "Yes! it is my mummy, the mummy of Inca Caxas. Now I shall learn how the Peruvians embalmed their royal dead. Mine! mine! mine!" He crooned like a mother over a child, caressing the

100

coffin; then suddenly drew himself upright and fixed Mrs. Jasher with an indignant eye. "So it was you, madam, who stole my mummy," he declared venomously, "and I thought of making you my wife. Oh, what an escape I have had. Shame, woman, shame!"

Mrs. Jasher stared, then her face grew redder than the rouge on her cheeks, and she stamped furiously in the neat Louis Quinze slippers in which she had injudiciously come out.

"How dare you say what you have said?" she cried, her voice shrill and hard with anger. "Mr. Hope has been saying the same thing. Are you both mad? I never set eyes on the horrid thing in my life. And only to-night you told me that you loved—"

"Yes, yes, I said many foolish things, I don't doubt, madam. But that is not the question. My mummy! my mummy!" he rapped the wood furiously—"how does my mummy come to be here?"

"I don't know," said Mrs. Jasher, still furious, "and I don't care."

"Don't care: don't care, when I look forward to your helping me in my lifework! As my wife—"

"I shall never be your wife," cried the widow, stamping again. "I wouldn't be your wife for a thousand or a million pounds. Marry your mummy, you horrid, red-faced, crabbed little—"

"Hush! hush!" whispered Lucy, taking the angry woman round the waist, "you must make allowances for my father. He is so excited over his good fortune that he—"

"I shall not make allowance," interrupted Mrs. Jasher angrily. "He practically accuses me of stealing the mummy. If I did that, I must have murdered poor Sidney Bolton."

"No, no," cried the Professor, wiping his red face. "I never hinted at such a thing. But the mummy is in your garden."

"What of that? I don't know how it came there. Mr. Hope, surely you do not support Professor Braddock in his preposterous accusation?"

"I bring no accusation," stuttered the Professor.

"Neither do I, Mrs. Jasher. You are excited now. Go in and sleep, and to-morrow you will talk reasonably." This brilliant speech was from Hope, and wrought Mrs. Jasher into a royal rage.

"Well," she gasped, "he asks me to be calm, as it I wasn't the very calmest person here. I declare: oh, I shall be ill! Lucy," she seized the girl's hand and dragged her towards the cottage, "come in and give me red lavender. I shall be in bed for days and days and days. Oh, what brutes men can be! But listen, you two horrors," she indicated Braddock and Hope, as she pushed open the door, "if you dare to say a word against me, I'll have an action for libel against you. Oh, dear me, how very ill I feel! Lucy, darling, help me, oh, help me, and—and—oh—oh—oh!" She flopped down on the threshold of her home with a cry.

"Archie! Archie! She's fainted."

Hope rushed forward, and raised the stout little woman in his arms. Jane, attracted by the clamor, appeared on the scene, and between the three of them they managed to get Mrs. Jasher placed on the sofa of the pink drawing-room. She certainly was in a dead faint, so Hope left her to the administrations of Lucy and the servant, and walked out again into the garden, closing the cottage door after him.

He found the heartless Professor quite oblivious to Mrs. Jasher's sufferings, so taken up was he with the newly found mummy. Cockatoo had been sent for a hand-cart, and while he was absent Braddock expatiated on the perfections of this relic of Peruvian civilization.

"Will you sell it to Don Pedro?" asked Hope.

"After I have done with it, not before," snapped Braddock, hovering round his treasure. "I shall want a percentage on my bargain also."

Archie thought privately that if Braddock unswathed the mummy, he would find the emeralds and would probably stick to them, so that his expedition to Egypt might be financed. It that case Don Pedro would no longer wish to buy the corpse of his ancestor. But while he debated as to the advisability of telling the Professor of the existence of the emeralds, Cockatoo returned with the hand-cart.

"You have lost Mrs. Jasher," said Hope, while he, assisted the Professor to hoist the mummy on to the cart.

"Never mind! never mind!" Braddock patted the coffin. "I have found something much more to my mind: something ever so much better. Ha! ha!"

CHAPTER XIV

THE UNEXPECTED HAPPENS

In spite of newspapers and letters and tape-machines and telegrams and such like aids to the speedy diffusion of news, the same travels quicker in villages than in cities. Word of mouth can spread gossip with marvelous rapidity in sparsely inhabited communities, since it is obvious that in such places every person knows the other—as the saying goes—inside out. In every English village walls have ears and windows have eyes, so that every cottage is a hot-bed of scandal, and what is known to one is, within the hour, known to the others. Even the Sphinx could not have preserved her secret long in such a locality.

Gartley could keep up its reputation in this respect along with the best, therefore it was little to be wondered at, that early next morning every one knew that Professor Braddock had found his long-lost mummy in Mrs. Jasher's garden, and had removed the same to the Pyramids without unnecessary delay. It was not particularly late when the hand-cart, with its uncanny burden, had passed along the sole street of the place, and several men had emerged from the Warrior Inn ostensibly to offer help, but really to know what the eccentric master of the great house was doing. Braddock brusquely rejected these offers; but the oddly shaped mummy case, stained green, having been seen, it needed little wit for those who had caught a sight of it to put two and two together, especially as the weird object had been described at the inquest and had been talked over ever since in every cottage. And as the cart had been seen coming out of the widow's garden, it naturally occurred to the villagers that Mrs. Jasher had been concealing the mummy. Shortly the rumor spread that she had also murdered Bolton, for unless she had done so, she certainly—according to village logic—could not have been possessed of the spoil. Finally, as Mrs. Jasher's doors and windows were small and the mummy was rather bulky, it was natural to presume that she had hidden it in the garden. Report said she had buried it and had dug it up just in time to be pounced upon by its rightful owner. From which it can be seen that gossip is not invariably accurate.

However this may be, the news of Professor Braddock's good fortune shortly came to Don Pedro's ears through the medium of the landlady. As she revealed what she had heard in the morning, the

103

Peruvian gentleman was spared a sleepless night. But as soon as he learned the truth—which was surprising enough in its unexpectedness—he hastily finished his breakfast and hurried to the Pyramids. As yet he had not intended to see Braddock so promptly, or at least not until he had made further inquiries at Pierside, but the news that Braddock possessed the royal ancestor of the De Gayangoses brought him immediately into the museum. He greeted the Professor in his usual grave and dignified manner, and no one would have guessed from his inherent calmness that the unexpected news of Braddock's arrival, and the still more unexpected information about the green mummy, had surprised him beyond measure. Being somewhat superstitious, it also occurred to Don Pedro that the coincidence meant good fortune to him in the recovery of his long-lost ancestor.

Braddock, already knowing a great deal about Don Pedro from Lucy and Archie Hope, was only too pleased to see the Peruvian, hoping to find in him a kindred spirit. As yet the Professor was not aware of the contents of the ancient Latin manuscript, which revealed the fact of the hidden emeralds, since Hope had decided to leave it to the Peruvian to impart the information. Archie knew very well that Don Pedro—as he had plainly stated—wished to purchase the mummy, and it was only right that Braddock should know what he was selling. But Hope forgot one important fact perhaps from the careless way in which Don Pedro had told his story—namely, that the Professor in a second degree was a receiver of stolen goods. Therefore it was more than probable that the Peruvian would claim the mummy as his own property. Still, in that event he would have to prove his claim, and that would not be easy.

The plump little professor had not yet unsealed the case, and when Don Pedro entered, he was standing before it rubbing his fat hands, with a gloating expression in his face. However, as Cockatoo had brought in the Peruvian's card, Braddock expected his visitor and wheeled to face him.

"How are you, sir?" said he, extending his hand. "I am glad to see you, as I hear that you know all about this mummy of Inca Caxas."

"Well, I do," answered De Gayangos, sitting down in the chair which his host pushed forward. "But may I ask who told you that this mummy was that of the last Inca?"

Braddock pinched his plump chin and replied readily, enough.

"Certainly, Don Pedro. I wished to learn the difference in embalming between the Egyptians and the ancient Peruvians, and looked about for a South American corpse. Unexpectedly I saw in several European newspapers and in two English journals that a green Peruvian mummy was for sale at Malta for one thousand pounds. I sent my assistant, Sidney Bolton, to buy it, and he managed to get it, coffin and all, for nine hundred. While in Malta, and before he started back in The Diver with the mummy, he wrote me an account of the transaction. The seller—who was the son of a Maltese collector—told Bolton that his father had picked up the mummy in Paris some twenty and more years ago. It came from Lima some thirty years back, I believe, and, according to the collector in Paris, was the corpse of Inca Caxas. That is the whole story."

Don Pedro nodded gravely.

"Was there a Latin manuscript delivered along with the mummy?" he asked.

Braddock's eyes opened widely.

"No, sir. The mummy came thirty years ago from Lima to Paris. It passed twenty years back into the possession of the Maltese collector, and his son sold it to me a few months ago. I never heard of any manuscript."

"Then Mr. Hope did not repeat to you what I told him the other night?"

The Professor sat down and his mouth grew obstinate.

"Mr. Hope related some story you told him and others about this mummy having been stolen from you."

"From my father," corrected the unsmiling Peruvian; keeping a careful eye on his host; "that is really the case. Inca Caxas is, or was, my ancestor, and this manuscript"—Don Pedro produced the same from his inner pocket—"details the funeral ceremonies."

"Very interesting; most interesting," fussed Braddock, stretching out his hand. "May I see it?"

"You read Latin," observed Don Pedro, surrendering the manuscript.

Braddock raised his eyebrows.

"Of course," he said simply, "every well-educated man reads Latin, or should do so. Wait, sir, until I glance through this document."

"One moment," said Don Pedro, as the Professor began to literally devour the discolored page. "You know from Hope, I have no doubt, how I chance upon my own property in Europe?"

Braddock, still with his eyes on the manuscript, mumbled

"Your own property. Quite so: quite so."

"You admit that. Then you will no doubt restore the mummy to me."

By this time the drift of Don Pedro's observations entirely

reached the understanding of the scientist, and he dropped the document he was reading to leap to his feet.

"Restore the mummy to you!" he gasped. "Why, it is mine."

"Pardon me," said the Peruvian, still gravely but very decisively, "you admitted that it belonged to me."

Braddock's face deepened to a fine purple.

"I didn't know what I was saying," he protested. "How could I say it was your property when I have bought it for nine hundred pounds?"

"It was stolen from me."

"That has got to be proved," said Braddock caustically.

Don Pedro rose, looking more like, Don Quixote than ever.

"I have the honor to give you my word and—"

"Yes, yes. That is all right. I cast no imputation on your honor."

"I should think not," said the other coldly but strongly.

"All the same, you can scarcely expect me to part with so valuable an object," Braddock waved his hand towards the case, "without strict inquiry into the circumstances. And again, sir, even if you succeed in proving your ownership, I am not inclined to restore the mummy to you for nothing."

"But it is stolen property you are keeping from me."

"I know nothing about that: I have only your bare word that it is so, Don Pedro. All I know is that I paid nine hundred pounds for the mummy and that it cost the best part of another hundred to bring it to England. What I have, I keep."

"Like your country," said the Peruvian sarcastically.

"Precisely," replied the Professor suavely. "Every Englishman has a bull-dog tenacity of purpose. Brag is a good dog, Don Pedro, but Holdfast is a better one."

"Then I understand," said the Peruvian, stretching out his hand to pick up the fallen manuscript, "that you will keep the mummy."

"Certainly," said Braddock coolly, "since I have paid for it. Also, I shall keep the jewels, which the manuscript tells me—from the glance I obtained of it—were buried with it."

"The sole jewels buried are two large emeralds which the mummy holds in its hands," explained Don Pedro, restoring the manuscript to his pocket, "and I wish for them so that I may get money to restore the fortunes of my family."

"No! no! no!" said Braddock forcibly. "I have bought the mummy and the jewels with it. They will sell to supply me with money to fit out my expedition to the tomb of Queen Tahoser."

"I shall dispute your claim," cried De Gayangos, losing his calmness.

Braddock waved his hand with supreme content.

"I can give you the address of my lawyers," he retorted; "any steps you choose to take will only result in loss, and from what you hint I should not think that you had much money to spend on litigation."

Don Pedro bit his lip, and saw that it was indeed a more difficult task than he had anticipated to make Braddock yield up his prize.

"If you were in Lima," he muttered, speaking Spanish in his excitement, "you would then learn that I speak truly."

"I do not doubt your truth," answered the Professor in the same language.

De Gayangos wheeled and faced his host, much surprised.

"You speak my tongue, senor?" he demanded.

Braddock nodded.

"I have been in Spain, and I have been in Peru," he answered dryly, "therefore I know classical Spanish and its colonial dialects. As to being in Lima, I was there, and I do not wish to go there again, as I had quite enough of those uncivilized parts thirty years ago, when the country was much disturbed after your civil war."

"You were in Lima thirty years ago," echoed Don Pedro; "then you were there when Vasa stole this mummy."

"I don't know who stole it, or even if it was stolen," said the Professor obstinately, "and I don't know the name of Vasa. Ah! now I remember. Young Hope did say something about the Swedish sailor who you said stole the mummy."

"Vasa did, and brought it to Europe to sell—probably to that man in Paris, who afterwards sold it to your Malteses collector."

"No doubt," rejoined Braddock calmly; "but what has all this to do with me, Don Pedro?"

"I want my mummy," raged the other, and looked dangerous.

"Then you won't get it," retorted Braddock, adopting a pugnacious attitude and quite composed. "This mummy has caused one death, Don Pedro, and from your looks I should think you would like it to cause another."

"Will you not be honest?"

"I'll knock your head off if you bring my honesty into question," cried the Professor, standing on tip-toe like a bantam. "The best thing to do will be to take the matter into court. Then the law can decide, and I have little doubt but what it will decide in my favor."

The Englishman and the Peruvian glared at one another, and Cockatoo, who was crouching on the floor, glanced from one angry face to another. He guessed that the white men were quarreling and perhaps would come to blows. It was at this moment that a knock came to the door, and a minute later Archie entered. Braddock glanced at him, and took a sudden resolution as he stepped forward.

"Hope, you are just in time," he declared. "Don Pedro states that the mummy belongs to him, and I assert that I have bought it. We shall make you umpire. He wants it: I want it. What is to be done?"

"The mummy is my own flesh and blood, Mr. Hope," said Don Pedro.

"Precious little of either about it," said Braddock contemptuously.

Archie twisted a chair round and straddled his long legs across it, with his arms resting on its back. His quick brain had rapidly comprehended the situation, and, being acquainted with both sides of the question, it was not difficult to come to a decision. If it was hard that Don Pedro should lose his ancestor's mummy, it was equally hard that Braddock—or rather himself—should lose the purchase money, seeing that it had been paid in good faith to the seller in Malta for a presumably righteously acquired object. On these premises the young Solon proceeded to deliver judgment.

"I understand," said he judiciously, "that Don Pedro had the mummy stolen from him thirty years ago, and that you, Professor, bought it under the impression that the Maltese owner had a right to possess it."

"Yes," snapped Braddock, "and I daresay the Maltese owner thought so too, since he bought it from that collector in Paris."

Hope nodded.

"And if Vasa sold it to the man in Paris," said he calmly, "he certainly would not tell the purchaser that he had looted the mummy in Lima, and the poor man would not know that he was receiving stolen goods. Is that right, Don Pedro?"

"Yes, sir," said the Peruvian, who had recovered his temper and his gravity; "but I declare solemnly that the mummy was stolen from my father and should belong to me."

"No one disputes that," said Archie cheerfully; "but it ought to belong to the Professor also, since he has bought it. Now, as it can't possibly belong to two people, we must split the difference. You, Professor, must sell back the mummy to Don Pedro for the price you paid for it, and then, Don Pedro, you must recompense Professor Braddock for his loss."

"I have not much money," said Don Pedro gravely; "still, I am willing to do as you say."

"I don't know that I am," protested Braddock noisily. "There are the two emeralds which are of immense value, as Don Pedro says, and they belong to me, since the mummy is my property."

"Professor," said Archie solemnly, "you must do right, even if you lose by it. I believe the story of Senor De Gayangos; and the mummy with its jewels belongs to him. Besides, you only wish to see the way in which the Inca race embalmed their dead. Well, then, unpack the mummy here in the presence of Don Pedro. When you have satisfied your curiosity, and when Senor De Gayangos signs a check for one thousand pounds, he can take away the corpse. You have had so much trouble over it, that I wonder your are not anxious to see the last of it."

"But the emeralds would sell for much money and would defray the expenses of my expedition into Egypt to search for that Queen's tomb."

"I understood from Lucy that Mrs. Jasher intended to finance that expedition when she became your wife."

"Humph!" muttered Braddock, stroking his fat chin. "I said a few foolish things to her last night when I was heated up. She may not forgive me, Hope."

"A woman will forgive anything to the man she loves," said Archie.

Braddock was no fool, and could not help casting a glance at his tubby figure, which was reflected in a near mirror. It seemed incredible that Mrs. Jasher could love him for his looks, and the fact that he might some day be a baronet did not strike him at the moment as a consideration. However, he foresaw trouble and expense should Don Pedro go to law, as he seemed determined to do. Taking all things into consideration, Braddock thought that Archie's judgment was a good one, and yielded.

"Well," he said after reflection, "let us agree. I shall open the case and examine the mummy, which after all is the reason why I bought it. When I have satisfied myself as to the difference between the modes of embalming, Don Pedro can give me a check and take away the mummy. I only hope that he will have less trouble with it than I have had," and, so speaking, Braddock, signing to Cockatoo to bring all the necessary tools, laid hands on the case.

"I am content," said Don Pedro briefly, and seated himself in a chair beside the young Daniel who had delivered judgment.

Hope offered to assist the Professor to open the case, but was dismissed with an abrupt refusal.

"Though I am glad you are present to see the mummy unpacked," said Braddock, laboring at the lid of the case, "for if the emeralds are missing, Don Pedro might accuse me of stealing them."

"Why should the emeralds be missing?" asked Hope quickly.

Braddock shrugged his shoulders.

"Sidney Bolton was killed," said he in a low voice, "and it was not likely that any one would commit a murder for the sake of this mummy, and then leave it stranded in Mrs. Jasher's garden. I have my doubts about the safety of the emeralds, else I would not have consented to sell the thing back again."

With this honest speech, the Professor vigorously attacked the lid of the case, and inserted a steel instrument into the cracks to prize up the covering. The lid was closed with wooden pegs in an antique but perfectly safe manner, and apparently had not been opened since the dead Inca had been laid to rest therein hundreds of years ago among the Andean mountains. Don Pedro winced at this desecration of the dead, but, as he had given his consent, there was nothing left to do but to grin and bear it. In a wonderfully short space of time, considering the neatness of the workmanship and the holding power of the wooden pegs, the lid was removed. Then the four on-lookers saw that the mummy had been tampered with. Swathed in green-stained llama wool, it lay rigid in its case. But the swathings had been cut; the hands protruded and the emeralds were gone—torn rudely from the hard grip of the dead.

CHAPTER XV

AN ACCUSATION

Both Don Pedro and Professor Braddock were amazed and angry at the disappearance of the jewels, but Hope did not express much surprise. Considering the facts of the murder, it was just what he expected, although it must be confessed that he was wise after the event.

"I refer you to your own words immediately before the case was opened, Professor," he remarked, after the first surprise had subsided.

"Words! words!" snapped Braddock, who was anything but pleased. "What words of mine do you mean, Hope?"

"You said that it was not likely that any one would commit a murder for the sake of the mummy only, and then leave it stranded in Mrs. Jasher's garden. Also, you declared that you had your doubts about the safety of the emeralds, else you would not have consented to sell the mummy again to its rightful owner."

The Professor nodded.

"Quite so: quite so. And what I say I hold to," he retorted, "especially as I have proved myself a true prophet. You can both see for yourselves," he waved his hand towards the rifled case, "that poor Sidney must have been killed for the sake of the emeralds. The question is, who killed him?"

"The person who knew about the jewels," said Don Pedro promptly.

"Of course: but who did know? I was ignorant until you told me about the manuscript. And you, Hope?" He searched Archie's face.

"Do you intend to accuse me?" questioned the young man with a slight laugh. "I assure you, Professor, that I was ignorant of what had been buried with the corpse, until Don Pedro related his story the other night to myself and Random, and the ladies."

Braddock turned impatiently to De Gayangos, as he did not approve of Archie's apparent flippancy.

"Does any one else know of the contents of this manuscript?" he demanded irritably.

Don Pedro nursed his chin and looked musingly on the ground.

"It is just possible that Vasa may."

"Vasa? Vasa? Oh yes, the sailor who stole the mummy thirty years ago from your father in Lima. Pooh! pooh! pooh! You tell me

111

that this manuscript is written in Latin, and evidently in monkish Latin at that, which is of the worst. Your sailor could not read it, and would not know the value of the manuscript. If he had, he would have carried it off."

"Senor," said the Peruvian politely, "I have an idea that my father made a translation of this manuscript, or at all events a copy."

"But I understood," put in Hope, still astride of his chair, "that you did not find the original manuscript until your father died."

"That is quite true, sir," assented the other readily, "but I did not tell you everything the other night. My father it was who found the manuscript at Cuzco, and although I cannot state authoritatively, yet I believe I am correct in saying that he had a copy made. But whether the copy was merely a transcript or actually a translation, I cannot tell. I think it was the former, as if Vasa, reading a translation, had learned of the jewels, he undoubtedly would have stolen them before selling this mummy to the Parisian collector."

"Perhaps he did," said Braddock, pointing to the rifled corpse. "You see that the emeralds are missing."

"Your assistant's assassin stole them," insisted Don Pedro coldly.

"We cannot be sure of that," retorted the Professor, "although I admit that no man would jeopardize his neck for the sake of a corpse."

Archie looked surprised.

"But an enthusiast such as you are, Professor, might risk so much."

For once in his life Braddock made a good-humored reply.

"No, sir. Not even for this mummy would I place myself in the power of the law. And I do not think that any other scientist would either. We savants may not be worldly, but we are not fools. However, the fact remains that the jewels are gone, and whether they were stolen by Vasa thirty years ago, or by poor Sidney's assassin the other day, I don't know, and, what is more, I don't care. I shall examine the mummy further, and in a couple of days Don Pedro can bring me a check for one thousand and remove his ancestor."

"No! no!" cried the Peruvian hurriedly; "since the emeralds are missing, I am not in a position to pay you one thousand English pounds, sir. I want to take back the body of Inca Caxas to Lima; as one must show respect to one's ancestors. But the fact is, I cannot pay the money."

112

"You said that you could," shouted the exasperated Professor in his bullying way.

"I admit it, senor, but I had hoped to do so when I sold the emeralds, which—as you can see—are not available. Therefore the body of my royal ancestor must remain here until I can procure the money. And it may be that Sir Frank Random will help me in this matter."

"He wouldn't help me," snapped Braddock, "so why should he help you?"

Don Pedro, looking more dignified than ever, drew himself up to his tall height.

"Sir Frank," he said, in a stately way, "has done me the honor of seeking to be my son-in-law. As my daughter loves him, I am willing to permit the marriage, but now that I have learned the emeralds are lost, I shall not consent until Sir Frank buys the mummy from you, Professor. It is only right that my daughter's hand should redeem her regal forefather from purely scientific surroundings and that she should take the mummy back to be buried in Lima. At the same time, sir, I must say that I am the rightful owner of the dead, and that you should surrender the mummy to me free of charge."

"What, and lose a thousand pounds!" cried Braddock furiously. "No, sir, I shall do nothing of the sort. You only wanted the mummy for the sake of the jewels, and now that they are lost, you do not care what becomes of your confounded ancestor, and you—"

The Professor would have gone on still more furiously, but that Hope, seeing Don Pedro was growing angry at the insult, chimed in.

"Let me throw oil on the troubled waters," he said, smoothly. "Don Pedro is not able to redeem the mummy until the emeralds are found. As such is the case, we must find the emeralds and enable him to do what is necessary."

"And how are we to find the jewels?" asked Braddock crossly.

"By finding the assassin."

"How is that to be done?" asked De Gayangos gloomily. "I have been doing my best at Pierside, but I cannot find a single clue. Vasa is not to be found."

"Vasa!" exclaimed Archie and the Professor, both profoundly astonished.

Don Pedro raised his eyebrows.

"Certainly. Vasa, if anyone, must have killed your assistant, since he alone could have known that the jewels were buried with Inca Caxas."

"But, my dear sir," argued Hope good-naturedly, "if Vasa stole the manuscript, whether translated or not, he certainly must have learned the truth long, long ago, since thirty years have elapsed. In

113

that event he must have stolen the jewels, as Professor Braddock remarked lately, before he sold the mummy to the Parisian collector."

"That may be so," said Don Pedro obstinately, while the Professor muttered his approval, "but we cannot be certain on that point. No one—I agree with the Professor in this—would have risked his neck to steal a mere mummy, therefore the motive for the committal of the crime must have been the emeralds. Only Vasa knew of their existence outside myself and my dead father. He, therefore, must be the assassin. I shall hunt for him, and, when I find him, I shall have him arrested."

"But you can't possibly recognize the man after thirty years?" argued Braddock disbelievingly.

"I have a royal memory for faces," said Don Pedro imperturbably, "and in the past I saw much of Vasa. He was then a young sailor of twenty."

"Humph!" muttered Braddock. "He is now fifty, and must have changed in thirty years. You'll never recognize him."

"Oh, I think so," said the Peruvian smoothly. "His eyes were peculiarly blue and full of light. Also, he had a scar on the right temple from a blow which he received in a street riot in which I also was concerned. Finally, gentlemen, Vasa loved a peon girl on my father's estate, and she induced him to have the sun encircled by a serpent—a Peruvian symbol—tattooed on his left wrist. With all these marks, and with my memory for faces, which never yet has failed me, I have no doubt but what I shall recognize the man."

"And then?"

"And then I shall have him arrested"

Hope shrugged his square shoulders. He had not much belief in Don Pedro's boasted royal memory, and did not think that he would recognize a young sailor of twenty in what would certainly be a grizzled old salt of fifty years. However, it was possible that the man might be right in his surmise, since Vasa alone could have known about the emeralds. The only doubt was whether he would have waited for thirty years before looting the mummy. Archie said nothing of these thoughts, as they would only serve to prolong an unprofitable discussion. But he made one suggestion.

"Your best plan," he said suggestively, "is to write a description of Vasa—who, by the way, has probably changed his name—and hand it to the police, with the promise of a reward if he is found."

"I am very poor, senor. Surely the Professor here—"

"I can offer nothing," said Braddock quickly, "as I am quite as poor as you are, if not more so, Sir Frank might help," he added sarcastically.

"I shall not ask," said Don Pedro loftily. "If Sir Frank chooses to become my son-in-law by purchasing back my royal ancestor, to which you have no right, I am willing that it should be so. But, poor as I am, I shall offer a reward myself, since the honor of the De Gayangoses is involved in this matter. What reward do you suggest, Mr. Hope?"

"Five hundred pounds," said the Professor quickly.

"Too much," said Hope sharply—"far too much. Make the reward one hundred pounds, Don Pedro. That is enough to tempt many a man."

The Peruvian bowed and noted down the amount.

"I shall go at once to Pierside and see Inspector Date, who had to do with the inquest," he remarked. "Meanwhile, Professor, please do not desecrate my royal ancestor's body more than you can help."

"I shall certainly not search for any more emeralds," retorted Braddock dryly. "Now, clear out, both of you, and leave me to examine the mummy. Cockatoo, show these gentlemen out, and let no one else in."

Don Pedro returned to the Warrior Hotel to inform his daughter of what had taken place, with the intention of going in the afternoon to Pierside. Meanwhile, he wrote out a full description of Vasa, making an allowance for the lapse of years and explaining the scar and the symbol on the left wrist. Hope also sought Lucy and related the latest development of the case. The girl was not surprised, as she likewise believed that the assassin had desired more than the mummy when he murdered Sidney Bolton.

"Mrs. Jasher did not know about the emeralds?" she asked suddenly.

"No," replied Archie, much surprised. "Surely you do not suspect her of having a hand in the devilment?"

"Certainly not," was the prompt answer. "Only I cannot understand how the mummy came to be in her garden."

"It was brought up from the river, I expect."

"But why to Mrs. Jasher's garden?"

Hope shook his head.

"I cannot tell that. The whole thing is a mystery, and seems likely to remain so."

"It seems to me," said the girl, after a pause, "that it would be best for my father to return this mummy to Don Pedro, and have done with it, since it seems to bring bad luck. Then he can marry Mrs. Jasher, and go to Egypt on her fortune to seek for this tomb."

"I doubt very much if Mrs. Jasher will marry the Professor now, after what he said last night."

"Nonsense, my father was in a rage and said what first came

into his mind. I daresay she is angry. However, I shall see her this afternoon, and put matters right."

"You are very anxious that the Professor should marry the lady."

"I am," replied Lucy seriously, "as I want to leave my father comfortably settled when I marry you. The sooner he makes Mrs. Jasher his wife, the readier will he be to let me go, and I want to marry you as soon as I possibly can. I am tired of Gartley and of this present life."

Of course to this speech Archie could make only one answer, and as that took the form of kissing, it was entirely satisfactory to Miss Kendal. Then they discussed the future and also the proposed engagement of Sir Frank Random to the Peruvian lady. But both left the subject of the mummy alone, as they were quite weary of the matter, and neither could suggest a solution of the mystery.

Meanwhile Professor Braddock had passed a very pleasant hour in examining the swathings of the mummy. But his pleasure was destined to be cut short sooner than he desired, as Captain Hiram Hervey unexpectedly arrived. Although Cockatoo—as he had been instructed—did his best to keep him out, the sailor forced his way in, and heralded his appearance by throwing the Kanaka head-foremost into the museum.

"What does this mean?" demanded the fiery Professor, while Cockatoo, with an angry expression, struggled to his feet, and Hervey, smoking his inevitable cheroot, stood on the threshold— "how dare you treat my property in this careless way."

"Guess your property should behave itself then," said the captain in careless tones, and sauntered into the room. "D'y think I'm goin' to be chucked out by a measly nigger and—Great Scott!"— this latter exclamation was extorted by the sight of the mummy.

Braddock motioned to the still angry Cockatoo to move aside, and then nodded triumphantly.

"You didn't expect to see that, did you?" he asked.

Hervey came to anchor on a chair and turned the cheroot in his mouth with an odd look at the mummy.

"When will he be hanged?"

Braddock stared.

"When will who be hanged?"

"The man as stole that thing."

"We haven't found him yet," Braddock informed him swiftly.

"Then how in creation did you annex the corpse."

The Professor sat down and explained. The lean, long mariner listened quietly, only nodding at intervals. He did not seem to be surprised when he heard that the corpse of the head Inca had been

116

found in Mrs. Jasher's garden, especially when Braddock explained the whereabouts of the property.

"Wal," he drawled, "that don't make my hair stand on end. I guess the garden was on his way and he used it for a cemetery."

"What are you talking about?" demanded the perplexed scientist.

"About the man who strangled your help and yanked away the corpse."

"But I don't know who he is. Nobody knows."

"Go slow. I do."

"You!" Braddock started and flung himself across the room to seize Hervey by the lapels of his reefer coat. "You know. Tell me who he is, so that I can get the emeralds."

"Emeralds!" Hervey removed Braddock's plump hands and stared greedily.

"Don't you know? No, of course you don't. But two emeralds were buried with the mummy, and they have been stolen."

"Who by?"

"No doubt by the assassin who murdered poor Sidney."

Hervey spat on the floor, and his weather-beaten face took on an expression of, profound regret.

"I guess I'm a fool of the best."

"Why?" asked Braddock, again puzzled.

"To think," said Hervey, addressing the mummy, "that you were on board my boat, and I never looted you."

"What!" Braddock stamped. "Would you have committed theft?"

"Theft be hanged!" was the reply. "It ain't thieving to loot the dead. I guess a corpse hasn't got any use for jewels. You bet I'd have gummed straightways onto that mummy, when I brought it from Malta in the old Diver, had I known it was a jeweler's shop of sorts. Huh! Two emeralds, and I never knew. I could kick myself."

"You are a blackguard," gasped the astonished Professor.

"Oh, shucks!" was the elegant retort, "give it a rest. I'm no worse than that dandy gentleman who added murder to stealing, anyhow."

"Ah!" Braddock bounded off his chair like an india-rubber ball, "you said that you knew who had committed the murder."

"Wal," drawled Hervey again, "I do and I don't. That is I suspect, but I can't swear to the business before a judge."

"Who killed Bolton?" asked the Professor furiously. "Tell me at once."

"Not me, unless it's made worth my while."

"It will be, by Don Pedro."

"That yellow-stomach. What's he got to do with it?"

"I have just told you the mummy belongs to him; he came to Europe to find it. He wants the emeralds, and intends to offer a reward of one hundred pounds for the discovery of the assassin."

Hervey arose briskly.

"I'm right on the job," said he, sauntering to the door. "I'll go to that old inn of yours, where you say the Don's stopping, and look him up. Guess I'll trade."

"But who killed Bolton?" asked Braddock, running to the door and gripping Hervey by his coat.

The mariner looked down on the anxious face of the plump little man with a grim smile.

"I can tell you," said he, "as you can't figure out the business, unless I'm on the racket. No, sir; I'm the white boy in thin circus."

The Professor shook the lean sailor in his anxiety.

"Who is he?"

"That almighty aristocrat that came on board my ship, when I lay in the Thames on the very afternoon I arrived with Bolton."

"Who do you mean?" demanded Braddock, more and more perplexed.

"Sir Frank Random."

"What! did he kill Bolton and steal my mummy?"

"And hide it in that garden on his way to the Fort? I guess he did."

The Professor sat down and closed his eyes with horror. When he opened them again, Hervey was gone.

CHAPTER XVI

THE MANUSCRIPT AGAIN

But the Professor was not going to let Captain Hervey escape without giving him full information. Before the Yankee skipper could reach the front door, Braddock was at his heels, gasping and blowing like a grampus.

"Come back, come back. Tell me all."

"I reckon not," rejoined the mariner, removing Braddock's grip. "You ain't the one to give the money. I'll go to the Don, or to Inspector Date of Pierside."

"But Sir Frank must be innocent," insisted Braddock.

"He's got to prove it," was the dry response. "Let me go."

"No. You must tell me on what grounds—"

"Oh, the devil take you!" said Hervey hastily, and sat down on one of the hall chairs. "It's this way, since you won't let me skip until I tell you. This almighty aristocrat came to Pierside on the same afternoon as I cast anchor. While Bolton was on board, he looked in to have a yarn of sorts."

"What about?"

"Now, how in creation should I know?" snapped the skipper. "I wasn't on hand, as I'd enough to do with unloading cargo. But his lordship went with Bolton to the state-room, and they talked for half an hour. When they came out, I saw that his lordship had his hair riz, and heard him saying things to Bolton."

"What sort of things?"

"Well, for one, he said, `You'll repent of this,' and then again, `Your life isn't safe while you keep it.'"

"Meaning the mummy?"

"I reckon that's so, unless I am mistaken," said Hervey serenely.

"Why didn't you go to the police with this information?"

"Me? Not much. Why, I saw no way of making dollars. And then, again, I did not think of putting things together, until I found that his lorship—"

"Meaning Sir Frank," interpolated the Professor, frowning.

"I'm talking Queen's, or King's, or Republican lingo, I guess, and I do mean his lorship," said the skipper dryly—"until I found that his lorship had been in the public-house where the crime was committed."

"The Sailor's Rest? When did he go there?"

"In the evening. After his talk with Bolton, and after a row—as they both seemed to have their hair off—he skipped over the side and went back to his yacht, which wasn't far away. Bolton took his blamed mummy ashore and got fixed at the Sailor's Rest. I gathered afterwards, from the second mate of The Diver (which ain't my ship now), that his lorship came into the hotel and had a drink. Afterwards my second mate saw him talking to Bolton through the window."

"In the same place as the woman talked?" questioned the Professor.

"That's so, only it was later in the evening that the woman came along to give chin-music through the window. I am bound to say," added the captain generously, "that no one I can place my hand on saw his lorship loafing about the hotel after dark. But what of that? He may have laid his plans, and arranged for the corpse to be found later, in that blamed packing case."

"Is this all your evidence?"

"It's enough, I guess."

"Not to procure a warrant."

"Why, a man in the States would be electrocuted on half the evidence."

"I daresay," retorted the little man with contempt, "but we are in a land where justice of the purest prevails. All your evidence is circumstantial. It proves nothing."

The captain was considerably nettled.

"I calculate that it proves Sir Frank wanted the mummy, else why did he come on board my ship to see your infernal assistant. The words he used showed that he was warning Bolton how he'd do for him. And then he talked through the window, and was in the public-house, which ain't a place for an almighty aristocrat to shelter in. I guess he's the man wanted by the police. Why," added Hervey, warming to his tale, "he'd a slap-up yacht laying near the blamed hotel, and could easily ship the corpse, after slipping it through the window. When he got tired of it, and looted the emeralds, he took it by boat, below the Fort, to Mrs. Jasher's garden and left it there, so as to pull the wool over the eyes of the police. It's as clear as mud to me. You search his lorship's shanty, and you'll find the emeralds."

"It is strange," muttered Braddock unwillingly.

"Strange, but not true," said a voice from the head of the stairs, and young Hope came down leisurely, with a pale face, but a very determined air. "Random is absolutely innocent."

"How do you know?" demanded the skipper contemptuously.

"Because he is an English gentleman and my very good friend."

120

"Huh! I guess that defense won't save him from being lynched."

Meanwhile Braddock was looking irritably at Archie.

"You've been listening to a private conversation, sir. How dare you listen?"

"If you hold private conversations at the top of your voices in the hall, you must be expected to be listened to," said Archie coolly. "I plead guilty, and I am not sorry."

"When did you come?"

"In time to hear all that Captain Hervey has explained. I was chatting with Lucy, and had just left her, when I heard your loud voices."

"Has Lucy heard anything?"

"No. She is busy in her room. But I'll tell her," Hope turned to mount the stairs; "she likes Random, and will no more believe him guilty than I do at this present moment."

"Stop!" cried Braddock, flying forward to pull Hope back, as he placed his foot on the first stair. "Tell Lucy nothing just now. We must go to the Fort, you—and I, to see Random. Hervey, you come also, and then you can accuse Sir Frank to his face."

"If he dares to do it!" said Archie, who looked and felt indignant.

"Oh, I'll accuse him right enough when the time comes," said Hervey in his coolest manner, "but the time isn't now. Savy! I am going to see the Don first and make sure of this reward."

"Faugh!" cried Hope with disgust, "Blood-money!"

"What of that? Ifs a man is a murderer he should be lynched."

"My friend, Sir Frank Random, is no murderer."

"He's got to prove, that, as I said before," rejoined the Yankee in a calm way, and strolled to the door. "So-long, gents both. I'll light out for the Warrior Inn and play my cards. And I may tell you," he added, pausing at the door, which he opened, "that I haven't got that blamed wind-jammer, so need money to hold out until another steamer comes along. One hundred pounds English currency will just fill the bill. So now you know the lay I'm on. So-long," and he walked quietly out of the house, leaving Archie and Braddock looking at one another with pale faces. The assurance of Hervey surprised and horrified them. Still, they could not believe that Sir Frank Random had been guilty of so brutal a crime.

"For one thing," said Hope after a pause, "Random did not know where the emeralds were to be found, or even that they existed."

"I understood that he did know," said Braddock reluctantly. "In my hearing, and in your own, you heard Don Pedro state that he had related the story of the manuscript to Random."

121

"You forget that I learned about the emeralds at the same time," said Hope quietly. "Yet this Yankee skipper does not accuse me. The knowledge of the emeralds came to Random's ears and to mine long after the crime was committed. To have a motive for killing Bolton and stealing the emeralds, Random would have had to know when he arrived in England."

"And why should he have not known?" asked the Professor, biting his lip vexedly. "I don't want to accuse Random, or even to doubt him, as he is a very good fellow, even though he refused to assist me with money when I desired a reward to be offered. All the same, he met Don Pedro in Genoa, and it is just possible that the man told him of the jewels buried with the mummy."

Archie shook his head.

"I doubt that," said he thoughtfully. "Random was as astonished as the rest of us, when Don Pedro told his Arabian Night story. However, the point can be easily settled by sending for Random. I daresay he is at the Fort."

"I shall send Cockatoo for him at once," said the Professor quickly, and walked into the museum to instruct the Kanaka. Archie remained where he was, and seated himself on a chair, with folded arms and knitted brows. It was incredible that an English gentleman with a stainless name and such a well-known soldier should commit so terrible a crime. And the matter of Hervey's accusation was complicated by the fact—of which Hervey was ignorant—that Don Pedro was willing that Random should become his son-in-law. Hope wondered what the fiery, proud Peruvian would say when he heard his friend denounced. His reflections on this point were cut short by the return of the Professor, who appeared at the door of the museum dismissing Cockatoo. When the Kanaka took his departure, Braddock beckoned to the young man.

"There is no reason why we should talk in the hall, and let the whole house know of this new difficulty," he said in a testy manner. "Come in here."

Hope entered and looked with ill-concealed repugnance at the uncanny shape of the green mummy, which was lying on a long table. He examined the portions where the swathings had been cut with some sharp instrument, to reveal the dry, bony hands, which formerly had held the costly jewels. The face was invisible and covered with a mask of dull beaten gold. Formerly the eyes had been jeweled, but these last were now absent. He pointed out the mask to the Professor, who was hovering over the weird dead with a large magnifying-glass.

"It is strange," said Hope earnestly, "that the mask of gold was not stolen also, since it is so valuable."

122

"Unless melted down, the mask could be traced," said Braddock after a pause. "The jewels, according to Don Pedro, are of immense value, and so could have been got rid of easily. Random was satisfied with those."

"Don't talk of him in that way, as though his guilt was certain," said Hope, wincing.

"Well, you must admit that the evidence against him is strong."

"But purely circumstantial."

"Circumstantial evidence has hanged many an innocent man before now. Humph!" said Braddock uneasily, "I hope it won't hang our friend. However, we shall hear what he has to say. I have sent Cockatoo to the Fort to bring him here at once. If Random is absent, Cockatoo is to leave a note in his room, on the writing-table."

"Would it not have been better to have told Cockatoo to give the note to Random's servant?"

"I think not," responded Braddock dryly. "Random's servant is certainly one of the most stupid men in the entire army. He would probably forget to give him the note, and as it is important that we should see Random at once, it is better that he should find it placed personally on his writing-table by Cockatoo, upon whom I can depend."

Archie abandoned the argument, as it really mattered very little. He took up another line of conversation.

"I expect if the criminal tries to dispose of the emeralds he will be caught," said he: "such large jewels are too noticeable to escape comment."

"Humph! It depends upon the cleverness of the thief," said the Professor, who was more taken up with the mummy than with the conversation, "He might have the jewels cut into smaller stones, or he might go to India and dispose of them to some Rajah, who would certainly say nothing. I don't know how criminals act myself, as I have never studied their methods. But I hope that the clue you mention will be hit upon, if only for Random's sake."

"I don't believe for one moment that Random is in danger," said Archie, "and, if he is, I shall turn detective myself."

"I wish you joy," replied Braddock, bending over the mummy. "Look, Hope, at the wonderful color of this wool. There are some arts we have lost completely—dyeing of this surprising beauty is one. Humph!" mused the archaeologist, "I wonder why this particular mummy is dyed green, or rather why it is wrapped in green bandages. Yellow was the royal color of the ancient Peruvian monarchs. Vicuna wool dyed yellow. What do you think, Hope? It is strange."

Archie shrugged his shoulders.

"I can say nothing, because I know nothing," he said sharply. "All I do know is that I wish this precious mummy had never been brought here. It has caused trouble ever since its arrival."

"Well," said Braddock, surveying the dead with some disfavor, "I must say that I shall be glad to see the last of it myself. I know now all that I wanted to know! Humph! I wonder if Don Pedro will allow me to strip the mummy? Of course! It is mine not his. I shall unswathe it entirely," and Braddock was about to lay sacrilegious hands on the dead, when Cockatoo entered breathlessly. He had been so quick that he must have run to the Fort and back again.

"I knock at door," said the Kanaka, delivering his message, "and I hear no voice. I go in and find no one, so I put the letter on the table. I come down and ask, and a soldier tells me, sir, his master is coming back in half an hour."

"You should have waited," said Braddock, waving Cockatoo aside. "Come along with me to the Fort, Hope."

"But Random will come here as soon as he returns."

"Very likely, but I can't wait. I am anxious to hear what he has to say in his defense. Come, Cockatoo, my coat, my hat, my gloves. Stir yourself, you scoundrel!"

Archie was not unwilling to go, since he was anxious also to hear what Random would say to the absurd accusation brought against him by the Yankee. In a few minutes the two men were walking smartly down the road through the village, the Professor striving to keep up with Hope's longer legs by trotting as hard as he could. Halfway down the village they met a trap, and in it Captain Hervey being driven to the Jessum railway station.

"Have you seen Don Pedro?" asked the Professor, stopping the vehicle.

"I reckon not," answered Hervey stolidly. "He's gone into Pierside to see the police. I'm off there also."

"You had better come with us," said Archie sternly;—"we are going to see Sir Frank Random."

"Give him my respects," said the skipper cold-bloodedly, "and say that he's worth one hundred pounds to me," he waved his hand and the trap moved away, but he looked back with a wry smile. "Say I'll square the matter for double the money and command of his yacht."

Braddock and Archie looked after the trap in disgust.

"What a scoundrel the man is!" said the Professor pettishly; "he'd sell his father for what he could get."

"It shows how much his word is to be depended upon. I expect this accusation of Random is a put-up job."

"I hope so, for Random's sake," said Braddock, trotting briskly along.

In a short time they arrived at the Fort and were informed that Sir Frank had not yet returned, but was expected back every moment. In the meanwhile, as Braddock and Hope were both extremely well known, they were shown into Random's quarters, which were on the first floor. When the soldier-servant retired and the door was closed, Hope seated himself near the window, while Braddock trotted round, looking into things.

"It's a dog kennel," said the Professor. "I told Random that."

"Perhaps we should have waited him in the mess," suggested Archie.

"No! no! no! We couldn't talk there, with a lot of silly young fools hanging about. I told Random that I would never enter the mess, so he invited me to come always to his quarters. He was in love with Lucy then," chuckled the Professor, "and nothing was too good for me."

"Not even the dog kennel," said Hope dryly, for the Professor's chatter was so rude as to be quite annoying.

"Pooh! pooh! pooh! Random doesn't mind a joke. You, Hope, have no sense of humor. Your name is Scotch also. I believe you are a Caledonian."

"I am nothing of the sort. I was born on this side of the border."

"You might have been born at the North Pole for all I care," said the little man politely. "I don't like artists: they are usually silly. I wish Lucy had married a man of science. Now don't talk rubbish. I know what you are going to say."

"Well," said Archie, humoring him, "what am I going to say?"

This non-plussed the irritable savant.

"Hum! Hum! hum! I don't know and don't care. Pouf! How hot this room is! What a number of books of travel Random has!" Braddock was now at the bookcase, which consisted of shelves swung by cords against the wall.

"Random travels a great deal," Archie reminded him.

"Quite so: quite so. Wastes his money on that silly yacht. But he hasn't traveled in South America. I expect he's going there. Come here, Hope, and see the many, many books about Peru and Chili and Brazil. There must be a dozen, and all library books too."

Archie sauntered towards the shelves.

"I expect Random is getting up the subject of South America, so as to talk to Donna Inez."

"Probably! probably!" snapped Braddock, pulling several of the books out of place. "Why, there isn't a—Ah, dear me! What a catastrophe!"

He might well say so, for in his desire to examine the books, they all tipped off the shelves and lay in a disorderly heap on the floor. Hope began to pick them up and replace them, and so did the author of the mischief. Among the books were several papers scribbled with notes, and Braddock bundled these all in a heap.. Shortly, he caught sight of the writing on one.

"Hullo! Latin," said he, and read a line or two. "Oh!" he gasped, "Hope! Hope! The manuscript of Don Pedro!"

"Impossible!"

Archie rose and stared at the discolored paper.

"Sorry to have kept you," said Random, entering at this moment.

"You villain!" shouted Braddock furiously, "so you are guilty after all?"

CHAPTER XVII

CIRCUMSTANTIAL EVIDENCE

Random was so taken aback by the fierce accusation of the Professor that he stood suddenly still at the door, and did not advance into the room. Yet he did not look so much afraid as puzzled. Whatever Braddock might have thought, Hope, from the expression on the young soldier's face, was more than ever satisfied of his innocence.

"What are you talking about, Professor?" asked Random, genuinely surprised.

"You know well enough," retorted the Professor.

"Upon my word I don't," said the other, walking into the room and unbuckling his sword. "I find you here, with the contents of my bookcase on the floor, and you promptly accuse me of being guilty. Of what, I should like to know? Perhaps you can tell me Hope."

"There is no need for Hope to tell you, sir. You are perfectly well aware of your own villainy."

Random frowned.

"I allow a certain amount of latitude to my guests, Professor," he said with marked dignity, "but for a man of your age and position you go too far. Be more explicit."

"Allow me to speak," intervened Archie, anticipating Braddock. "Random, the Professor has just had a visit from Captain Hiram Hervey, who was the skipper of The Diver. He accuses you of having murdered Bolton!"

"What?" the baronet started back, looking thunderstruck.

"Wait a moment. I have not finished yet. Hervey accuses you of this murder, of stealing the mummy, of gaining possession of the emeralds, and of placing the rifled corpse in Mrs. Jasher's garden, so that she might be accused of committing the crime."

"Exactly," cried Braddock, seeing that his host remained silent from sheer surprise. "Hope has stated the case very clearly. Now, sir, your defense?"

"Defense! defense!" Random found his tongue at last and spoke indignantly. "I have no defense to make."

"Ah! Then you acknowledge your guilt?"

"I acknowledge nothing. The accusation is too preposterous for any denial to be necessary. Do you believe this of me?" He looked from one to the other.

"I don't," said Archie quickly, "there is some mistake."

"Thank you, Hope. And you, Professor?"

Braddock fidgeted about the room.

"I don't know what to think," he said at length. "Hervey spoke very decisively."

"Oh, indeed," returned Random dryly, and, walking to the door, he locked it. "In that case, I must ask you for an explanation, and neither of you shall leave this room until one is given. Your proofs?"

"Here is one of them," snapped Braddock, throwing the manuscript on the table. "Where did you get this?"

Random took up the discolored paper with a bewildered air.

"I never set eyes on this before," he said, much puzzled. "What is it?"

"A copy of the manuscript mentioned by Don Pedro, which describes the two emeralds buried with the mummy of Inca Caxas."

"I see." Random understood all in a moment. "So you say that I knew of the emeralds from this, and so murdered Bolton to obtain them."

"Pardon me," said Braddock with elaborate politeness. "Hervey says that you murdered my poor assistant, and although my discovery of this manuscript proves that you must have known about the jewels, I say nothing. I wait to hear your defense."

"That's very good of you," remarked Sir Frank ironically. "So it seems that I am in the dock. Perhaps the counsel for the prosecution will state the evidence against me," and he looked again from one to the other.

Archie shook the baronet by the hand very warmly.

"My dear fellow," he declared decidedly, "I don't believe one word of the evidence."

"In that case there must be a flaw in it," retorted Random, but did not seem to be unmoved by Hope's generous action. "Sit down, Professor; it appears that you are against me."

"Until I hear your defense," said the old man obstinately.

"I cannot make any until I hear your evidence. Go on. I am waiting," and Sir Frank flung himself into a chair, where he sat calmly, his eyes steadily fixed on the Professor's face.

"Where did you get that manuscript?" asked Braddock sharply.

"I got it nowhere: this is the first time I have seen it."

"Yet it was hidden amongst your books."

"Then I can't say how it got there. Were you looking for it?"

"No! Certainly not. To pass the time while waiting, I examined your library, and in pulling out a book, your case, being a swing one, over-balanced and shot its contents on to the floor. Amongst the papers which fell with the books, I caught a glimpse of the manuscript, and, noting that it was written in Latin, I picked it up, surprised to think that a frivolous young man, such as you are, should study a dead language. A few words showed me that the manuscript was a copy of the one referred to by Don Pedro."

"One moment," said Archie, who had been thinking. "Perhaps this is the original manuscript, which De Gayangos has given to you, Random."

"It is good of you to afford me a loophole of escape," said Sir Frank, leaning back with folded arms, "but De Gayangos gave me nothing. I saw the manuscript in his hands, when he showed it to us all at Mrs. Jasher's. But whether this is the original or a copy I can't say. Don Pedro certainly did not give it to me."

"Has Don Pedro been in your quarters?" asked Hope thoughtfully.

"No. He has only visited me in the mess. And even if Don Pedro did come in here—for I guess what is in your mind—I really do not see why he should slip a manuscript which he values highly amongst my books."

"Then you really never saw this before?" said Braddock, indicating the paper on the table, and impressed by Random's earnestness.

"How often do you want me to deny it?" retorted the young man impatiently. "Perhaps you will state on what grounds I am accused?"

Braddock nodded and cleared his throat.

"Captain Hervey declared that your yacht arrived at Pierside almost at the same time as his steamer."

"Quite right. When Don Pedro received a wire from Malta stating that the mummy had been sold to you, and that it was being shipped to London on The Diver, I got up steam at once, and chased the tramp to that port. As the tramp was slow, and my boat was fast, I arrived on the same day and almost at the same hour, even though Hervey's boat had the start of mine."

"Why were you anxious to follow The Diver?" asked Hope.

"Don Pedro wished to get back the mummy, and asked me to follow. As I was in love with Donna Inez, and still am, I was only too willing to oblige him."

Braddock nodded again.

"Hervey says that you went on board The Diver, and had an interview with Bolton."

"That is perfectly true, and my visit was paid for the same reason as I followed the steamer to London—that is, I acted on behalf of Don Pedro. I wished to ascertain for certain that the mummy was on board, and having done so from Bolton, I urged

129

him to induce you to give back the same, free of charge, to De Gayangos, from whom it had been stolen. He refused, as he declared that he intended to deliver it to you."

"I knew I could always trust Bolton," said the Professor enthusiastically. "It would have been better for you to have come to me, Random."

"I daresay; but I wished, as I told you, to make certain that the mummy was on board. That was the real reason for my visit; but, being in Bolton's company, I naturally told him that Don Pedro claimed the mummy as his property, and warned him that if you or he kept the same, that there would be trouble."

"Did you use threats?" asked Hope, remembering what he had overheard.

"No; certainly not."

"Yes, you did," cried Braddock quickly. "Hervey declares that you told Bolton that he would repent of keeping the mummy, and that his life would not be safe while he held it."

To the surprise of both visitors, Random admitted using these serious threats without a moment's hesitation.

"Don Pedro told me that many Indians, both in Lima and Cuzco, who look upon him as the lawful descendant of the last Inca, are anxiously expecting the return of the royal mummy. He also stated that when the Indians knew who held the mummy they would send one of themselves to get it back, if he—Don Pedro, that is—did not fetch it. To get back the mummy Don Pedro declared that these Indians would not stop short of murder. Hence my warning to Bolton."

"Oh!" Archie jumped up with widely opened eyes. "Then perhaps this solves the problem. Bolton was murdered by some Peruvian Indian."

Random shook his head gravely.

"Again you offer me a loophole of escape, my dear fellow," he said sententiously, "but that theory will not hold water. At present the Indians in Lima and Cuzco do not know that the mummy has been found. Don Pedro only chanced upon the paper which announced the sale by accident and had no time to communicate with his barbaric friends in South America. Failing to get the mummy from you, Professor, he would have returned to Peru and then would have told who possessed the corpse of Inca Caxas, leaving the Indians to deal with the matter. In that case my warning to Bolton would be necessary. But at the time I told him, it was not necessary. However, Bolton remained true to you, Professor, and declined to surrender the mummy. I therefore wired to Don Pedro at Genoa that the mummy was on board The Diver and was being sent to Gartley. I also advised him to come to me here in order to be introduced to you. The rest you know."

There was a moment's silence. Then Archie, to test if Random was willing to admit everything—as an innocent man certainly would—asked significantly,

"Did you see Bolton again after your interview on board ship?"

It was then that the baronet proved his good faith.

"Oh, yes," he said easily and without hesitation. "I was walking about Pierside later, and, passing along that waterside alley near the Sailor's Rest, I saw a window on the ground floor open, and Bolton looking out across the river. I stopped and asked him when he proposed to take the mummy to Gartley, and if it was on shore. He admitted that it was in the hotel, but declined to say when he would send it on to you, Professor. When he closed the window, I afterwards went into the hotel and had a drink in order to ask casually when Mr. Bolton intended to leave. I gathered—not directly, of course, but in a roundabout way—that he had arranged to go next morning and to send on his luggage. Then I left and went to London. In the course of time I returned here and learned of the murder and the disappearance of the corpse of Inca Caxas. And now," Random stood up, "having admitted all this, perhaps you will believe me to be innocent."

"You have no idea who murdered Bolton and placed his body in the packing case?" asked Braddock, manifestly disappointed.

"'No. No more than I have any idea of the person who placed the mummy case and its contents in Mrs. Jasher's garden."

"Oh, you know that!" said Archie quickly.

"Yes. The news was all over the village this morning. I could hardly help knowing it. And I believe that the mummy has been taken to your house, Professor."

"It has," admitted Braddock dryly. "I took it myself from Mrs. Jasher's arbor in a hand-cart, with the assistance of Cockatoo. But when I made an examination this morning in the presence of Hope and Don Pedro, I found that the swathings of the body had been ripped up, and that the emeralds mentioned in that manuscript had been stolen."

"Strange!" said Random with a frown; "and by whom?"

"No doubt by the assassin of Sidney Bolton."

"Probably." Random kicked a mat straight with his foot. "At any rate the theft of the emeralds shows that it was not any Indian who killed Bolton. None of them would rifle so sacred a corpse."

"Besides which—as you say—the Indians in Peru do not know that the mummy has reappeared after thirty years' seclusion," chimed in Hope, rising. "Well, and what is to be done now?"

131

For answer Sir Frank picked up the manuscript which still remained on the table.

"I shall see Don Pedro about this," he said quietly, "and ascertain if it is the original or a copy."

Braddock rose slowly and stared at the paper.

"Do you know Latin?" he asked.

"No," rejoined Random, knowing what the savant meant. "I learned it, of course, but I have forgotten much. I might translate a word or two, but certainly not the hedge-priest Latin in which this is written." He looked carefully at the manuscript as he spoke.

"But who could have placed it in your room?" questioned Archie.

"We cannot learn that until we see Don Pedro. If this is the original manuscript which we saw the other night, we may learn how it passed from the possession of De Gayangos to my bookcase. If it is a copy, then we must learn, if possible, who owned it."

"Don Pedro said that a transcript or a translation had been made," mentioned Hope.

"Evidently a transcript," said Braddock, glaring at the paper in Random's hand. "But how could that find its way from Lima to this place?"

"It might have been packed up with the mummy," suggested Archie.

"No," contradicted Random decisively, "in that event, the man in Malta from whom the mummy was bought would have discovered the emeralds, and would have taken them."

"Perhaps he did. We have nothing to show that Bolton's assassin committed the crime for the sake of the jewels."

"He must have done so," cried the Professor, irritably, "else there is no motive for the commission of the crime. But I think myself that we must start at the other end to find a clue. When we discover who placed the mummy in Mrs. Jasher's garden—"

"That will not be easy," murmured Hope thoughtfully, "though, of course, the same must have been brought by river. Let us go down to the embankment and see if there are any signs of a boat having been brought there last night," and he moved to the door. "Random?"

"I cannot leave the Fort, as I am on duty," replied the officer, putting the manuscript away in a drawer and locking the same, "but this evening I shall see Don Pedro, and in the meanwhile I shall endeavor to learn from my servant who visited me lately while I was absent. The manuscript must have been brought here by someone. But I trust," he added as he escorted his two visitors to the door, "that you now acquit me of—"

"Yes! yes! yes!" cried Braddock, hastily cutting him short and shaking his hand. "I apologize for my suspicions. Now I maintain that you are innocent."

"And I never believed you to be guilty," cried Hope heartily.

"Thank you both," said Random simply, and, having closed the door, he returned to a chair near the fire to smoke a pipe, and meditate over his future movements. "An enemy hath done this," said Random, referring to the concealment of the manuscript, but he could think of no one who desired to harm him in any way.

CHAPTER XVIII

RECOGNITION

Lucy and Mrs. Jasher were having a confidential conversation in the small pink drawing-room. True to her promise, Miss Kendal had come to readjust matters between the fiery little Professor and the widow. But it was not an easy task, as Mrs. Jasher was righteously indignant at the rash words used to her.

"As if I knew anything about the matter," she repeated again and again in angry tones. "Why, my dear, he as good as told me I had murdered—"

Lucy did not let her finish.

"There! there!" she said, speaking as she would have done to a fretful child, "you know what my father is."

"It seems to me that I am just beginning to learn," said the widow bitterly, "and knowing how ready he is to believe ill of me, I think it is better we should part for ever."

"But you'll never be Lady Braddock."

"Even if I married him, I am not sure that I should be, since I learn that his brother is singularly healthy and comes of a long-lived family. And it will not be pleasant to live with your father when he has such a temper."

"That was only because he was excited. Think of your salon, and of the position you wish to hold in, London."

"Ah, well," said Mrs. Jasher, visibly softening, "there is something to be said there. After all, one can never find a man who is perfection. And a very amiable man is usually a fool. One can't expect a rose to be without thorns. But really, my dear," she surveyed Lucy with mild surprise, "you appear to be very anxious that I should marry your father."

"I want to see my father made comfortable before I marry Archie," said the girl with a blush. "Of course my father is quite a child in household affairs and needs everything done for him. Archie—I am glad to say—is now in a position to marry me in the spring. I want you to be married about the same time, and then you can live in Gartley, and—"

"No, my dear," said Mrs. Jasher firmly, "if I marry your father, he wishes us to go at once to Egypt in search of this tomb."

"I know that he wants you to help with the money left to you by your late brother. But surely you will not go up the Nile yourself?"

"No, certainly not," said the widow promptly. "I shall remain in Cairo while the Professor goes on his excursion into Ethiopia. I know that Cairo is a very charming place, and that I shall be able to enjoy myself there."

"Then you have decided to forgive my father for his rash words?"

"I must," sighed Mrs. Jasher. "I am so tired of being an unprotected widow without a recognized position in the world. Even with my brother's money,—not that it is so very much—I shall still be looked upon askance if I go into society. But as Mrs. Braddock, or Lady Braddock, no one will dare to say a word against me. Yes, my dear, if your father comes and, asks my pardon he shall have it. We women are so weak," ended the widow virtuously, as if she was not making a virtue of necessity.

Things being thus settled, the two talked on amiably for some time, and discussed the chances of Random marrying Donna Inez. Both acknowledged that the Peruvian lady was handsome enough, but had not a word to say for herself.

While thus chattering, Professor Braddock trotted into the room, looking brisk and bright from his stroll in the cold frosty air. Gifted as he was with scientific assurance, the little man was not at all taken aback by the cold reception of Mrs. Jasher, but rubbed his hands cheerfully.

"Ah, there you are, Selina," said he, looking like a bright-eyed robin. "I hope you are feeling well."

"How can you expect me to feel well after what you said?" remarked Mrs. Jasher reproachfully, and anxious to make a virtue of forgiveness.

"Oh, I beg pardon: I beg pardon. Surely, Selina, you are not going to make a fuss over a trifle like that?"

"I did not give you permission to call me Selina."

"Quite so. But as we are to be married, I may as well get used to your Christian name, my dear."

"I am not so sure that we will be married," said Mrs. Jasher stiffly.

"Oh, but we must," cried Braddock in dismay. "I am depending upon your money to finance my expedition to Queen Tahoser's tomb."

"I see," observed the widow coldly, while Lucy sat quietly by and allowed the elder woman to conduct the campaign, "you want me for my money. There is no love in the question."

"My dear, as soon as I have the time—say during our voyage to Cairo, whence we start inland up the Nile for Ethiopia—I shall make love whenever you like. And, confound it, Selina, I admire you no end—to use a slang phrase. You are a fine woman and a sensible woman, and I am afraid that you are throwing yourself away on a snuffy old man like myself."

"Oh no! no! Pray do not say that," cried Mrs. Jasher, visibly moved by this flattery. "You will make a very good husband if you will only strive to govern your temper."

"Temper! temper! Bless the woman—I mean you, Selina—I have the very best temper in the world. However, you shall govern it and myself also if you like. Come," he took her hand, "let us be friends and fix the wedding day."

Mrs. Jasher did not withdraw her hand.

"Then you do not believe that I have anything to do with this terrible murder?" she asked playfully.

"No! no! I was heated last night. I spoke rashly and hastily. Forgive and forget, Selina. You are innocent—quite innocent, in spite of the mummy being in your confounded garden. After all, the evidence is stronger against Random than against you. Perhaps he put it there: it's on his way to the Fort, you see. Never mind. He has exonerated himself, and no doubt, when confronted with Hervey, will be able to silence that blackguard. And I am quite sure that Hervey is a blackguard," ended Braddock, rubbing his bald head.

The two ladies looked at one another in amazement, not knowing what to say. They were ignorant of the theft of the emeralds and of the accusation of Sir Frank by the Yankee skipper. But, with his usual absentmindedness, Braddock had forgotten all about that, and sat in his chair rubbing his head quite pink and rattling on cheerfully.

"I went down with Hope to the embankment," he continued, "but neither of us could see any sign of a boat. There's the rude, short jetty, of course, and if a boat came, a boat could go away without leaving any trace. Perhaps that is so. However, we must wait until we see Don Pedro and Hervey again, and then—"

Lucy broke in desperately.

"What are you talking about, father? Why do you bring in Sir Frank's name in that way?"

"What do you expect me to say?" retorted the little man. "After all, the manuscript was found in his room, and the emeralds are gone. I saw that for myself, as did Hope and Don Pedro, in whose presence I opened the mummy case."

Mrs. Jasher rose in her astonishment.

"Are the emeralds gone?" she gasped.

"Yes! yes! yes!" cried Braddock irritably. "Am I not telling you so? I almost believe in Hervey's accusation of Random, and yet the boy exonerated himself very forcibly—very forcibly indeed."

"Will you explain all that has happened, father?" said Lucy, who was becoming more and more perplexed by this rambling chatter. "We are quite in the dark."

"So am I: so is Hope: so is every one," chuckled Braddock. "Ah, yes: of course, you were not present when these events took place."

"What events?—what events?" demanded Mrs. Jasher, now quite exasperated.

"I am about to tell you," snapped her future husband, and related all that had taken place since the arrival of Captain Hervey in the museum at the Pyramids. The women listened with interest and with growing astonishment, only interrupting the narrator with a simultaneous exclamation of indignation when they heard that Sir Frank was accused.

"It is utterly and wholly absurd," cried Lucy angrily. "Sir Frank is the soul of honor."

"So I think, my dear," chimed in Mrs. Jasher. "And what does he say to—?"

Braddock interrupted.

"I am about to tell you, if you will stop talking," he cried crossly. "That is so like a woman. She asks for an explanation and then prevents the man from giving it. Random offers a very good defense, I am bound to say," and he detailed what Sir Frank had said.

When the history was finished, Lucy rose to go.

"I shall see Archie at once," she said, moving hastily, towards the door.

"What for?" demanded her father benignly.

Lucy turned.

"This thing can't go on," she declared resolutely. "Mrs. Jasher was accused by you, father—"

"Only in a heated moment," cried the Professor, excusing himself.

"Never mind, she was accused," retorted Lucy stubbornly, "and now this sailor accuses Sir Frank. Who knows who will be charged next with committing the crime? I shall ask Archie to take the matter up, and hunt down the real criminal. Until the guilty person is found, I foresee that we shall never have a moment's peace."

"I quite agree with you," said Mrs. Jasher earnestly. "For my own sake I wish the matter of this mystery to be cleared up. Why don't you help me?" she added, turning to Braddock, who listened placidly.

"I am helping," said Braddock quietly. "I intend to set Cockatoo on the trail at once. He shall take up his abode in the Sailor's Rest on some pretext, and no doubt will be able to find a clue."

"What?" cried the widow incredulously, "a savage like that?"

"Cockatoo is much cleverer than the average white man," said Braddock dryly, "especially in following a trail. He, if any one, will learn the truth. I would much rather trust the Kanaka than young Hope."

"Nonsense!" cried Lucy, standing up for her lover. "Archie is the one to discover the assassin. I'll see him at once. And you, father?"

"I, my dear," said the Professor calmly, "shall remain here and make my peace with the future Mrs. Braddock."

"You have made it already," said the widow graciously, and extended her hand, which the Professor kissed unexpectedly, and then sat back in his chair, looking quite abashed at his outburst of gallantry.

Seeing that everything was going well, Lucy left the elderly couple to continue their courting, and hurried to Archie's lodgings in the village. However, he happened to be out, and his landlady did not know when he would return. Rather annoyed by this, since she greatly desired to unbosom herself, Miss Kendal walked disconsolately towards the Pyramids. On the way she was stopped by Widow Anne, looking more dismal and funereal than ever, and garrulous with copious draughts of gin. Not that she was intoxicated, but her tongue was loose, and she wept freely for no apparent reason. According to herself, she had stopped Lucy to demand back from Mr. Hope through the girl certain articles of attire which had been borrowed for artistic purposes. These, consisting of a shawl and a skirt and a bodice, were of extraordinary value, and Mrs. Bolton wanted them back or their equivalent in value. She mentioned that she would prefer the sum of five pounds.

"Why do you not ask Mr. Hope yourself?" said Lucy who was too impatient to bear with the old creature's maunderings. "If you gave him the things he will no doubt return them."

"If they aren't spiled with paint," wailed Widow Anne. "He told my Sid as he wanted them for a model to wear while being painted. Sid asked me, and I gave 'em to Sid, and Sid, he passed 'em along to your good gentleman. There was a skirt, as good as new, and a body of the dress trimmest beautiful, and a tartan shawl as I got from my mother. But no," the old woman corrected herself, "it was a dark shawl with red spots and—"

"Ask Mr. Hope, ask Mr. Hope," cried Miss Kendal impatiently. "I know nothing about the things," and she tore her dress from Widow Anne's detaining hand to hurry home. Mrs. Bolton wailed aloud at this desertion, and took her way to Hope's lodgings, where she declared her determination to remain until the artist restored her apparel.

Lucy for the moment thought little of this interview; but on reflection she thought it strange that Archie should borrow clothes from Mrs. Bolton through Sidney. Not that there was anything strange in Archie's procuring such garments, since he may have wanted them to clothe a model with. But he could easily have got such things from his landlady, or, if from Widow Anne, could have borrowed them direct without appealing to Sidney. Why, then, had the dead man acted as an intermediate party? This question was hard to answer, yet Lucy greatly wished for a reply, since she suddenly remembered how a woman in a dark dress and with a dark shawl over her head had been seen by Eliza Flight, the housemaid of the Sailor's Rest, talking to Bolton through the window. Were the garments borrowed as a disguise, and did the person who had borrowed them desire that it should be supposed that Widow Anne was talking to her son? There was a chill hand clutching Lucy's heart as she went home, for the words of Mrs. Bolton seemed indirectly to implicate Hope in the mystery. She determined to ask him about the matter straight out, when he came in that night to pay his usual visit.

At dinner the Professor was in excellent spirits, and actually became so human as to compliment Lucy on her housekeeping. He also mentioned that he hoped Mrs. Jasher would cater as excellently. Over coffee he informed his step-daughter that he had entirely won the widow's heart by abasing himself at her feet and withdrawing the accusation. They had arranged to be married in May, one or two weeks after Lucy became Mrs. Hope. In the autumn they would start for Egypt, and would remain abroad for a year or more.

"In fact," said the Professor, setting down his cup and preparing to take his departure, "everything is now settled excellently. I marry Mrs. Jasher: you, my dear, marry Hope, and—"

"And Sir Frank marries Donna Inez," finished Lucy quickly.

"That," said Braddock stiffly, "entirely depends upon what De Gayangos says to this accusation of Hervey's."

"Sir Frank is innocent."

"I hope so, and I believe so. But he will have to prove his innocence. I shall do my best, and I have sent round to Don Pedro to come here. We can then talk it over."

"Can Archie and I come in also?" asked Miss Kendal anxiously.

Somewhat to her surprise, the Professor yielded a ready assent.

"By all means, my dear. The more witnesses we have, the better it will be. We must do all in our powers to bring this matter to a successful issue."

So things were arranged, and when Archie came up to the drawing-room, Lucy informed him that Braddock was in the museum with Don Pedro, telling all that had happened. Hope was glad to hear that Lucy had secured the Professor's consent that they should be present, for the mystery of Bolton's terrible death was piquing him, and he dearly desired to learn the truth. As a matter of fact, although he was unaware of it, he was suffering from an attack of detective fever, and wished to solve the mystery. He therefore went gladly into the museum with his sweetheart. Oddly enough—as Lucy recollected when it was too late to speak—she quite forgot to relate what Widow Anne had said about the borrowed clothes.

Don Pedro, looking more stiff and dignified than ever, was in the museum with Braddock. The two men were seated in comfortable chairs, and Cockatoo, some distance away, was polishing with a cloth the green mummy case of the fatal object which had brought about all the trouble. Lucy had half expected to see Donna Inez, but De Gayangos explained that he had left her writing letters to Lima in the Warrior Inn. When Miss Kendal and Hope were seated, the Peruvian expressed himself much surprised at the charge which had been brought against Sir Frank.

"If I can speak of such things in the presence of a lady," he remarked, bowing his head to Lucy.

"Oh yes," she answered eagerly. "I have heard all about the charge. And I am glad that you are here, Don Pedro, for I wish to say that I do not believe there is a word of truth in the accusation."

"Nor do I," asserted the Peruvian decisively.

"I agree—I agree," cried Braddock, beaming. "And you, Hope?"

"I never believed it, even before I heard Random's defense," said Archie with a dry smile. "Did you not see Captain Hervey yourself, sir?" he added, turning to Don Pedro; "he started for Pierside to look you up."

"I have not seen him," said De Gayangos in his stately way, "and I am very sorry, as I desire to examine him about the accusation he had dared to bring against my very good friend, Sir Frank Random. I wish he were here at this very minute, so that I could tell him what I think of the charge."

Just as Don Pedro spoke the unexpected happened, as though some genie had obeyed his commands. As though transported into the room by magic, the American skipper appeared, not through the floor, but by the door. A female domestic admitted him and announced his name, then fled to avoid the anger of her master, seeing she had violated the sacred precincts of the museum.

Captain Hervey, amused by the surprise visible on every face, sauntered forward, hat on head and cheroot in mouth as usual. But when he saw Lucy he removed both with a politeness scarcely to be expected from so rude and ready and rough a mariner.

"I beg pardon for coming here uninvited," said Hervey awkwardly, "but I've been chasing the Don all over Pierside and through this village. They told me at the police office that you"—he spoke to De Gayangos "had doubled on your trail, so here I am for a little private conversation."

The Peruvian looked gravely at Hervey's face, which was clearly revealed in the powerful light of the many lamps with which the museum was filled, and rose to bow.

"I am glad to see you, sir," he said politely, and with a still more searching glance. "With the permission of our host I shall ask you to take a chair," and he turned to Braddock.

"Certainly! certainly!" said the Professor fussily. "Cockatoo?"

"Pardon, allow me," said De Gayangos, and brought forward a chair, still keeping his eyes on the skipper, who was rather confused by the courtesy. "Will you be seated, senor: then we can talk."

Hervey sat down quietly close to the Peruvian; who then leaned forward to address him.

"You will have a cigarette?" he asked, offering a silver case.

"Thanks, no. I'll smoke a cheroot if the lady don't mind."

"Not at all," replied Lucy, who, along with Archie and the Professor, was puzzled by Don Pedro's manner. "Please smoke!"

In taking back the case Don Pedro allowed it to drop. As he made no motion of picking it up, Hervey, although annoyed with himself for his politeness towards a yellow-stomach, as he called De Gayangos, was compelled to stretch for it. As he handed it back to Don Pedro, the Peruvian's eyes lighted up and he nodded gravely.

"Thank you, Vasa," said De Gayangos, and Hervey, changing color, leaped from his seat as though touched by a spear-point.

CHAPTER XIX

NEARER THE TRUTH

For a few moments there was silence. Lucy and Archie sat still, as they were too much surprised by Don Pedro's recognition of Captain Hervey as the Swedish sailor Vasa to move or speak. But the Professor did not seem to be greatly astonished, and the sole sound which broke the stillness was his sardonic chuckle. Perhaps the little man had progressed beyond the point of being surprised at anything, or, like, Moliere's hero, was only surprised at finding virtue in unexpected places.

As for the Peruvian and the skipper, they were both on their feet, eyeing one another like two fighting dogs. Hervey was the first to find his very useful tongue.

"I guess you've got the bulge on me," said he, trying to outstare the Peruvian, for which nationality, from long voyaging on the South American coast, he entertained the most profound contempt.

But in De Gayangos he found a foeman worthy of his steel.

"I think not," said Don Pedro quietly, and facing the pseudo-American bravely. "I never forget faces, and yours is a noticeable one. When you first spoke I fancied that I remembered your voice. All that business with the chair was to get close to you, so that I could see the scar on your right temple. It is still there, I notice. Also, I dropped my cigarette case and forced you to pick it up, so that, when you stretched your arm, I might see what mark was on your left wrist. It is a serpent encircling the sun, which Lola Farjados induced you to have tattooed when you were in Lima thirty years ago. Your eyes are blue and full of light, and as you were twenty when I knew you, the lapse of years has made you fifty—your present age."

"Shucks!" said Hervey coolly, and sat down to smoke.

Don Pedro turned to Archie and Braddock.

"Mr. Hope! Professor!" he remarked, "if you remember the description I gave of Gustav Vasa, I appeal to you to see if it does not exactly fit this man?"

"It does," said Archie unhesitatingly, "although I cannot see the tattooed left wrist to which you refer."

Hervey, still smoking, made no offer to show the symbol, but Braddock unexpectedly came to the assistance of Don Pedro.

"The man is Vasa right enough," he remarked abruptly.

"Whether he is Swedish or American I cannot say. But he is the same man I met when I was in Lima thirty years ago, after the war."

Hervey slowly turned his blue eyes on the scientist with a twinkle in their depths.

"So you recognized me?" he observed, with his Yankee drawl.

"I recognized you at the moment I hired you to take The Diver to Malta to bring back that mummy," retorted Braddock, "but it didn't suit my book to let on. Didn't you recognize me?"

"Wal, no," said Hervey, his drawl more pronounced than ever. "I haven't got the memory for faces that you and the Don here seem to possess. Huh!" He wheeled his chair and faced Braddock squarely. "I'd have thought you wiser not to back up the Don, sir."

Braddock's little eyes sparkled.

"I am not afraid of you," said he with great contempt. "I never did anything for which you could get money out of me for, Captain Hervey or Gustav Vasa, or whatever your name might be."

"You were always a mighty spry man," assented the skipper coolly, "but spry men, I take it, make mistakes from being too almighty smart."

Braddock shrugged his shoulders, and Don Pedro intervened.

"This is all beside the point," he remarked angrily. "Captain Hervey, do you deny that you are Gustav Vasa in the face of this evidence?"

Hervey drew up the left sleeve of his reefer jacket, and showed on his bared wrist the symbol of the sun and the encircling serpent.

"Is that enough?" he drawled, "or do you want to look at this?" and he turned his head to reveal his scarred right temple.

"Then you admit that you are Vasa?"

"Wal," drawled the captain again, "that's one of my names, I guess, though I haven't used it since I traded that blamed mummy in Paris, thirty years ago. There's nothing like owning up."

"Are you not Swedish?" asked Lucy timidly.

"I am a citizen of the world, I guess," replied Hervey with great politeness for him, "and America suits me for headquarters as well as any other nation. I might be Swedish or Danish or a Dago for choice. Vasa may be my name, or Hervey, or anything you like. But I guess I'm a man all through."

"And a thief!" cried Don Pedro, who had resumed his seat, but was keeping quiet with difficulty.

"Not of those emeralds," rejoined the skipper coolly: "Lord, to think of the chance I missed! Thirty years ago I could have looted them, and again the other day. But I never knew—I never knew," cried Hervey regretfully, with his vividly blue eyes on the mummy. "I could jes' kick myself, gentlemen, when I think of the miss."

"Then you didn't steal the manuscript along with the emeralds?"

"Wal, I did," cried Hervey, turning to Archie, who had spoken, "but it was in a furren lingo, to which I didn't catch on. If I'd known I'd have learned about those blamed emeralds."

"What did you do with the copy of the manuscript you stole?" asked Don Pedro sharply. "I know there was a copy, as my father told me so. I have the original myself, but the transcript—and not a translation, as I fancied—appeared in Sir Frank Random's room to-day, hidden behind some books."

Hervey made no move, but smoked steadily, with his eyes on the carpet. However, Archie, who was observing keenly, saw that he was more startled than he would admit. The explanation had taken him by surprise.

"Explain!" cried the Peruvian sharply.

Hervey looked up and fixed a pair of very evil eyes on the Don.

"See here," he remarked, "if the lady wasn't present, I'd show you that I take no orders from any yellow—that is, from any low-down Don."

"Lucy, my dear, leave us," said Braddock, rising, much excited; "we must have this matter sifted to the bottom, and if Hervey can explain better in your absence, I think you should go."

Although Miss Kendal was very anxious to hear all that was to be heard, she saw the advisability of taking this advice, especially as Hope gave her arm a meaning nudge.

"I'll go," she said meekly, and was escorted by her lover to the door. There she paused. "Tell me all that takes place," she whispered, and when Archie nodded, she vanished promptly. The young man closed the door and returned to his seat in time to hear Don Pedro reiterate his request for an explanation.

"And 'spose I can't oblige," said the skipper, now more at his ease since the lady was out of the room.

"Then I shall have you arrested," was the quick reply.

"For what?"

"For the theft of my mummy."

Hervey laughed raucously.

"I guess the law can't worry me about that after thirty years, and in a low-down country like Peru. Your Government has shifted fifty times since I looted the corpse."

This was quite true, and there was absolutely no chance of the skipper being brought to book. Don Pedro looked rather disconsolate, and his gaze dropped under the glare of Hervey's eyes, which seemed unfair, seeing that the Don was as good as the captain was evil.

"You can't expect me to condone the theft," he muttered.

"I reckon I don't expect anything," retorted Hervey coolly "I looted the corpse, I don't deny, and—"

"After my father had treated you like a son," said Don Pedro bitterly. "You were homeless and friendless, and my father took you in, only to find that you robbed him of his most precious possession."

The skipper had the grace to blush, and shifted uneasily in his chair.

"You can't say truer than that," he grumbled, averting his eyes. "I guess I'm a bad lot all through. But a friend of mine wanted the corpse, and offered me a heap of dollars to see the business through."

"Do you mean to say that some one asked you to steal it?"

"No," put in Braddock unexpectedly, "for I was the friend."

"You!" Don Pedro swung round in great astonishment, but the Professor faced him with all the consciousness of innocence.

"Yes," he remarked quietly, "as I told you, I was in Peru thirty years ago. I was then hunting for specimens of Inca mummies. Vasa—this man now called Hervey—told me that he could obtain a splendid specimen of a mummy, and I arranged to give him one hundred pounds to procure what I wanted. But I swear to you, De Gayangos," continued the little man earnestly, "that I did not know he proposed to steal the mummy from you."

"You knew it was the green mummy?" asked Don Pedro sharply.

"No, I only knew that it was a mummy."

"Did Vasa get it for you?"

"I guess not," said the gentleman who confessed to that name. "The Professor went to Cuzco and got into trouble—"

"I was carried off to the mountains by some Indians," interpolated the Professor, "and only escaped after a year's captivity. I did not mind that, as it gave me the opportunity of studying a decaying civilization. But when I returned a free man to Lima, I found that Vasa had left the country with the mummy."

"That's so," assented Hervey, waving his hand. "I got a berth as second mate on a wind-jammer sailing to Europe, and as the country wasn't healthy for me since I'd looted the green mummy, I took it abroad and yanked it to Paris, where I sold it for a couple of hundred pounds. With that, I changed my name and had a high old time. I never heard of the blamed thing again until the Professor here turned up with Mr. Bolton at Pierside, asking me to bring it in The Diver from Malta. It was what you'd call a coincidence, I reckon," added Hervey lazily; "but I did cry small when I heard the

Professor here had paid nine hundred for a thing I'd let slip for two hundred. Had I known of those infernal emeralds, I'd have ripped open the case on board and would have recouped myself. But I knew nothing, and Bolton never told me."

"How could he," asked Braddock quietly, "when he did not know that any jewels were buried with the dead? I did not know either. And I have explained why I wanted the mummy. But it never struck me until I hear what you say now, that this mummy," he nodded towards the green case, "was the one which you had stolen at Lima from De Gayangos. But you must do me the justice, Captain Hervey, to tell Don Pedro that I never countenanced the theft."

"No! you were square enough, I guess. The sin is on my own blessed shoulders, and I don't ask it to be shifted."

"What did you do with the copy of the manuscript?" asked Don Pedro.

Hervey ruminated.

"I can't think," he mused. "I found a screed of Latin along with the mummy, when I looted it from your Lima house, but it dropped out of my mind as to what became of it. Maybe I passed it along to the Paris man, and he sold it along with the corpse to the Maltese gent."

"But I tell you this copy was found in Sir Frank's room," insisted De Gayangos. "How did it come to be there?"

Captain Hervey rose and took a turn up and down the room. When Cockatoo came in his way he calmly kicked him aside.

"What do you think, Mr. Hope?" he asked, coming to a full stop before Archie, while Cockatoo crept away with a very dark scowl.

"I don't know what to think," replied that young gentleman promptly, "save that Sir Frank is my very good friend, and that I take his word that he knows nothing of how the manuscript came to be hidden in his bookcase."

"Huh!" said Hervey scornfully, and took another turn up and down the room in silence. "I surmise that your friend isn't a white man."

Hope leaped to his feet.

"That's a lie," he said distinctly.

"I'd have shot you for that down Chili way," snapped the skipper.

"Possibly," retorted the artist dryly, "but I happen to be handy with my revolver also. I say again that you lie. Random is not the man to commit so foul a crime."

"Then how did the manuscript get into his room?" questioned Hervey.

"He is trying to learn, and, when he does, will come here to let us all know, Captain Hervey. But I ask you on what grounds you accuse him? Oh I know all you said to-day," added Hope scornfully, waving his hand; "but you can't prove that Random got the manuscript."

"If it's in his room, as you acknowledge, I can," said Hervey, speaking in a much more cultivated tone. "See here. As I said before, that copy must have been passed along with the corpse to the Maltese man. Well, then, the Professor here bought the corpse, and with it the manuscript."

"No," contradicted the little man, prodigiously excited. "Bolton wrote to me full particulars of the mummy, but said nothing about any manuscript."

"Well, he wouldn't," replied Hervey calmly, "seeing that he'd know Latin."

"He did know Latin," admitted Braddock uneasily; "I taught him myself. But do you mean to say that he got that manuscript and read it and intended to keep the fact of the emeralds secret?"

Hervey nodded three times, and twisted his cheroot in his mouth.

"How else can you figure the business out?" he demanded quietly, and with his eyes fixed on the excited Professor. "Bolton must have got that manuscript, as I can't remember what I did with it, save pass it along with the corpse. He—as you admit—doesn't tell you about it when he writes. Well, then, I reckon he calculated getting this corpse to England, and intended to steal the emeralds when safely ashore."

"But he could have done that on the boat," said Archie quickly.

"I guess not, with me about," said Hervey coolly. "I'd have spotted his game and would have howled for shares."

"You dare to say that?" demanded De Gayangos fiercely.

"Keep your hair on. I dare to say anything that comes up my darned back, you bet. I'm not going to knuckle down to a yellow-stomach—"

Out flew Don Pedro's long arm, and Hervey slammed against the wall. He slipped his hand around to his hip pocket with an ugly smile, but before he could use the revolver he produced, Hope dashed up his arm, and the ball went through the ceiling. "Lucy!" cried the young man, knowing that the drawing-room was overhead, and in a moment was out of the door, racing up the stairs at top speed. Some sense of shame seemed to overpower Hervey as he thought that he might have shot the girl, and he replaced the revolver in his pocket with a shrug.

"I climb down and apologize," he said to Don Pedro, who bowed gravely.

"Hang you, sir; you might have shot my daughter," cried Braddock. "The drawing-room, where she is sitting, is right overhead, and-"

As he spoke the door opened, and Lucy came in on Archie's arm. She was pale with fright, but had sustained no damage. It seemed that the revolver bullet had passed through the floor some distance away from where she was sitting.

"I offer my humble apologies, miss," said the cowed Hervey.

"I'll break your neck, you ruffian!" growled Hope, who looked, and was, dangerous. "How dare you shoot here and—"

"It's all right," interposed Lucy, not wishing for further trouble. "I am all safe. But I shall remain here for the rest of your interview, Captain Hervey, as I am sure you will not shoot again in the presence of a lady."

"No, miss," muttered the captain, and when again invited by the angry Professor to speak, resumed his discourse in low tones. "Wal, as I was saying," he remarked, sitting down with a dogged look, "Bolton intended to clear with the emeralds, but I guess Sir Frank got ahead of him and packed him in that blamed case, while he annexed the emeralds. He then took the manuscript, which he looted from Bolton's corpse, and hid it among his books, as you say, while he left the blamed mummy in the garden of the old lady you talked about. I guess that's what I say."

"It's all theory," said Don Pedro in vexed tones.

"And there isn't a word of truth in it," said Lucy indignantly, standing up for Frank Random.

"It ain't for me to contradict you, miss," said Hervey, who was still humble, "but I ask you, if what I say ain't true, how did that copy of the manuscript come to be in that aristocrat's room?"

There was no reply made to this, and although every one present, save Hervey, believed in Random's innocence, no one could explain. The reply came after some further conversation, by the appearance of the soldier himself in mess kit. He walked unexpectedly into the room with Donna Inez on his arm, and at once apologized to De Gayangos.

"I called to see you at the inn, sir," he said, "and as you were not there, I brought your daughter along with me to explain about the manuscript."

"Ah, yes. We talk of that now. How did it come into your room, sir?"

Random pointed to Hervey.

"That rascal placed it there," he said firmly.

CHAPTER XX

THE LETTER

At this second insult Archie quite expected to see the skipper again draw his revolver and shoot. He therefore jumped up rapidly to once more avert disaster. But perhaps the fiery American was awed by the presence of a second lady—since men of the adventurous type are often shy when the fair sex is at hand—for he meekly sat where he was and did not even contradict. Don Pedro shook hands with Sir Frank, and then Hervey smiled blandly.

"I see you don't believe in my theory," said he scoffingly.

"What theory is that?" asked Random hastily.

"Hervey declares that you murdered Bolton, stole the manuscript from him, and concealed it in your room," said Archie succinctly.

"I can't suggest any other reason for its presence in the room," observed the American with a grim smile. "If I'm wrong, perhaps this almighty aristocrat will correct me."

Random was about to do so, and with some pardonable heat, when he was anticipated by Donna Inez. It has been mentioned before that this young lady was of the silent order. Usually she simply ornamented any company in which she found herself without troubling to entertain with her tongue. But the accusation against the baronet, whom she apparently loved, changed her into a voluble virago. Brushing aside the little Professor, who stood in her way, she launched herself forward and spoke at length. Hervey, cowering in the chair, thus met with an antagonist against whom he had no armor. He could not use force; she dominated him with her eye and when he ventured to open his mouth his few feeble words were speedily drowned by the torrent of speech which flowed from the lips of the Peruvian lady. Every one was as astonished by this outburst as though a dog had spoken. That the hitherto silent Donna Inez de Gayangos should speak thus freely and with such power was quite as great a miracle.

"You—are a dog and a liar," said Donna Inez with great distinctness, and speaking English excellently. "What you say against Sir Frank is madness and foolish talk. In Genoa my father did not speak of the manuscript, nor did I, who tell you this. How, then, could Sir Frank kill this poor man, when he had no reason to slay him—"

149

"For the emeralds," faltered Hervey weakly.

"For the emeralds!" echoed the lady scornfully. "Sir Frank is rich. He does not need to steal to have much money. He is a gentleman, who does not murder, as you have done."

Hervey started to his feet, dismayed but defiant, and saw that he was ringed with unfriendly faces.

"As I have done. Why, I am—"

Donna Inez interrupted.

"You are a murderer. I truly believe that you—yes, that you" she pointed a scornful finger at him "killed this poor man who was bringing the mummy to the Professor. If you were in my own country, I should have you lashed like the dog you are. Pig of a Yankee, vile scum of the—"

"That will do, Inez," said De Gayangos imperiously. "We wish to make this gentleman tell the truth, and this is not the way to go about the matter."

"Gentleman," echoed the angry Peruvian, "he is none. Truth! There is no truth in him, the pig of pigs!" and then, her English failing, she took refuge in Spanish, which is a fairly comprehensive language for swearing in a polite way. The words fairly poured from her mouth, and she looked as fierce as Bellona, the goddess of war.

Archie, listening to her words and watching her beautiful face distorted out of all loveliness, secretly congratulated himself upon the fact that he was not her prospective bridegroom. He wondered how Sir Frank, who was a mild, good-tempered man himself, could dare to make such a fiery female Lady Random.

Perhaps the young man thought himself that she was going a trifle too far, for he touched her nervously on the arm. At once the anger of Donna Inez died down, and she submitted to be led to a chair, whispering as she went, "It was for your sake, my angel, that I was angry," she said, and then relapsed into silence, watching all future proceedings with flashing eyes but compressed mouth.

"Wal," muttered Hervey with his invariable drawl, "now that the lady has eased her mind, I should like to know why this aristocrat says I placed that manuscript in his room."

"You shall know, and at once," said Random promptly. "Did you not call to see me a day or so ago?"

"I did, sir. I wished to tell you what I had discovered, so that you might pay me to shut my mouth if you felt so inclined. I asked where your room was, sir, and walked right in, since your flunky was not at the door."

"Quite so. You were in my room for a few minutes—"

"Say five," interpolated the American imperturbably.

"And then came down. You met my servant, who told you that I would not be back for five or six hours."

"That's just as you state, sir. I was sorry to miss you, but, my time being valuable, I had to get back to Pierside. Failing you, I later came to see the Professor here, and told him what I had discovered."

"You merely discovered a mare's nest," said Random contemptuously; "but this is not the point. I believe that you, and you only, could have hidden that manuscript among my books, intending that it should be discovered, so that I might be implicated in this crime."

"Did your flunky tell you that much?" inquired Hervey coolly.

"My servant told me nothing, save that you had been in my room, where you had no right to be."

"Then," said the American quietly and decisively, "I can't see, sir, how you can place the ticket on me."

"You accuse me, so why should I not accuse you?" retorted Random.

"Because you are guilty, and I ain't," snapped the American.

"You join issue: you join issue," murmured Braddock, rubbing his hands.

Random took no notice of the interruption.

"I have heard from Mr. Hope and Professor Braddock of the grounds upon which you base your accusation, and I have explained to them how I came to be on board your ship and both in and out of the Sailor's Rest."

"And the explanation is quite satisfactory," said Hope smartly.

"I agree," Donna Inez nodded with very bright eyes. "Sir Frank has explained to me also. He knew nothing of the manuscript."

"And you, sir," said Don Pedro quietly to Captain Hervey, "apparently did, since you stole it along with the mummy from Lima."

"I confess the theft, but I didn't know what the manuscript contained," said the skipper dryly, "or I reckon you wouldn't have to ask who stole the emeralds. No, sir, I should have looted them."

"I believe you did, and murdered Bolton," cried Random hotly.

"Shucks!" retorted Hervey, rising with a shrug, "if I had wished to get rid of Bolton, I'd have yanked him overboard and then would have written `accident' in my blamed log-book."

Braddock looked at Don Pedro, and Archie at Sir Frank. What the skipper said was plausible enough. No man would have been such a fool as to have murdered Bolton ashore, when he could have done so without suspicion on board the tramp. Moreover, Hervey spoke with genuine regret, since he had missed the emeralds and

151

assuredly would not have hesitated to steal them even at the cost of Bolton's life, had he known of their whereabouts. So far he had made a good defense, and, seeing the impression produced, he strolled to the door. There he halted.

"If you gents want to lynch me," he said leisurely, "I'll be found at the Sailor's Rest for the next week. Then I'm going as skipper of The Firefly steamer, Port o' London, to Algiers. You can send the sheriff along whenever you choose. But I mean to have my picnic first, and to-morrow I'm going to Inspector Date with my yarn. Then I guess that almighty aristocrat wilt find himself in quod."

"Wait a moment," cried Braddock, running to the door. "Let me talk to you and arrange what is best to be done. If you will—"

He proceeded no further, for without vouchsafing him a reply, Hervey, now quite master of the situation, passed through the door, and the Professor hastily followed him. Those who remained looked at one another, scarcely knowing what to say, or how to act.

"They will arrest thee, my angel," cried Donna Inez, clasping Random's arm.

"Let them," retorted the young man defiantly. "They can prove nothing. With all my heart and soul I believe Hervey to be the guilty person. Hope, what do you say?—and you, Miss Kendal?"

"Hervey has certainly made an excellent defense," said Archie cautiously. "He wouldn't have been such a fool as to murder Bolton ashore when he could have done it so easily when on the narrow seas."

"I agree with you there," said Random quickly. "But if he is innocent; if he did not bring the manuscript into my room, who did?"

"I wonder if Widow Anne herself is guilty?" said Lucy in a musing tone.

All present turned and looked at the girl.

"Who is Widow Anne?" asked Don Pedro with a puzzled air.

"She is the mother of Sidney Bolton, the man who was murdered," said Hope quickly. "My dear Lucy, why do you say that?"

Lucy paused before replying and then answered the question by asking another one.

"Did you ask Sidney to get you some clothes from his mother to clothe a model?"

"Never in my life," said Hope promptly, and, as Lucy, saw, truly.

"Well, I accidentally met Mrs. Bolton to-day, and she insisted that her son had borrowed from her a dark shawl and a dark dress for you."

"That is not true," said Hope hotly. "Why should the woman tell such a lie?"

"Well," said Lucy slowly, "it struck me that the woman who spoke with Sidney through the Sailor's Rest window might be Widow Anne herself, and that she has invented this story of the clothes being lent to account for their being worn, should she be discovered."

"It's certainly odd she should speak like this," said Random thoughtfully; "but you forget, Miss Kendal, that she proved an alibi."

"What of that?" cried Don Pedro hurriedly, "alibis can be manufactured."

"It will be best to see this woman and question her," suggested Donna Inez.

Archie nodded.

"I shall do so to-morrow. By the way, does she ever come to your room in the Fort, Random?"

"Oh yes, she is my laundress, you know, and at times brings back the clothes herself. My servant is usually in, though. I see what you mean. That she might have received the manuscript from Bolton, and have left it in my room."

"Yes, I think that," said Archie slowly. "I should not be at all surprised to learn that a portion of Hervey's theory is correct. Bolton may have found the manuscript packed up in the mummy, amongst the graveclothes, in fact. If he read it—as he would and could, seeing that he was an excellent Latin scholar, thanks to Professor Braddock's training—he might have formed a design to steal the emeralds when he was in the Sailor's Rest. Then someone saved him the trouble, and packed him off to Gartley instead of the mummy."

"But why should Widow Anne leave the manuscript in my room?" argued Random.

"Can't you see? Bolton knew that you wanted the mummy for Don Pedro, and was aware how you had—so to speak—used threats in the presence of witnesses, since you spoke out aloud on the deck."

"Only to warn Bolton against the Indians," pleaded Random.

"Exactly; but your words were capable of being twisted as Hervey has twisted them. Well, if Widow Anne really went to see her son—and from the lie about the borrowed clothes it looks like it—he may have given her the manuscript, so as to throw the blame on you."

"The murder?"

"No, no," said Archie testily. "Bolton did not expect to be murdered. But I really believe that he intended to fly with the emeralds, and hoped that when the manuscript was found in your

153

room you would be accused. The idea was suggested to him, I believe, by your visit to The Diver."

"What do you think, Miss Kendal?" asked Random nervously.

"I fancy that it is possible."

Sir Frank turned to the Peruvian.

"Don Pedro," he said proudly, "you have heard what Hervey says; do you believe that I am guilty?"

For answer De Gayangos took his daughter's hand and placed it in that of the young soldier.

"That will show you what I think," he said gravely.

"Thank you, sir," said Random, moved, and shook his future father-in-law heartily by the hand, while Donna Inez, throwing all restraint to the winds, kissed her lover exultingly on the check. In the midst of this scene Professor Braddock returned, looking very pleased.

"I have induced Hervey to hold his tongue for a few days until we can look into this matter," he said, rubbing his hands "that is, if you think it wise, all of you. Otherwise, I am quite willing to go myself to-morrow and tell the police."

"No," said Archie rapidly, "let us thresh out the matter ourselves. We will save Sir Frank's name from a police court slur at all events."

"I do not think there is any chance of Sir Frank being arrested," said Don Pedro politely; "the evidence is insufficient. And at the worst he can provide an alibi."

"I am not so sure of that," said Random anxiously. "I went to London certainly, but I did not go to any place where I am known. However," he added cheerfully, "I daresay I'll be able to defend myself. Still, the fact remains that we are no nearer to learning who killed Bolton than we were."

"I am sending Cockatoo to Pierside to-morrow to stop at the Sailor's Rest for a time," said Braddock quickly. "He will watch Hervey, and if there is anything suspicious about his movements, we shall soon know."

"And I turn amateur detective to-morrow and question Widow Anne," said Hope, after which remark he had to explain matters to Braddock, who had been out of the room when Mrs. Bolton's strange request had been discussed.

Meanwhile Donna Inez had been whispering to her lover and pointing to the mummy. Don Pedro followed her thoughts and guessed what she was saying. Random proved the truth of his guess by, turning to him.

"Do you really want to take back the mummy to Peru, sir?" he asked quietly.

154

"Certainly. Inca Caxas was my forefather. I do not wish to leave him in this place. His body must be restored to its tomb. All the Indians, who look upon me as their present Inca expect me to bring the body back. Although," added De Gayangos gravely, "I did not come to Europe to look for the mummy, as you know."

"Then I shall buy the mummy," said Random impetuously. "Professor, will you sell it to me?"

"Now that I have examined it thoroughly I shall be delighted," said the little man, "say for two thousand pounds."

"Not at all," interposed Don Pedro; "you mean one thousand."

"Of course he does," said Lucy quickly; "and the check must be paid to Archie, Sir Frank."

"To me! to me!" cried Braddock indignantly. "I insist."

"The money belongs to Archie," said Lucy obstinately. "You have seen what you desired to see, father and as Archie only lent you the money, it is only fair that he should have it again."

"Oh, let the Professor have it," said Hope good-naturedly.

"No! no! no!"

Random laughed.

"I shall make the check payable to you, Miss Kendal, and you can give it to whomsoever you choose," he said; "and now, as everything has been settled so far, I suggest that we should retire."

"Come to my rooms at the inn," said Don Pedro, opening the door. "I have much to say to you. Good night, Professor; to-morrow let us go to Pierside and see if we cannot get at the truth."

"And to-morrow," cried Random, "I shall send the check, sir."

When the company departed, Lucy had another wrangle with her father about the check. As Archie had gone away, she could speak freely, and pointed out that he was enjoying her mother's income and was about to marry Mrs. Jasher, who was rich.

"Therefore," argued Lucy, "you certainly do not want to keep poor Archie's money."

"He paid me that sum on condition that I consented to the wedding."

"He did nothing of the sort," she cried indignantly. "I am not going to be bought and sold in this manner. Archie lent you the money, and it must be returned. Don't force me to think you selfish, father."

The upshot of the argument was that Lucy got her own way, and the Professor rather unwillingly agreed to part with the mummy and restore the thousand pounds. But he regretted doing so, as he wished to get all the money he could to go towards his proposed Egyptian expedition, and Mrs. Jasher's fortune, as he assured his step-daughter, was not so large as might be thought. However, Lucy overruled him, and retired to bed, congratulating herself that she would soon be able to marry Hope. She was beginning to grow a trifle weary of the Professor's selfish nature, and wondered how her mother had put up with it for so long.

Next day Braddock did not go with Don Pedro to Pierside, as he was very busy in his museum. The Peruvian went alone, and Archie, after a morning's work at his easel, sought out Widow Anne to ask questions. Lucy and Donna Inez paid an afternoon visit to Mrs. Jasher and found her in bed, as she had caught a mild sort of influenza. They expected to find Sir Frank here, but it seemed that he had not called. Thinking that he was detained by military business, the girls thought nothing more of his absence, although Donna Inez was somewhat downcast.

But Random was detained in his quarters by a letter which had arrived by the mid-day host, and which surprised him not a little. The postmark was London, and the writing, evidently a disguised hand, was almost illegible in its crudeness. The contents ran as follows, and it will be noticed that there is neither date nor address, and that it is written in the third person:

"If Sir Frank Random wants his character to be cleared and all suspicion of murder to be removed from him, he can be completely exonerated by the writer, if he will pay the same five thousand pounds. If Sir Frank Random is willing to do this, let him appoint a meeting-place in London, and the writer will send a messenger to receive the money and to hand over the proofs which will clear Sir Frank Random. If Sir Frank Random plays the writer false, or communicates with the police, proofs will be forthcoming which will prove him to be guilty of Sidney Bolton's death, and which will bring him to the scaffold without any chance of escape. A couple of lines in the Agony Column of The Daily Telegraph, signed `Artillery,' and appointing a meeting-place, will suffice; but beware of treachery."

CHAPTER XXI

A STORY OF THE PAST

Mrs. Jasher's influenza proved to be very mild indeed.

When Donna Inez de Gayangos and Lucy paid a visit to her on the afternoon of the day succeeding the explanations in the museum, she was certainly in bed, and explained that she had been there since the Professor's visit on the previous day. Lucy was surprised at this, as she had left Mrs. Jasher perfectly well, and Braddock had not mentioned any ailment of the widow. But influenza, as Mrs. Jasher observed, was very rapid in its action, and she was always susceptible to disease from the fact that in Jamaica she had suffered from malaria. Still, she was feeling better and intended to rise from her bed on that evening, if only to lie on the couch in the pink drawing-room. Having thus detailed her reasons for being ill, the widow asked for news.

As no prohibition had been placed upon Lucy with regard to Hervey's visit and as Mrs. Jasher would be one of the family when she married the Professor, Miss Kendal had no hesitation in reporting all that had taken place. The narrative excited Mrs. Jasher, and she frequently interrupted with expressions of wonder. Even Donna Inez grew eloquent, and told the widow how she had defended Sir Frank against the American skipper.

"What a dreadfully wicked man!" said Mrs. Jasher, when in possession of all the facts. "I really believe that he did kill poor Sidney."

"No," said Lucy decisively, "I don't think that. He would have murdered him on board had he intended the crime, as he could have done so with more safety. He is as innocent as Sir Frank."

"And no one dare say a word against him," cried Donna Inez with flashing eyes.

"He has a good defender, my dear," said the widow, patting the girl's hand.

"I love him," said Donna Inez, as if that explained everything, and perhaps it did, so far as she was concerned.

Mrs. Jasher smiled indulgently, then turned for further information to Lucy.

"Can it be possible," she said, "that Widow Anne is guilty?"

"Oh, I don't think so. She would not murder her own son, especially when she was so very fond of him. Archie told me, just

157

before we came here, that he had called to see her. She still insists that Sidney borrowed the clothes, saying that Archie wanted them."

"What do you make of that, my dear?"

"Well," said Miss Kendal, pondering, "either Widow Anne herself was the woman who talked to Sidney through the Sailor's Rest window, and has invented this story to save herself, or Sidney did get the clothes and intended to use them as a disguise when he fled with the emeralds."

"In that case," said Mrs. Jasher, "the woman who talked through the window still remains a problem. Again, if Sidney Bolton intended to steal the emeralds, he could have done so in Malta, or on board the boat."

"No," said Lucy decisively. "The mummy was taken directly from the seller's house to the boat, and perhaps Sidney did not find the manuscript until he looked at the mummy. Then Captain Hervey kept an eye on Sidney, so that he could not open the mummy to steal the emeralds."

"Still, according to your own showing, Sidney looked at the actual mummy—he opened the mummy case, that is, else he could not have got the manuscript."

Lucy nodded.

"I think so, but of course we cannot be sure. But the packing case in which the mummy was stowed was placed in the hold of the steamer, and if Sidney had wished to steal the emeralds, he could not have done so without exciting Captain Hervey's suspicions."

"Then let us say that Sidney robbed the mummy when in the Sailor's Rest, and took the clothes he borrowed from his mother in order to fly in disguise. But what of the woman?"

Lucy shook her head.

"I cannot tell. We may learn more later. Don Pedro has gone to Pierside to search, and my father says that he will send Cockatoo there also to search."

"Well," sighed Mrs. Jasher wearily, "I hope that all this trouble will come to an end. That green mummy has proved most unlucky. Leave me now, dear girls, as I feel somewhat tired."

"Good-bye," said Lucy, kissing her. "I hope that you will be better this evening. Don't get up unless you feel quite able."

"Oh, I shall take my ease in the drawing-room."

"I thought you always called it the parlor," laughed the girl.

"Ah," Mrs. Jasher smiled, "you see I am practicing against the time when I shall be mistress of the Pyramids, You can't call that large room there a parlor," and she laughed weakly.

Altogether, Mrs. Jasher impressed both Lucy and Donna Inez with the fact that she was very weak and scarcely able, as she put it, to draw one leg after the other. Both the girls would have been surprised to see what a hearty meal Mrs. Jasher made that evening, when she was up and dressed. Perhaps she felt that her strength needed keeping up, but she certainly partook largely of the delicate dinner provided by Jane, who was a most excellent cook.

After dinner, Mrs. Jasher lay on a pink couch in the pink parlor by a splendid fire, for the night was cold and raw with a promise of rain. The widow had a small table at her elbow, on which stood a cup of coffee and a glass of liquor. The rose-colored curtains were drawn, the rose-shaded lamps were lighted, and the whole interior of the cottage looked very comfortable indeed. Mrs. Jasher, in a crocus-yellow tea-gown trimmed with rich black lace, reclined on her couch like Cleopatra in her barge. In the pink light she looked very well preserved, although her face wore an anxious expression. This was due to the fact that the mail had come in and the three letters brought by the postman had to do with creditors. Mrs. Jasher was always trying to make both ends meet, and had a hard struggle to keep her head above water. Certainly, since she had inherited the money of her brother, the Pekin merchant, she need not have looked so worried. But she did, and made no disguise of it, seeing that she was quite alone.

After a time she went to her desk and took out a bundle of bills and some other letters, also an account book and a bank book. Over these she pored for quite an hour. The clock struck nine before she looked up from this unpleasant task, and she found her financial position anything but satisfactory. With a weary sigh she rose and stared at herself in the mirror over the fireplace, frowning as she did so.

"Unless I can marry the Professor at once, I don't know what will happen to me," she mused gloomily. "I have managed very well so far, but things are coming to a crisis. These devils," she alluded to her creditors, "will not keep off much longer, and then the crash will come. I shall have to leave Gartley as poor as when I came, and there will be nothing left but the old nightmare life of despair and horror. I am getting older every day, and this is my last chance of getting married. I must force the Professor to have a speedy marriage. I must! I must!" and she began to pace the tiny room in a frenzy of terror and well-founded alarm.

As she was trying to calm herself and succeeding very badly, Jane entered the room with a card. It proved to be that of Sir Frank Random.

"It is rather a late hour for a visit," said Mrs. Jasher to the servant. "However, I feel so bored, that perhaps he will cheer me up. Ask him to come in."

When Jane left, she stood still for a moment or so, trying to think why the young man had called at so untoward an hour. But when his footsteps were heard approaching the door, she swept the books and the bills and the letters into the desk and locked it quickly. When Random appeared at the door, she was just leaving the desk to greet him, and no one would have taken the smiling, plump, well-preserved woman for the creature who lately had looked so haggard and careworn.

"I am glad to see you, Sir Frank," said Mrs. Jasher, nodding in a familiar manner. "Sit down in this very comfortable chair, and Jane shall bring you some coffee and kummel."

"No, thank you," said Random in his usual stiff way, but very politely. "I have just left the mess, where I had a good dinner."

Mrs. Jasher nodded, and sank again on the couch, which was opposite the chair which she had selected for her visitor.

"I see you are in mess kit," she said gayly; "quite a glorified creature to appear in my poor little parlor. Why are you not with Donna Inez? I have heard all about your engagement from Lucy. She was here to-day with Senorita De Gayangos."

"So I believe," said Random, still stiffly; "but you see I was anxious to come and see you."

"Ah!" said Mrs. Jasher equably, "you heard that I was ill. Yes; I have been in bed ever since yesterday afternoon, until a couple of hours ago. But I am now better. My dinner has done me good. Pass me that fan, please. The fire is so hot."

Sir Frank did as he was told, and she held the feather fan between her face and the fire, while he stared at her, wondering what to say.

"Don't you find this atmosphere very stuffy?" he remarked at length. "It would be a good thing to have the windows open."

Mrs. Jasher shrieked.

"My dear boy, are you mad? I have a touch of the influenza, and an open window would bring about my death. Why, this room is delightfully comfortable."

"There is such a strong perfume about it," sniffed Random pointedly.

"I should think you knew that scent by this time, Sir Frank. I use no other and never have done. Smell!" and she passed a flimsy handkerchief of lace.

Random took the handkerchief and placed it to his nostrils. As he did so a strange expression of triumph crept into his eyes.

"I think you told me once that it was a Chinese perfume," he said, returning the handkerchief.

Mrs. Jasher nodded, well pleased.

160

"I get it from a friend of my late husband who is in the British Embassy at Pekin. No one uses it but me."

"But surely some other person uses it?"

"Not in England; and I do not know why you should say so. It is a specialty of mine. Why," she added playfully, "if you met me in the dark you should know me, by this scent."

"Can you swear that no one else has ever used this perfume?" asked Random.

Mrs. Jasher lifted her penciled eyebrows.

"I do not know why you should ask me to swear," she said quietly, "but I assure you that I keep this perfume which comes from China to myself. Not even Lucy Kendal has it, although she greatly desired some. We women are selfish in some things, my dear man. It's a most delicious perfume."

"Yes," said Sir Frank, staring at her, "and very strong."

"What do you mean by that?"

"Nothing. Only I should think that such a perfume would be good for the cold you contracted by going to London last night."

Mrs. Jasher turned suddenly pale under her rouge, and her hand clenched the fan so tightly as to break the handle.

"I have not been to London for quite a month," she faltered. "What a strange remark!"

"A true one," said the baronet, fumbling in the pocket of his jacket. "You went to London last night by the seven o'clock train to post this," and he held out the anonymous letter.

The widow, now quite pale, and looking years older, sat up on the couch with a painful effort, which suggested old age.

"I don't understand," she said, trying to speak calmly. "I was not in London, and I did not post any letter. If you came here to insult me—"

"There can be no insult in asking a few questions," said Random, throwing aside his stiffness and speaking decisively. "I received this letter, which bears a London postmark, by the mid-day post. The handwriting is disguised, and there is neither address nor signature nor date. You manufactured your communication very cleverly, Mrs. Jasher, but you forgot that the Chinese perfume might betray you."

"The perfume! the perfume!" Mrs. Jasher gasped and saw in a moment how the late conversation had led her to fall into a trap.

"The letter retains traces of the perfume you use," went on the baronet relentlessly. "I have a remarkably keen sense of smell, and, as scent is a most powerful aid to memory, I speedily recollected that you used this especial perfume. You told me a few moments ago that no one else used it, and so you have proved the truth of my statement that this letter"—he tapped it—"is written by you."

"It's a lie—a mistake," stuttered Mrs. Jasher, now at bay and looking dangerous. Her society veneer was stripped off, and the adventuress pure and simple came to the surface.

Indignant at the way in which she had deceived everyone, and having much at stake, Random did not spare her.

"It is not a mistake," he insisted; "neither is it a lie. When I became aware that you must have written the letter, I drove at once to Jessum to see if you had gone to London, as you had posted it there. I learned from the station master and from a porter that you went to town by the seven o'clock train and returned by the midnight."

Mrs. Jasher leaped to her feet.

"They could not recognize me. I wore—" Then she stopped, confused at having so plainly betrayed herself.

"You wore a veil. All the same, Mrs. Jasher, you are too well known hereabouts for anyone to fail to recognize you. Besides, your remark just now proves that I am right. You wrote this blackmailing letter, and I demand an explanation."

"I have none to give," muttered the woman fiercely, and fighting every inch.

"If you refuse to explain to me you shall to the police," said Sir Frank, rising and making for the door.

Mrs. Jasher flung herself forward and clung to him.

"For God's sake, don't!"

"Then you will explain? You will tell me?"

"Tell you what?"

"Who murdered Sidney Bolton."

"I do not know. I swear I do not know," she cried feverishly.

"That is ridiculous," said Random coldly. "You say in this letter that you can hang me or save me. As you know that I am innocent, you must be aware who is guilty."

"It's all bluff. I know nothing," said Mrs. Jasher, releasing his arm and throwing herself on the couch. "I only wished to get money."

"Five thousand pounds—eh? Rather a large order," sneered Random, replacing the letter in his pocket. "You would not ask that sum for nothing: you must be aware of the truth. I suspected many people, Mrs. Jasher, but never you."

The woman rose and flung out her arms.

"No," she said in a deep voice, and fighting like a rat in a corner. "I tricked you all down here. Sir Frank, I will tell you the truth."

"About the murder?"

162

"I know nothing of that. About myself."

Random shrugged his shoulders.

"I'll hear about yourself first," he said. "I can learn details concerning the murder later. Go on."

"I know nothing of the murder or of the theft of the emeralds—"

"Yet you hid the mummy in this house, and afterwards placed it in your arbor to be found by the Professor, for some reason."

"I know nothing about that either," muttered Mrs. Jasher doggedly, and with very white lips. "That letter you have traced to me is all bluff."

"Then you admit having written it?"

"Yes," she said sullenly. "You know too much, and it is useless for me to deny the truth in the face of the evidence you bring against me. I would fight though," she added, raising her head like a snake its crest, "if I was not sick and tired of fighting."

"Fighting?"

"Yes, against trouble and worry and money difficulties and creditors. Oh," she struck her breast, "what do you know of life, you rich, easy-going man? I have been in the depths, and not through my own fault. I had a bad mother, a bad husband. I was dragged in the mire by those who should have helped me to rise. I have starved for days; I have wept for years; in all God's earth there is no more miserable a creature than I am."

"Kindly talk without so much melodrama," said Random cruelly.

"Ah," Mrs. Jasher sat down and locked her hands together, "you don't believe me. I daresay you don't understand, for life, real life, is a sealed book to you. It is useless for me to appeal to your sympathy, for you are so very ignorant. Let us stick to facts. What do you wish to know?"

"Who killed Sidney Bolton: who has the emeralds."

"I can't tell you. Listen! With my past life you have nothing to do. I will commence from the time I came down here. I had just lost my husband, and I managed to scrape together a few hundred pounds—oh, quite in a respectable way, I assure you," she added scoffingly, on seeing her listener wince. "I came here to try and live quietly, and, if possible, to secure a rich husband. I knew that the Fort was here and thought that I might marry an officer. However, the Professor's position attracted me, and I decided to marry him. I am engaged, and but for your cleverness in tracing that letter I should be Mrs. Braddock within a very short time. I have exhausted all my money. I am deeply, in debt. I cannot hold out longer."

"But the money you inherited—"

"That is all bluff also. I never had a brother. I inherit no money.

163

I know nothing of Pekin, save that a friend of mine sends that scent to me as a yearly Christmas present. I am an adventuress, but perhaps not so bad as you think me. Lucy and Donna Inez have heard no wickedness from my lips. I have always been a good woman in one sense—a moral woman, that is—and I did wish to marry the Professor and live a happy life. Seeing that I was at the end of my resources, and that Professor Braddock expected a legacy with me before marriage, I looked round to, see how I could get the money. I heard that you were accused by Captain Hervey, and so last night I wrote that letter and posted it in London, thinking that you would yield to save yourself from arrest."

Random laughed cynically.

"You must have thought me weak," he muttered.

"I did," said Mrs. Jasher frankly. "To tell you the truth, I thought that you were a fool. But by tracing that letter and withstanding my demand, you have proved yourself to be more clever than I took you to be. Well, that is all. I know nothing of the murder. My letter is sheer bluff to extort from you five thousand pounds. Had you paid I should have passed it off to the Professor as the money left to me by my brother. But now—"

"Now," said Random, rising to go, "I shall tell what you have told me to the Professor, and—"

"And hand me over to the police," said Mrs. Jasher, shrugging her plump shoulders, "Well, I expected that. Yet I fancied for old times' sake that you might have been more lenient."

"We were never anything but acquaintances, Mrs. Jasher," said Random coldly, "so I fail to see why you should expect mercy after the way in which you have behaved. You expect to blackmail me, and yet go free. I must punish you somehow, so I shall tell Professor Braddock, as you certainly cannot marry him. But I shall not hand you over to the police."

"You won't?" Mrs. Jasher stared, scarcely able to believe her ears.

"No. Give me a day to think over matters, and I shall arrange what to do with you. I think there is some good in you, Mrs. Jasher, and so I shall see if I can't assist you. In the meantime I shall have your cottage watched, so that you may not run away."

"In that case, you may as well hand me over to the police," she said bitterly.

"Not at all," rejoined Random coolly. "I can trust my servant, who is stupid but honest and is devoted to me. I'll see that everything is kept quiet. But if you attempt to run away I shall have you arrested for blackmail. You understand?"

"Yes. You are treating me very well," she gasped. "When shall I see you?"

"To-morrow evening. I must talk the matter over with Braddock. To-morrow I shall arrange what to do, and probably I shall give you a chance of leading a new life in some other part of the world. What do you say?"

"I accept. Indeed, there is nothing else left for me to do."

"That is an ungrateful speech," said Random severely.

"I daresay. However, we can talk of gratitude to-morrow. Meanwhile, please leave me."

Sir Frank went to the door and there paused.

"Remember," he said distinctly, "that your cottage is being watched. Try to escape and I shall have you arrested."

Mrs. Jasher groaned and buried her face in the sofa cushion.

CHAPTER XXII

A WEDDING PRESENT

Mrs. Jasher had thought Random exceedingly clever in acting as he had done to trap her. She would have thought him still more clever had she known that he trusted to the power of suggestion to prevent her from trying to escape. Sir Frank had not the slightest intention of setting his soldier-servant to watch, as such was not the duty for which such servants are hired. But having impressed firmly on the adventuress's mind that he would act in this way, he departed, quite certain that the woman would not attempt to run away. Although no one was watching the cottage, Mrs. Jasher, believing what had been told her, would think that sharp eyes were on her doors and windows day and night, and would firmly believe that if she tried to get away she would be captured forthwith by the Pierside police, or perhaps by the village constable. Like an Eastern enchanter, the baronet had placed a spell on the cottage, and it acted admirably. Mrs. Jasher, although longing to escape and hide herself, remained where she was, cowed by a spy who did not exist.

The next day Random went to the Pyramids as soon as his duties permitted and saw the Professor. To the prospective bridegroom he explained all that had happened, and displayed the anonymous letter, with an account of how he had proved Mrs. Jasher to be the writer. Braddock's hair could not stand on end, as he had none, but he lost his temper completely, and raged up and down the museum in a way which frightened Cockatoo out of his barbaric wits. When more quiet he sat down to discuss the matter, and promptly demanded that Mrs. Jasher should be handed over to the police. But he might have guessed that Sir Frank would refuse to follow this extreme advice.

"She has acted badly, I admit," said the young man. "All the same, I think she is a better woman than you may think, Professor."

"Think! think! think!" shouted the fiery little man, getting up once more to trot up and down like an infuriated poodle. "I think she is a bad woman, a wicked woman. To deceive me into thinking her rich and—"

"But surely, Professor, you wished to marry her also for love?"

"Nothing of the sort, sir: nothing of the sort. I leave love and such-like trash to those like yourself and Hope, who have nothing else to think about."

"But a marriage without love—"

"Pooh! pooh! pooh! Don't argue with me, Random. Love is all moonshine. I did not love my first wife—Lucy's mother—and yet we were very happy. Had I made Mrs. Jasher my second, we should have got on excellently, provided the money was forthcoming for my Egyptian expedition. What am I to do now, I ask you, Random? Even the thousand pounds you pay for the mummy goes back to that infernal Hope because of Lucy's silly ideas. I have nothing— absolutely nothing, and that tomb is amongst those Ethiopian hills, I swear, waiting to be opened. Oh, what a chance I have missed!— what a chance! But I shall see Mrs. Jasher myself. She knows about this murder."

"She declares that she does not."

"Don't tell me! don't tell me!" vociferated the Professor. "She would not have written that letter had she known nothing."

"That was bluff. I explained all that."

"Bluff be hanged!" cried Braddock, only he used a more vigorous word. "I do not believe that she would have dared to act on such a slight foundation. I shall see her myself this very afternoon and force her to confess. In one way or another I shall find the assassin and make him disgorge those emeralds under the penalty of being hanged. Then I can sell them and finance my Egyptian expedition."

"But you forget, Professor, that the emeralds, when found, belong to Don Pedro."

"They don't," rasped the little man, turning purple with rage. "I refuse to let him have them. I bought the mummy, and the contents of the mummy, including those emeralds. They are mine."

"No," said Random sharply. "I buy the mummy, from you, so they pass into my possession and belong to De Gayangos. I shall give them to him."

"You'll have to find them first," said Braddock savagely; "and as to the mummy, you shan't have it. I decline to sell it. So there!"

"If you don't," said Random very distinctly, "Don Pedro will bring an action against you, and Captain Hervey will be called as a witness to prove that the mummy was stolen."

"Don Pedro hasn't the money," said Braddock triumphantly; "he can't pay lawyer's fees."

"But I can," rejoined the young man very dryly. "As I am going to marry Donna Inez, it is only just that I should help my future father-in-law in every way. He has a romantic feeling about this relic of poor humanity and wishes to take it back to Peru. He shall do so."

"And what about me?—what about me?"

"Well," said Random, speaking slowly with the intention of still further irritating the little man, whose selfishness annoyed him, "if I were you I should marry Mrs. Jasher and settle down quietly in this house to live on what income you have."

Braddock turned purple again and spluttered.

"How dare you make a proposition like that to me, sir?" he bellowed. "You ask me to marry this low woman, this adventuress, this—this—this—" Words failed him.

Of course Random had no intention of advising such a marriage, although he did not think so badly of Mrs. Jasher as did the Professor. But the little man was so venomous that the young man took a delight in stirring him up, using the widow's name as a red rag to this particular bull.

"I do not think Mrs. Jasher is a bad woman," he remarked.

"What! what! what! After what she has done? Blackmail! blackmail! blackmail!"

"That is bad, I admit, but she has failed to get what she wanted, and, after all, you indirectly are the cause of her writing that blackmailing letter."

"I am?—I am? How dare you?"

"You see, she wanted to get five thousand out of me as her dowry."

"Yes, and told me lies about her damned brother who was a Pekin merchant, when after all he never existed."

"Oh, I don't defend that," said Random coolly. "Mrs. Jasher has behaved badly on the whole. Still, Professor, I think there is good in her, as I said before. She evidently had bad parents and a bad husband; but, so far as I can gather, she is not an immoral woman. The poor wretch only came here to try and drag herself out of the mire. If she had married you I feel sure that she would have made you a most excellent wife."

The Professor was in such a rage that he suddenly became calm.

"Of course you talk absolute rubbish," he said caustically. "Had I my way this woman would be whipped at a cart's tail for the shameful way in which she has deceived us all. However, I shall see her to-day and make her confess who murdered Bolton."

"Don Pedro will be greatly obliged if you do. He wants those emeralds."

"So do I, and if I get them I shall keep them," snapped Braddock; "and if you haven't anything more to say you can leave me. I'm busy."

As there was nothing more to be done with the choleric little man, Sir Frank took the hint and departed. He went forthwith to the Warrior Inn to see Don Pedro and also Donna Inez. But it so happened that the girl had gone to the Pyramids on a visit to Miss Kendal, and Random was sorry that he had missed her. However, it was just as well, as he could now talk freely to De Gayangos. To him he related the whole story of Mrs. Jasher, and discovered that the Peruvian also, as Braddock had done, insisted that Mrs. Jasher knew the truth.

"She would not have written that letter if she did not know it," said Don Pedro.

"Then you think that she should be arrested?"

"No. We can deal with this matter ourselves. At present she is quite safe, as she certainly will not leave her cottage, seeing that she thinks it is being watched. Let us permit Braddock to interview her, and see what he can learn. Then we can discuss the matter and come to a decision."

Random nodded absently.

"I wonder if Mrs. Jasher was the woman who talked to Bolton through the window?" he remarked.

"It is not impossible. Although that does not explain why Bolton borrowed a female disguise from this mother."

"Mrs. Jasher might have worn it."

"That would argue some understanding between Bolton and Mrs. Jasher, and a knowledge of the manuscript before Bolton left for Malta. We know that he could only have seen the manuscript for the first time at Malta. It was evidently stowed away in the swathings of the mummy by my father, who forgot all about it when he gave me the original."

"Hervey forgot also. I wonder if that is true?"

"I am certain it is," said Don Pedro emphatically, "for, if Hervey, or Vasa, or whatever you like to call him, had found that manuscript and had got it translated, he certainly would have opened the mummy and have secured the emeralds. No, Sir Frank, I believe that his theory is partly true. Bolton intended to run away with the emeralds, and send the empty mummy to Professor Braddock; for, if you remember, he arranged that the landlord of the Sailor's Rest should forward the case next morning, even if he happened to be away. Bolton intended to be away—with the emeralds."

"Then you do not believe that Hervey placed the manuscript in my room?"

"He declared most emphatically that he did not," said Don Pedro, "when at Pierside yesterday I went to the Sailor's Rest and saw him. He told Braddock only the other day that he had lost his chance of a sailing vessel, and, as yet, had not got another one. But when he returned to Pierside he found a letter waiting him—so he told me—giving him command of a four thousand ton tramp steamer called The Firefly. He is to sail at once—to-morrow, I believe."

"Then what is he going to do about this murder business?"

"He can do nothing at present, as, if he remains in Pierside, he will lose his new command. To-morrow he drops down stream, but meantime he intends to write out the whole story of the theft of the mummy. I have promised to give him fifty pounds for doing so, as I want to get back the mummy, free of charge, from Braddock."

"I think Braddock will stick to the mummy in any event," said Random grimly.

"Not when Hervey writes out his evidence. He will not have it completed by the time he sails, as he is very busy. But he has promised to send off a boat to the jetty near the Fort to-morrow evening, when he is dropping down stream. I shall be there with fifty pounds in gold."

"Supposing he fails to stop or send the boat?"

"Then he will not get his fifty pounds," retorted Don Pedro. "The man is a rascal, and deserves prison rather than reward, but since the mummy was stolen by him thirty years back, he alone can prove my ownership."

"But why take all this trouble?" argued the baronet. "I can buy the mummy from Braddock."

"No," said Don Pedro. "I have a right to my own property."

Random lingered until late in the afternoon and until darkness fell, as he was anxious to see Donna Inez. But she did not appear until late. Meanwhile Archie Hope put in an appearance, having come to see Don Pedro with an account of his interview with Widow Anne. Before coming to the inn he had called on Professor Braddock, and from him had heard all about the wickedness of Mrs. Jasher. His surprise was very great.

"I should not have believed it," he declared. "Poor woman!"

"Ah," said Random, rather pleased, "you are more merciful than the Professor, Hope. He calls her a bad woman."

"Humph! I don't think that Braddock is so good that he can afford to throw a stone," said Archie rather sourly. "Mrs. Jasher has not behaved well, but I should like to hear her complete story before judging. There must be a lot of good in her, or Lucy, who has been with her a great deal, would have found her out long ago. I go by a woman's judgment of a woman. But Mrs. Jasher must have been anxious to marry."

"She was; as Professor Braddock knows," said Random quickly.

"I am not thinking of that so much as of what Widow Anne told me."

"Oh," said Don Pedro, looking up from where he was seated, "so you have seen that old woman? What does she say about the clothes?"

"She sticks to her story. Sidney, she declares, borrowed the clothes to give to me for a model. Now, I never asked Bolton to do this, so I fancy the disguise must have been intended for himself, or for Mrs. Jasher."

"But what had Mrs. Jasher to do with him?" demanded Random sharply.

"Well, it's odd," replied Hope slowly, "but Mrs. Bolton declares that her son was in love with Mrs. Jasher, and when he returned from Malta intended to marry her."

"Impossible!" cried Sir Frank. "She engaged herself to Braddock."

"But only after Bolton's death, remember."

Don Pedro nodded.

"That is true. But what you say, Mr. Hope, proves the truth of Hervey's theory."

"In what way?"

"Mrs. Jasher, as we know from what Random told us, wanted money. She would not marry a man who was poor. Bolton was poor, but of course the emeralds would make him wealthy, as they are of immense value. Probably he intended to steal them in order to marry this woman. This implicates Mrs. Jasher in the crime."

"Yes," assented Sir Frank, nodding. "But as Bolton did not know that the emeralds existed before he bought the mummy in Malta, I do not see why he should borrow a disguise beforehand for Mrs. Jasher to meet him at the Sailor's Rest."

"The thing is easily settled," said Hope impatiently. "Let us both go to Mrs. Jasher's this evening, and insist upon the truth being told. If she confesses about her secret engagement to Sidney Bolton, she may admit that the clothes were borrowed for her."

"And she may admit also that she placed the manuscript in my room," said Sir Frank after a pause. "Hervey did not place it there, but it is just possible that Mrs. Jasher, having got it from Bolton when she talked to him through the window, may have done so."

"Nonsense!" said Hope with vigorous commonsense. "Mrs. Jasher would be spotted in a moment if she had gone to your quarters. She had to pass the sentry, remember. Then, again, we have not yet proved that she was the woman in Mrs. Bolton's clothes who spoke through the window. That can all be settled if we speak to her this evening."

"Very good." Random glanced at his watch. "I must get back.

Don Pedro, will you tell Inez that I shall come in this evening? We can then talk further about these matters. Hope?"

"I shall stop here, as I wish to consult Don Pedro."

Random nodded and took a reluctant departure. He dearly wished, as an engaged lover should, to remain on the chance that Donna Inez might return, but duty called him and he was forced to obey.

The night was very dark, although it was not particularly late. But there was no rain, and Random walked rapidly through the village and down the road to the Fort. He caught a glimpse of the lights of Mrs. Jasher's cottage twinkling in the distance, and smiled grimly as he thought of the invisible spell he had placed thereon. No doubt Mrs. Jasher was shivering in her Louis Quinze shoes at the idea of being watched. But then, she deserved that much punishment at least, as Random truly thought.

When entering the Fort, the sentry saluted as usual, and Random was about to pass, when the man stepped forward, holding out a brown paper package.

"Please, sir, I found this in my sentry box," he said, saluting.

Sir Frank took the packet.

"Who placed it there? and why do you give it to me?" he demanded in surprise.

"Please, sir, it's directed to you, sir, and I don't know who put it in my box, sir. I was on duty, sir, and I 'spose someone must have dropped it on the floor of the box, sir, when I was at the other end of my beat, sir. It was as dark as this, sir, and I saw nothing and heard nothing. When I come back, sir, I stepped into the box out of the rain and felt it with my feet. I struck a light, sir, and found it was for you."

Sir Frank slipped the package into his pocket and went away after a grim word or so to the sentry, advising him to be more on the alert. He was puzzled to think who had left the packet in the sentry box, and curious to know what it contained. As soon as he got to his own room, he cut the string which bound loosely the brown paper. Then, in the lamplight, there rolled out from the carelessly-tied parcel a glorious sea-green emerald of great size, radiating light like a sun. A scrap of white paper lay in the brown wrapping. On it was written, "A wedding gift for Sir Frank Random."

CHAPTER XXIII

JUST IN TIME

Of all the surprises in connection with the tragedy of the green mummy, this was surely the greatest. Sidney Bolton had undoubtedly been murdered for the sake of the emeralds, and the assassin had escaped with the spoil, for which he had sold his soul. Yet here was one of the jewels returned anonymously to Random, who could pass on the same to its rightful owner. In the midst of his amazement Sir Frank could not help chuckling when he thought how enraged Professor Braddock would be at Don Pedro's good fortune. At the eleventh hour, as it were, the Peruvian had got back his own, or at least a portion of his own.

Placing the emerald in his drawer, Random gave orders to his servant that the sentry, when off duty, should be brought before him. Just as Random finished dressing for mess—and he dressed very early, so as to devote his entire attention to solving this new problem—the soldier who had been on guard appeared. But he could tell nothing more than he had already related. When doing sentry-go immediately outside the gate of the Fort, the packet had been slipped into the box, while the man was at the far end of his beat. It was quite dark when this was done, and the soldier confessed that he had not heard a sound, much less had he seen anyone. The person who had brought the glorious gem had watched his opportunity, and, soft-footed as a cat, had stolen forward in the darkness to drop the precious parcel on the floor of the sentry box. There the man had found it by the feel of his feet, when he stepped in some time later to escape a shower. But what time had elapsed from the placing of the parcel to its discovery by the sentry it was impossible to say. It must, however, as Random calculated, have been within the hour, since, before then, it would not have been dark enough to hide the approach of the person, whether male or female, who carried a king's ransom in the brown paper parcel.

At first Random was inclined to place the sentry under arrest for having failed so much in his duty as to allow anyone to approach so near the Fort; but, as he had already reprimanded the man, and, moreover, wished to keep the fact of the recovered jewel quiet, he simply dismissed him. When alone, he sat down before the fire, wondering who could have dared so very greatly, and for what reason the emerald had been handed to him. If it had been sent to

Don Pedro, or even to Professor Braddock, it would have been much more reasonable.

It first occurred to him that Mrs. Jasher, out of gratitude for the way in which he had treated her, had sent him the jewel. Remembering his former experience, he smelt the parcel, but could detect no sign of the famous Chinese scent which had proved a clue to the letter. Of course the direction on the packet and the inscribed slip of paper were in feigned handwriting, so he could gather nothing from that. Still, he did not think that Mrs. Jasher had sent the emerald. She was desperately hard up, and if she had become possessed of the gem by murder—presuming her to have been the woman who talked to Bolton through the window—she assuredly would have sold it to supply her own needs. Certainly, if guilty, she would still possess the other emerald, of equal value; but undoubtedly, had she risked her neck to gain a fortune, she would have kept the entire plunder which was likely to cost her so dear. No; whomsoever it was who had repented at the eleventh hour, Mrs. Jasher was not the person.

Perhaps Widow Anne was the woman who had talked through the window, and who had restored the emerald. But that was impossible, since Mrs. Bolton habitually took more liquor than was good for her, and would not have the nerve to deliver the jewel, much less commit the crime, the more especially as the victim was her own son. Of course she might have found out Sidney's scheme to run away with the jewels, and so would have claimed her share. But if she had been in Pierside on that evening—and her presence in Gartley had been sworn to by three or four cronies—she would have guessed who had strangled her boy. If so, not all the jewels in the world would have prevented her denouncing the criminal. With all her faults—and they were many—Mrs. Bolton was a good mother, and looked upon Sidney as the pride and joy of her somewhat dissipated life. Mrs. Bolton was certainly as innocent as Mrs. Jasher.

There remained Hervey. Random laughed aloud when the name came into his puzzled head. That buccaneer was the last person to surrender his plunder or to feel compunction in committing a crime. Once the skipper got his grip on two jewels, worth endless money, he would never let them go—not even one of them. Arguing thus, it seemed that Hervey was out of the running, and Random could think of no one else. In this dilemma he remembered that two heads were better than one, and, before going into dinner, he sent a note to Archie Hope, asking him to come to the Fort as speedily as possible.

Sir Frank was somewhat dull at dinner on that evening, and scarcely responded to the joking remarks of his brother officers.

174

These jocularly put his preoccupation down to love, for it was an open secret that the baronet admired the fair Peruvian, although no one as yet knew that Random was legally engaged with Don Pedro's consent. The young man good-humoredly stood all the chaff hurled at him, but seized the opportunity to slip away to his quarters as soon as coffee came on the table and the smoking began. It was nine o'clock before he returned to his room, and here he found Hope waiting for him impatiently.

"I see you have been dining at the Pyramids," said Random, seeing that Hope was in evening dress.

Archie nodded.

"Yes. I don't put on this kit to have my humble chop at my lodgings. But the Professor asked me to dinner to talk over matters."

"What does he say?" asked Random, looking for the cigarette box.

"Oh, he is very angry with Mrs. Jasher, and considers that she has swindled him. He called to see her this afternoon, and—so he says—had a stormy interview with her."

"I don't wonder at that, if he speaks as he generally does," said the other grimly, and pushing along the cigarettes, "There you are! The whisky and soda are on yonder table. Make yourself comfortable, and tell me what the Professor intends to do."

"Well," said Archie, turning half round from the side table where he was pouring out the whisky, "he had already started action, by sending Cockatoo to live at the Sailor's Rest and spy on Hervey."

"What rubbish! Hervey is, going away to-morrow in The Firefly, bound for Algiers. Nothing is to be learned from him."

"So I told the Professor," said Hope, returning to the armchair near the fire, "and I mentioned that Don Pedro had induced the skipper to write out a full account of the theft of the mummy from Lima thirty years ago. I also said that the signed paper would be handed in at the Gartley jetty when The Firefly came down stream to-morrow night."

"Humph! And what did Braddock say to that?"

"Nothing much. He merely stated that whatever Hervey said toward proving the ownership of your future father-in-law, that he intended to stick to the embalmed corpse of Inca Caxas, and also that he intended to claim the emeralds when they turned up."

Random rose and went to the drawer of his desk.

"I am afraid he has lost one emerald, at all events," he said, unlocking the drawer.

"What's that?" said Hope sharply. "Why did you—oh, gosh!" He jumped up with an amazed look as Random held up the magnificent gem, from which streamed vividly green flames in the mellow lamplight. "Oh, gosh!" gasped the artist again. "Where the devil did you get that?"

"I sent for you to tell you," said Sir Frank, giving the jewel into his friend's hand and coming back to his seat. "It was found in the sentry box."

Hope stared at the great jewel and then at the soldier.

"What do you mean by that?" he demanded. "How the dickens could it be found in a sentry box? You must be making a mistake."

"Not a bit of it. It was found on the floor of the box by the sentry, as I tell you, and I have sent to consult with you as to how the deuce it got there."

"Hervey," muttered Archie, fascinated by the gem.

Random shrugged his square shoulders.

"Catch that Yankee Shylock returning anything he got his grip on, even as a wedding present."

"A wedding present," said Hope, more at sea than ever. "If you don't mind giving me details, old chap, my head would buzz less."

"I rather think that it will buzz more," said Random dryly, and, producing the brown paper in which the gem had been wrapped, and the inscribed paper found within, he related all that had happened.

Archie listened quietly and did not interrupt, but the puzzled look on his face grew more pronounced.

"Well," ended Random, seeing that no remark was made when he had finished, "what do you think?"

"Lord knows! I'll go out of my mind if these sort of things come along. I am a simple sort of chap, and have no use for mysteries which beat all the detective stories I have ever read. That sort of thing is all very well in fiction, but in real life—humph! What are you going to do?"

"Give back the emerald to Don Pedro."

"Of course, though, it is given to you for a wedding present. And then?"

"Then"—Random stared into the fire—"I don't know. I asked you in to assist me."

"Willingly; but how?"

Random pondered for a few moments.

"Who sent that emerald to me, do you think?" he asked, looking squarely at the artist.

Hope meditatively turned the jewel in his long fingers.

"Why not ask Mrs. Jasher?" he suggested suddenly.

"No!" Sir Frank shook his head. "I fancied it might be her, but it cannot be. If she is guilty—as she must be, should she have sent the

176

emerald—she would not part with her plunder when she is so hard up. I am beginning to believe, Hope, that what she said was true about the letter."

"How do you mean exactly?"

"That the letter was mere bluff and that she really knows nothing about the crime. By the way, did Braddock learn anything?"

"Not a thing. He merely said that the two of them fought. I expect Braddock stormed and Mrs. Jasher retorted. Both of them have too much tongue-music to come to any understanding. By the way—to echo, your own phrase—you had better put away this gem or I shall be strangling you myself in order to gain possession of it. The mere sight of that gorgeous color tempts me beyond my strength."

Random laughed and locked the jewel in his drawer. Hope suggested that with such a flimsy lock it was unsafe, but the baronet shook his head.

"It is safer here than in a woman's jewel case," he asserted. "No one looks to my drawer, and certainly no one would expect to find a crown jewel of this description in my quarters. Well," he came back to his seat, slipping his keys into his trouser pocket, "the whole thing puzzles me."

"Why not do as I suggest and go to Mrs. Jasher? In any case you are going there to-night, are you not?"

"Yes. I want to decide what to do about the woman. I had intended to go alone, but as you are here you may as well come also."

"I shall be delighted. What do you intend to do?"

"Help her," said Random briefly.

"She doesn't deserve it," replied Hope, lighting a fresh cigarette.

"Does anyone ever deserve anything?" asked Sir Frank cynically. "What does Miss Kendal think of the business? I suppose Braddock told her. He has too long a tongue to keep anything to himself."

"He told her at dinner, when I was present. Lucy is quite on your side. She says that she had known Mrs. Jasher for months and that there is good in her, although I am bound to say that Lucy was a trifle shocked."

"Does she want Mrs. Jasher to marry her father now?"

"Her step-father," corrected Archie immediately. "No, that is out of the question. But she would like Mrs. Jasher to be helped out of her difficulties and have a fair start. It was only by the greatest diplomacy that I prevented Lucy going to see the wretched woman this evening."

"Why did you prevent her?"

Archie colored.

"I daresay I am a trifle prudish," he replied, "but after what has happened I do not wish Lucy to associate with Mrs. Jasher. Do you blame me?"

"No, I don't. All the same, I don't think that Mrs. Jasher is an immoral woman by any means."

"Perhaps not; but we needn't discuss her character, as we know precious little of her past, and she no doubt told you the story that best suited herself. I think it will be best to make her tell all she knows this evening, and then send her away with a sum of money in her pocket to begin a new life."

"I shall help her certainly," said Random, with his eyes on the fire, "but can't say exactly how. It is my opinion that the poor wretch is more sinned against than sinning."

"You are a soldier with a conscience, Random."

The other laughed.

"Why shouldn't a soldier have a conscience? Do you take your idea of officers from the lady novelist, who makes us out to be all idle idiots?"

"Not exactly. All the same, many a man would not take the trouble to behave as you are doing to this unlucky woman."

"Any man, who was a man, whether soldier or civilian, would help such a poor creature. And I believe, Hope, that you will help her also."

The artist leaped to his feet impulsively.

"Of course. I'm with you right along, as Hervey would say. But first, before deciding what we shall do to set Mrs. Jasher on her legs again, let us hear what she has to say."

"She can say nothing more than she has said," remonstrated Random.

"I don't believe that," replied Hope, reaching for his overcoat. "You may choose to believe that the letter was the outcome of bluff. But I really and truly think that Mrs. Jasher is in the know. What is more, I believe that Bolton got her those clothes, and that she was the woman who talked to him—went there to see how the little scheme was progressing."

"If I thought that," said Random coldly, "I would not help Mrs. Jasher."

"Oh, yes, you would. The greater the sinner the more need she or he has of help, you know, my dear fellow. But get your coat on, and let us toddle. I don't suppose we need pistols."

Sir Frank laughed, as, aided by the artist, he struggled into his military greatcoat.

"I don't suppose that Mrs. Jasher will be dangerous," he

remarked. "We'll get what we can out of her, and then arrange what is best to be done to recoup her fallen fortunes. Then she can go where she chooses, and we can,—as the French say—return to our muttons."

"I think Donna Inez and Lucy would be annoyed to hear themselves called muttons," laughed Archie, and the two men left the room.

The night was darker than ever, and a fine rain was falling incessantly. When they left the dimly lighted archway of the fort through the smaller, gate set in the larger one they stepped into midnight blackness such as must have been spread over the land of Egypt. In accordance with the primitive customs of Gartley inhabitants, one of them at least should have been furnished with a lantern, as it was no easy task to pick a clean way through the mud.—-However, Archie, knowing the surroundings better even than Random, led the way, and they walked slowly through the iron gate on the hard high road which led to the Fort. Immediately beyond this they turned towards the narrow cinder path which led through the marshes to Mrs. Jasher's cottage, and toiled on cautiously through the misty rain, which fell continuously. The fog was drifting up from the mouth of the river and was growing so thick that they could not see the somewhat feeble lights of the cottage. However, Archie's instincts led him aright, and they blundered finally upon the wooden gate. Here they paused in shocked surprise, for a woman's scream rang out wildly and suddenly.

"What, in heaven's name, is that?" asked Hope, aghast.

"We must find out," breathed Random, and raced through the white cotton-wool of the fog up the path. As he reached the veranda the door opened and a woman came running out screaming. But other screams inside the cottage still continued.

"What is the matter?" cried Random, seizing the woman.

She proved to be Jane.

"Oh, sir, my mistress is being murdered—"

Hope plunged past her into the corridor, not waiting to hear more. The cries had died down to a low moaning, and he dashed into the pink parlor to find it in smoky darkness. Striking a match, he held it above his head. It showed Mrs. Jasher prone on the floor, and a dark figure smashing its way through the flimsy window. There was a snarl and the figure vanished as the match went out.

CHAPTER XXIV

A CONFESSION

Jane was still being held by Sir Frank at the floor, and was still screaming, fully convinced that her captor was a burglar, in spite of having recognized him by his voice. Random was so exasperated by her stupidity that he shook her.

"What is the matter, you fool?" he demanded. "Don't you know that I am a friend?"

"Y-e-s, s-i-r," gasped Jane, fetching her breath again after the shaking; "but go for the police. My mistress is being murdered."

"Mr. Hope is looking after that, and the screams have ceased. Who was with your mistress?"

"I don't know, sir," sobbed the servant. "I didn't know anyone had called, and then I heard the screaming. I looked into the parlor to see what was the matter, but the lamp had been thrown over and had gone out, and there was a dreadful struggle going on in the darkness, so I screamed and ran out and then I—oh—oh" Jane showed symptoms of renewed hysteria, and clutched Random tightly, as a man came cautiously round the corner.

"Are you there, Random?" asked Hope's voice.

"It's so infernally dark and foggy that I have missed him."

"Missed who?"

"The man who was trying to murder Mrs. Jasher, He got her down when I entered and struck a match. Then he dashed through the window before I could catch him or even recognize him. He's vanished in the mist."

"It's no use looking for him anyhow," said Random, peering into the dense blackness, which was thick with damp. "We had better see after Mrs. Jasher."

"Whom have you got there?"

"Jane—who seems to have lost her head."

"It's a mercy I haven't lost my life, sir, with burglars and murderers all about the place," sobbed the girl, dropping on to the veranda.

Random promptly hauled her to her feet.

"Go and get a candle, and keep calm if you can," he said in an abrupt military voice. "This is no time to play the fool."

His sharpness had great effect on the girl, and she became much more her usual self. Hope lighted another match, and the trio

180

proceeded through the passage towards the kitchen, where Jane had left a lamp burning. Seizing this from its bracket, Sir Frank retraced his way along the passage to the pink parlor, followed closely by Hope and timorously by Jane. A dreadful scene presented itself. The dainty little room was literally smashed to pieces, as though a gigantic bull had been wallowing therein. The lamp lay on the floor, surrounded by several extinguished candles. It was a mercy that all the lights had been put out when overturned, else the gim-crack cottage would have been long since in a blaze. Chairs and tables and screens were also overturned, and the one window had its rose-hued curtains torn down and its glass broken, showing only too clearly the way in which the murderer had escaped. And that the man who had attacked Mrs. Jasher was a murderer could be seen from the stream of blood that ran slowly from Mrs. Jasher's breast. Apparently she had been stabbed in the lungs, for the wound was on the right side. There she lay, poor woman, in her tawdry finery, crumpled up, battered and bruised, dead amongst the ruins of her home. Jane immediately began to scream again.

"Stop her, Hope," cried Random, who was kneeling by the body and feeling the heart. "Mrs. Jasher is not dead. Hold your noise, woman, and go for a doctor." This was to Jane, who, prevented from screaming, took to whimpering.

"I had better go," said Hope quickly; "and I'll go to the Fort and alarm the men. Perhaps they may catch the man."

"Can you describe him?"

"Of course not," said Archie indignantly. "I only caught a glimpse of him by the feeble light of a lucifer match. Then he leaped through the window and I after him. I made a grab at him, but lost him in the mist. I don't know in the least what he is like."

"Then how can anyone arrest him?" snapped Random, raising Mrs. Jasher's head. "Give what alarm you like, but race for Robinson up the village. We must save this poor woman's life, if only to learn who killed her."

"But she isn't dead yet—she isn't dead yet," wailed Jane, clapping her hands, while Hope, knowing the value of time, promptly ran out of the house to get further assistance.

"She soon will be," said Sir Frank, whose temper was not of the best at so critical a moment in dealing with a fool. "Go and bring me brandy at once, and afterwards linen and hot water. We must do our best to staunch this wound and revive her."

For the next quarter of an hour the man and the woman labored hard to save Mrs. Jasher's life. Random bound up the wound in a rough and ready fashion, and Jane fed the pale lips of her mistress with sips of brandy. Mrs. Jasher gradually became more alive, and a faint sigh escaped from her lips, as her wounded bosom rose and fell with recovered breath. When Sir Frank was in hopes that she would speak, she suddenly relapsed again into a comatose state. Luckily at that moment Archie returned with young Dr. Robinson at his heels, and also was followed by Painter, the village constable, who had luckily been picked up in the fog.

Robinson whistled as he looked at the insensible woman.

"She's had a narrow squeak," he muttered, lifting the body with the assistance of Random.

"Will she recover?" questioned Hope anxiously.

"I can't tell you yet," answered the doctor; and with Sir Frank he carried the heavy body of the widow into her bedroom. "How did it happen?"

"That is my business," said Painter, who had followed, and who was now filled with importance. "You look after the body, sir, and I'll question these gentlemen and the servant."

"Servant yourself! Such sauce!" muttered Jane, with an angry toss of her cap at the daring young policeman. "I know nothing. I left my mistress in the parlor writing letters, and never heard anyone come in. The bell didn't sound anyhow. The first thing I knew that anything was wrong was on hearing the screams. When I looked into the parlor the candles and the lamp were out, and there was a struggle going on in the dark. Then I cried out, very naturally, I'm sure, and ran straight into the arms of these gentlemen, as soon as I could get the front door open."

After delivering this address, Jane was called away to assist the doctor in the bedroom, and along with Archie and Random the constable repaired to the pink parlor to hear what they had to say. Of course they could tell him even less than Jane had told, and Archie protested that he was quite unable to describe the man who had dashed out of the window.

"Ah," said Painter sapiently, "he got out there; but how did he enter?"

"No doubt by the door," said Random sharply.

"We don't know that, sir. Jane says she did not hear the bell."

"Mrs. Jasher might have let the man in, whomsoever he was, secretly."

"Why should she, sir?"

"Ah! now you are asking more than I can tell you. Only Mrs. Jasher can explain, and it seems to me that she will die."

Meanwhile, in some mysterious way the news of the crime had spread through the village, and although it was growing late—for it was past ten o'clock—a dozen or so of villagers came along. Also there arrived a number of soldiers under a smart sergeant, and to him Sir Frank explained what had happened. In the fainthearted way—for the mist was now like cotton-wool—the military and the civilians hunted through the marshes round the cottage, hoping to come across the assassin hiding in a ditch. Needless to say, they found no one and nothing, for it was worse than looking for a needle in a bundle of hay. The man had come out of the mist, and, after executing the deed, had vanished into the mist, and there was not the very slightest chance of finding him. Gradually, as it drew towards midnight, the soldiers went back to the Fort, and the villagers to their homes. But, along with the doctor and the constable, Hope and his military friend stopped on. They were determined to get at the root of the mystery, and when Mrs. Jasher became sensible she would be able to reveal the truth.

"It's all of a piece with the sending of the emerald," said Random to the artist, "and that is connected, as we know, with the death of Bolton."

"Do you think that this man who has struck down Mrs. Jasher is the same one who strangled Sidney Bolton?"

"I should think so. Perhaps Mrs. Jasher sent the emerald after all, and this man killed her out of revenge."

"But how would he know that she had the emerald?"

"God knows! She may have been his accomplice."

Archie knit his brows.

"Who the devil can this mysterious person be?"

"I can only reply as you have done, my friend. God knows."

"Well, I am certain that God will not let him escape this time. This will bring Gartley once more into notoriety," went on Hope. "By the way, I saw one of the servants from the Pyramids here. I hope the fool won't go home and frighten Lucy's life out of her."

"Go to the Pyramids and see her," suggested Sir Frank. "Mrs. Jasher is still unconscious, and will be for hours, the doctor tells me."

"It is too late to go to the Pyramids, Random."

"If they know of this new tragedy there, I'll bet they are not in bed."

Hope nodded.

"All the same, I'll remain here until Mrs. Jasher can speak," he said, and sat smoking with Random in the dining-room, as the most comfortable room in the house.

Constable Painter camped, so to speak, in the drawing-room, keeping guard over the scene of the crime, and had placed the Chinese screen against the broken window to keep out the cold. In the bedroom Jane and Dr. Robinson looked after the dying woman. And dying she was, according to the young physician, for he did not think she would live much longer. Round the lonely cottage the sea-mist drifted white and thick, and the darkness deepened, until—as the saying goes—it could have been cut with a knife. Never was there so eerie and weary and sinister a vigil.

Towards four o'clock Hope fell into a doze, while resting in an arm-chair; but he was suddenly aroused from this by an exclamation from Sir Frank, who had remained wide awake, smoking cigar after cigar. In a moment the artist was on his feet, alert and quick-brained.

"What is it?"

Random made for the dining-room door rapidly.

"I thought I heard Painter call out," he declared, and hastily sought the parlor, followed by Hope.

The room was empty, but the screen before the broken window had been thrown down, and they could see Painter's bulky form immediately outside.

"What the deuce is the matter?" demanded Random, entering. "Did you call out, Painter. I fancied I heard something."

The constable came in again.

"I did call out, sir," he confessed. "I was half asleep in that chair, when I suddenly became wide awake, and believed I saw a face looking at me round the corner of the screen. I jumped up, calling for you, sir, and upset the screen."

"Well? well?" demanded Sir Frank impatiently, and seeing that the man hesitated.

"I saw no one, sir. All the same, I had an idea, and I have still, that a man came through the window and peered at me from behind the screen."

"The man who attacked Mrs. Jasher?"

"I can't say, sir. But there was someone. At any rate he's gone again, if he really did come, and there is no chance of finding him. It's like pea-soup outside."

Hope and Random simultaneously stepped through the window, but could not see an inch before them, so thick was the sea-fog and so dense was the darkness. Returning, they replaced the screen, and, telling Painter to be more on the alert, went back shivering to the fire in the dining-room. When they were seated again, Archie put a question.

"Do you think that policeman was dreaming?" he asked meditatively.

"No," replied Random sharply. "I believe that the man who assaulted Mrs. Jasher is hanging about, and ventured back into the room, relying on the fog as a means of escape, should he be spotted."

"But the man wouldn't be such a fool as to return into danger."

"Not unless he wanted something very badly," said Random significantly.

Hope let the cigarette he was lighting fall.

"What do you mean?"

"I may be wrong, of course. But it is my impression that there is something in the parlor which this man wants, and for which he tried to murder Mrs. Jasher. We interrupted him, and he was forced to flee. Hidden in the fog, he is lurking about to see if he can't obtain what he has risked his neck to secure."

"What can it be?" murmured Archie, struck by the feasibility of this theory.

"Perhaps the second emerald," remarked Sir Frank grimly.

"What! You don't think that—"

"I don't think anything. I am too tired to think at all. However, Painter will keep his eyes open, and in the morning we can search the room. The man has been in the house twice to get what he wanted. He won't risk another attempt, now that he is aware we are on the alert. I'm going to try and get forty winks. You keep watch, as you have had your sleep."

Hope was quite agreeable, but just as Random composed himself to uneasy slumber, Jane, haggard and red-eyed, came hastily into the dining-room.

"If you please, gentlemen, the doctor wants you to come and see mistress. She is sensible, and—"

The two waited to hear no more, but went hastily but softly into the room wherein lay the dying woman. Robinson sat by the bedside, holding his patient's hand and feeling her pulse. He placed his finger on his lips as the men entered gently, and at the same moment Mrs. Jasher's voice, weak from exhaustion, sounded through the room, which was dimly illuminated by one candle. The newcomers halted in obedience to Robinson's signal.

"Who is there?" asked Mrs. Jasher weakly, for, in spite of the care exercised, she had evidently heard the footsteps.

"Mr. Hope and Sir Frank Random," whispered the doctor, speaking into the dying woman's ear. "They came in time to save you."

"In time to see me die," she murmured; "and I can't die, unless I tell the truth. I am glad Random is there; he is a kind-hearted boy, and treated me better than he need have done. I—oh—some brandy—brandy."

Robinson gave her some in a spoon.

"Now lie quietly and do not attempt to speak," he commanded. "You need all your strength."

185

"I do—to tell that which I wish to tell," gasped Mrs. Jasher, trying to raise herself. "Sir Frank! Sir Frank!" Her voice sounded hoarse and weak.

"Yes, Mrs. Jasher," said the young man, coming softly to the bedside.

She thrust out a weak hand and clutched him.

"You must be my father-confessor, and hear all. You got the emerald?"

"What!" Random recoiled in astonishment, "Did you—"

"Yes, I sent it to you as a wedding present. I was sorry and I was afraid; and I—I—" She paused again, gasping.

The doctor intervened and gave her more brandy.

"You must not talk," he insisted severely, "or I shall turn Sir Frank and Mr. Hope out of the room."

"No! no! Give me more brandy—more—more." and when the doctor placed a tumbler to her lips, she drank so greedily that he had to take the glass away lest she should do herself harm. But the ardent spirit put new life into her, and with a superhuman effort she suddenly reared herself in the bed.

"Come here, Hope—come here, Random," she said in a much stronger voice. "I have much to tell you. Yes, I took the emerald after dark and threw it into the sentry box when the man wasn't looking. I escaped your spy, Random, and I escaped the notice of the sentry. I walked like a cat, and like a cat I can see in the dark. I am glad you have got the emerald."

"Where did you get it?" asked Random quietly.

"That's a long story. I don't know that I have the strength to tell it. I have written it out."

"You have written it out?" said Hope quickly, and drawing near.

"Yes. Jane thought that I was writing letters, but I was writing out the whole story of the murder. You were good to me, Random, you dear boy, and on the impulse of the moment I took the emerald to you. I was sorry when I got back, but it was too late then to repent, as I did not dare to go near the Fort again. Your spy who watched might have discovered me the second time. I then thought that I would write out the story of the murder, so as to exonerate myself."

"Then you are not guilty of Bolton's death?" asked Sir Frank, puzzled, for her confession was somewhat incoherent.

"No. I did not strangle him. But I know who did. I have written it all down. I was just finishing when I heard the tapping at the window. I let him in and he tried to get the confession, for I told him what I had done."

"Who did you tell?" asked Hope, much excited.

186

Mrs. Jasher took no notice.

"The confession is lying on my desk—all the sheets of paper are loose. I had no time to bind them together, for he came in. He wanted the emerald, and the confession. I told him that I had given the emerald to you, Random, and that I had confessed all in writing. Then he went mad and flew at me with a dreadful knife. He knocked over the candles and the lamp. Everything went out and all was darkness, and I lay crying for help, with that devil stabbing—stabbing—ah—"

"Who, in heaven's name, is the man?" demanded Random, standing up in his eagerness. But Mrs. Jasher had fallen back in a faint, and Robinson was again supplying her with brandy.

"You had better leave the room, you two," he said, "or I can't be answerable for her life."

"I must stay and learn the truth," said Random determinedly, "and you, Hope, go into the parlor and find that confession. It is on the desk, as she said, all loose sheets. No doubt it was the confession which the man she refers to tried to secure when he came back the second time. He may make another attempt, or Painter may go to sleep. Hurry! hurry!"

Archie needed no second telling, as he realized what hung on the securing of the confession. He stole swiftly out of the room, closing the door after him. Faint as was the sound, Mrs. Jasher heard it and opened her eyes.

"Do not go, Random," she said faintly. "I have yet much to say, although the confession will tell you all. I am half sorry I wrote it out—at least I was—and perhaps should have burnt it had I not met with this accident."

"Accident!" echoed Sir Frank scornfully. "Murder you mean."

The sinister word galvanized the dying woman in sudden strong life, and she reared herself again on the bed.

"Murder! Yes, it is murder," she cried loudly. "He killed Sidney Bolton to get the emeralds, and he killed me to make me close my mouth."

"Who stabbed you? Speak! speak!" cried Random anxiously.

"Cockatoo. He is guilty of my death and Bolton's," and she fell back, dead.

CHAPTER XXV

THE MILLS OF GOD

In the cold gray hours of the morning, Hope and his friend left the cottage wherein such a tragedy had taken place. The dead woman was lying stiff and white on her bed under a winding sheet, which had already been strewn with many-hued chrysanthemums taken from the pink parlor by the weeping Jane. The wretched woman who had led so stormy and unhappy a life had at least one sincere mourner, for she had always been kind to the servant, who formed her entire domestic staff, and Jane would not hear a word said against the dead. Not that anyone did say anything; for Random and Hope kept the contents of the confession to themselves. There would be time enough for Mrs. Jasher's reputation to be smirched when those same contents were made public.

When the poor woman died, Random left the doctor and the servant to look after the corpse, and went into the parlor. Here he met Hope with the confession in his hand. Luckily, Painter was not in the room at the moment, else he would have prevented the artist from taking away the same. Hope—as directed by Mrs. Jasher—had found the confession, written on many sheets, lying on the desk. It broke off abruptly towards the end, and was not signed. Apparently at this point Mrs. Jasher had been interrupted—as she had said—by the tapping of Cockatoo at the window. Probably she had admitted him at once, and on her refusal to give him the emerald, and on her confessing what she had written, he had overturned the lights for the purpose of murdering her. Only too well had the Kanaka succeeded in his wickedness.

Archie slipped the confession into his pocket before the policeman returned, and then left the cottage with Random and the doctor, since nothing else could now be done. It was between seven and eight, and the chilly dawn was breaking, but the sea-mist still lay heavily over the marshes, as though it were the winding sheet of the dead. Robinson went to his own house to get his trap and drive into Jessum, there to catch the train and ferry to Pierside. It was necessary that Inspector Date should be informed of this new tragedy without delay, and as Constable Painter was engaged in watching the cottage, there was no messenger available but Dr. Robinson. Random indeed offered to send a soldier, or to afford

Robinson the use of the Fort telephone, but the doctor preferred to see Date personally, so as to detail exactly what had happened. Perhaps the young medical man had an eye to becoming better known, for the improvement of his practice; but he certainly seemed anxious to take a prominent part in the proceedings connected with the murder of Mrs. Jasher.

When Robinson parted from them, Random and Hope went to the lodgings of the latter, so as to read over the confession and learn exactly to what extent Mrs. Jasher had been mixed up in the tragedy of the green mummy. She had declared herself innocent even on her death-bed, and so far as the two could judge at this point, she certainly had not actually strangled Sidney Bolton. But it might be—and it appeared to be more than probable—that she was an accessory after the fact. But this they could learn from the confession, and they sat in Hope's quiet little sitting-room, in which the fire had been just lighted by the artist's landlady, with the scattered sheets neatly ranged before them.

"Perhaps you would like a cup of coffee, or a whisky and soda," suggested Archie, "before starting to read?"

"I should," assented Random, who looked weary and pale. "The events of the night have somewhat knocked me up. Coffee for choice—nice, black, strong, hot coffee."

Hope nodded and went to order the same. When he returned he sat down, after closing the door carefully, and proceeded to read. But before he could speak Random raised his hand.

"Let us chat until the coffee comes in," he said; "then we shall not be interrupted when reading."

"All right," said Hope. "Have a cigar!"

"No, thanks. I have been smoking all the night. I shall sit here by the fire and wait for the coffee. You look chippy yourself."

"And small wonder," said Archie wearily. "We little thought when we left the Fort last night what a time we were going to have. Fancy Mrs. Jasher having sent you the emerald after all!"

"Yes. She repented, as she said, and yet I dare say—as she also said—she was sorry that she acted on her impulse. If she had not been stabbed by that damned Cockatoo, she would no doubt have destroyed that confession. I expect she wrote that also on the impulse of the moment."

"She confessed as much," said Hope, leaning his head on his hand and staring into the fire. "She must have been cognizant of the truth all along. I wonder if she was an accessory before or after the fact?"

"What I wonder," said Random, after a moment's thought, "is, what Braddock has to do with the matter?"

Hope raised his head in surprise.

"Why, nothing. Mrs. Jasher did not say a word against Braddock."

"I know that. All the same, Cockatoo was completely under the thumb of the Professor, and probably was instructed by him to strangle Bolton."

"That is impossible," cried the artist, much agitated. "Think of what you are saying, Random. What a terrible thing it would be for Lucy if the Professor were guilty in such a way as you suggest!"

"Really, I fail to see that. Miss Kendal is no relation to Braddock save by marriage. His iniquities have nothing to do with her, or with you."

"But it's impossible, I tell you, Random. Throughout the whole of this case Braddock has acted in a perfectly innocent way."

"That's just it," said Sir Frank caustically; "he has acted. In spite of his pretended grief for the loss of the emeralds, I should not be surprised to learn from that," he nodded towards the confession on the table, "that he was in possession of the missing gem. Cockatoo had no reason to steal the emeralds himself, setting aside the fact that he probably would not know their value, being but a semi-civilized savage. He acted under orders from his master, and although Cockatoo strangled Bolton, the Professor is really the author and the gainer and the moving spirit."

"You would make Braddock an accessory before the fact."

"Yes, and Mrs. Jasher an accessory after the fact. Cockatoo is the link, as the actual criminal, who joins the two in a guilty partnership. No wonder Braddock intended to make that woman his wife even though he did not love her, for she knew a jolly sight too much for his peace of mind."

"This is horrible," murmured Hope desperately; "but it is mere theory. We cannot be sure until we read the confession."

"We'll be sure soon, then, for here comes the coffee."

This last remark Random made when a timid knock came to the door, and a moment later the landlady entered with a tray bearing cups, saucers, and a jug of steaming coffee. She was a meek, reticent woman who entered and departed in dismal silence, and in a few moments the two young men were quite alone with the door closed. They drank a cup of coffee each, and then Hope proceeded to read the confession.

The story told by Mrs. Jasher commenced with a short account of her early life. It appeared that her father was a ruined gentleman and a gambler, and that her mother had been an actress. She was dragged up in a Bohemian sort of way until she attained a marriageable age, when her mother, who seemed to have been both

190

wicked and hard-hearted, forced her to marry a comparatively wealthy man called Jasher. The elderly husband—for Jasher was not young—treated his wife very badly, and, infected with the spirit of gambling by her father, lost all his money. Mrs. Jasher then went with him to America and performed on the stage in order to keep the home together. She had one child, but it died, much to her grief, yet also much to her relief, as she was so miserable and poor. Mrs. Jasher gave a scanty account of sordid years of trouble and trial, of failure and sorrow. She and her husband roamed all over America, and then went to Australia and New Zealand, where they lived a wretched existence for many years. Finally the husband died of strong drink at an advanced age, leaving Mrs. Jasher a somewhat elderly widow.

The poor woman again took to the stage and tried to earn her bread, but was unsuccessful. Afterwards she lectured. Then she kept a boarding establishment, and finally went out as a nurse. In every way, it would seem, she tried to keep her head above water, and roamed the world like a bird of passage, finding rest nowhere for the sole of her foot. Yet throughout her story both the young men could see that she had always aspired to a quiet and decent, respectable existence, and that only force of circumstances had flung her into the whirlpool of life.

"As I said," remarked Random at this stage, "the miserable creature was more sinned against than sinning."

"Her moral sense seemed to have become blunted, however," said Archie doubtfully.

"And small wonder, amidst such surroundings; but it seems to me that she was much better under the circumstances than many another woman would have been. Go on."

In Melbourne Mrs. Jasher made a lucky speculation in mines, which brought her one thousand pounds. With this she came to England, and resolved to make a bid for respectability. Chance led her into the neighborhood of Gartley, and thinking that if she set up her tent in this locality she might manage to marry an officer from the Fort—since amidst such dismal surroundings a young man might be the more easily fascinated by a woman of the world—she took the cottage amidst the marshes at a small rent. Here she hoped to eke out what money she had left—a few hundreds—until the coveted marriage should take place. Afterwards she met Professor Braddock and determined to marry him, as a man more easy to manage. She was successful in enlisting Lucy on her side, and until the green mummy brought its bad luck to the Pyramids everything went capitally.

It was in connection with the name of Bolton that the first

mention was made of the green mummy. Sidney was a clever young man, although very lowly born, and having been taken up by Professor Braddock as an assistant, could hope some day to make a position. Braddock was educating him, although he paid him very little in the way of wages. Sidney fell in love with Mrs. Jasher, and in some way—she did not mention how—gained her confidence. Perhaps the lonely woman was glad to have a sympathetic friend. At all events she told her past history to Sidney, and mentioned that she desired to marry Braddock. But Sidney insisted that she should marry him, and promised to make enough money to satisfy her that he was a good match, setting aside his humble birth, for which Mrs. Jasher cared nothing.

It was then that Sidney related what he had discovered. Braddock, when in Peru many years before, had tried to get mummies for some scientific reason. When Hervey—then known as Vasa—promised to procure him the mummy of the last Inca, Braddock was extremely pleased. Hervey stole the mummy and also the copy of the manuscript which was written in Latin. He sent this latter to Braddock—who was then at Cuzco—as an earnest of his success in procuring the mummy, and when the Professor returned to Lima the mummy was to be handed to him. Unfortunately, Braddock was carried into captivity for one year, and when he escaped Vasa had disappeared with the mummy. As the Professor had deciphered the Latin manuscript, he knew of the emeralds, and for years had been hunting for the mummy—sure to be recognized from its peculiar green color—in order to get the jewels, and thus secure money for his Egyptian expedition. All through, it seems, the Professor was actuated by purely scientific enthusiasm, as in the abstract he cared very little for hard cash. Bolton told Mrs. Jasher that Braddock explained how much he desired to get the mummy, but he did not mention about the jewels. For a long time Sidney was under the impression that his master merely wanted the mummy to see the difference between the Egyptian and Peruvian modes of embalming.

Then one day Sidney chanced on the Latin manuscript, and learned that Braddock's real reason for getting the mummy was to procure the emeralds which were held in the grip of the dead. Sidney kept this knowledge to himself, and Braddock never guessed that his assistant knew the truth. Then unexpectedly Braddock stumbled across the advertisement describing the green mummy for sale in Malta. From the color he made sure that it was that of Inca Caxas, and so moved heaven and earth to get money to buy it. At length he did, from Archie Hope, on condition that he consented to the marriage of his step-daughter with the young man. Thinking that Sidney was ignorant of the jewels, he sent him to bring the mummy home.

Sidney told Mrs. Jasher that he would try and steal the jewels in Malta or on board the tramp steamer. Failing that, he would delay the delivery of the mummy to Braddock on some excuse and rob it at Pierside. To make sure of escaping, he borrowed a disguise from his mother, alleging that Hope wanted the same to clothe a model. Sidney intended to take these clothes with him, and, after stealing the jewels, to escape disguised as an old woman. As he was slender and clean-shaven and a capital actor, he could easily manage this.

Then he arranged that Mrs. Jasher should join him in Paris, and they would sell the emeralds, and go to America, there to marry and live happily ever afterwards, like a fairy tale.

Unfortunately for the success of this plan, Mrs. Jasher thought that the Professor would make a more distinguished husband, so she betrayed all that Sidney, had arranged.

"What a beastly thing to do!" interrupted Random, disgusted. "It is not as if she wanted to help Braddock. I think less of Mrs. Jasher than ever I did. She might have remembered that there is honor amongst thieves."

"Well, she is dead, poor soul!" said Hope with a sigh. "God knows that if she sinned, she has paid cruelly for her sin," after which remark, as Sir Frank was silent, he resumed his reading.

Braddock was furious when he learned of his assistant's projected trickery, and he determined to circumvent him. He agreed to marry Mrs. Jasher, as, if he had not done so, she could have warned Sidney and he could have escaped with both the mummy and the jewels by conniving with Hervey. The Professor could not risk that, as, remembering Hervey as Gustav Vasa, he was aware how clever and reckless he was. Whether Braddock ever intended to marry the widow in the end it is hard to say, but he certainly pretended to consent to the engagement, which was mainly brought about by Lucy. Then came the details of the murder so far as Mrs. Jasher knew.

One evening—in fact on the evening when the crime was committed—the woman was walking in her garden late. In the moonlight she saw Braddock and Cockatoo go down along the cinderpath to the jetty near the Fort. Wondering what they were doing, she waited up, and heard and saw them—for it was still moonlight—come back long after midnight. The next day she heard of the murder, and guessed that the Professor and his slave—for Cockatoo was little else—had rowed up to Pierside in a boat and there had strangled Sidney and stolen the mummy. She saw Braddock and accused him. The Professor had then opened the case, and had pretended astonishment when discovering the corpse of the man whom Cockatoo had strangled, as he knew perfectly well.

Braddock at first denied having been to Pierside, but Mrs. Jasher insisted that she would tell the police, so he was forced to make a clean breast of it to the woman.

"Now for it," said Random, settling himself to hear details of the crime, for he had often wondered how it had been executed.

"Braddock," read Archie from the confession, for Mrs. Jasher did not trouble herself with a polite prefix—"Braddock explained that when he received a letter from Sidney stating that he would have to remain with the mummy for a night in Pierside, he guessed that his treacherous assistant intended to effect the robbery. It seems that Sidney by mistake had left behind the disguise in which he intended to escape. Aware of this through me"—Mrs. Jasher referred to herself—"he made Cockatoo assume the dress and row up the river to the Sailor's Rest. The Kanaka easily could be mistaken for a woman, as he also, like Sidney, was slender and smooth-chinned. Also, he wore the shawl over his head to disguise his mop of frizzy hair as much as possible, and for the purpose of concealing his tattooed face. In the darkness—it was after nine o'clock—he spoke to Sidney through the window, as he had seen him there earlier, when searching for him. Cockatoo said that Sidney was much afraid when he heard that his purpose had been discovered by the Professor. He offered a share of the plunder to the Kanaka, and Cockatoo agreed, saying he would come back late, and that Sidney was to admit him into the bedroom so that they could open the mummy and steal the jewels. Sidney quite believed that Cockatoo was heart and soul with him, especially as the cunning Kanaka swore that he was weary of his master's tyranny. It was when Cockatoo was talking thus that he was seen by Eliza Flight, who mistook him—very naturally—for a woman. Cockatoo then returned by boat to the Gartley jetty and told his master. Afterwards, the Professor, at a much later hour, went down to the jetty and was rowed up to Pierside by the Kanaka."

"That was when Mrs. Jasher saw them," said Random, much interested.

"Yes," said Archie. "And then, if you remember; she watched for the return of the couple."

"It was nearly midnight when the boat was brought alongside the sloping stone bank of the alley which ran past the Sailor's Rest. No one was about at that hour, not even a policeman, and there was no light in Sidney Bolton's window. Braddock was much agitated as he thought that Sidney had already escaped. He waited in the boat and sent Cockatoo to knock at the window. Then a light appeared and the window was silently opened. The Kanaka slipped in and remained there for some ten minutes after closing the window. When he returned, the light was extinguished. He whispered to his master that Sidney had opened the packing case and the mummy coffin, and had ripped the swathings to get the jewels. When Sidney would not hand over the jewels to the Kanaka, as the latter wanted him to, Cockatoo, already prepared with the window cord, which he had silently taken from the blind, sprang upon the unfortunate assistant and strangled him. Cockatoo told this to his horrified master, and wanted him to come back to hide the corpse in the packing case. Braddock refused, and then Cockatoo told him that he would throw the jewels—which he had taken from Sidney's body—into the river. The position of master and servant was reversed, and Braddock was forced to obey.

"The Professor slipped silently ashore and into the room. The two men relighted the candle and pulled down the blind. They then placed the corpse of Sidney in the packing case, and screwed the same down in silence. When this was completed, they were about to carry the mummy in its coffin—the lid of which they had replaced—to the boat, when they heard distant footsteps, probably those of a policeman on his beat. At once they extinguished the candle, and—as Braddock told Mrs. Jasher—he, for one, sat trembling in the dark. But the policeman—if the footsteps were those of a policeman—passed up another street, and the two were safe. Without relighting the candle, they silently slipped the mummy through the window, Cockatoo within and Braddock without. The case and its contents were not heavy, and it was not difficult for the two men to take it to the boat. When it was safely bestowed, Cockatoo—who was as cunning as the devil, according to his master returned to the bedroom, and unlocked the door. He afterwards passed a string through the joining of the upper and lower windows, and managed to shut the snib. Afterwards he came to the boat and rowed it back to Gartley. On the way Cockatoo told his master that Sidney had left instructions that the packing case should be taken next morning to the Pyramids, so there was nothing to fear. The mummy was hidden in a hole under the jetty and covered with grass."

"Why didn't they take it up to the house?" asked Random, on hearing this.

"That would have been dangerous," said Hope, looking up from the manuscript, "seeing that the mummy was supposed to have been stolen by the murderer. It was easier to hide it amongst the grasses under the jetty, as no one ever goes there. Well"—he turned over a few pages—"that is practically all. The rest is after events."

"I want to hear them," said Random, taking another cup of coffee.

Hope ran his eyes swiftly over the remaining portion of the paper, and gave further details rapidly to his friend.

"You know all that happened," he said, "the Professor's pretended surprise when he found the corpse he had himself helped to pack and—"

"Yes! yes! But why was the mummy placed in Mrs. Jasher's garden?"

"That was Braddock's idea. He fancied that the mummy might be found under the jetty and that inconvenient inquiries might be made. Also, he wished if possible to implicate Mrs. Jasher, so as to keep her from telling to the police what he had told her. He and Cockatoo went down to the river one night and removed the mummy to the arbor silently. Afterwards he pretended to be astonished when I found it. I must say he acted his part very well," said Hope reflectively, "even to accusing Mrs. Jasher. That was a bold stroke of genius."

"A very dangerous one."

"Not at all. He swore to Mrs. Jasher that if she said anything, he would tell the police that she had taken the clothes provided by Sidney from the Pyramids and had gone to speak through the window, in order to fly with Sidney and the emeralds. As the fact of the mummy being found in Mrs. Jasher's garden would lend color to the lie, she was obliged to hold her tongue. And after all, as she says, she didn't mind, since she was engaged to the Professor, and possessed at least one of the emeralds."

"Ah! the one she passed along to me. How did she get that?"

Hope referred again to the manuscript.

"She insisted that Braddock should give it to her as a pledge of good faith. He had to do it, or risk her splitting. That was why he placed the mummy in her garden, so as to bring her into the matter, and render it more difficult for her to speak."

"What of the other emerald?"

"Braddock took that to Amsterdam, when he went to London that time—if you remember, when Don Pedro arrived. Braddock sold the emerald for three thousand pounds, and it is now on its way to an Indian rajah. I fear Don Pedro will never set eyes on that again."

"Where is the money?"

"He banked it in a feigned name in Amsterdam, and intended to account for it when he married Mrs. Jasher by saying it was left to her by that mythical Pekin merchant brother of hers. Savvy!"

196

"Yes. What an infernal little villain! And I expect he sent Cockatoo down last night for the other emerald."

"That is not related in the manuscript," said Archie, laying down the last sheet and taking up his coffee. "The confession ends abruptly—at the time Cockatoo tapped at the window, I expect. But she said, when dying, that the Kanaka asked for the second emerald. If she had not sent it to you in a fit of weakness, I expect she would have passed it along. I can't make out," added Archie musingly, "why Mrs. Jasher confessed when everything was so safe."

"Well," said Random, nursing his chin, and staring into the fire, "she made a mistake in trying to blackmail me, though why she did so I can't tell, seeing she had the whiphand of Braddock. Perhaps she wanted the five thousand to spend herself, knowing that the Professor's plunder would be wasted on his confounded expedition. At any rate she gave herself away by the blackmail, and I expect she grew frightened. If the house had been searched—and it might have been searched by the police, had I arrested her for blackmail the emerald would have been found and she would have been incriminated. She therefore got rid of it cleverly, by passing it along to me as a wedding gift. Then she again grew afraid and wrote out this confession to exonerate herself."

"But it doesn't," insisted Hope. "She makes herself out plainly as an accessory after the fact."

"A woman doesn't understand these legal niceties. She wrote that out to clear herself in case she was arrested for the blackmail, and perhaps in case Braddock refused to help her—as he certainly did, if you remember."

"He was hard on her," confessed Archie slowly.

"Being such a villain himself," said Random grimly. "However, Cockatoo arrived unluckily on the scene, and when he found she had parted with the emerald, and had written out the truth, he stabbed her. If we hadn't come just in the nick of time, he would have annexed that confession, and the truth would never have become known. No one," ended Random, rising and stretching himself, "would connect Braddock or Cockatoo with the death of Mrs. Jasher."

"Or with the death of Sidney Bolton either," said Hope, also rising and putting on his cap. "What an actor the man is!"

"Where are you going?" demanded Sir Frank, yawning.

"To the Pyramids. I want to see how Lucy is."

"Will you tell her about that confession?"

"Not until later. I shall give this to Inspector Date when he arrives. The Professor has made his bed, so he must lie on it. When I marry Lucy, I'll take her away from this damned place."

197

"Marry her at once, then," advised Random, "while the Professor is doing time, and while Cockatoo is being hanged. Meanwhile, I think you had better put on your overcoat, unless you want to walk through the village in crumpled evening dress, like a dissipated undergraduate."

Archie laughed in spite of his weariness, and assumed his greatcoat at the same moment as Random slipped into his. The two young men walked out into the village and up to the Pyramids, for Random wished to see Braddock before returning to the Fort. They found the door of the great house open and the servants in the hall.

"What is all this?" demanded Hope, entering. "Why are you here, and not at work? Where is your master?"

"He's run away," said the cook in a shrill voice. "Lord knows why, sir."

"Archie! Archie!" Lucy came running out of the museum, pale-faced and white, "my father has gone away with Cockatoo and the green mummy. What does it mean? And just when poor Mrs. Jasher is murdered too."

"Hush, darling! Come in, and I'll explain," said Hope gently.

CHAPTER XXVI

THE APPOINTMENT

Poor Lucy Kendal was terribly grieved and shocked when the full account of her step-father's iniquity was revealed to her. Archie tried to break the news as delicately as possible, but no words could soften the sordid story. Lucy, at first, could not believe it possible that a man, whom she had known for so long, and to whom she was related, would behave in such a base way. To convince her Hope was forced to let her read the account in Mrs. Jasher's handwriting. When acquainted with the contents, the poor girl's first desire was to have the matter hushed up, and she implored her lover with tears to suppress the damning document.

"That is impossible," said Hope firmly; "and if you think again, my dear, you will not repeat such a request. It is absolutely necessary that this should be placed in the hands of the police, and that the truth should become as widely known as possible. Unless the matter is settled once and for all, someone else may be accused of this murder."

"But the disgrace," wept Lucy, hiding her face on her lover's shoulder.

He slipped his arm round her waist.

"My darling, the disgrace exists whether it be public or private. After all, the Professor is no relation."

"No. But everyone knows that I am his step-daughter."

"Everyone," echoed Archie, with an assumed lightness. "My dear, everyone in this instance only means the handful of people who live in this out-of-the-way village. Your name will not appear in the papers. And even if by chance it does, you will soon be changing it for mine. I think the best thing that can be done is for you to come with me to London next week and marry me. Then we can go to the south of France for the rest of the winter, until you recover. When we return and set up house in London—say in a year—the whole affair will be forgotten."

"But how can you bear to marry me, when you know that I come of such a bad stock?" wept Lucy, a trifle more comforted.

"My dear, must I remind you again that you are no relation to Professor Braddock; you have not a drop of his wicked blood in your veins. And even if you had, I should still marry you. It is you I love, and you I marry, so there is no more to be said. Come, darling, say that you will become my wife next week."

"But the Professor?"

Archie smiled grimly. He found it difficult to forgive Braddock for the disgrace he had brought on the girl.

"I don't think we'll ever be troubled again with the Professor," he said, after a pause. "He has bolted into the unknown with that infernal Kanaka."

"But why did he fly, Archie?"

"Because he knew that the game was up. Mrs. Jasher wrote out this confession, and told Cockatoo, when he entered the room to get the emerald, that she had written it. To save his master the Kanaka stabbed the wretched woman, and, had Random and I not arrived, he would have secured the confession. I really believe he came back again out of the mist in the small hours of the morning to steal it. But when he found that all was vain, he returned here and told the Professor that the story of the murder had been written out. Therefore there was nothing left to Braddock but to fly. Although," added Hope, with an afterthought, "I can't imagine why those two fugitives should drag that confounded mummy with them."

"But why should the Professor fly?" asked Lucy again. "According to what Mrs. Jasher writes, he did not strangle poor Sidney."

"No. And I will do him the justice to say that he had no idea of having his assistant murdered. It was Cockatoo's savage blood which came out in the deed, and maybe it can be explained by the Kanaka's devotion to the Professor. It was the same way in the murder of Mrs. Jasher. By killing Bolton, the Kanaka hoped to save the emeralds for Braddock: in stabbing Mrs. Jasher, he hoped to save the Professor's life."

"Oh, Archie, will they hang my father?"

Hope winced.

"Call him your step-father," he said quickly. "No, dear, I do not think he will be hanged; but as an accessory after the fact he will certainly be condemned to a long term of imprisonment. Cockatoo, however, assuredly will be hanged, and a good job too. He is only a savage, and as such is dangerous in a civilized community. I wonder where they have gone? Did anyone hear them going?"

"No," said Lucy unhesitatingly. "Cook came up this morning to my room, and said that my father—I mean my step-father—had gone away with Cockatoo and with the green mummy. I don't know why she should have said that, as the Professor often went away unexpectedly."

"Perhaps she heard rumors in the village and put two and two together. I cannot tell. Some instinct must have told her. But I daresay Braddock and his accomplice fled under cover of the mist and in the small hours of the morning. They must have known that the confession would bring the officers of the law to this house."

"I hope they will escape," murmured Lucy.

"Well, I am not sure," said Hope hesitatingly. "Of course, I should like to avoid a scandal for your sake, and yet it is only right that the two of them should be punished. Remember, Lucy dear, how Braddock has acted all along in deceiving us. He knew all, and yet not one of us suspected him."

While Archie was thus comforting the poor girl, Gartley village was in an uproar. Everyone was talking about this new crime, and everyone was wondering who had stabbed the unlucky woman. As yet the confession of Mrs. Jasher had not been placed in the hands of the police and everyone was ignorant that Cockatoo was the criminal who had escaped in the fog. Inspector Date speedily arrived with his myrmidons on the scene and made the cottage his headquarters. Later in the day, Hope, having taken a cold bath to freshen himself up, came with the confession. This he gave to the officer and explained the whole story of the previous night.

Date was more than astonished: he was astounded. He read the confession and made notes; then he sent for Sir Frank Random, and examined him in the same strict way as he had examined the artist. Jane was also questioned. Widow Anne was put in the witness box, so as to report about the clothes, and in every way Date gathered material for another inquest. At the former one he had only been able to place scanty evidence before the jury, and the verdict had been unsatisfactory to the public. But on this occasion, seeing that the witnesses he could bring forward would solve the mystery of the first death as well as the second, Inspector Date exulted greatly. He saw himself promoted and his salary raised, and his name praised in the papers as a zealous and clever officer. By the time the inquest came to be held, the inspector had talked himself into believing that the whole mystery had been solved by himself. But before that time came another event happened which astonished everyone, and which made the final phase of the green mummy crime even more sensational than it had been. And Heaven knows that from beginning to end there had been no lack of melodrama of the most lurid description.

Don Pedro de Gayangos was exceedingly amazed at the unexpected turn which the case had taken. That he should have been trying to solve a deep mystery for so long, and that the solution, all the time, had been in the hands of the Professor, startled him exceedingly. He admitted that he had never liked

201

Braddock, but explained that he had not expected to hear that the fiery little scientist was such a scoundrel. But, as Don Pedro confessed, it was an ill wind which blew him some good, when the upshot of the whole mysterious tragic business was the restoration of at least one emerald. Sir Frank brought the gem to him on the afternoon of the day succeeding Mrs. Jasher's death, and while the whole village was buzzing with excitement. It was Random who gave all details to Donna Inez and her father, leading from one revelation to another, until he capped the whole extraordinary story by producing the splendid gem.

"Mine! mine!" said Don Pedro, his dark eyes glittering. "Thanks be to the Virgin and the Saints," and he bowed his head to make the sign of the cross devoutly on his breast.

Donna Inez clapped her hands and her eyes flashed, for, like every woman, she had a profound love for jewels.

"Oh, how lovely, Frank! It must be worth no end of money."

"Professor Braddock sold the other to some Indian rajah in Amsterdam—through an agent, I presume for three thousand pounds."

"I shall get more than that," said Don Pedro quickly. "The Professor sold his jewel in a hurry and had no time to bargain. But sooner or later I shall get five thousand pounds for this." He held the gem in the sunlight, where it glowed like an emerald sun. "Why, it is worthy of a king's crown."

"I fear you will never get the other gem," said Random regretfully. "I believe that it is on its way to India, if Mrs. Jasher can be trusted."

"Never mind. I shall be content with this one, senor. I have simple tastes, and this will do much to restore the fortunes of my family. When I go back with this and the green mummy, all those Indians who know of my descent from the ancient Incas will be delighted and will pay me fresh reverence."

"But you forget," said Random, frowning, "the green mummy has been taken away by Professor Braddock."

"They cannot have gone far with it," said Donna Inez, shrugging.

"I don't know so much about that, dearest," said Sir Frank. "Apparently, since they handled it at the time of the murder, it is easier carried about than one would think. And then they fled last night, or rather in the small hours of this morning, under cover of a dense fog."

"It is clear enough now," said De Gayangos, peering through the window, where a pale winter sun shone in a clear steel-hued sky. "They are bound to be caught in the long run."

"Do you wish them to be caught?" asked Random abruptly.

"Not the Professor. For Miss Lucy's sake I hope he will escape; but I trust that the savage who killed these two unfortunate people will be brought to the gallows."

"So do I," said Random. "Well, Don Pedro, it seems to me that your task in Gartley is ended. All you have to do is to wait for the inquest and see Mrs. Jasher buried, poor soul! Then you can go to London and remain there until after Christmas."

"But why should I remain in London?" asked the Peruvian, surprised.

Random glanced at Donna Inez, who blushed.

"You forget that you have given your consent to my marriage with—"

"Ah, yes," Don Pedro smiled gravely. "I return with the jewel to Lima, but I leave my other jewel behind."

"Never mind," said the girl, kissing her father; "when Frank and I are married we will come to Callao in his yacht."

"Our yacht," said Random, smiling.

"Our yacht," repeated Donna Inez. "And then you will see, father, that I have become a real English lady."

"But don't entirely forget that you are a Peruvian," said Don Pedro playfully.

"And a descendant of Inca Caxas," added Donna Inez. Then she flirted her fan, which she was rarely without, and laughed in her English lover's face. "Don't forget, senor, that you marry a princess."

"I marry the most charming girl in the world," he replied, catching her in his arms, rather to the scandal of De Gayangos, who had stiff Spanish notions regarding the etiquette of engaged couples.

"There is one thing you must do for me, senor," he said quietly, "before we leave this most unhappy case of murder and theft for ever."

"What is that?" asked Sir Frank, turning with Inez in his arms.

"To-night at eight o'clock, Captain Hervey—the sailor Gustav Vasa, if you prefer the name—steams down the river in his new boat The Firefly. I received a note from him"—he displayed a letter—"stating that he will pass the jetty of Gartley at that hour, and will burn a blue light. If I fire a pistol, he will send off a boat with a full account of the theft of the mummy of Inca Caxas, written by himself. Then I will hand his messenger fifty gold sovereigns, which I have here," added Don Pedro, pointing to a canvas bag on the table, "and we will return. I wish you to go with me, senor, and also I wish your friend Mr. Hope to come."

203

"Do you anticipate treachery from Captain Hervey?" asked Random.

"I should not be surprised if he tried to trick me in some way, and I wish you and your friend to stand by me. Were this man alone, I would go alone, but he will have a boat's crew with him. It is best to be safe."

"I agree with you," said Random quickly. "Hope and I will come, and we will take revolvers with us. It doesn't do to trust this blackguard. Ho! ho! I wonder if he knows of the Professor's flight."

"No. Considering the terms upon which the Professor stood with Hervey, I should think he would be the last person he would trust. I wonder what has become of the man."

More people than Don Pedro wondered as to the whereabouts of Braddock and his servant, for everyone was inquiring and hunting. The marshes round the cottage were explored: the great house itself was searched, as well as many cottages in the village, and inquiries were made at all the local stations. But all in vain. Braddock and Cockatoo, along with the cumbersome mummy in its case, had vanished as completely as though the earth had swallowed them up. Inspector Date's idea was that the pair had taken the mummy to Gartley Pier, after the search made by the soldiers, and there had launched the boat, which Cockatoo—judging from his visit to Pierside—apparently kept hidden in some nook. It was probable, said Date, the two had rowed down the river, and had managed to get on board some outward-bound tramp. They could easily furbish up some story, and as Braddock doubtless had money, could easily buy a passage for a large sum. The tramp being outward-bound, her captain and crew would know nothing of the crime, and even if the fugitives were suspected, they would be shipped out of England if the bribe was sufficiently large. So it was apparent that Inspector Date had not much opinion of tramp-steamer skippers.

However, as the day wore on to night, nothing was heard of Braddock or Cockatoo or the mummy, and when night came the village was filled with local reporters and with London journalists asking questions. The Warrior Inn did a great trade in drink and beds and meals, and the rustics reaped quite a harvest in answering questions about Mrs. Jasher and the Professor and the weird-looking Kanaka. Some reporters dared to invade the Pyramids, where Lucy was weeping in sorrow and shame, but Archie, reinforced by two policemen, sent to his aid by Date, soon sent them to the right about. Hope would have liked to remain with Lucy all the evening, but at half-past seven he was forced to meet Don Pedro and Random outside the Fort in order to go to Gartley Jetty.

CHAPTER XXVII

BY THE RIVER

As the hunt for the fugitives had continued all day, everyone, police, villagers and soldiers, were weary and disheartened. Consequently, when the three men met near the Fort, there seemed to be few people about. This was just as well, as they would have been followed to the jetty, and obviously it was best to keep the strange meeting with Captain Hervey as secret as possible. However, Don Pedro had taken Inspector Date into his confidence, as it was impossible to get past the cottage of the late Mrs. Jasher, in which the officer had taken up his quarters, without being discovered. Date was quite willing that the trio should go, but stipulated that he should come also. He had heard all about Captain Hervey in connection with the mummy, and thought that he would like to ask that sailor a few leading questions.

"And if I see fit I shall detain him until the inquest is over," said Date, which was mere bluff, as the inspector had no warrant to stop The Firefly or arrest her skipper.

The three men therefore were joined by Date, when they came along the cinder path abreast of the cottage, and the quartette proceeded further immediately, walking amongst the bents and grasses to the rude old wooden jetty, near which Hervey intended to stop his ship. The night was quite clear of fog, strange to say, considering the late sea-mist; but a strong wind had been blowing all day and the fog-wreaths were entirely dispersed. A full moon rode amongst a galaxy of stars, which twinkled like diamonds. The air was frosty, and their feet scrunched the earth and grasses and coarse herbage under foot, as they made rapidly for the embankment.

When they reached the top they could see the jetty clearly almost below their feet, and in the distance the glittering lights of Pierside. Vague forms of vessels at anchor loomed on the water, and there was a stream of light where the moon made a pathway of silver. After a casual glance the three men proceeded down the slope to the jetty. Three of them at least had revolvers, since Hervey was an ill man to tackle; but probably Date, who was too dense to consider consequences, was unarmed. Neither did Don Pedro think it necessary to tell the officer that he and his two companions were prepared to shoot if necessary. Inspector Date, being a prosy

Englishman, would not have understood such lawless doings in his own sober, law-abiding country.

When they reached the jetty Don Pedro glanced at his watch, illuminating the dial by puffing his cigar to a ruddy glow. It was just after eight o'clock, and even as he looked an exclamation from Date made him raise his head. The inspector was pointing out-stream to a large vessel which had steamed inshore as far as was safe. Probably Hervey was watching for them through a night-glass, for a blue light suddenly flared on the bridge. Don Pedro, according to his promise, fired a pistol, and it was then that Date learned that his companions were armed.

"What the devil did you do that for?" he inquired angrily. "It will bring my constables down on us."

"I do not mind, since you can control them," said De Gayangos coolly. "I had to give the signal."

"And we all have revolvers," said Random quickly. "Hervey is not a very safe man to tackle, inspector."

"Do you expect a fight?" said Date, while they all watched a boat being lowered. "If so, you might have told me, and I should have brought a revolver also. Not that I think it is needed. The sight of my uniform will be enough to show this man that I have the law behind me."

"I don't think that will matter to Hervey," said Archie dryly. "So much as I have seen of him suggests to me that he is a singularly lawless man."

Date laughed good-humoredly.

"It seems to me, gentlemen, that you have brought me on a filibustering expedition," he said, and seemed to enjoy the novel situation. Date had been wrapped up in the cotton-wool of civilization for a long time, but his primitive instincts rose to the surface, now that he had to face a probable rough-and-tumble fight. "But I don't expect there will be any scrap," he said regretfully. "My uniform will settle the matter."

It certainly seemed to annoy Captain Hervey considerably, for, as the boat approached the shore, and the moonlight revealed a distinctly official overcoat, he gave an order. The man stopped rowing and the boat rocked gently, some distance from the jetty.

"You've got a high old crowd with you, Don Pedro," sang out Hervey, in great displeasure. "Is that angel in the military togs, with the brass buttons, the almighty aristocrat!"

"No. I am here," cried out Random, laughing at the description, which he recognized. "My friend Hope is with me, and Inspector Date. I suppose you have heard what has happened?"

"Yes, I've taken it all in," said Hervey sourly. "I guess the news is all over Pierside. Well, it's none of my picnic, I reckon. So chuck that gold over here, Don Pedro, and I'll send along the writing."

"No," said Don Pedro, prompted by Date. "You must come ashore."

"I guess not," said Hervey vigorously. "You want to run me in."

"For that theft of thirty years ago," laughed De Gayangos. "Nonsense! Come along. You are quite safe."

"Shan't take your damned word for it," growled Hervey. "But if those two gents can swear that there's no trickery, I'll come. I can depend on the word of an English aristocrat, anyhow."

"Come along. You are quite safe," said Sir Frank, and Hope echoed his words.

Thus being made certain, Hervey gave an order and the boat was rowed right up to the beach, immediately below the jetty. The four men were about to descend, but Hervey seemed anxious to avoid giving them trouble.

"Hold on, gents," said he, leaping ashore. "I'll come up 'longside."

Date, ever suspicious, thought it queer that the skipper should behave so politely, as he had gathered that Hervey was not usually a considerate man. Also, he saw that when the captain was climbing the bank, the boat, in charge of a mate—as the inspector judged from his brass-bound uniform—backed water to the end of the jetty, where it swung against one of the shell-encrusted piles. Hervey finally reached the jetty level, but refused to come on to the same. He beckoned to Don Pedro and his companions to walk forward to the ground upon which he was standing. Also, he seemed exceedingly anxious to take time over the transaction, as even after he had handed the scroll of writing to the Peruvian, and had received the gold in exchange, he engaged in quarrelsome conversation. Pretending that he doubted if De Gayangos had brought the exact sum, he opened the canvas bag and insisted on counting the money. Don Pedro naturally lost his temper at this insult, and swore in Spanish, upon which Hervey responded with such volubility that anyone could see he was a pastmaster in Castilian swearing. The row was considerable, especially as Random and Hope were laughing at the quarrel. They thought that Hervey was the worse for drink, but Date—clever for once in his life—did not think so. It appeared to him that the boat had gone to the end of the jetty for some reason connected with the same reason which induced the skipper to spin out the time of the meeting by indulging in an unnecessary quarrel.

The skipper also kept his eyes about him, and insisted that the four men should keep together at the head of the pier.

"I daresay you're trying to play low down on me," he said with a scowl, after satisfying himself that the money was correct, "but I've got my shooter."

"So have I," cried Don Pedro indignantly, and slipped his hand round to his hip pocket, "and if you talk any further so insulting I shall—"

"Oh, you bet, two can play at that game," cried Hervey, and ripped out his own weapon before the Spaniard could produce his Derringer. "Hands up or I shoot."

But he had reckoned without his host. While covering De Gayangos, he overlooked the fact that Random and Hope were close at hand. The next moment, and while Don Pedro flung up his hands, the ruffian was covered by two revolvers in the hands of two very capable men.

"Great Scott!" cried Hervey, lowering his weapon. "Only my fun, gents. Here, you get back!"

This was to Inspector Date, who had been keeping his ears and eyes open, and who was now racing for the end of the jetty. Peering over, he uttered a loud cry.

"I thought so—I thought so. Here's the nigger and the mummy!"

Hervey uttered a curse, and, plunging past the trio, careless of the leveled weapons, ran down to the end of the jetty, and, throwing his arms round Date, leaped with him into the sea. They fell just beside the boat, as Random saw when he reached the spot. A confused volley of curses arose, as the boat pushed out from the encrusted pile, the mate thrusting with a boat-hook. Hervey and Date were in the water, but as the boat shot into the moonlight, Random—and now Hope and De Gayangos, who had come up—saw a long green form in amongst the sailors; also, very plainly, Cockatoo with his great mop of yellow hair.

"Shoot! shoot!" yelled Date, who was struggling with the skipper in the shallow water near shore. "Don't let them escape."

Hope ran up the jetty and fired three shots in the air, certain that the firing would attract the attention of the four or five constables on guard at the cottage, which was no very great distance away. Random sent a bullet into the midst of the boatload, and immediately the mate fired also. The bullet whistled past his head, and, crazy with rage, he felt inclined to jump in amongst the ruffians and have a hand-to-hand fight. But De Gayangos stopped him in a voice shrill with anger. Already the shouts and noise of the approaching policemen could be heard. Cockatoo gripped the green mummy case desperately, while the sailors tried to row towards the ship.

Then De Gayangos gave a shout, and leaped, as the boat swung past the jetty. He landed right on Cockatoo, and although a cloud drifted across the moon, Random heard the shots coming rapidly from his revolver. Meanwhile Hervey got away from Date, as the constables came pounding down the jetty and on to the beach.

"Chuck the mummy and nigger overboard and make for the ship," he yelled, swimming with long strokes towards the boat.

This order was quite to the sailors' minds, as they had not reckoned on such a fight. Half a dozen willing hands clutched both Cockatoo and the case, and, in spite of the Kanaka's cries, both were hurled overboard. As the case swung overside, De Gayangos, balancing himself at the end of the boat, fired at Cockatoo. The shot missed the Kanaka, and pierced the mummy case. Then from it came a piercing yell of agony and rage.

"Great God!" shouted Hope, who was watching the battle, "I believe Braddock is in that damned thing."

The next moment De Gayangos was swung overboard also, and the sailors were lifting Hervey into the boat. It nearly upset, but he managed to get in, and the craft rowed for the vessel, which was again showing a flaring blue light. Random sent a shot after the boat, and then with the policemen ran down to help De Gayangos, who was struggling in the water. He managed to pull him out, and when he had him safe and breathless on shore, he saw that the boat was nearing the ship, and that Date, torn and wet and disheveled, with three policemen, was up to his waist in water, struggling to bring ashore Cockatoo and the mummy case, to which he clung like a limpet. Hope ran down to give a hand, and in a few minutes they had the Kanaka ashore, fighting like the demon he was. Random and De Gayangos joined the breathless group, and Cockatoo was held in the grasp of two strong men—who required all their strength to hold him—while Date, warned by Hope's cry of what was in the case, tore at the lid. It was but lightly fastened and soon came off. Then those present saw in the moonlight the dead face of Professor Braddock, who had been shot through the heart. As they looked at the sight, Cockatoo broke from those who held him, and, throwing himself on his master, howled and wept as though his heart would break. At the same moment there came a derisive whistle from The Firefly, and they saw the great tramp steamer slowly moving down stream, increasing her speed with almost every revolution of the screw. Braddock had been captured, but Hervey had escaped.

At the inquest on the Professor and on the body of Mrs. Jasher, it was proved that Cockatoo had warned his master that the game was up, and had suggested that Braddock should escape by hiding in the mummy case. The corpse of Inca Caxas was placed in an empty Egyptian sarcophagus—in which it was afterwards found—and Braddock, assisted by his faithful Kanaka, wheeled the case down to the old jetty. Here, in a nook where Cockatoo had formerly kept the boat, the Professor concealed himself all that night and all next day. Cockatoo, having got rid of his boat long since (lest it might be used in evidence against him and his master), ran through the dense mist and the long night up to Pierside, where he saw Captain Hervey and bribed him with a promise of one thousand pounds to save his master. Hervey, having assured himself that the money was safe, since it was banked in a feigned name in Amsterdam, agreed, and arranged to ship the Professor in the mummy case.

Thus it was that Hervey kept the four men talking up the jetty, as he knew that Cockatoo with his own sailors was shipping the Professor in the mummy case underneath, and well out of sight. Cockatoo had come down stream with The Firefly, and in this way had not been discovered. Throughout that long day the miserable Braddock had crouched like a toad in its hole, trembling at every sound of pursuit, as he knew that the whole of the village was looking for him. But Cockatoo had hidden him well in the case, in the lid of which holes had been bored. He had brandy to drink and food to eat, and he knew that he could depend upon the Kanaka. Had Date not been suspicious, the ruse might have been successful, but to save himself Hervey had to sacrifice the wretched Professor, which he did without the slightest hesitation. Then came the unlucky shot from the revolver of De Gayangos, which had ended Braddock's wicked life. It was Fate.

At the inquest a verdict of "wilful murder" was brought against the Kanaka, but a verdict of "justifiable homicide" was given in favor of the Peruvian. Thus Cockatoo was hanged for the double murder and Don Pedro went free. He remained long enough in London to see his daughter married to the man of her choice, and then returned to Lima.

Of course the affair caused more than a nine days' wonder, and the newspapers were filled with accounts of the murder and the projected escape. But Lucy was saved from all this publicity, as, in the first place, her name was kept out of print as much as possible, and, in the second, Archie promptly married her, and within a fortnight of her step-father's death took her to the south of France, and afterwards to Italy. What with his own money and the money she inherited from her mother—in which Braddock had a life interest—the young couple had nearly a thousand a year.

Six months later Sir Frank came into the small San Remo where Mr. and Mrs. Hope lived, with his wife on his arm. Lady

Random looked singularly charming and was assuredly more conversational. This was the first time the two sets of lovers had met since the tragedy, and now each girl had married the man she loved. Therefore there was great joy.

"My yacht is over at Monte Carlo," said Random, "and I am, going with Inez to South America. She wants to see her father."

"Yes, I do," said Lady Random; "and we want you to come also, Lucy—you and your dear husband."

Archie and his wife looked at one another, but declined unanimously.

"We would rather stay here in San Remo," said Mrs. Hope, becoming slightly pale. "Don't think me unkind, Inez, but I could not bear to go to Peru. It is associated too much in my own mind with that terrible green mummy."

"Oh, Don Pedro has taken that back to the Andes," explained Sir Frank, "and it is now reposing in the sepulchre in which it was placed, hundreds of years ago, by the Indians, faithful to Inca Caxas. Inez and I are going up to a kind of forbidden city, where Don Pedro reigns as Inca, and I expect we shall have a jolly time. I hear there is some big game shooting there."

"What about your soldiering?" asked Hope, rather, surprised at this extended tour being arranged.

"Oh, my husband has left the army," pouted Inez. "His duties kept him away from me nearly all the day, and I grew weary of being left alone."

"So you see, Mrs. Hope," laughed Random gayly, "that I have had to succumb to my fireside tyrant. We shall go and see this fairy city and then return to my home in Oxfordshire. There Inez will settle down as a real English wife and I'll turn a country squire. So, after all our troubles, peace will come."

"And as you will not come to my country," said Lady Random to her hostess, "you cannot refuse to visit Frank and myself at the Grange. We have had so much trouble together that we cannot lose sight of each other."

"No," said Lucy, kissing her. "We will come to Oxfordshire."

So it was arranged, and the next day Mr. and Mrs. Hope went over to Monte Carlo to see the last of Sir Frank and his wife. They stood on the heights watching the pretty little steamer making for South America. Archie noticed that his wife's face was somewhat sad.

"Are you sorry we did not go, sweetheart?"

"No," she replied, placing her arm within his own. "I only want to be with you."

"That is all right." He patted her hand. "Now that we have sold

211

all the furniture in the Pyramids, and have got rid of the lease, there will be nothing to remind you of the green mummy."

"Yet I can't help thinking of my unfortunate step-father, and of poor Mrs. Jasher, and of Sidney Bolton. Oh, Archie, little as we can afford it, I am glad that we allow Mrs. Bolton a small sum a year. After all, it was through my step-father that her son met with his death."

"I don't quite agree with you, dear. Cockatoo's innate savagery was the cause, as Professor Braddock did not intend or desire murder. But there, dear, do not think any more about these dismal things. Dream of the time when I shall be the president of the Royal Academy, and you my lady."

"I am your lady now. But," added Lucy, perhaps from an association of ideas of color and the Academy, "I shall hate green for the rest of my life."

"That's unlucky, considering it is Nature's color. My dear, in a year or two this tragedy, or rather the three tragedies, will seem like a dream. I won't listen to another word now. The green mummy has passed out of our lives and has taken its bad luck with it."

"Amen, so be it," said Lucy Hope, and the happy couple went home, leaving all their sorrows behind them, while the smoke of the steamer faded on the horizon.

THE END

Milton Keynes UK
Ingram Content Group UK Ltd.
UKHW040156211124
451476UK00007B/53